A Cord of Three
Strands

A NOVEL

Books by Christy Distler

A Cord of Three Strands

The Heart Knows the Way Home

A Cord of Three
Strands

A NOVEL

Christy Distler

Published by Avodah Books
www.avodahbooks.com

Library of Congress Cataloging-in-Publication Data

Names: Distler, Christy, author.
Title: A cord of three strands : a novel / Christy Distler.
Description: Warminster, PA: Avodah Books, 2020.
Identifiers: LCCN: 2020906687 | ISBN: 978-1-7347789-0-8 (paperback) | 978-1-7347789-4-6 (casebound) | 978-1-7347789-1-5 (ebook)
Subjects: LCSH United States--History--French and Indian War, 1754-1763--Fiction. | Horsham (Pa. : Township)--Fiction. | Quakers--Pennsylvania--Fiction. | Delaware Indians--Pennsylvania--History--Fiction. | Frontier and pioneer life--Pennsylvania--Fiction. | Love stories. | Christian fiction. | Historical fiction. | BISAC FICTION / Historical / Colonial America & Revolution | FICTION / Christian / Historical | FICTION / Historical / General
Classification: LCC PS3604.I868 C67 2020 | DDC 813.6--dc23

All Scripture, whether quoted or paraphrased, is from the Geneva Bible, 1599 Edition. Published by Tolle Lege Press. All rights reserved. Used by permission.

Publisher's Note: This work is in part a historical reconstruction, and as such, some secondary characters, most locations, and Friends' roles in relations with the Lenape and in refuting slavery are historically accurate. All other characters and the story itself are fictional, and any resemblance to actual persons, living or dead, is coincidental.

Cover design by Hannah Linder Designs

Endorsements

The appealing characters and the dilemmas they faced quickly drew me into Christy Distler's *A Cord of Three Strands*. The details of Friends' faith and daily lives were fascinating. Distler portrays the historical setting in vivid, accurate strokes, weaving real events into the characters' stories quite believably, particularly in how deeply Isaac was torn between two worlds. The historical notes are interesting and helpful in illuminating the context of the Pennsylvania Quakers during this period. I've extensively researched the Lenape during the French and Indian War, and I appreciate how Distler presents all sides in the conflict realistically and with sympathy. The story's resolution was heartwarming. I highly recommend *A Cord of Three Strands*.

J. M. Hochstetler
author of the American Patriot Series
and coauthor of the Northkill Amish Series

Although I admit that I initially checked the accuracy of the vocabulary and practices vividly described in the first chapters, it wasn't long before I settled into my trust of Christy Distler's well-researched, captivating depiction of the Pennsylvania Quakers and the Lenape in 1756. Distler has captured period vocabulary and scene descriptions of not only rural settings but also Philadelphia during the era of the French and Indian War. More than 265 years later, I am certain that contemporary Quaker readers will identify with the experiences of Isaac Lukens, of mixed Lenape and French ancestry; Elisabeth Alden, a birthright English Quaker; and find many of the aspects of A Cord of Three Strands, as told from their alternating perspectives, relevant to their own lives. The book would delight lovers of U.S. history as well.

Barbara Luetke
reviewer for *Friends Journal*

Beautifully written with engaging characters, *A Cord of Three Strands* is a historical romance rich with period details. Distler leaves you turning the pages until the end.

Tanya Eavenson
award-winning author of *The Rescue*

For Mom—
my lifelong best friend and biggest fan;
the illustrator of the first book I wrote, at age seven;
and the one who introduced me to our Lukens family.
I love you.

In memory of Penny (2006–2020)—
the sweetest dog ever and my inspiration for
Penny (and Mwekane) in the story.
Fourteen years with you wasn't nearly enough.

There is that near you
[the Inward Light, the voice of
Christ within].
which will guide you:
oh! wait for it, and be sure ye keep to it.

ISAAC PENINGTON
LETTER TO WOMEN FRIENDS AT ARMSCOT, 1678

Note to the Reader

Days and months: Quakers did not (some still do not) use the traditional names for days and months because of their pagan origins. Instead, they numbered them: First Day (Sunday), Second Day (Monday), First Month, Second Month, etc. On the Gregorian calendar, First Month began on March 25 (the first day of the year). The Julian calendar replaced the Gregorian calendar in 1752, and January 1 (the new first day of the year) began First Month. This is why May is Second Month in this book's prologue but February is Second Month in chapter one.

Friend vs. friend: *Friend* (capitalized) means Quaker, whereas *friend* (lowercase) means a social friend. *Friend* and *Quaker* are synonymous, with *Friend* preferred by Friends and *Quaker* preferred by non-Friends.

Thee vs. thou (plain speech): In archaic language, when one person spoke to another, *thou* was used as a grammatical subject and *thee* as a grammatical object. By the 1750s, when this book is set, Quakers were using *thee* for subjects and objects. For example, instead of saying, "How art thou?" they would say, "How is thee?" This may sound odd to modern readers, but it is historically accurate in plain speech. *Thee* is singular and its plural is *you*, so both words are used in this novel depending on the context.

Glossary

Convinced Friend: A person who was not born into a
Quaker family but joined a Friends Meeting by choice.

Disorderly walker: A Friend deemed to be acting
contrary to Quaker beliefs and practice.

Inward Light/Light Within: The power and inspiration of Christ within a person.

Meeting for worship: Friends' gathering to worship
God. Friends often gathered on First Days and midweek.

Meeting for worship with a concern for business:
A meeting held monthly to address and approve/disapprove
business (marriage requests, births or deaths to be recorded,
members' inapt behavior, etc.).

Mennist: An eighteenth-century term for a Mennonite.

Public Friend: An itinerant Friends minister.

Rise of meeting: The conclusion of meeting for worship.

Stop in my heart: Quaker saying referring to felt but not easily understood scruples about an activity or action.

Wanishi: The Lenape word for *thank you*.

Way will open: Quaker saying implying that a resolution to a problem will come about.

Weighty Friend: A Friend recognized for having wisdom.

Women's Meeting: Although considered equal spiritually, men and women met separately for business meetings. The Men's and Women's Meetings handled different issues.

Yearly Meeting: A group of Friends Meetings that meet together yearly (similar to a church district).

PROLOGUE

Isaac

Mid-Second Month (May) 1744
Horsham, Pennsylvania

Does it still hurt terribly?"

Beside me at the trestle table in the kitchen area of her home's common room, Elisabeth took my hand and pulled away the cloth wrapped around it. The linen had been soaked in chill water from the springhouse as soon as we'd arrived from school, but now it was barely cool.

My bruised and swollen knuckles still ached even three hours after our schoolmaster had put his ferule to them six times. "Not as much as it did."

She caught her lower lip between her teeth, as she always did when upset. With her two top teeth missing, the funny way her lip filled the gap made me grin.

"What, pray tell, does thee find humorous, Isaac?" She scowled, and for a moment I thought she might cry. "'Tis hardly trifling, thy injury and how thee took the rapping for my knuckles as well. I laughed too."

Aye, and how could she not? When my dog, Penny, leapt through the schoolhouse's open window, our schoolmaster had jumped nearly two feet in the air, knocking his spectacles on the floor and then stepping on them. Other children laughed as well, though they hadn't received any reprimand beyond a stare that chased every sound from the room.

I still found amusement in the image of our schoolmaster's twisted spectacles sitting cockeyed on his nose as he'd admonished me, "How dare a scholar summon that mangy beast into an environment intended for learning and then chortle at its disgraceful interruption?" Perhaps I wouldn't have laughed if he wasn't always so disagreeable.

Of course, I'd surely find less humor in the incident when Father and Mother saw my hand. But I wouldn't think about that now. "Thee is of too tender an age for such punishment, Beth Alden."

She swiped away the tear that slid down her cheek. "Papa says eight years is old enough to endure the consequence required of an offense. And thee is only two years older."

"Two and a half—almost." Still, I would never allow unnecessary harm to come to her. She was so much smaller than I, and a boy couldn't ask for a more loyal friend, even if she was a girl. "I didn't want him to hurt thee. A friend loves at all times."

She smiled, but only until she looked upon my knuckles again.

I stood. "I mustn't tarry. I told Mother I wouldn't stay

long today." As well, Elisabeth's mama awaited her help in the garden. Soon she would be calling for her—or worse, would come inside and see my hand.

"Wait. Remember what I was saying this morning?" Elisabeth rose and withdrew to the bedchamber she shared with her baby brother, then returned with her sewing hussif. "I still need some of thy hair."

I should have listened more to her chattering on our way to school instead of searching the field we crossed for small critters. "Remind me?"

"Yesterday in meeting for worship, thy father spoke about a threefold cord—how 'tis not easily broken."

Threefold? "I thought he said three-*folded*."

"Nay, three*fold*. A cord of three strands, braided."

Now I understood. I couldn't imagine what he'd meant by—

"Entwined, the strands are stronger. That reminded me of us, thee and me and Jesus together. I want to make a cord for a page marker in my Bible." As she spoke, she'd cut a piece of white embroidery thread. Now she released the tie that held my hair in a queue and knotted the thread close to my scalp halfway up my head. Then she tied another piece of thread near the end of my hair before picking up her scissors.

I grabbed her hand. "How much is thee cutting?"

"Only a small piece. 'Twill not even be noticeable." The scissors snipped, and in her hand lay a slim lock of hair about eight inches long. "See? I'm going to braid it with the piece I cut from my hair and the spun lamb's wool I dyed red because Christ shed his blood for us."

From within her hussif she pulled similar locks of dark-red yarn and blond hair, both knotted at each end like the length of my hair. At one end she tied all three together with another piece of white thread, then she had me hold one end while she braided them and tied the other end.

She used a needle to pull off the original ties on the three pieces before holding out the result of her work. "This cord will always remind us that no matter what happens, because we have each other and Jesus, we will not easily be broken."

What a silly girl she was.

But when I took the cord from her and looked over the woven red, black, and blond, what she'd just said and done made sense. Perfect sense.

Why this girl who was so much more intelligent than I chose me as her dearest friend, I didn't know. But I did know one thing: just as our lives had been tied together from the time of her birth—entwined, she had said—I intended to keep them that way.

For the rest of our days.

CHAPTER 1

Isaac

*Late Second Month (February) 1756
Northampton County, Pennsylvania*

Even before we saw the smoke, I smelled it. Not the sweet, welcoming scent that curled from a frontier cabin's chimney but a faint yet acrid odor that foretold a scorching destruction.

I scanned the barren treetops on both sides of the road, listening. No other sound accompanied the soft crunching of snow beneath our moccasins. Still, the skin on my shoulders tightened and prickled.

"Isaac." Beside me, Sam Milham backhanded my arm and stopped. His pale-blue eyes narrowed beneath the beaver fur of his woolen cap as he scanned the clear sky and surrounding forest. Finally, he jutted his chin toward the summit fifty paces ahead. "That way."

Gripping the arms of our travois tighter, I set out for the crest. My longer strides and the weight of his ration sack put me several steps ahead of him, but he caught up when I slowed.

Thick gray smoke rose from a clearing in the trees, about one hundred and fifty yards into the vale below and thirty yards east of the road. Dense haze blanketed the area, its concentration diminishing as the wind drove it southeastward.

Sam swore. "It's a settler plantation. You think it's Wolf Clan?"

God forbid it. But with the increasing war parties that ravaged the frontier, that seemed more likely than an inadvertent cabin or barn fire. "Let's go." I plunged through the ankle-deep snow as quickly as the road's slope allowed.

We had almost reached the wagon path to the plantation when gunshots rang out. A woman's cry resonated through the trees, and whoops followed. Moments later a shriek pierced the air. Then silence.

I stopped, lowering the travois to the ground, then crept into the wood. My heart pounded, stealing my breath. Far off, a hawk screed. Distant sounds of laughter echoed.

"They're intent on revenge." Sam's coarse whisper came from behind. "We can do nothing."

We didn't know that. Not for certain.

Navigating the trees, I headed for the upwind end of the clearing. Sam cursed again but followed.

None of what I'd seen and heard in our village last month—the warriors' reprehensible stories, the scalps they displayed atop spears, or the bound, exhausted captives they dragged behind them—prepared me for what awaited in the glade.

The cabin smoldered, one end still burning. Flames had already blackened the barn beyond. Amidst the smoke and floating ash, bodies lay strewn—a man and a boy of possibly fourteen near the barn, a younger boy by the cabin, and a woman at the edge of the wood. Crystalized blood stained the snow around their heads, confirming their fate.

Bitterness rose to my throat, and I swallowed it before it choked me. Surely this family had committed no offense, yet they had been butchered like animals.

As I neared the prostrate woman, four buckskin-clad warriors trotted from between the cabin and barn, their scalp locks swinging. Only the leader, who held a hunting gun against his shoulder, didn't use an arm to shield his nose and mouth from the pungent smoke.

They emerged from the haze, and the leader's lips contorted into a sneer. The contrast of white teeth against his black-painted face added to its malice. "Walks In Two Worlds," he called in Lenape. "Has the half-breed and his yellow-haired friend finally decided to join us?"

The others snickered and lowered their arms, baring their faces.

Wolf Clan indeed. Walks In Two Worlds was what that clan's warriors from the west, those who had forsaken our tribe's peace with the province, called me with contempt. Their thin frames and smooth skin purported they were younger than I. Even their leader had likely seen no more than twenty winters. Already they were murderers.

"These people did nothing to you!" I started toward them, shaking with anger. For the first time in many months, speaking our native language felt foreign. "Have you no conscience?"

The leader stopped five paces from where I stood, his expression sobering. Then his smirk returned. "What would our great sachems say now, seeing the one who once spewed pleadings for peace now consumed by fury?" He swept out his hand. "They took what was not theirs—our land. We are taking it back."

Sam grabbed my arm, halting my advance.

A child's shrieks carried from within the forest, then another warrior emerged with a young boy who flailed and cried out for his mama. As they approached, the warrior, no older than fifteen winters, exuded the pride of a young hunter who'd shot his first deer.

"I told you I would find him." He dropped the boy at his feet, then grabbed the child's tousled brown hair and unsheathed the knife at his waist.

Charging forward, I knocked the knife from his hand and shoved him to the ground. "Coward! He is a child."

The young warrior jumped to his feet, glaring. "So were William Penn's sons, once. If we had destroyed them in their youth, this land would still be ours. Our families would be thriving here, not starving and dying of white man's sickness."

I stood over the trembling boy. "Taking his life will neither right the wrongs nor bring back what we have lost. You will not lay a hand on him again."

Sam drew his pistol. Despite his short stature and how his veins contained not a drop of Indian blood, his thirteen years in the wilderness, apt aim, and hand-fighting skill had earned him the reputation of a man not to be crossed. But gratitude for Sam's unapologetic defense succumbed to recognition of my hypocrisy.

The young warrior spat at me. "Walks In Two Worlds speaks our language with a forked tongue. Though he is Lenape, he clings to the white man's Quaker religion. Many applaud the peace he promotes, but he is a traitor to his suffering people."

The leader swung his hunting gun toward me, but Sam trained his pistol on him and cocked the hammer before the leader could shoulder his weapon.

Scowling, the leader grabbed his gun by the barrel and dropped its butt to the ground. "The boy is ours." Spread out behind him, the others made no move. Their glares confirmed their refusal to yield.

Our rations.

"Let's trade, then." I nodded at where the wagon path entered the clearing. "Two and a half bushels of shelled corn sit on a travois near the road. Take them."

The young warrior scoffed. "Shelled corn?"

"Are you not only a coward but also a fool?" The furious words left my mouth before I could temper them. "Parched, the corn will feed your families. The boy will not."

The leader jerked his head, and one of the others ran off to the path. After peering through the wood toward the road, he turned back and nodded.

"We go," the leader said.

Sam didn't stand down. "Leave the travois."

The young warrior glowered at me as he trailed the others. "Walks In Two Worlds' days are numbered," he hissed as he passed us. "Soon he will walk only in one—the spirit world."

Sam pursed his lips as they disappeared into the forest. "That was to feed *our* village, my friend."

As if I didn't know that. The two of us had spent weeks trapping beavers for pelts we needed to barter for corn and other rations, not to mention our week traveling to and from the trading post. The rations still filled his sack, but without the corn, the gnawing hunger in our bellies would not soon relent. "They would have taken his life."

He snorted. "Now they will try to take yours."

The warriors gone, I knelt beside the boy, who wore only breeches, a shirt, and stockings. He cowered when I placed my hand on his shoulder, drawing up his knees and covering his head with his arms.

"'Tis all right. I won't hurt thee," I said in English. After lifting him to his feet, I eased his hands from his face. He trembled as his teeth chattered, and the tears pooled in his bulging brown eyes slid down his cheeks. When he tried to look around, I cupped his chin and held it fast. "My name is Isaac. What is thine?"

He gulped, his face deathly pale against the darker skin of my hand. "J-Jeremiah." By the odor about him, he'd urinated on himself.

"We won't let them harm thee, Jeremiah." I doffed my buckskin frock and wrapped it around him. "Which way is thy closest neighbor?"

He turned, pointing to another trail into the wood, fortunately in the opposite direction of the road. As his gaze settled on the woman lying twenty-five paces away, he gasped. "Mama?" He pulled free and lurched toward her. "Mama!"

I caught him by the arm and stood, picking him up and pressing his face to my chest.

Behind us, wood creaked and groaned. The barn's front wall slowly caved in, sending the remainder of the roof crashing down. Out rushed a hot billow of smoke thick with embers and ash, and I turned away.

Sam shielded his face in the crook of his arm and moved toward the trail. "Nothing more we can do."

With Jeremiah still clutched to my chest, I followed. We had no choice but to pass the woman, and I couldn't look away from her. She had been shot through the back and partially scalped, with much of her light hair now matted red.

Elisabeth.

I stopped, reminded of my beloved childhood friend. From behind, the long, wavy hair and slight frame could have been hers.

My burning throat clenched, and I moved on before I retched. The woman had lost her life, probably trying to save her boy's. Now he had no family, orphaned just as I'd been when I wasn't much younger than he.

As we tramped through the forest, Jeremiah clung to the front of my shirt. "I want Mama," he said again and again, sobbing. "I want my mama."

Tears smarted my eyes as I held him tighter. "I know thee does." And I did, for suddenly I longed for my mother as well.

Chinkanning Indian Village
Tunkhannock, Pennsylvania

By the time Sam and I reached our village four days later, word of our encounter with the warriors from the west had already arrived. Many of the people regarded me in silence, not even responding to my greeting as we walked between the lines of *wikwams*.

Part of me couldn't blame them. I'd traded much-needed corn for a white child's life, in their minds stealing food from their mouths and insulting our tribe by placing importance on a boy born of people who'd taken so much from them. Those who'd once esteemed my endeavors to advocate for the Lenape, both with the Six Nations who controlled us and with the province, now considered me a disgrace.

The only thing that troubled me more was the plight of young Jeremiah. The neighbor family had welcomed him with much affection, sorrowfully promising to see to the burial of his kin, but no amount of love would expunge the agony of violently losing his parents and brothers. The despair that hollowed his stare had reawakened the anguish of losing my first parents, even though I had no memory of them.

Then came my summons. Our leader wished to speak with me.

Afterward, Sam stepped into pace beside me as I left the village seeking solace. "What did Teedyuscung want?"

I slowed but didn't look at him. "He said 'tis time I leave the village."

Sam grabbed my arm, stopping me. "No."

Despite myself, I smiled. In the two years I'd known him, rarely had he shown sentiment for anyone. He'd lived alone in the wilderness for years until our tribe had come north to our former village in Wyomink and met him nearby. He made no secret of how he often preferred solitude. "Thee will miss me, then?"

He crossed his arms. "After everything you've done for them, they now want you to leave because you confronted a bunch of boys playing warrior and called one a coward?"

I shook my head. The fault was mine alone. "The wrath I showed has undermined the gentleness and reconciliation I've always encouraged. They think I've sided with the settlers. Teedyuscung also believes I must leave for my own safety. The warrior I shamed vows revenge, and I will not retaliate. Teedyuscung fears my life will be quickly taken."

Sam clapped a hand on my shoulder. "Not while I'm around, my friend."

I matched his gesture, obliged. Despite our ten-year age difference and how he dismissed the nonviolence I embraced, his loyalty was unparalleled. "I thank thee, but Teedyuscung is right." Releasing his shoulder, I started to walk again. To where, I didn't know, but I could not remain still. "I cannot stay here any longer. Too many now forsake peace, and my strivings for harmony are no longer welcome, even amongst my own Turtle Clan."

Even Teedyuscung, a fellow Turtle and once a close companion in building the chain of friendship between the Lenape and the province, had turned to retaliation of the most vile kind. "Despite our differences now, he wishes no harm come to me. 'Tis time I returned to Horsham."

"No." He seized my arm again.

"Sam, I'd decided even before he summoned me. More

than two years have passed since I've seen my family. Never did I intend to stay away so long. The tribe will be moving to Diahoga when the cold spell ends, and I cannot travel any farther from home." I sighed and clasped his shoulder again. "Lord willing, I leave tomorrow."

Clenching his jaw, he stalked away. "Or maybe you're a coward as well, Isaac Lukens."

Maybe I was.

～

Lecha River Valley (Lehigh Valley), Pennsylvania

I didn't know what I loathed more, the biting cold that stung my face or the gnawing hunger that consumed my belly. After four days of travel by night, both made me yearn for a place to tarry, for the warmth of a blazing fire and a hot meal. But where?

I'd traveled the Nescopeck Path many times, but the blue-black veil of early morn and the newest blanket of snow obscured any familiarity with the landscape. Considering the moon's change in position since I'd passed Gnaden-hutten—or the burned remains of the Moravian mission—surely I neared Bethlehem.

Or perhaps my disorientation came from exhaustion. Never had I longed for home more, and that pushed me on despite the ache of my limbs from plodding through snow since nightfall. With the mountainous terrain now miles behind me, the promise of easier travel over rolling hills kept me moving.

Wind clicked the bare branches high above me, and an owl hooted in the distance, breaking the hushed stillness of the snow. Something rustled within the wood, heightening my senses. I glanced through the trees on either side, searching for the glow of eyes. 'Twasn't the first time I'd sensed animal presence along the path, and hopefully, whatever it was didn't share my level of hunger.

Just as my fingers found the bone haft of the knife sheathed at my waist, the sound of movement through the snow spun me around.

Nothing there. I listened for several moments, and at hearing only silence, turned to continue. Fifteen paces ahead, a silhouette stepped from behind a tree at the road's edge, a hunting gun pointed at me. A shorter shadow emerged onto the path behind him, his gun also at the ready.

"Vhat's your name and vher are you going?" the taller one asked.

I held out my hands. "Please. I—"

"He has a knife," the other yelled.

Footsteps crunched behind me, turning me around again. A thunderous sound echoed, and a blow to my back staggered me. I tried to face my attacker, but the fire that seared through my side spun the world atilt.

When I opened my eyes, four men stood above me, two with guns trained on my face. The beating of my heart thudded in my ears. "Please," I rasped. Every breath intensified the agony that sliced through me. "I mean thee . . . no harm."

"Vhat?" One of them knelt beside me and leaned closer. "*Ach*, I know dis man." He huffed. "You shot da Quaker peacemaker who lives vith da Lenape."

Shot?

"How was I supposed to know that, him travelin' by night dressed like a savage?" a gruff voice said. "He coulda been traveling with others, looking to ambush like the ones that massacred Hayes' militia."

"Looks a whole lot more Indian than Quaker to me," another voice said, followed by guffaws from at least two of them.

"*Ruhe!*" A hand clutched my arm as they provided the silence he demanded. "Vhat's your name again?"

I swallowed, gritting my teeth. "Isaac . . . Lukens."

"*Ja.*" He stood. "Shtand him up."

"What'll we do with him?"

"I vill take him to Tom McCue's. Now help me shtand him up."

Hands gripped my arms and heaved me to my feet.

The pain exploded into engulfing blackness.

The brightening deep-blue sky of dawn stretched above me. My side throbbed, the pain sharpening to a torment that stole my breath with every jostle. I lifted my head but then dropped it back onto the hay beneath me. Wooden wagon sides rose around me, and a thick blanket that smelled of damp wool and livestock covered my body.

So tired. My eyes closed, but I forced them open. Where was I, and where was I being taken?

The wagon jolted through a rut, forcing a groan from deep in my throat. I held my breath until the sting eased, then moved my hand to where it hurt most. Sticky warmth soaked my shirt. When I pulled my arm from beneath the blanket, blood stained my hand.

Aye. The men on the Nescopeck Path, the crack of the

hunting gun, the insufferable pain. A destination mentioned, but what was it? I couldn't remember.

Another jar of the wagon brought a grunt through clenched teeth.

"Ve're halfvay der." The booming voice came from somewhere above my head. "My name is Dieter Kolb. Vher ver you going?"

"Horsham. North of Philadelphia." Despair flooded me. With a bullet wound, 'twould be days before I could finish my journey.

"*Gut.* You vill be safe vher I take you—and safer yet when you get to your Horsham."

Safe? I desired not safety but peace. Peace between the people of my father, white settlers seeking religious freedom in America, and those of my mother, the Lenape who'd long inhabited the lands but had them stripped away. Reconciliation now seemed hopeless.

I closed my eyes, my heart rent. For the second time in less than three years, I was taking leave of a place where I didn't belong. I hadn't found my mother's or father's family, and I could only hope the Friends who'd reared me would extend love and grace despite the selfishness I'd displayed in departing from them.

Chapter 2

Elisabeth

Second Day, Third Month 8th, 1756
Horsham, Pennsylvania

Eventide often proved the most lonesome time of day for me. This night was no exception. As much as the care of my young siblings added to my other responsibilities tired me, I often preferred their unrelenting needs to the taunting silence that filled the house once they were abed.

Now, in the quietness save for the crackle of the fire, I had turned to the reading of Scripture to comfort me.

"What is the Almighty impressing upon thy heart tonight, daughter?"

I looked up from my Bible. Papa watched me from his usual place in the wingback chair, the *Pennsylvania Gazette* he'd been reading now folded on his lap.

Jon-Isaac stirred in the cradle beside my rocker, and I reached down and patted him. When he calmed, I returned my attention to Papa. "The book of Luke, chapter eight. The parable of the candle."

"Does any verse speak to thee particularly?"

Indeed one did, and I made the brazen decision to share it. "'For nothing is secret, that shall not be evident: neither anything hid, that shall not be known, and come to light.'" Swallowing, I met his gaze.

His dark eyebrows knit as he shook his head. "We have discussed this. As thy father, 'tis my charge to protect thee."

I sighed. There he sat in his black breeches and waistcoat, white shirt, and cravat—as plain a Friend as I'd ever seen—yet he disregarded one of our steadfast Quaker tenets. "As Friends we embrace truth. According to Christ, it sets us free."

"'Tis Christ's truth that sets us free. Not all truth. And some truth is—" He canted his head, then stood.

A horse's muffled neigh came from outside, and I rose when Papa started for the door.

He opened it enough to step into the gap. "Hello?"

"Inside. Make haste," a familiar voice said. I couldn't immediately place it.

Papa backed up, swinging the door wide, and quick footfall sounded on the porch. A man in a dark woolen coat and hat ushered in two women fully shrouded in hooded cloaks.

Papa shut the door behind them.

The man looked up, and the glow of the candles and hearth fire illuminated his weathered face. Abner Jones, a Friend who lived a few miles to the north. "Please forgive the late intrusion, Jonathan. These two are in need of Friends' assistance." He turned to me. "Thy help especially."

Mine? The women huddled close together, one much taller than the other and both with their heads lowered to conceal their faces. "In any way I can."

Abner drew back the hoods. "This is Samson and Ruthie."

My breath caught. Before me stood a young man, about seventeen years, with thick black hair and the darkest skin I'd ever seen. His emotionless eyes, their whites yellowed, met mine momentarily before he averted them. Ruthie, with lighter skin, finer features, and a mass of long curly hair, lifted her head only slightly before crying out and clutching her middle.

Samson and Abner grabbed her arms as I moved closer. By the way she moaned, and Abner's comment to me, I suspected not illness but labor of childbirth.

"Breathe, Ruthie." I leaned over beside her and rubbed her lower back. "Breathe until it eases."

Her groans finally ceased. Straightening, she leaned against Samson.

She was but a child herself, fifteen years at most. Though likely five years younger than I, she would soon be a mother.

I disregarded that thought to attend what mattered most. "How close together are thy pains?"

She shook her head. "Don't know."

"I found them hiding in our barn tonight," Abner said. "Their master has men chasing them. Ruthie said her bag of waters broke this forenoon, and her labor started a few hours afterward." He looked to Papa. "I took them to Susannah Lukens, but no one was at home. I know she has been training Elisabeth in midwifery, and word is you both have helped the enslaved before. I hope you do not mind—"

"Of course not." I untied the strings at Ruthie's neck, and

Abner slipped the cloak from her shoulders. "Come. We shall get thee more comfortable."

Samson removed his own cloak, then loosed the ties of the petticoat fastened low about his hips. He stepped out of it and handed it to Abner.

"These men pursuing you," Papa said to Samson, "are they close behind?"

Samson nodded once. "Near caught us last night."

Papa picked up the candle on the table beside his chair, then crossed the room to the kitchen area. After tossing back the braided rug, he lifted the door to the root cellar. "Down here."

Samson and I helped Ruthie, and Abner followed. Soon we were all in the cool, damp room that smelled of dirt, potatoes, and parsnips. By the flickering light of the candle, Papa and Abner unstacked the wooden crates behind the ladder, revealing the narrow opening in the dirt-and-stone wall. Papa slipped through first and had lit all the lanterns in the hidden room by the time the rest of us followed.

Abner looked around, taking in the sleeping pallets, basin and pitcher on a washstand, two chairs, and chamber pot. "Thee built this, Jonathan?"

"The root cellar I did." Even in the dim light, I could see Papa's expression darken. "Isaac walled in this room while he was living with us."

"I had no idea."

"'Tis safest that way." Papa glanced at me. "I shall get water and blankets. Abner, thee should go."

"Clean rags as well," I said. "And my bag."

With the two men gone, I faced Samson and Ruthie. Their clothing was filthy and tattered, even threadbare in places, and Ruthie shivered continuously, though that could have been from her labor. "Come rest." I led her to one of the pallets and knelt to help her sit.

"What can I do, mistress?" Samson asked.

"First, thee may call me Elisabeth. In the Almighty's eyes, I am no more valuable than thee. Therefore I deserve—and desire—no fancy title. And second, thee may sit behind her for support."

He did as instructed, not even hesitating at the impropriety of a man assisting, and I eased Ruthie against him.

His impassive expression softened. "You helped slaves before?"

"A few times, when the opportunity arose."

"And you birthed babies before?"

I pulled my handkerchief from my apron pocket and patted the perspiration from Ruthie's forehead. "Aye."

Just not by myself, not in a root cellar, and not when the baby's mother was a child herself and its parents were pursued by slave catchers.

Between the pains that gripped her, I helped Ruthie get undressed, washed down, into a clean shift, and settled on the blanket we placed over the pallet's straw tick. She turned onto her side, and I covered her with another blanket to ward off the chill.

The floor creaked above us as Papa, having brought down everything I needed as well as clean clothing for Samson, now moved about in the common room.

I knelt by Ruthie and drew the blanket partly aside. "Is the time right for thy confinement?"

She opened her eyes and rolled onto her back. "I reckoned it not for another month."

I felt around on her belly to determine the baby's position. Praise be to God, its head was downward and I felt quickening. "How old is thee?"

"Almost seventeen." Her face twisted, and she gritted her teeth as her belly contracted.

I let her squeeze my hand till the pain eased, then dabbed her forehead with a dampened cloth. "Is Samson thy husband?"

She smiled, albeit faintly. "He ain't, but he loves me. He will be someday."

"The baby isn't mine." Samson's quiet words startled me, and I looked over my shoulder. He now stood behind me, having finished using the cellar's main room to wash and dress in Papa's old work clothing. "I wouldn't never compromise her. Our master, he did this to her."

Inconceivable. How any human could condone such an evil as slavery confounded me. Then I realized his narrowed eyes reflected affront toward me, not the situation. "Of course. I didn't think—" I searched for apposite words. "'Tisn't my intention to judge, only to understand so I can best help to birth this baby and keep you safe."

His expression eased.

"Please, come and sit behind her. Thy support will be a comfort."

He resumed his previous position, cradling her, and she looked up at him. With a sigh, she shifted her gaze to me. "We knew we were taking a chance, running with my time of confinement nearing, but our master found out about us—about our feelings for each other. He was gonna sell Samson. We couldn't wait."

I nodded, my heart convicted. I had spent much of the day lamenting to God about my life, and now its conditions seemed so trifling. Surely Samson and Ruthie would have traded places with me without a moment's thought. "You were brave to run, and we will do all we can to assist you."

Another pain seized her, this one so intense that she struggled to stay quiet and take the shallow breaths I demonstrated. When it ended, she relaxed against Samson but then clapped a hand over her mouth and pointed to the washstand.

I grabbed the basin, caught her grimy hair back from her face, and held the bowl as she vomited what little was in her stomach. She dry heaved a few last times, then leaned back, panting, and ran the back of her hand across her chin. "Sorry."

I set the basin aside. "No need to apologize. 'Tisn't uncommon during labor. Often, it means that birth is nearing." After re-dampening the cloth, I wiped her face again. "Does thee want to rinse thy mouth?"

She nodded.

I lowered my cupped hand into the bucket of water, then tipped it against her lower lip until a small amount of water flowed into her mouth. "Try to rest now."

She swallowed and closed her eyes.

Samson kissed the top of her head. When he rested his cheek on it, his eyes shone.

My heart went out to him. "She is doing well."

He nodded. "I love her more than anything. Despise to see her hurting. Wish I could bear the pain for her."

"You've already beared enough pain for me," she whispered. "Got the scars on your back to prove it."

He scowled. "And I'll do it again if I have to."

Tears welled in my own eyes as contradictory emotions overwhelmed me. My mind filled with fury toward an abhorrent system that treated humans as property to be used for selfish gain, yet my heart swelled with admiration—and a twinge of longing—for the bond they shared.

Sadness followed, for until a few years before, I had enjoyed such a sweet companionship with Isaac, my friend and protector from a tender age. Despite how his abrupt departure from our community still stewed bitterness deep within me, betimes I follishly allowed myself to imagine, even hope, for his return. Especially when trials came, and there had been no shortage of them since he had left.

For three more hours Ruthie labored. I tended her needs, recited the Scriptures Susannah Lukens used to comfort the women she attended, and prayed aloud for Ruthie, her baby, and our safety.

Another strong pain racked her, and this time she tried to sit up. "Need to use the chamber pot."

I stayed her with a hand on her forearm. "That's the baby thee is feeling. 'Tis time."

She nodded wildly, clenching her teeth.

How I wished we had Susannah's birthing chair—and her reassuring composure and knowledge. My legs, fortunately hidden beneath my petticoats and apron, quivered as I stood. "Samson, help her up so she can squat. Then kneel behind her, loop thy arms up under her shoulders, and steady her."

He did, and I placed a clean blanket on the floor beneath her, then lifted her shift to the tops of her legs. "Grab the fronts of thy legs now, Ruthie. Then with the next pain, bear down no matter how much it hurts."

The next contraction soon came, and with venerable

strength and resolve, she bore down hard. The baby's head, covered with sodden black hair, appeared. It slipped back in when she stopped pushing but reappeared and then fully emerged with her next strain. I supported it with my hand. "Good. Now take another breath and bear down again."

She did, and after three more pushes, the baby slid out into my hands.

I turned the little girl over, lowering her head and patting her back to clear her mouth and nose. Her color looked good, but . . .

Breathe, baby. Please breathe.

Placing the infant on the blanket, I rubbed her with it to stimulate breathing and clean off the blood and pasty covering. She squeaked, coughed a few times, and then kicked her legs and wailed.

Relief flooded me. *Oh, thank thee, Father.*

I looked up at Ruthie, whose tears now reflected not misery but joy. "Thy daughter is beautiful and has a fine set of lungs."

"My daughter," she choked out, then looked back at Samson. "Our daughter."

He nodded, smiling, and kissed her cheek. "Our *free* daughter."

~

Third Day, Third Month 9th

As soon as the sun rose the next morning, Papa sent my young stepsister, Abigail, through the wood to fetch our neighbor. Both Susannah Lukens and her elderly mother returned, and Abigail was then sent off to school, aware even at seven years of age that she mustn't mention those who hid in our root cellar. Mary Lukens stayed in the common room to care for Ethan and Jon-Isaac while Susannah and I took porridge and milk below.

Susannah examined the baby girl as Samson and Ruthie ate heartily, then handed her over to me so she could examine Ruthie.

I cradled the tiny infant close and swayed back and forth to quiet her fussing. "There, there, sweet girl." Taking in her pinched, reddening face, I considered the life she would live had her parents not fled. How I hoped she would never know such hardship.

"Thee did a fine job." Susannah's compliment came from behind, and she rested a hand on my back. "I knew thee would, when the time came."

I stroked the baby's soft cheek. "Her parents deserve the commendation, as does the Lord for his favor."

Rapid steps crossed the floor over our heads. "Elisabeth! Susannah!" Papa's voice carried into the cellar from above. "Men are riding in!"

My stomach constricted. Men? The slave catchers?

Ruthie's eyes bulged as she shook her head. "Oh, have mercy, Jesus. Have mercy on us."

Susannah took the baby. "Go back up. Close the cellar door and replace the rug." She laid the baby in Ruthie's arms. "Put her to thy breast to nurse. We must keep her quiet." She glanced back at me. "Make haste."

My heart fluttered as I left the hidden room and then climbed the ladder. My feet stumbled just as I grasped Papa's hand, and he yanked me up by one arm, then closed the door. I drew the rug overtop before hurrying to the table with him.

Sitting on the bench beside four-year-old Ethan, I cautioned, "Say not a word."

Within a minute, pounding shook the door, startling me despite how I'd expected it.

Papa calmly walked to the door and opened it.

Two men, both taller than Papa and dressed like frontiersmen, stood there. "We're lookin' for runaway slaves. Boy's eighteen, tall, black as tar. Girl's sixteen, thin but carryin' a child, brown skin, unkempt hair. You seen 'em?" The one speaking peered around Papa into the house.

Papa stepped back. "Look around if you must. You may look in the forge and barn as well."

They pushed past him, and Papa remained by the door as they entered each of the bedchambers and then returned to the common room. The one wearing a fox-fur cap started toward the table, eyeing me with a repulsive rotten-toothed grin as he crossed the braided rug. The root-cellar door creaked differently when he stepped on it, and he stopped and scowled down at it.

The crates! In my rush to leave the cellar, I'd forgotten to stack them.

Jon-Isaac fussed and reached for me, and I rose on unsteady legs and lifted him from his high chair.

Both men glanced around the common room, taking in the kitchen and sitting areas, then moved toward the front door. As they neared Papa, a whimper carried from below.

The other man spun around so quickly that his cap nearly fell off. "What was that?"

I slipped my hand beneath Jon-Isaac's petticoat and pinched his chubby leg as hard as I could.

He let out a screech, then started to wail.

"My apologies. Strangers frighten him." I held him closer and kissed his forehead.

The man beside Papa grunted. "C'mon. It's just the baby squallin'. They ain't here, and I can't stand babies cryin'. Check the forge and barn, but didn't I tell ya they're gone? This area's teemin' with these Quaker sort. The way some of them are against slavery, one o' them probably got 'em outta here durin' the night."

The other stared me down, then clomped toward the open doorway.

Papa closed the door after them. The rest of us stayed motionless for several moments, till Papa edged to the front window, staying out of sight.

I turned toward the table and handed Jon-Isaac his coral teething ring, but he pushed it away. "I'm sorry, sweet boy," I whispered and kissed his cheek.

Ethan tugged at my petticoat. "What's wrong with Jon-Isaac?"

"He's fine now." I sat next to him, holding Jon-Isaac close, and offered the ring again. This time he grabbed it with a chubby hand. He held the ring as his sobs abated, then leaned against me and gummed it.

Across the table, Mary smiled, nodding slightly.

Papa rejoined us several minutes later. "They are taking leave." He lowered himself to the bench beside me and used one finger to stroke Jon-Isaac's blond hair to the side of his forehead. "To everything there is a season, daughter." His blue eyes peered into mine. "Seasons to speak truth, and seasons when truth must be concealed. Thee understands this?"

I swallowed, still too shaken to protest. "Aye, Papa."

Sixth Day, Third Month 12th

"Does thee think Papa will return tonight?"

At Abigail's question, I looked up from watching Jon-Isaac in my arms. He slumbered deeply now, and I tucked him into his cradle, then joined her at the window. A mixture of snow and sleet pelted the glass, at times so fiercely that Abigail cringed.

When Papa had left with Abner Jones, Samson, Ruthie, and the baby early that morning, he'd told us he would be home by eventide. But that had been before the northeast snowstorm blew in. "He and Abner may have felt it safer to stay the night in Philadelphia."

She looked up at me, concern drawing her light brows together and filling her large green eyes. "Thee doesn't think danger befell them, does thee?"

I placed my hand on her shoulder. While I'd kept my temperament cheerful all day, hoping she wouldn't fret, even at her tender age she understood the risks of their trip. If Papa and Abner were discovered to be aiding runaways, they would be heavily fined—and 'twasn't uncommon for slave catchers, in their pursuit, to harm those who assisted slaves. "I think 'tis more likely they stayed in Philadelphia to weather the storm." I glanced at the wall clock. "'Tis nearly eight. Time for bed."

"Can thee ready Ethan first? I want to watch for a while longer."

I smiled lightly. She wished for Papa's return as much as I did. "Aye. Come, Ethan." I started toward where he sat playing with his toys.

"Wait, he's coming." She rushed to the front door.

Praise be to God.

I met her there and cracked it open enough to look out. Amidst the driving snow, the wagon neared the house, then the horses halted ten paces from the porch.

"Elisabeth, help me!" 'Twas Abner Jones's voice that called out as the driver jumped down.

My stomach soured. Something was wrong. "Stay here," I bid the children, then trod across the porch and through the snow. "Abner?"

He pulled a limp figure from the back of the wagon. "Help me get him inside."

Papa!

"What—"

"Get his legs."

I did, struggling with their weight, and we carried him into the house. "Abigail, bring a candle. Let's take him into his bedchamber." There we laid him on the bed, and Abigail set the candle on the table beside it. Even in the dimness, blood clearly covered the left side of his head and face and discolored his coat.

Abigail started to cry.

I opened the coat and placed my hand on his chest. At least he still breathed. If he had other injuries, they weren't visible. "Hush now. Take Ethan and get some water and clean rags."

"The wagon got stuck in a rut about a mile from here," Abner said, huffing to catch his breath. "He gave me the reins and climbed down to lead the horses. The wind gusted, and a limb overhanging the road cracked. I yelled to him, but he couldn't get out of the way quickly enough. It came down right on him."

My throat threatened to close as my mind swam. I'd treated wounds before but never one so serious—and not Papa's.

He grasped my shoulder. "Staunch the bleeding. I shall go for Dr. Crossley."

I swallowed. "Take Midnight, the black stallion. He's faster. And stop to summon Susannah Lukens on thy way." Susannah knew almost as much about treating injuries as she did about midwifery. She also could be here in minutes, long before Abner could ride the two and a half miles to Hatborough to fetch the doctor and then return.

Abner squeezed my shoulder, then left.

Abigail and Ethan came back into the room, she carrying a bucket of water and he with arms full of linen rags. "Will Papa be all right?" she whispered.

My heart nearly broke at the tears in their frightened eyes. Only eight months ago, they had asked the same question about their mother. Within a day she had drawn her last breath.

But I mustn't dwell on such. "Lord willing. Now bring another candle and then watch for Susannah."

They obeyed without another word, and I used a dampened rag to start cleaning the blood from Papa's head. *Father, spare him,* I begged.

Papa and I might not have always agreed, but without him I'd be lost.

Chapter 3

Isaac

Smoke stung my eyes and seized my throat. The cabin and barn in the glade before me burned, fully engulfed in flames. Gunshots echoed, followed by high-pitched cries of terror and whoops of vile pleasure. Amidst the haze, a settler family scattered, pursued by black-painted warriors.

Not again!

But no matter how I tried, my legs wouldn't propel me forward and my mouth wouldn't open. I couldn't stop the warriors, nor could I gather the settlers into the prospective fortification of the forest.

"Isaac!" A woman's shriek came from near the cabin. Strangely, it now looked like the log house that had once been my home.

A tall warrior, his face painted black, forced a woman to her knees. He pulled the white cap from her head, loosing waves of long blond hair, then shoved her to the ground with a foot atop her back. Grabbing her hair and twisting it around his wrist in one motion, he raised his other hand, wielding a glinting knife above her forehead.

"Isaac!" Her terrified cry, this time more familiar, echoed again.

The warrior yanked her head upward, revealing the sweet face and bright-blue eyes I knew so well.

"Elisabeth!" My bellow resounded in my ears as everything vanished into darkness. "Elisabeth!" I gasped for breath as my heart hammered.

A hand pressed my forehead, holding my head down. "Just a dream," a female voice soothed. "'Twas just a dream."

Breaths gradually came easier and my heart slowed, but the pallet I lay on still shook violently. So very cold. My head throbbed, and for all my effort, I couldn't lift my eyelids. My limbs felt too heavy to move.

"Just rest," the woman said.

The voice sounded different, but I could hope. "Beth? Is it—"

A damp cloth stroked my brow, cool against its heat. "I'm here. Rest now. I'm here."

I exhaled. Thanks be to God. She was unharmed.

Blackness closed in around me.

A chill tingled over my chest. Dimness surrounded me, the only light a flickering glow. I squeezed my crusted eyes closed and then opened them fully. A slim Indian woman of about forty years stood over me, her shiny black hair falling to her waist in a braid as she held a white cloth. Everything beyond her blurred.

Apprehension swelled in my chest. I had left Chinkanning, I knew I had, yet somehow I was back there on a pallet.

"How do you feel?" The woman's English was quite clear, unlike that of the village women. And surely I'd remember such a kind, gentle countenance.

I tried to speak, but my parched throat and swollen tongue produced no sound.

She lifted my head and held a cup to my mouth. Cold water pooled into it, more sweet and refreshing than I'd ever tasted. She allowed me two swallows, then lay my head back.

I closed my eyes. "Where am I?"

The chilling tingle moved down my arm, and I opened my eyes to find her washing my skin. "The home of Thomas McCue, near Bethlehem."

Remnants of memories slowly returned.

My vision cleared enough that I could now make out white walls. A wardrobe stood in the far corner, a fire burned low in a hearth, and a small table sat beside the bed I lay on.

Bethlehem—more than halfway to Horsham.

She smiled. "My name is Jerusha McCue."

"Thee is Lenape?"

"I am. The Moravians at Gnadenhutten taught me about Jesus, and I became a Christian. Then I met Tom and left them to marry him." She canted her head. "Five days ago, Dieter Kolb brought you here to us after you were shot."

Nearly a week had passed?

After dipping the cloth in a basin, she wrung it out. "Your wound was not serious, but it festered. For three days, you suffered high fevers and shaking chills, rarely awakening. Nightmares and delirium besieged you." She blotted my brow. "We prayed for you day and night. Last night your fever finally broke."

"What day is it?"

"March thirteenth."

I looked to the window and the pale light beyond it. "Dawn or dusk?"

"Dawn." She set the cloth in the water. "In a few days you should have strength to finish your journey." The grin returned to her lips. "Back to your Elisabeth?"

Elisabeth. Surely seeing her had been in dreams, the nightmares that Jerusha mentioned. "The raids—have they moved as far south as Philadelphia?"

"No."

Thanks be to God.

"Rest. I will bring you some broth and toasted bread."

As she left the room, I inhaled and released my breath. Aye, I would need strength—not only for my journey but to face those I'd left behind.

Christ's parable of the lost son came to mind. In some ways, our flights were similar. I, too, had gone in search of what I thought I wanted only to find more sorrow than I'd left behind—as well as the realization that I still didn't know who I was or where I belonged.

Third Day, Third Month 16th

"Isaac!" Tom McCue's holler carried into the barn three mornings later.

I patted the chestnut mare I'd just given hay and left the barn. Tom stood by a wagon hitched to two horses, speaking with a man as tall as I and a few years older. Brawny and with blond hair, his plain clothing and hat resembled those of the Mennists who lived northwest of Horsham.

Tom, a striking contrast in buckskin and with a beard that reached his chest, motioned me over. "This is Johannes Kolb, Dieter's nephew," he said as I neared. "He's on his way home to Rockhill, and Dieter asked him to stop and inquire about you. If you're up to traveling, he can take you as far as the turn off Minsi Trail to his plantation."

Rockhill, only fifteen miles from home. I could walk that distance in four hours' time—well, longer with my injury, but still. God bless Dieter Kolb.

"Isaac Lukens." I held out my hand. "I would be much obliged."

Johannes grasped it as he looked over my buckskin breeches, dark-blue trade-cloth shirt, and moccasins, which Jerusha had somehow scrubbed clean of blood. "Lukens? You are kin to Abraham and Joseph, then?" His German accent was discernible, though not as strong as his uncle's.

Of course. Living in Rockhill, he could know of my uncles who had settled about ten miles from there in Towamensing. "They're my Quaker father's brothers." I released his hand. "With so many in fear of Indian raids, I've been traveling by night for safety. Will my company endanger thee?"

"We will trust *Gott* for protection." Johannes's tone proved he harbored no qualms.

Tom smiled. "It's time you got home, Isaac."

Home. If my journey went as planned, I'd be in Horsham by the end of the night.

I headed to the house to gather my belongings, and soon

afterward stood by the wagon again, now with Jerusha as well as the two men.

I clasped hands with Tom, then turned to her.

She had initially protested my traveling so soon after injury and illness, but her expression now reflected peace with my decision. Taking me by the arms, she pulled me down to kiss my cheek. "You are a good man. You have done all you can for our people—and not without suffering for it. We are indebted to you for that." She looked me in the eye. "God go with you on your return to your Elisabeth and the Friends who have loved you as their own. God spared your life. Surely he has great plans for you."

How I longed to believe that. When she hugged me, I wrapped my arms around her. Tears of gratitude came to my eyes. "Without thee, I surely would have died. I'm grateful for thy care—and for thy encouragement." We released each other, and I faced Tom, who drew Jerusha to his side. "I cannot thank thee enough for opening thy home to me."

Tom nodded. "Safe journey, and Godspeed."

Johannes and I climbed into the wagon. As the sun reached the eight-of-the-clock station in the sky, we set out in the direction of Bethlehem.

"How much time has passed since you were home?" Johannes asked after we'd traveled only minutes.

Too long. I stared at Bethlehem's mountain that rose a few miles ahead of us and drew a breath. "Two and a half years."

He arched his eyebrows. "A long time. May I ask what led you to Wyomink?"

I hesitated, not inclined to discuss it, but felt obligated since he had been so kind in offering me passage. "I went in search of the families of my parents who gave me life. They lived north of the Forks of the Delaware."

"But you were reared by Friends?"

"When I was a child of only two years, my parents and I journeyed to Philadelphia, though I know not why. We all contracted influenza while there. My mother and father died, and the woman who cared for me in my illness took me in."

"Were you able to find your family?"

"Nay."

"*Onkel* Dieter said you were a peacemaker between the Indians and settlers?"

"On my way north, I took shelter at Gnadenhutten during treacherous weather. I met Teedyuscung there, and we became friends. I supported his peacemaking efforts and went with him when he and a large group of Christian Indians left the Moravians and went north to Wyomink." I inhaled and released my breath. "But he, too, has now forsaken peace."

Johannes nodded. "I pray God's mercy for all, white and Indian. The attacks on the frontier are revolting but not unprovoked."

I looked at him, taken aback.

"Uncommon words from a white man, not?" he said.

"Aye. But thee is right. The Lenape have lost so much."

We lapsed into silence as the horses plodded along the trail. Rolling hills of dormant meadows and bare-branched woods outspread on both sides of us. Soon springtime would bring new beginnings of life in the greenness of the grass and the budding of the trees—and hopefully, a new beginning for me.

"Who awaits you at home?" Johannes asked.

I turned my attention to him.

He grinned. "The Lenape *fraa* seemed to believe you have a young woman awaiting your return."

"Elisabeth? So she thinks. When my fever raged, I reckoned her to be Elisabeth, but 'tis not as she implied. Elisabeth lived on neighboring land, and her father was the blacksmith with whom I apprenticed. I lived with them from the time I was twelve, and she was like a sister to me."

"How glad you must be. Being separated from my family for a few days when I make the journey to *Onkel* Dieter's is difficult enough, let alone for longer."

I had felt the same way once. Now, as much as I anticipated my reunion with Friends, concern for how I'd be received overshadowed that. My decision to leave had aggrieved many, especially Elisabeth, and had likely caused our Friends Meeting to disown me.

I changed the subject. "Who awaits thee at home?"

"My *fraa* and our four children. Rockhill has never suffered harm at the hands of Indians, and I trust my family's safety to *Gott*, but I was hesitant to leave them this time with all the turmoil not so far away."

"That is one of the reasons I'm returning home."

He shook his head. "*Schade*. Such a pity. A man needn't be a yeoman to understand that those who plant weed seeds will not harvest grain in season. Whatsoever a man sows, that shall he also reap."

Truer words had never been spoken. And I feared the time of reaping had come.

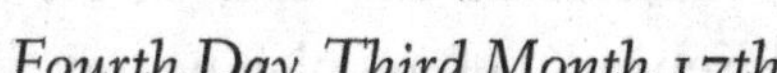

Fourth Day, Third Month 17th

Having left Rockhill early in the morning, I'd turned off the Minsi Trail onto the road that led from Montgomery to Horsham at daybreak. My plan had been to start my trek as soon as we reached Johannes's home the evening prior, but he'd encouraged me to eat supper with his family and sleep at least a few hours. Exhausted and sore from the daylong wagon ride, I agreed. Then this morning I'd departed the Kolb plantation when Johannes rose to tend his livestock.

Now, two hours after daybreak, pangs of relief and hesitance stirred within me as I approached the home Mother shared with my sister Susannah. Two stories and built of fieldstone with black-shuttered windows and a slate roof, the house looked just as it always had. Hopefully, its inhabitants' health fared as well.

I opened the front door, and the consolation of familiarity greeted me as I stepped into the center hall. After placing my snapsack on the floor, I walked to the doorway leading into the parlor. The cozy room also appeared no different from when I'd left. Only a few decorations adorned the whitewashed walls, the furniture was austere but of high quality, and the Oriental rug I'd played on as a child covered the floor.

Before the fireplace, Mother sat in her rocking chair, her head back and eyes closed, her hands palm up on the open Bible in her lap. Throughout the years, I'd found her in that position many times, listening so intently for God's whisper that she heard nothing else. Yet age now lined her face more deeply and her frame seemed thinner.

Guilt riddled my gut.

I crossed the floor to the chair, then knelt, kissing her forehead before placing my hand over her much smaller ones. "Mother?"

She lifted her head. When her blue eyes focused on me, they filled with tears. "Isaac," she said, smiling, and took my face in her hands. "Thee has returned."

I grinned. "I have." Never had her touch been such a comfort and joy.

She embraced me, whispering several times, "My son has returned. Praise be to God." Then after adjusting her linen cap, she wiped her eyes with the handkerchief pulled from the waistband of her apron, closed her Bible, and set both on the table next to her chair. "Thee must be hungry. Come to the kitchen. Susannah isn't here, but she will return soon."

I shook my head. "I've eaten. Don't trouble thyself."

She placed her hand on the side of my head and ran it down the length of my hair. "Thee has been living on the frontier?"

"I was, with a group of Lenape and Mahican many miles north of here."

"Was thy journey long?"

Much longer than I'd expected. "Several days. Thee has fared well?"

"I have. These old bones get stiff when the weather is cold and damp, but Susannah takes good care of me."

I searched her face. Indeed she looked older, but I saw something more. Her eyes lacked the serenity I remembered. So much could have happened in the time I was gone that I hesitated to ask, but I would find out soon enough. "Something troubles thee?"

She swallowed. "Jonathan Alden was badly injured on Sixth Day of last week."

The food Johannes's wife had provided for my journey grew heavy in my stomach. "Injured?"

"He and Abner Jones were returning from the city during the snowstorm. He alighted the wagon to lead the horses, and a large branch overhanging the road fell onto him."

Nay.

"He has awoken only a few times, and he started with fever two days ago."

At least he was alive. But I knew well the graveness of infection. "I'm sorry, Mother. I should go to them."

She nodded. "Thee go. They need thee right now."

I hugged her again and kissed her cheek, then stood and headed for the door.

As I took off toward the path through the wood, the difficulties that forced my departure from Chinkanning suddenly held little significance in comparison to those that awaited me at the Alden home.

I hastened through the dim wood as quickly as the pain in my side allowed. The forest floor's heady spring aroma, once a smell that invigorated me, only served to intensify the lead weight in my belly. Although the Aldens lived only a couple of minutes' walk from Mother's, I couldn't get there quickly enough.

Soon I came to the stream that cut through the trees. After crossing the plank bridge, I slowed my pace and stopped at the edge of the Alden clearing. The log house, harvested vegetable and herb gardens, woodshed, barn, and forge showed few signs of change.

A young girl with long blond braids appeared at the path's entrance to the wood. She stopped, her eyes widening when they met mine. Dropping her armload of sticks, she ran for the house so swiftly that her loosely tied cap slid off the back of her head.

"Wait!" I hurried after her.

"Indian!" She stumbled on her petticoat about ten paces from the house and landed prostrate, allowing me to close the distance between us.

I dropped to one knee. "Fear not. I won't hurt thee."

"Indian! Indian!" Her screeches pierced my ears.

As I righted her, a kick to my middle took all my breath and sent blistering pain through my side. No doubt she'd reopened the scab that covered my wound. I finally sucked in air, but dizziness warned me not to get up yet.

"We are Friends. If thee comes in peace, thee is welcome here." Although cautious in tone, the familiar female voice that called out was surely the sweetest sound I'd ever heard.

I stood, ignoring another wave of imbalance. My pulse quickened at seeing her standing near the porch. "Elisabeth."

"Isaac?" She stepped forward, her mouth agape, then clapped her hand over it. Grabbing and lifting her petticoat, she rushed toward me.

Elation clogged my throat and brought tears to my eyes as she flung her arms around me, and I held her tightly despite the aching in my side.

Eventually, she drew back.

While the homestead looked no different, Elisabeth did. She stood inches taller, nearly the height of my shoulder, and her slight frame had rounded into that of a young woman. A beautiful young woman.

She wiped tears from her flushed cheeks and tucked her neck kerchief back into the bodice of her gown. "Has thee been to see thy mother?"

"Aye. Thy papa, how is he?"

She shook her head, suddenly stricken. "He rarely awakens. Now he burns with fever as well." After a few moments, she scowled and looked away.

Clearly, I stared too intently. "My apologies. Thee looks so much older, so mature."

She took a step back and folded her arms. "Thee has been away all of two years and then some. Did thee expect I would still look like a seventeen-year-old girl?"

"I . . ." My chest constricted at the resentment that stole the joy from her face and clipped her words. Not that I didn't deserve her exasperation. "Nay."

She narrowed her eyes and set her mouth. "How long will thee be staying?"

I moved toward her. Heartened by the passion with which she'd greeted me, I'd dared to hope she held no ill will. Wrong. "Elisabeth." She retreated again, and I stayed myself. "I'm not leaving."

"We did not expect thee to return," she said, her arms still crossed. "When Isaac Norris brought word from thee after you happened to meet at the Albany Congress, he said thee had assimilated into the Lenape culture. After another year passed with no word, we expected thee had found thy home."

I exhaled. Excuses would be futile. "I'm not leaving. I have seen how Mother is aging, and I could never leave thee alone with thy papa as he is."

Her expression softened but only for a moment. "I'm not alone." She turned toward the house, where the little girl stood in the doorway with a sandy-haired boy who, although quite young, was already breeched. "'Tis all right. Come here to me."

They came off the porch and peeked at me from behind her.

"Thee has met Abigail—and her very able foot. And this is Ethan." She rested a hand on each of their heads. "Papa married Barbara Edwards from Abington in the spring of the year before last. They are the children from her first marriage." She looked down at them. "Isaac is Aunt Mary's son and Susannah's brother. Thee needn't fear him."

Abigail glanced at me. "I thought he was an Indian."

Elisabeth eyed me from head to foot. "Thee is correct. His first mother was Lenape, and when his parents died, Aunt Mary became his mother."

"He's like us?"

"Aye." Elisabeth returned her attention to me. "Their mother died in Seventh Month."

Meaning their care rested wholly on Elisabeth.

The little girl inched to Elisabeth's side, peering up at her. "Is Jon-Isaac named for him and Papa?"

Elisabeth adjusted Abigail's cap. "Aye."

"Jon-Isaac?" I repeated.

"Our baby brother," Ethan said. Unlike Abigail, he watched me with only interest in his brown eyes. Eyes so much like Jeremiah's, and they shared similar loss.

Elisabeth raised her gaze to mine.

"Thy papa gave him the middle name Isaac?" I asked.

"Nay. I did. Come inside. Surely thee wants to see Papa." Turning, she guided the children toward the house.

I followed.

Perhaps she didn't hate me as much as I'd feared.

CHAPTER 4

Elisabeth

I finished stirring the chicken stew that bubbled in a pot over the low fire, then straightened. Only the occasional crackle of wood broke the stillness that filled the house. While Jon-Isaac slept in his cradle, Abigail sat at the table writing letters on her slate and Ethan played with his toys on the braided rug in the sitting area.

Movement drew my attention across the room to the doorway of Papa's bedchamber. Isaac still sat in the chair by Papa's bed, where he had spent most of the afternoon. I folded my arms, irritation replacing the surge of sympathy I'd felt. While he genuinely loved Papa, he had left, rendering Papa heartbroken over the loss of the apprentice he had loved as his own son.

Father, forgive me. 'Twasn't my place to judge another.

I walked to the table. "I need to milk Sally and get water from the springhouse."

Abigail looked up, her eyes wide. "Please. I want to go with thee."

"Nay. I shan't be gone long, and I need thee to stay with Ethan and Jon-Isaac."

She glanced toward Papa's bedchamber, and her eyes glimmered when she looked back at me. She shook her head and stood. "I don't want to stay here with him."

I sighed. She still feared Isaac, having not even ventured near him all day. I couldn't blame her. Clad in frontiersman's garb, bone necklaces, and a pewter cross hanging from one ear—and with his long hair unbound—Isaac barely resembled the young man who'd once worn plain clothing and his hair in a queue. "Abby, he will not hurt thee. I wouldn't leave thee with him if he would."

"I'll go." Isaac now stood in the doorway. "What needs to be done?"

I opened my mouth to protest, but his going might be best. "Daniel's boys have been tending the animals since Papa's injury, but Sally kicks too much for them, so I've been milking her."

"That goat was always fine with me. Anything else?"

"Just water from the springhouse."

Without a word, he headed for the back door.

"Isaac." I followed him.

He waited, his hand on the latch.

"She doesn't mean to be hurtful," I said softly upon reaching him. "Children at school have told her stories about Indian attacks, and they've frightened her. She just needs time to understand thee will not hurt her."

He drew a breath. "I'd like to stay here so I can help with whatever thee might need. I'll stay in the forge quarters—if thee is agreeable."

Despite my great relief, I refused to show it. If he wanted to stay, so be it, but I wouldn't employ guilt to coerce him. "This is thy home, and thee is welcome here."

By the somber look in his eyes when he nodded once and opened the door, my words had not been in any way convincing.

Fifth Day, Third Month 18th

"Elisabeth!"

Abigail's cry brought me to my feet as I helped Ethan dress the next morning. Hearing the urgency in her voice—joyful urgency—I fastened his breeches and rushed to her.

"What is it?" I asked at entering Papa's bedchamber.

Abigail sat on the edge of Papa's bed, one hand on his cheek. "He opened his eyes. He said my name."

Such happiness washed through me that my heart skipped a beat. I leaned over the bed, looking at him closely. High fever still flushed his face below the bleached linen strips that formed a thick bandage from above his blackened eyes to the crown of his head, but his eyelids fluttered. "Papa?"

His eyes opened slightly, and he moaned. The hint of a smile twitched at the corner of his mouth.

"Hurry. Go outside and summon Isaac."

Abigail didn't move, and I met her gaze. She slid off the

bed, shaking her head, then went to the wall where Ethan stood in his shirt, breeches, and stockings.

As much as I didn't want to leave Papa, I hastened to the back door and out into the morning chill. "Isaac!" No answer came from the barn or forge. "Isaac!"

He hurried out of the barn still holding a pitchfork.

"'Tis Papa! He has awoken!" I rushed back inside.

By the time I reached Papa's bedchamber, Isaac was close behind. He followed me into the room and sat on the chair by the bed.

I lowered myself onto the tick. "Papa?"

"Jon?" Isaac placed a hand on his shoulder.

"Look, Papa. Isaac is here." I turned his head to the side. "He's come home."

When he opened his eyes they shone, but he raised his eyebrows in recognition. "Isaac," he breathed out, his voice barely a whisper. His slight smile reappeared. "Thee . . . has returned."

Isaac squeezed his shoulder gently. "I have."

Papa swallowed. "I always . . . knew thee would."

I stroked his cheek with the backs of my fingers. "Does thee want anything? Some tea? Thee has had little to eat or drink for days."

He stared into my eyes. "Thee is . . . so much like thy mama. How I . . . loved her . . . my Catharine." He looked back to Isaac and struggled to free his arms from the covers. When I drew down the quilt, he gripped Isaac's forearm. "I must . . . ask of thee . . ."

Isaac leaned closer. "Anything."

"Take care of . . ." He glanced at me before returning his gaze to him and attempting to sit up. "Take care of her . . . and the children. Will thee . . . do that?"

"Papa, thee mustn't talk that way," I said.

Isaac nodded. "I will. Thee knows I will."

Papa opened his mouth to speak but instead fell back onto his pillow, panting.

"Rest now." I touched his hot, unshaven face again. "Thee must build thy strength. We will be here when thee awakens."

"Indeed," Isaac said. "We'll be right here."

Papa cradled my face in his large hand and ran his roughened thumb over my lips. With a weak smile, he dropped his arm to the bed.

I took his hand in mine, and he squeezed it and closed his eyes.

Joy now replaced the dread that had plagued me for days. Papa was awake.

~

Seventh Day, Third Month 20th

Wind drove the chilly drizzle that fell from the dismal sky as we stood at Papa's gravesite two days later. John Cadwallader, a weighty Friend and longtime friend of Papa's, afforded words of comfort, and I did my best to smile and nod. While the stories shared by Friends during the memorial meeting had touched my heart, reality set in again as I stared at the small gray stone with the inscription *J. A. 1756*.

A hand on my shoulder startled me, and I looked up to find more people gathered around us. They offered condolences to Isaac and me and any assistance we might need, and we thanked them for their care.

"Does thee wish to stay longer?" Isaac asked once most everyone had left.

I looked down at the children beneath my cloak, Jon-Isaac asleep against my shoulder and Abigail with her arm around my waist. "Nay. We should get them out of the weather."

My throat ached terribly as Isaac, with his own cloak over Ethan, led me away from the grave.

Papa was gone. Barely more than a week before, he'd been fine—working in his forge, laughing with those who came to him for blacksmithing, and playing with the children. Now the shell of his body lay beneath cold, dark clumps of earth.

At our wagon, Isaac lifted Ethan into the back and reached for Abigail.

She cowered, stepping around behind me.

"Abigail." I shifted Jon-Isaac to one arm and grasped her shoulder to urge her forward. "Let Isaac help thee."

After a hesitation, she allowed him to pick her up.

Resentment pricked me when my gaze returned to the lines of markers. The small crescent-shaped gravestones seemed an unworthy representation of the faithful Friends whose physical bodies lay forever silent beneath them. Did they not deserve more for their deep love for God and their devout ways—more than just their initials, if even that, etched into stone?

Thou art dust, and to dust shalt thou return. The words from Scripture admonished me, followed by those of Papa: *"Who are we, that the Almighty is mindful of us? Yet he is. We must put away all vanity, for glory belongs to him alone."*

"Forgive me, Father," I murmured.

"Elisabeth?"

I turned at Isaac's voice. Daniel and Hannah Lukens, Isaac's brother and sister-in-law, now stood with us. Since Papa's injury, their family had helped us in every way they could.

Daniel nodded at me, sending droplets of water sliding off the brim of his hat. "I know thee requested no community gathering, but if you would like us to visit today, Hannah and the children and I would be most willing."

They could not have been better neighbors, but hosting company seemed unbearable. Simply breathing required all my effort. "Thank thee, Daniel, but I think we would like to rest."

"Of course."

Hannah embraced me. "We shall send the boys to help Isaac tend the animals this evening. Let us know if thee would like the assistance of one of the older girls."

I released her. "I will."

Daniel rested a hand on Isaac's shoulder briefly, then led Hannah away.

Isaac helped me into the wagon, and I sat and adjusted my cloak around Jon-Isaac. Behind me, Abigail and Ethan huddled beneath a woolen blanket. In their short lives, they had lost a mother and two fathers. I'd at least had a mother for twelve years and a father for twenty. They had only me now.

I held Jon-Isaac closer. Not that I wouldn't be a proper mother for them. I'd taken over most of their care when Barbara took ill not long after she and Papa married, and her death had placed the entirety of that responsibility on me.

But being a mother was one thing. How would I be their mother and now, without Papa, their father as well?

I awoke to a low, vaguely familiar voice. Someone was singing. But Friends neither sang nor participated in any other type of music.

Upon opening my eyes, I found myself in Papa's bedchamber, now mine. The events of the day—Papa's burial and Isaac's persuading me to rest after we returned to the house—came back, bringing heaviness to my heart. I slid out of bed and made my way to the common room.

Isaac sat in the rocking chair before the hearth, holding Jon-Isaac on his lap as he crooned a chant-like song that certainly wasn't English. Jon-Isaac watched with attentive eyes as he batted at the cross hanging from Isaac's ear. At seeing me, he gave an exultant two-toothed smile and shook his arms in excitement.

Love for him eased the emptiness within my soul. What a welcome reprieve his sweet innocence brought.

Isaac turned, his expression contrite. "He started to cry, and I didn't want him to wake thee."

I shook my head. "'Tis all right. I've hummed to him as well at times."

"How did thee sleep?"

"Fine." While initially discomfited by the thought of taking Papa's bedchamber for my own, I'd napped well, feeling Papa's presence more strongly and savoring the silence and stillness of not sharing a bed with Abigail and Ethan.

I lowered myself onto the footstool beside the chair, watching Jon-Isaac. His awe as he beheld Isaac came as no surprise. When we were growing up, Isaac had simply been Isaac to me, but now the salience of his darker skin, slate-blue eyes, and black hair stood out. Never had I considered the countenance of a man beautiful—until now. "Isaac enchants thee, doesn't he, sweet boy?"

"Aah-gaah," Jon-Isaac babbled and grabbed a handful of Isaac's hair.

We laughed, and the familiar sound of it brought comfort initially but then bitterness at how much I'd missed our relationship. Jon-Isaac pulled his hair, and I untangled his chubby little fist.

Isaac met my gaze. "He reminds me of Henry."

The thought of my two-year-old brother who had died when I was almost nine burgeoned my already overwhelming grief. Papa had once said the same thing, and I bit back a curt reply. 'Twasn't Isaac's fault that I barely remembered what Henry looked like—nor my three-year-old sister Lucy, stillborn brother Timothy, or even Mama at times.

Jon-Isaac reached for me, and I took him. "Thee must be ready for a fresh clout and some pap."

Isaac stood. "I'll go tend Sally so you have fresh milk for him."

"Shall I prepare some supper?"

"I don't have a stomach for much."

Nor did I. "Some tea?"

"Please."

He started for the door, and remorse pricked me. Isaac had taken over all of Papa's tasks since returning, as well as a few of mine. He had treated me kindly, even when my words held unwarranted impudence, and had responded to Abigail's fear of him with gentleness. Yet I still resented him.

A lump formed in my throat as I watched Jon-Isaac gnaw

on his thumb. To teach the children to show mercy and grace, I would need to display those traits myself. But what if I couldn't?

Never had I felt so unfit for the lot I faced.

Chapter 5

Isaac

I saac." Daniel's greeting came from behind as I pulled the pail from beneath Sally.

Glancing over my shoulder, I found him standing in the doorway of the barn, a lantern held chest high. I patted the nanny goat's rump, then rose from the milking stool and carried the pail out of the stall.

My brother neared, his concerned gaze never leaving mine, and hung the lantern on the wall. The brightness in the large room increased, and I averted my eyes, wishing for the protective disguise of the previous dimness. "How is thee?"

He and Hannah had helped Elisabeth and me prepare Jonathan's body early that morning, but we'd had no time to speak in confidence. I'd expected he would visit before the day was done, but still hadn't determined a truthful answer to that anticipated question. "As well as can be expected." I set the pail by the wall.

"Precious in the sight of the Lord is the death of his saints. Jonathan died in the Lord. But while a victory for him, 'tis a great loss for those of us left with his absence. To thee and Elisabeth and the children especially."

And to Daniel, as he and Jonathan had been neighbors and good friends for twenty years. I paced away from him, beleaguered with guilt. "I should have been here." If the settler had not shot me on the Nescopeck Path, I likely would have been. Then I could have accompanied Jonathan to Philadelphia. I clenched my hands to keep from striking the wall. "If I had . . ."

"Thee mustn't blame thyself." He followed me to where I'd leaned against the fencing of a stall. "The Almighty appoints our time on earth, and 'twas Jonathan's time to receive his riches in heaven." He sat on the bench against the wall, and I followed suit. "How long will thee be staying?"

His words, though not undeserved, cut deep. "I can't leave, not now. Elisabeth could never manage the children and the homestead on her own, even with the assistance of Friends. I made a promise to Jonathan. When he awoke before he died, he requested that I take care of them. I won't go back on my word."

"I see." He removed his hat, revealing the scant gray that now streaked his light-brown hair. "But does thee truly want to stay?"

Another uncertainty. While I'd longed for Horsham before arriving, doubts now afflicted me. Some Friends observed me with reticence, and how long would it be before I longed for the freedom of the wilderness I'd come to love almost as much as Sam did?

"I'm not sure what I want right now. But as long as Elisabeth allows it, I will do my best to care for her and the children. I owe that to Jonathan—and to her." I stared at our feet, his in black leather and mine in worn moccasins. "I owe it to Mother to be here as well. She cared for me as my mother, and I should be here to care for her as her son."

He nodded. "Where is thee staying?"

"In the quarters in the forge."

"Good. Even though thee always slept in the house loft, much has changed. Thee and Elisabeth are adults now, and Meeting will not approve your living under the same roof without the oversight of another."

"Mother and Susannah have said as much. I cannot say I'd be welcome in the house anyway."

He arched his eyebrows. "Why would thee be unwelcome? Elisabeth has missed thee terribly."

If so, she had a peculiar way of showing it. "Elisabeth knows not how she feels about me. We have occasional moments where 'tis as if I never left and we are still as close as ever, but the rest of the time she barely speaks to me." I leaned my elbows on my legs and rubbed my hands over my face. "And then there is Abigail, who thinks I want to scalp her."

Daniel grunted. "When a stone is tossed into water, a ripple always follows. Much the same, our actions always have consequences. Is thee still a Christian?"

I sat up straighter. "Of course I—" Hearing the defensiveness in my tone, I stopped. His question was not unwarranted. "My beliefs have not changed."

"Thanks be to God for that." He sighed as his gaze lowered, taking in my garb. "Perchance if thee returned to dressing plainly and cut thy hair, 'twould put Abigail's fears to rest—as well as assuage the worries of Friends."

No one had mentioned my appearance, but 'twould be only a matter of time. Though my old clothing was still in the clothing press in the house's loft, I hadn't donned any of it save the cloak I wore to Jonathan's burial. Not that my breeches would fit well, considering I was thinner now than when I left. "Aye."

"I will pray for thee, Isaac, and thee needs to pray and mind the Light within thee. Thy intentions for staying are honorable, but I fear if thee is not happy here, thee will not be the help truly needed. God has given thee a gift for mediation, and this may be the place he has called thee to, or it may not. Aye, thee gave thy word to Jonathan, but I believe he would want thee to go if God called thee elsewhere. Consider that."

I could only nod in acquiescence.

First Day, Third Month 21st

A noise woke me from drowsing the next afternoon. I sat forward in the wingback chair, looking around. The doors to Elisabeth's and the children's bedchambers remained open only a crack, and no sounds came from beyond them. As I leaned back again, someone rapped on the front door.

I answered it before the visitor could knock again. There in the bright daylight stood John Cadwallader and Jabez Holt. My expectation that I'd soon be visited by weighty Friends was correct, and it heartened me that both knew me well.

With a nod, I invited them inside.

Jabez glanced around the common room. "Is thee here alone?"

"Nay. Elisabeth and the children are sleeping. Abigail had belly pains and trouble sleeping much of the night. She finally fell asleep around eight this morning, and then Elisabeth lay down once Ethan and Jon-Isaac were abed for their naps." I gestured to the couch and returned to the chair I'd been resting in.

"You were missed this morning at meeting for worship," Jabez said as they sat down. "Of course, Friends understand that the last few days have been difficult for you."

Difficult hardly described our anguish. "But if not for Abigail's illness, we would have been there."

John smiled. "We are glad to hear that. I know having thee home has been a comfort and help to Elisabeth." His expression then sobered. "When I spoke with Daniel today, he stated that thee has expressed intention to remain in Horsham. This is good news as well, but we do want to discuss where thee stands in thy life."

"And fully ascertain those intentions," Jabez added.

Even I had yet to ascertain those intentions, so all I could do was explain what I did know. "The Lenape are kind, honorable people who wanted peace with the white settlers, and I was humbled when God saw fit to use me in that process." Stretching out my legs, I looked from him to John. "But the unfair treatment of the tribes has caused wrath to replace peace in the hearts of some."

"We have received word of many Indian attacks on the frontier in the last months," Jabez said before I could continue.

A loosening seam on my moccasins caught my eye.

'Twould be a simple repair. If only the unravelings of my life could be so easily mended. "Aye."

His thick gray eyebrows nearly reached the brim of his hat when I finally glanced up at him. "But thee was never a partaker of such attacks?"

I pursed my lips until I trusted my tone wouldn't offend. "Never."

"Isaac, we are not implying we believe thee was," John said, and the sincerity of his expression and tone gave further assurance. "Thee has always had a gentle heart and a strong faith."

"Thy care for Elisabeth and the children since returning has clearly reflected that," Jabez went on. "But we must hold to the truth. At times, what our eyes see changes what our hearts feel. Thy countenance reveals a heart that is distraught, possibly from more than the loss of Jonathan."

I slowly breathed in and out, of no mind to broach that subject. "I do not wish to discuss what my eyes have seen. But this I can tell you without doubt: never was I a part of malevolence against another. As a Christian, I could not engage in such behavior, and that is one of the reasons I have returned."

John nodded. "We thank thee for confirming that with graciousness. Should any Friends question us, we can now declare thy goodwill to all."

That Friends could think I would participate in such behavior hurt. "Elisabeth has acknowledged that Meeting disowned me. I expect you would like to speak about that as well."

"Thee is not the first Friend to be disowned for absconding to parts unknown." Jabez's slack jowls quivered as he shook his head with vehemence. "Thee left in anger and did not request a certificate. In spite of the tenderness that many felt for thee in light of Hugh and Margaret Roberts's unbecoming and follish treatment, when thee did not return or even send word, we were tasked with disowning thee."

"I didn't leave in anger at Friends. I left to search for the families of my mother and father who gave me life." And because I could no longer bear the shame I felt every time Friends looked upon me with pity. "I couldn't request a certificate because I didn't know where I was going, or if there was a Meeting nearby. I knew only that I was headed north."

"Even so. Thy disownment was not an easy decision for us, and nothing beneficial can come from quibbling about it." As always, John spoke firmly yet with kindness. "However, we do wish to discuss thy intentions. Friends are exceedingly glad that thee has returned, and we wholeheartedly want thee back under care, but that is ultimately thy decision."

Jabez folded his hands in his lap. "Does thee wish to condemn thy behaviors and come under the care of Friends again?"

I nodded. "I will write an acknowledgment of my transgressions. And read it in meeting if required."

"That will not be necessary," John said. "Thy acknowledgment and regular attendance in meeting will be adequate evidence of thy repentance."

Jabez cocked his head as he looked at me. "Thee does understand that thy present clothing—and decorative adornments—are unsuitable for a Friend?"

I did, though 'twas ironic. Friends' garb, though considered more plain, was certainly more extravagant. "My former clothing is in the loft, and I shall resume wearing it."

Both nodded.

When we walked to the door at the conclusion of their visit, John clasped my arm. "Thy return is an answer to the prayers of many. I know Daniel and Hannah have been of much help, but if other assistance is needed, please do not hesitate to inform us."

"We will do that."

I nodded at Jabez, then closed the door behind them. When I turned around, Elisabeth carried Jon-Isaac out of her bedchamber.

"Who was here?" she asked.

"John Cadwallader and Jabez Holt."

Jon-Isaac grinned and reached for me as they neared. Like Ethan, he had taken to me almost right away, and their sweet admiration eased the distress of readjusting to life in Horsham. He squealed when Elisabeth handed him to me, then grabbed at the cross hanging from my ear.

I caught his hand and removed the earring. "I'm afraid thee will need to find a new toy, since such adornments are not befitting a Friend."

Elisabeth's expression brightened. "Will thee need thy clothing altered, then? Thee is a bit leaner now."

Her offer and expression of approval came as a relief since part of me had feared how she would react if I asked her to add another task to her responsibilities. "My breeches, at least. If thee has time. I can ask Susannah if thee doesn't."

"No need. After the children are abed this evening?"

The hopefulness in her tone heartened me further. If nothing else, she wished for my reinstatement in Meeting. "Aye."

The chance to spend some time alone with her suddenly made my decision to return to plain dress a bit more appealing.

CHAPTER 6

Isaac sat on the settle by the hearth, his Bible open in his lap, when I returned to the common room after rocking Jon-Isaac to sleep.

He looked up at me as I neared him, the slightest smile on his lips.

Something stirred in my chest. Not irritation this time, but something much different. An optimistic anticipation, perhaps. During his years living with us, Isaac and I had passed many evenings together, with him carving small pieces of wood while I cross-stitched or embroidered. We'd talked and laughed, often long after Papa was abed. Now I had time with him again.

"Thee is not too weary?" he asked.

I set my sewing hussif on the rocking chair, then lit another candle. "Not at all. Go up and change thy clothing."

Minutes later, he descended the ladder from the loft in brown breeches and a white linen shirt. He held a handful of cloth at the waist to keep the breeches from falling down.

I sat forward in my chair, opened my hussif, and took Isaac's arm to turn him toward the hearth's firelight. Raising the hem of his shirt, I grasped the left-side waist of his breeches and started making small tucks with pins. I moved to his right side to make equal tucks on that side, but his shirt fell down over my hands. He lifted it for me, and I pushed his hand higher.

My breath caught. Below his ribs was a deeply gouged wound the size of half a walnut shell. Reddened skin surrounded the black-rimmed scab. Immediately I thought of how he had grabbed his side when Abigail kicked him. But such an injury had come from much more than that. "Isaac, what happened?"

He looked away from me, but I could see his throat move as he swallowed. "I was shot." His words barely reached my ears.

Shot? "By whom?"

"A white settler . . . north of Bethlehem." He shook his head. "'Tisn't what thee thinks. On my journey home, I came upon a group of settlers early one morning. One of them thought I was a warrior and panicked."

As much as I wished to stand and face him, his stiff posture told me to refrain. "What does thee mean, 'tisn't what I think?"

"I never took part in a war party."

"Why would thee—" Then I remembered what I'd heard him discussing with the visiting Friends that afternoon. "Isaac, I would never—*could* never—believe thee would do such a thing."

He nodded, his gaze still fixed on something across the room.

I almost challenged him further, incredulous that he would think I would entertain such a thought, but stayed myself. *"I do not wish to discuss what my eyes have seen."* My heart had lurched at overhearing him say that, and sadness now replaced my annoyance. Whatever he had seen had changed him—allowed him to think I would judge him—and I thanked God for harnessing my tongue.

I carefully pressed the area around the scab with my fingertips. "'Tis quite inflamed. Does it hurt?"

"The scabbed area is tender to touch and certain movements." His posture eased a bit, and he turned to reveal a smaller, better-healed wound on his back. "That is where the bullet entered. It exited the front."

"When did it happen?" He had returned only days ago, yet it didn't look fresh.

"Two weeks past. The bullet damaged only muscle and skin, but the wound festered. Four days I fought the infection, and then 'twas another three days before I could resume my journey."

I placed my palm over the area, but he recoiled and caught my hand in his.

"My apologies." Withdrawing my hand, I peered up at him. Oddly, his eyes seemed to reflect not pain but surprise. "I just wanted to be sure it wasn't hot to touch."

He didn't respond, and his solemn reserve curtailed my beseeching of more information.

I finished pinning tucks until the breeches fit his waist, then sent him back to the loft to change into the buckskin breeches he'd been wearing. When he returned carrying all his plain breeches, I used the pinned pair as a pattern to alter the waists of the others and started sewing the tucks.

He sat on the settle with the Bible again, but neither of us said a word.

My throat ached at our silence. How I wished he would speak, to tell me about his visit with John and Jabez or read aloud the verses. He had been my dearest friend for the first seventeen years of my life, yet that had ceased when Margaret Roberts deceived him and he made the decision to find the family of his first parents. Though he had returned, the closeness we once shared had not.

I folded the breeches on my lap once they were all altered, then set my hussif on the floor next to the rocking chair.

He looked up. "Would thee mind cutting my hair?"

But his hair was lovely. 'Twas longer than I had seen on a man before, but its black shine and the way he wore it loose with the front tied back appealed to me. "Is thee certain that is what thee wants?"

He scowled, though not in anger. "'Tis quite long, and 'twould be a hazard in the forge."

True, but . . . "Thee could wear it in a braid and tie it up while working."

His stare softened into a grin. "Thee prefers it as it is?"

I stood, encouraged by his brightened disposition. "I do. It suits thee, and I don't think thee should cut it unless thee truly wants to."

He closed the Bible and placed it on the settle, then rose. "I shall consider that. We're both weary, so I shall retire now."

Oh, not yet! Despite my conflicting feelings, I wanted to say so much to him, to share so much. But I had no idea where to begin. How I longed for more time with him, even if only in silence, but I nodded.

"I thank thee. Sleep well."

I could only watch as he headed for the door, and tears filled my eyes when it closed behind him.

Eventide again became the loneliest time of my day.

Fourth Day, Third Month 24th

The front door groaned open as I finished changing Jon-Isaac's clout and pilch, and moments later Isaac's voice reached my bedchamber. "Beth?"

The pilch ties slipped from my fingers, and I grabbed them before Jon-Isaac squirmed and I'd need to start over. Isaac had not used that name for me since he returned, and hearing it somehow bothered and encouraged me alike. After lifting Jon-Isaac from the bed, I carried him into the common room.

Inside the front door, Isaac stood with a shorter, stout visitor. The man's face was hidden as he mopped it with a handkerchief, but I immediately recognized the fine, gaily colored clothing.

I'd suspected he would soon visit, but that didn't preclude the nervousness that resulted. His many tales of the places he visited always provided a welcome diversion from the humdrum of my life, yet his dutiful attention surprised me. In comparison I seemed so naive, and at times even felt immature in his presence.

"Hiram." On my way to greet him, I set Jon-Isaac on the rug to play with Ethan.

"My deepest condolences, dear heart." He pocketed his handkerchief. "I came upon Robert Iredell on the road here, and he told me what happened. Had I known, I would have come straightaway, but I returned from Baltimore only yesterday."

Looking into the hazel eyes behind his spectacles, I tried to smile. "I know thee would have." Then I realized the men should be properly introduced. "Clearly, thee has met Isaac. He used to be Papa's apprentice and returned last week from working as a peacemaker amongst the Indians."

I turned to Isaac. "Hiram and his older brother own a carriage-building company in Philadelphia. This past summer one of his horses needed shoeing soon after he left from visiting Thomas Graeme, and he came to Papa. Since then he's had Papa making some special hardware for his carriages."

Isaac raised an eyebrow. "Thee has no closer, equally skilled blacksmiths in Philadelphia?"

Hiram smiled. "I do"—he directed his grin at me—"but none with as charming a daughter."

Warmth tingled on my cheeks, and I lowered my gaze to the floor. "Hiram."

"'Tis true," he said. "And naught to be self-conscious about. Thee cannot help thy loveliness." He faced Isaac. "I trust thee can search the forge for my order?"

Isaac never looked away from me. "I'll do that now."

Once Isaac left, Hiram offered his arm. "Let us sit for a bit. I have missed thee."

I allowed him to lead me to the couch.

"How has thee been?" He grimaced as if his own words slapped him. "My apologies. It sounds as if I'm making trifle talk. Surely this has been a trying time."

"Indeed. Having Isaac back has been a comfort."

He sat and took my hand when I lowered myself beside him. "Mmm, Isaac. An interesting fellow, I must say. Thy father had mentioned his former apprentice but never said he was an Indian."

"Half. He's half Lenape."

"Only half? Intriguing." He removed his hat and set it on the table next to the couch, then dropped his chin and smoothed his light-brown hair. "Oh." He started at raising his head to find Ethan standing before him. "Hello. What is thy name again?"

Ethan smiled, blinking his long lashes. "Ethan."

"Of course. Ethan. Thee may return to thy playing, young man." Hiram watched as he rejoined Jon-Isaac, who sat on the floor clacking together two wooden blocks, then shifted his gaze to me. "I did not realize thee is also called Beth."

"Only Isaac does that. When we were young, he couldn't pronounce Elisabeth. He still uses it betimes." Like when he wished to emphasize to another the closeness of our relationship, apparently.

"A pet name, then." He cleared his throat. "It concerns me that he is living here. Friends have not protested?"

I'd assumed he would question that. "For the children's and my sake, they have consented to his staying in the forge quarters. He lived here for several years before, and besides, he is like family to me."

"Of course." He patted my hand. "Caring for a home and children is much responsibility for a young woman."

"'Tis. But with Isaac's and Friends' assistance, it has been quite doable."

"No doubt. Thee is an able woman. But I presume they

will be under thy care only until determination of who will take them in permanently?"

I looked at the boys. "Who will take them in?"

"Well, Jon-Isaac is thy half-brother, I know. But the little girl and"—he paused—"Ethan, were they not thy papa's wife's children? I simply assumed they would have kin who would take them in now."

Not if I had say in the matter. "Barbara's husband had no family here in the Colonies. Her parents died before she married Papa, and she had but one brother and they had not spoken in years. I have cared for the children the past two years and wish to continue doing so."

"But thee is young and unmarried, dear heart. Raising such young children will require two parents. Friends know this. Surely thy Meeting will be tasked with appointing a committee to determine the future of their care, will they not?"

I tried to swallow but couldn't. Though I had not considered this, he was correct. When children under the care of Friends were orphaned of both parents, the Meeting appointed a committee to determine who would rear them and to ensure they received their rightful inheritance. "I . . . I suppose."

He squeezed my hand gently. "Oh dear. All this talk about the loss of thy father is upsetting thee. I should have been more sensitive to thy fragile state."

I shook my head. He misinterpreted what troubled me, and perhaps that was best.

Hiram was regaling me with an evocative narrative of his trip to Baltimore when Isaac came in the front door.

"I've loaded all the hardware into thy carriage," he said at nearing where we sat. His jaw tightened when his gaze rested on our interlaced hands. "I'll just need thee to ensure 'tis all there."

"Of course." Hiram finished his tea, then lifted my hand and kissed its back. "I shall take my leave now. I have much business to attend, having just returned."

I nodded, jolted back to reality and the grave implications of our previous discussion. That, coupled with the unending ache of grief, suddenly threatened my composure, and I clenched my teeth.

He stood. "No need for thee to rise, my dear. I shall call again soon, when time allows."

As Hiram strode toward the door, I looked at Isaac. His gaze held mine, then he crossed his arms as Hiram passed. Without a word, he followed him outside.

As soon as the door closed behind them, I drew a calming breath. If only Hiram could have stayed longer. Despite our conversation regarding the children, the rest of his visit had brightened my day.

Ethan jumped up and approached me, smiling sweetly. "I waited patiently. May I have some dried apples now?"

I pulled him close and savored the delight of his little arms around me. "Aye."

The children were my only family now. Surely Friends wouldn't see fit to take them from my care.

CHAPTER 7

Isaac

Elisabeth sat in the rocker by the hearth when I returned to the common room, her sampler on her lap and her rapt attention on the flames.

She looked at me and sighed when I sat on the settle. "Thy help with the children is appreciated. I don't know what had them so unruly tonight, and I feared losing patience with them."

I grinned. "A story settled them down."

She smiled, possibly for the first time since I'd come inside from loading Hiram Biddle's carriage that afternoon. "That makes three nights thee has told them a story. Soon they will want one every night."

Not that I'd mind. Growing up with much-older siblings, I'd always been surrounded by younger nieces and nephews, and I adored children. Abigail and Ethan were appropriately reserved, having just lost their stepfather, but Abigail now tolerated my presence, and at times I caught glimpses of their humor and silliness. "I enjoy it as well. Storytelling is revered by the Lenape. They use it for many reasons—to pass down history, to impart knowledge, to teach lessons."

"Is that what thee has been telling them?" Her tenor gave no indication of whether she approved.

"Does that bother thee?"

"Nay. Thee would never tell them a story that is not appropriate for their tender years. I know that." She looked down at the sampler, her expression sobering. "Thee is so good with them, so patient. I would do well to take instruction from thee."

Surely she didn't believe that. "Now that is not true." I stood and retrieved my bag of wood blocks and carving tools from the mantel, then sat on the stool beside the rocker. "Thee cares for them morning, noon, and night." I waited for her to look at me. "'Tis a great responsibility, and thee handles it with devoted love and compassion."

"By the grace of God alone some days, but I thank thee for thy encouragement—and for thy tenderness with Abigail. I wish thee could have seen the joy on her face when she awoke this morning and found the little dolls thee carved for her. She started playing with them as soon as she returned from school."

The sparkle in Abigail's eyes when she'd thanked me had been worth every moment I'd spent whittling, even the one when the knife slipped and bit a piece out of my knuckle. "She's a good girl."

"She is. Feisty at times but sweet."

I chuckled. "Like thee was at her age."

"'Tis true."

The beautiful smile she returned warmed me and provided courage to broach the matter that had hounded me all day. "Thee has never mentioned thy courtship."

Her expression darkened as she looked at the fire. "Hiram? We are not courting."

Was that what she believed? "It appears he is not of the same opinion."

She shook her head, but the widening of her eyes belied her conviction. "He came to Papa for hardware. I offered him tea and respite since he had traveled a distance, but I would afford anyone such a kindness."

"Beth, 'tis five hours' journey from Philadelphia by carriage, and he came with his coachman. Blacksmiths abound in the city, and even if they didn't, he could just send his coachman or another man in his stead. As well, he made it quite clear he returned to thy papa for hardware for more than one reason."

She lifted her chin. "He is a good friend of Dr. Graeme as well, and he often stays the night at Graeme Park. Besides, we are hardly of the same social circle. What interest would a man of his resources have in a blacksmith's daughter?"

"Apparently that is of little importance to him, given his compliments to thee and your hand holding. And Dr. Graeme spends only his summers here." I stopped, exhaling. The last thing I wanted was to argue with her, but her misconstruing their relationship could have dire consequences for both of them. "He has visited multiple times since Dr. Graeme returned to the city, has he not?"

She bit her lip as she watched the fire again. Perhaps, in innocence, she truly hadn't realized his intentions?

"Aye." Her lips tightened, and she looked at me. "I expect thee would not approve of such a courtship?"

I balked, searching for a response that would allow us constructive discussion. "I didn't say that. But he appears to be twice thy age."

"He is nine and thirty years."

"Only seven years younger than thy papa. How did he feel about his visits?"

Her gaze shifted downward to her sampler. "He encouraged me to get to know him better, and said I would be well provided for should we marry."

So she did realize courtship was a possibility—and, surely in Hiram's mind, a reality.

"Even so, I have never pursued his affection."

Her demeanor troubled me. She'd never been one to lie, and I suspected her drawn countenance reflected not apology but afflicting confusion. "What are thy thoughts about that? Marrying him would be quite a change, going from living here to living in Philadelphia. And while he may be a Friend, there are differences between some Philadelphia Friends and Friends here. Clearly, he is accustomed to an extravagant lifestyle. As well, thee always said how much thee loves Horsham, how thee couldn't imagine living anywhere else."

"That was years ago," she said softly. "So much has changed since then."

Most definitely. Regrettably, I'd been a part of that. But the Elisabeth I knew cherished our quiet, close-knit community and would never be happy in Philadelphia's high society. "Enough to make thee want to leave the only home thee has known and the Friends who love thee?"

Her head snapped up. "Is that not what thee did?"

"Elisabeth." But she was right. "I'm not trying to upset

"But thy intuition says . . ."

My intuition told me 'twould be best if he found another blacksmith—in Philadelphia. "I know Elisabeth, or at least I did. I would like to think I still do. I cannot see her happily married to a businessman who's old enough to be her father and travels often, leaving her alone—in the city, no less." I shook my head. "We were talking last night, and I reminded her that she has always loved living here. She told me that was years ago and much has changed."

Concern, or possibly sadness, tinged her expression. "The last few years have brought many changes to her life, Isaac. Some have been quite taxing." She rested her hand on mine as it lay on the table. "Elisabeth has always loved thee, and there's no doubt in my mind that she still does. Be patient and love her back, even if she makes it difficult. She needs thee . . . and I suspect she will need thee even more in the days to come."

I'd looked out the window at hearing raindrops pelt the glass, but her words captured my attention. "Thee is not telling me something."

She didn't respond.

"Susannah."

"I'm sorry." She now spoke in little more than a whisper. "I fear I have already said more than I should."

The rain fell harder, and I stood. "I should take my leave. Someone is bringing some tools for repair this afternoon, and I told Ethan he could watch me in the forge after his nap. Never have I met so small a child with such an interest in smithing."

She walked me to the back door. "Thee is a good man, Isaac, and Elisabeth *is* glad to have thee back despite how her actions may say otherwise."

Susannah was the second woman to use those words—*a good man*—to describe me. Still, I doubted I would believe them until I heard them from Elisabeth.

And I feared she would never say them.

First Day, Third Month 28th

The sun shone and the birds sang as Friends gathered after meeting for worship on First Day morning. Elisabeth, the children, and I moved amongst the groups of people outside the meeting house, exchanging pleasantries and thanking them for their visits and the meals they'd provided that week.

Tacy Jerret, one of Elisabeth's friends, soon approached. She greeted us warmly, her focus on Elisabeth. "Several of us are gathering at our house this afternoon for tea and to work on our samplers. If thee is able, we would be most happy to have thee join us."

Elisabeth gave a wavering smile as she balanced Jon-Isaac on her hip. "I thank thee, Tacy. The boys will be napping, however, so perhaps another time."

"I'll stay with them," I said.

"Thee is welcome to bring Abigail," Tacy added. "Some others are bringing their younger sisters."

Abigail smiled and folded her hands beneath her chin. "Oh, please, Elisabeth. May we attend?"

Elisabeth's brow furrowed, and she rested a hand on Abigail's head. "Another time."

"Why?" She scowled. "If the boys are napping and Isaac stays with them, why can't we—"

"Abigail." I gently gripped her shoulder.

Clamping her mouth, she looked down.

Elisabeth leaned over to address Ethan, who persistently pulled at her cloak to get her attention.

Tacy watched her for a few moments, eyes rife with sympathy, then looked back to me. "Another time, then."

When I turned back to Elisabeth, she conversed with Daniel and Hannah. Abigail giggled with their daughter Anna, her sullenness seemingly forgotten. Several paces beyond them, my niece Martha waved from where she stood with my sister Alice and a few other women.

I joined her. "How is thee, Martha?"

She smiled. "Quite well. And thee?"

"Likewise. Has thee a moment to speak in confidence?"

"Certainly." She led me away from the women and slowed to a stroll. "What is on thy mind?"

I hesitated, hoping I hadn't been presumptuous in asking her away like that, especially considering what I wanted to speak about. "Elisabeth."

"Did she decline Tacy's invitation?" Although she phrased her words as a question, I expected she already knew the answer.

"She did, even though I offered to stay with the boys. I want to believe she declined because she is still grieving, but I fear there is more to it than that."

She only stared at the ground as she walked.

"She barely speaks of those with whom she was such good friends before I left—even thee," I continued. "It seems that Hannah, Susannah, and my mother are the only ones with whom she has a close relationship."

She nodded and adjusted her tied-on straw hat against the breeze. "The children don't allow her much time for herself. Mother thinks she feels out of place with those of us without children."

That seemed plausible. "Does thee think the same?"

Martha stared off into the distance. "I do."

"But thee has other opinions as well?"

She looked at me and opened her mouth but then closed it again.

"I'm asking merely out of concern for Elisabeth."

She stopped and faced me. "I don't know." After a glance around us, she sighed. "Last spring, she was ill for about two weeks, even missing four meetings for worship. After that, she wasn't the same. I tried to keep up our friendship, but she never had time to socialize with anyone our age. The children became her priority, especially after Jon-Isaac was born and Barbara died." Sadness crinkled her face. "Our friendship has suffered ever since."

That could have been all it was, Elisabeth feeling isolated from the others because they no longer shared similar responsibilities. While two of her friends had married during my absence, none had children yet. "I thank thee, Martha. I hope I haven't discomfited thee."

"Thee is only concerned for Elisabeth."

As we made our way back toward the meeting house, I glanced across the clusters of people. Elisabeth caught my eye and then quickly looked away, almost as if she suspected we'd been speaking about her.

Martha smiled at me when we neared Alice and the other women. "I'm glad thee has returned, Isaac—for thy sake and for hers."

My gaze settled on Elisabeth again. If only she felt the same way.

CHAPTER 8

Elisabeth

Third Day, Third Month 30th

How is thee faring?" Susannah asked.

Tender gazes rested on me as I visited with the women who knew me best. Susannah, who had become like a mother to me when my own died, and Hannah, the kindest neighbor I could ask for, sat across the table. Beside me, Mary had her arm about my waist.

I glanced around the common room. The house was clean and tidy, the laundry washed and hung to dry, the livestock tended, and our food supply ample. Abigail was at school, Jon-Isaac napped, and Ethan played happily with Hannah's youngest boy. Even the forge fire blazed again, now under Isaac's able management. We lacked nothing.

Except Papa.

"We're managing. Abigail and Ethan sleep well again, and her belly pains have subsided."

"And thee?" Hannah asked.

My throat ached, and I took a sip of tea to ease it. The too-hot liquid burned its way down to my stomach. Fitting. If only it could singe away the uncharitable feelings that surfaced too often since Isaac's return.

To say I was faring well would be a lie, and they knew me well enough to sense such duplicity. "I must confess, since Papa's death, I'm bitter. I know I shouldn't be, but I am." When tears filled my eyes, I swallowed. "I miss him so very much . . . and the anger I feel shames me."

Mary tightened her arm around me. "Anger in and of itself is not a sin."

"Even Jesus experienced anger," Hannah added. "Such as with the changers of money in the temple and with the hardened hearts of the Pharisees. The Bible does not instruct that we mustn't be angry. What it warns against is sinning in our anger."

Mary set her cup on the table. "When Jacob's and my Ruth died in infancy, I experienced anger as well. I sought counsel from one of the Women's Meeting elders, and what I learned is that with anger, we must ask questions to determine its appropriateness. What is its motivation? On what is it focused? Is it properly controlled? Is its duration suitable? And does it have an apt result?"

I took a shaky breath, considering her queries. While her guidance intended to provide wisdom, their truth convicted me more.

"Has Isaac's return been a struggle for thee as well?" Susannah asked.

I looked at her, my first instinct denial, but the gentleness of her expression eased my reluctance to be honest. They loved me just as they loved Isaac and would not harbor ill will if I spoke freely.

"While he was gone, I often pondered whether he lived or had died," I murmured. "In my heart, I kept hope that he still lived—and I believed that I'd know it in my soul if his life was extinguished. But my head told me otherwise, because the Isaac I knew never would have separated himself from those who loved him, and from those he loved, for such a length of time."

Hannah nodded. "And now he has returned and thee is hurt because he was able to stay away for so long?"

I had never considered that before, but she was correct. "Aye."

She swallowed a sip of tea. "Has thee shared thy feelings with him?"

"Nay."

Susannah smiled. "Thee needs to speak truthfully with him. Does thee not agree that would nurture understanding between you and allow peace and trust to be worked toward?"

She made it sound so simple, and yet it wasn't. "Indeed. But I also hesitate. At times his eyes hold so much turmoil. He is hurting as well, and I don't want to wound him more."

Mary drew me closer. "Thee has such a compassionate heart."

"Has he shared with thee his experiences while he was gone?" Susannah asked.

"Only what I've heard him tell the children in stories. I have wanted to ask about other things but refrained. He plainly told John and Jabez that he didn't wish to speak about some of the things he's seen."

"Not with them. But he has always trusted thee with what he would not share with others"—Susannah glanced at Mary—"even Mother or me. I think if he would tell anyone, 'twould be thee."

Perhaps, or perhaps not. "He wouldn't talk to me about what happened with the Robertses."

"Not at the time," Mary said, "but perchance now that the sting of pain has dulled."

Except that now I begrudged him, and why would he confide in someone who treated him so?

I nodded and sipped my tea, but its warmth didn't untwist the knot in my stomach as I'd hoped.

While I always valued my friends' wise counsel, today's advice left me disconcerted. I had much heart-searching to do—and, I presumed, much forgiveness to not only give but also to request.

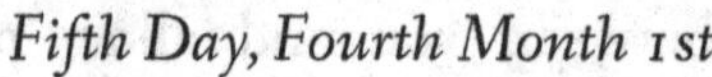

Fifth Day, Fourth Month 1st

I'd just placed the maize bread batter in the hearth oven when Isaac called from outside, "Abigail! Ethan! Come. I have a friend for you to meet!"

The children looked at me from where they played with Jon-Isaac in the sitting area. "A friend for us to meet? Whomever could he mean?" Abigail asked.

Childhood memories came to mind. When we were growing up, Isaac often called me outside to meet his *friends* —usually animals he found while traversing the forest. Toads, baby squirrels, snakes. Even an orphaned fawn. "I suppose you will need to go find out."

The children jumped up and hurried toward the open front door.

I crossed the floor and took Jon-Isaac from his baby-tender. "Hopefully, 'tis not a snake this time."

He squealed as if he understood.

The children's delighted cries quickened my pace to the door. Outside, Isaac knelt in the grass holding a wriggling black puppy that licked at the children's faces. The sound of their merry laughter surprised me. Although only about three weeks had passed since Papa's injury, it seemed like months since I'd heard proof of their happiness.

Abigail looked at him, her eyes bright. "Is it ours?"

Isaac smiled. "If you would like her, she is all yours."

A dog? If there was one thing we didn't need—

"Oh, I would!" She bounced on her heels and then kissed the puppy's head. "What's her name?"

"She doesn't have one yet. What would thee and Ethan like to name her?"

The puppy licked Isaac's neck and chin, bringing more laughter from all of them. He set her on the ground, and Abigail and Ethan knelt to stroke her head and back.

"How does thee say *dog* in Lenape?" Abigail asked.

"Dog? *Mwekane*. And puppy would be *mwekanètët*."

She scowled. "Mwek . . . What is *dog* again?"

"*Mwekane*."

"Mwek-ah-nee," she enunciated. "Oh, I like that. May we name her Mwekane?"

The puppy scampered away, and they followed.

Isaac stood as I approached. His expression dulled, confirming how poorly I hid my frustration. "I know I should have asked thee first. Daniel had several people showing interest in the litter. When he offered me first pick, I obliged because I knew how Abigail loved this one especially."

I sighed and handed him Jon-Isaac, who'd reached for him. "Thy intentions are good, but puppies require much time and training." And I already had more duties than seemed manageable at times. "I don't think now is the best time—"

"We can't keep her?"

Abigail's distraught interruption made me look down. With my attention on Isaac, I had not realized she'd carried the puppy to me. The anguish crumpling her face stabbed my heart. How could I be so selfish as to refuse them the one thing that eased the heartache that overshadowed their lives? "Of course we can. She shall make a fine addition to the family."

She bounced on her heels again, almost losing her grip on the puppy.

I caught the dog and lifted her little body into my arms. She licked my cheek, making me smile and turn my face to hers. I'd forgotten how I loved the sweet smell of a puppy.

"May we name her Mwekane?" Abigail asked.

"You may." I stroked the dog's head and set her on the ground.

Mwekane ran off as quickly as her legs would carry her, and Abigail made chase, calling her new name.

Ethan hurried to where Abigail knelt in the grass with the puppy in her arms, then dropped to his knees and giggled when Mwekane licked his face. She wiggled out of Abigail's arms and scurried off again, clearly enjoying the attention.

Mwekane ran toward us, and as they passed, Abigail stopped and wrapped her arms around Isaac's hips. "I thank thee, Isaac. I love her so much."

He shifted Jon-Isaac into one arm and rested his other hand on her head. "Thee is welcome."

A flood of emotion overwhelmed me, bringing tears to my eyes as Abigail dashed after Mwekane and Ethan—joy and reprieve at seeing their solemnity replaced by delight, yet a pang of resentment at . . . what? How the children had grown fond of Isaac, even after I'd prayed they would become comfortable with him?

My self-regard disgraced me. I pressed a hand to my mouth, controlling my breathing to keep composure.

Isaac stepped closer and placed a hand on my back.

His attempt to comfort me only increased my contrition. "I need to attend to the maize bread," I said, then fled toward the house.

I sat in the rocking chair in my bedchamber that night, listening as Isaac's voice drifted through the opening of the shared fireplace that served both Abigail and Ethan's bedchamber and my own. His stories now played a beloved part in their nightly routine, and their hushed voices consoled me as I rocked Jon-Isaac after tucking them into bed.

Once Jon-Isaac slumbered, I laid him in his cradle and returned to the common room. Mwekane opened her eyes, then wagged her tail and rose from where she lay. I sat in the rocking chair and lifted her to my lap, smiling when she licked my face. "Thee is such a sweet girl."

"Thank thee. But I'm not a girl."

I looked up to find Isaac approaching with a mischievous grin on his face. "Nay, thee is not." Neither was he the adolescent I remembered. During his time away, he had become a man, inwardly and outwardly. My smile faded. "I owe thee an apology for my exasperation earlier. 'Twas uncalled for."

He stroked Mwekane's head and sat on the stool beside my feet. "I will provide all her care and training. She will be my responsibility, not thine."

I peered into Mwekane's brown eyes and then set her on the floor when she tried to get down. "She is good for the children. Not that they will forget the loss of Papa, but she provides distraction from the perpetual sorrow. They are too young to be sad all the time."

"As is thee."

Had he so soon forgotten the despair of losing Papa? "I've lost every blood relative I know aside from Jon-Isaac. That is difficult."

"Indeed it is." His voice, though soft, held an intensity I had not expected. "It leaves a hollowness deep within that I cannot explain even after twenty years without my parents. Despite the abundant love I've been given, part of me longs for the presence of those with whom I share blood. It hurts."

I closed my eyes, chastened. If anyone were to understand how I felt, 'twould be Isaac. Really, he'd lost three fathers—his first father whom he couldn't remember, his Quaker father who took him in and reared him, and Papa, who had taught him to be a blacksmith. Then hurt pricked me. "Thee never told me thee felt that way."

"I only realized it right before I left." He inhaled. "Beth, I need thee to talk to me. Never have I seen thee so cross, and I know 'tis directed at me. Ignoring it will only allow it to bolster, and neither I nor thee want that. Please, will thee talk to me?"

I swallowed, still unable to look at him. "'Tis not only with thee."

"Still, I know my leaving aggrieved thee, and I truly regret that. I was hurting in a way I'd never felt before, and I reckon that blinded me to all else."

I looked him in the eye. "I understood that." Margaret Roberts's showing interest in his courtship when she intended to use it only to antagonize her father was conniving, and Hugh's disapproval of him simply for his Lenape heritage was reprehensible. "What I couldn't understand was thy refusal to talk to me about it."

"I didn't want to talk about it."

"Aye. Because I was a child."

He clenched his teeth. "I never should have said that. I was upset, not only about Margaret but also with myself because thee had warned me about her."

"She didn't deserve thy courtship. She may have caught every young man's eye with her charm and beauty, but in her heart she struggled with animosity toward her father and self-seeking."

He stood and paced toward the hearth. "I should have heeded thy words. But she was the first girl to show interest in courting me, and I believed . . ." When he turned and his eyes met mine, the sadness that knit his brows weighed on my heart. "I sincerely believed her interest was genuine."

"I know." My words sounded strangled, but I continued, knowing 'twould be a fruitless attempt if I tried to temper the sentiments raging within me. "It hurt me too, seeing thy pain, but that didn't hold a candle to losing the relationship I had with thee"—I rose and moved toward him—"and then losing thee altogether when thee left."

"Oh, Beth." His eyes shone as he placed his hand on my

shoulder. Moving it to the back of my neck, he drew me close.

I embraced him, though hesitant at first, but the familiar comfort of his closeness eased my reticence. As much as I'd kept my distance since his return, at the same time I had yearned so for the friendship we'd always shared.

After a few moments, he rested his chin on my head. "Forgive me?"

I nodded, my throat too tight to speak.

He finally released me.

My heart felt lighter as I lowered myself onto the rocker again, but not as much as it should have. When our gazes met as he sat on the settle, I realized why.

Forgiving him was one thing. Fully trusting him again was another.

CHAPTER 9

Isaac

Remorse needled me. The hurt reflected in Elisabeth's eyes brought such guilt that I despised myself. Growing up, she'd been the most loyal friend I could ask for. She'd tromped through mud and creeks with me, patiently helped when I struggled with schoolwork, and defended me when classmates called me addled. When my Quaker father died when I was twelve and I refused to leave the barn loft for two days after his burial, she spent both days with me—despite my muteness—and sneaked out at night to sleep beside me in the hay.

Yet years later I broke her heart. The blindness of ire and humiliation allowed me to disregard her, and I walked away from the girl who'd never left my side. What gall I had to now expect her to act as if that hadn't happened.

"Isaac." Elisabeth interrupted my thoughts.

I looked up from the floor as she sat on the settle next to me, nestling Mwekane on her lap.

"She was whimpering for thy attention."

When I placed my hand on the dog's head, she wagged her tail so rapidly that Elisabeth clutched her tighter to keep her on her lap.

"Thee is a good girl." I rubbed the dog's ear.

Elisabeth laughed softly. "Her coloring reminds me of Penny. Remember her?"

Both the sweet sound and memory warmed me inside. "How could I not? She was my best friend from the time I was five until I was fifteen. Next to thee."

"She was the best dog, the way she went everywhere with us." Her blue eyes sparkled in the firelight. "I still remember the day she found her way to the schoolhouse and gave Schoolmaster such a fright."

I grinned. "I still remember the sting of his ferule."

"I'm certain thee does, especially since thee took the rapping that should have been for my knuckles as well."

"Thee was so young—barely older than Abigail." I shook my head, then cupped the pup's tiny chin in my hand. "But no schoolroom visits for you, *mwekanètët*."

Elisabeth stroked her head. "How much of the Lenape language does thee understand?"

I drew a long, slow breath. While we'd spoken only sparingly about my time with the Lenape, her interest showed. I also expected some of the questions she would pose might be difficult for me to answer. "A fair amount. Some of the Lenape and Mahicans I lived with had been converted to Christianity by Moravian missionaries. They spoke some English at least, but after we left Gnadenhutten, they preferred to speak their native tongue, and I wished to learn it."

Her eyes widened. "Thee was at Gnadenhutten?"

"I was, but many months before it was raided and burned this last fall. We left there for Wyomink in Fourth Month of the spring before last."

She returned to petting Mwekane, who curled up on her lap. "I've heard some of the stories thee has told the children about Wyomink. It sounds like a lovely place."

"The first time I set my eyes upon the valley, the trees and flowers were in bloom, and the sky was perfectly blue above the mountains and the river. Teedyuscung called it paradise, our garden of Eden."

"Teedyuscung is the . . . chief?"

"He calls himself the king of the Lenape. He was our leader, and his intentions were admirable at first. He truly wanted to build the chain of friendship between the tribes and the white settlers, and we became good friends." I stared into the hearth. So many nights he and I had sat by a fire, discussing reconciliation and hopes for the future. And now . . . "But with the ill treatment of the Lenape, he turned his back on the peace for which he'd once striven."

"And did terrible things," she added.

Images flashed through my mind. Teedyuscung, his sons, and the other warriors bearing scalps and dragging ragged captives behind them. Their gratified smiles born of evil deeds. Jeremiah's mother, prostrate and bloodied. And the little boy's lifeless stare as I said good-bye to him.

I shook my head to eschew the lurid thoughts. "More than terrible."

She slid her hand under my arm and clasped the crook of my elbow. "Isaac—"

"I know thee has questions." Hearing my terseness, I placed my hand on hers and recovered my composure. "As much as I want to answer them, some of the things I've seen, I—"

"Do not wish to speak of. I know."

"You heard—"

"I awoke while John and Jabez were visiting." She looked down at Mwekane. "While I had no intention of eavesdropping, I also didn't want to interrupt your conversation. It was impossible not to overhear what was said."

My pulse suddenly raced, lightening my head and warming my face and neck. I needed air—and to end this conversation before I had to explain how the memories tormented me at times. "'Tis late. We should retire now."

She stood, handed over Mwekane, and followed me to the back door. There I faced her and forced a smile. Fortunately, movement seemed to settle my angst. "Sleep well."

"Isaac, I . . ." Her brow furrowed. "I understand that thee has seen unspeakable acts and that talking about them would only remind thee of what thee wishes to forget. But if ever thee does want to talk . . ."

Love for her swept through me. Despite what I'd done, her compassion remained—and it gave me hope that the friendship we once shared could be reclaimed. "If I do, thee will be the first to know."

I opened the door and stepped outside, then lifted Mwekane toward my face as I headed for the shop. She licked my chin while wagging her tail against my side, and my nerves settled as I brushed my cheek against her silky head.

Maybe she would be as much a help for me as she was for the children.

First Day, Fourth Month 4th

The familiar stillness of First Day meeting for worship surrounded me as I sat on the bench beside Daniel and his sons. Friends remained quiet this forenoon, even those who regularly gave testimony, which exaggerated the occasional rustles of fidgeting children that echoed through the room.

I withheld a grin. Mother's glance, solemn yet gentle, had silenced me more times than I could count when I sat in meeting as a child. When that hadn't worked, Susannah had taken pity and led me outside so I could expend my energy while she sat on the well-worn bench beside the door.

A familiar whimpering came from the women's side. Jon-Isaac. His sporadic protests continued for a few minutes, each followed by hushing whispers. Finally, a bench creaked, then footsteps headed toward the back of the room.

Poor Elisabeth. Since my return, she'd never once made it through meeting for worship without taking Ethan or Jon-Isaac out at some point. At least the day's weather, warmer than usual, was more pleasant than when I'd first returned to Horsham.

I stood and made my way to the door behind the last row of benches.

Outside, Elisabeth gave a weary smile from where she sat in the same place Susannah occupied so many times when I was small. In her haste to leave, she'd left her cloak inside.

Jon-Isaac smiled, babbling and reaching for me.

I lifted him into my arms. "'Tis hard for a boy to be quiet for so long, isn't it?" I glanced at her. "I'll stay out here with him if thee wishes to go back inside."

She got up. "Is thee certain?"

When our eyes met again, I couldn't take mine off her. The coolness of the air had flushed her cheeks with a rosiness that contrasted against her fair skin, and the light-gray color of her gown seemed to brighten the blue of her eyes. She was one of the loveliest women I'd ever met, yet somehow I'd never seen that beauty until I returned.

I forced my attention back to our conversation. "I don't mind a—"

An odd bird call interrupted me. When it repeated moments later, the skin across my shoulders prickled.

"What kind of bird is that?" Elisabeth curiously peered out over the meeting house's grassy yard with its occasional tall trees. "That is the second time I've heard it. I thought it was a dove's coo the first time, but it sounds different."

I scanned the surrounding landscape. Nothing appeared amiss. No movement caught my eye, and no sounds came from in the burying ground or around the schoolhouse. "'Tis not a bird's call," I said quietly and handed Jon-Isaac to her. "Go back inside."

"Why? What—"

The call resonated again, closer.

I stepped in front of her, holding out my arm to keep her behind me. "Go inside. Make haste."

"Isaac—"

Could she be any more stubborn? "Now!" I whispered. "Do as I say."

The undulating coo echoed from the same distance, and this time I recognized its originator.

"Show thyself, Sam!"

He emerged from behind the large oak by the corner of

the building. "Isaac, my friend. Your ears always were keen as a dog's." He chuckled as he approached, clad in a green trade-cloth shirt, a buckskin frock, and buckskin breeches and moccasins. A black band of fabric tied about the top of his head held back his unruly long hair from his unshaven face.

"Thee knows this man?" Elisabeth's question reminded me that she remained.

I wanted to order her inside again but kept my gaze trained on Sam. Although he had seemingly come around to my decision to return to Horsham, even traveling a few hours' time with me when I left, his presence unnerved me. "Who is with thee, Sam?"

He stopped and looked about, then held out both hands from his sides. "No one."

I moved nearer, still taking in everything around us. "Thee is alone? Give me thy word."

Sam stared at me. "You have my word. The northern frontier is crimson with bloodshed. No one's safe. Not white, not Indian. More and more Lenape join the French. My oldest sister lives outside Wilmington. I'm going to stay with her until I figure out where I'll head next." He proffered his hand. "You have my word."

While I wished to believe him, doubt nagged. I closed the gap between us, although keeping watch. "How is thee, Sam?"

"Glad to see you." He clapped my shoulder. "You're looking well."

"So is thee."

He nodded at Elisabeth, who watched us as she held Jon-Isaac close. "Would you be Elisabeth?"

Despite her solemnity, she showed no intimation of fear

as she came to stand beside me. "Elisabeth Alden. Sam is thy name?"

He nodded. "Sam Milham. I've heard much about you. Pleasure to make your acquaintance."

"Sam was living in Wyomink when we arrived there," I said. "He and I shared a *wikwam* in our village there and in Chinkanning."

She smiled. "Welcome to Horsham." The sounds of movement emanated from within the meeting house, and she looked behind us for a moment. "I believe Friends are at the rise of meeting, but thee is welcome to join us for dinner."

"Much obliged." He returned his attention to me. "If you're in agreement."

"Of course. Come. We'll introduce thee to Friends."

He and Elisabeth started for the meeting house. I followed but not without taking in the surroundings again. I truly hoped Sam had been truthful about the reason for his journey—and that he indeed traveled alone.

Sam's gaze followed Elisabeth as she crossed the common room floor carrying Jon-Isaac and leading Ethan by the hand. He watched as they disappeared into the children's bedchamber, then glanced around the inside of the house. Moments later she exited the room, pulling the door behind her, and he watched her take Jon-Isaac into her bedchamber and close the door.

When he continued to stare after her, I cleared my throat.

He smiled at me. "She is hardly the *girl* you described, my friend."

I didn't respond, and his grin disappeared and he returned his attention to his food. "Let me be honest. One of the reasons I came here was to see if you'd want to go south with me, to the backcountry west of Virginia, but—"

"Thee is not on the way to thy sister's?"

"I am," he said through a mouthful of maize bread. Swallowing, he shook his head. "But town life doesn't suit me. It never has, and after nearly two years in Wyomink, I was sure it didn't suit you either. Now I'm starting to reconsider that."

I shrugged, although unsure why I felt the need to convince him otherwise. "Horsham's not town life. 'Tis farms and forest. When I want the company of others, I have it. And when I want solitude, acres and acres of wood abound."

"It's not the same. But no matter. I doubt I could talk you into leaving if I tried."

"Leaving?" Abigail turned from where she stood at the wash basin stacking our plates, her face almost stricken. "Thee will not leave us, will thee?"

"Of course not, Abby."

She approached, though hesitantly. "Promise?"

"Thee has my word."

Still solemn, she collected the utensils and carried them off.

Sam looked from her to me, then inhaled and blew out his breath. "I don't know who surprises me more, Elisabeth or you." He kept his voice low. "Hardly expected to find you settled down, having taken over a business—and the care of a woman and children. Is that what you want, or do you feel you must because of the circumstances?"

With no intention to discuss this here, I stood. "Let's continue our conversation outside."

He grinned and got up.

"May I accompany you?" Abigail asked.

I turned to find her nearing me again.

"'Tis too nice to be inside. May I come along?"

"Elisabeth asked thee to start tidying up," I said. "Thee do that, and when she returns from rocking Jon-Isaac, ask her."

Her hopeful expectation waned, but she nodded.

"Good girl." I headed for the door, where Sam already stood waiting.

He snorted when our gazes met. "I always did prefer outside to in. So did you."

CHAPTER 10

Elisabeth

When I returned from rocking Jon-Isaac to sleep, Abigail stood at one of the front windows, staring through it.

"Did Isaac and Sam go outside?"

She looked at me with a frown on her face. "Aye. Isaac said Sam is his friend, but I think he's cross with him."

Cross? I stopped behind her and peered out the window. Through the distortion of the glass, I could see the men standing by the garden fence. Isaac pointed at something in the garden as they spoke. "We mustn't assume, Abby. If thee is uncertain, 'tis best not to speak than to say what may be untrue."

She looked down. "Aye."

I put my arm around her, feeling a bit guilty. How many times had I been chastised for the same thing as a child?

More times than I needed to remind Abigail, for certain. "What makes thee think Isaac is cross?"

"He spoke to him sternly." She peered up at me. "What is the backcountry nest of Virginia?"

The backcountry nest of— "Perhaps thee means the backcountry *west* of Virginia?"

"Aye, west. That is where Sam is going. He wants Isaac to go with him."

My heart skipped a beat, and I looked through the window again. The men were laughing, and Isaac showed no hint of irritation—though now I wished he did. "Sam said that?"

"Aye. I asked Isaac if he was leaving, and he gave his word that he isn't."

"Then thee has naught to worry about." Hopefully.

"May we join them after tidying up? 'Tis a fine day."

The less time Sam and Isaac spent alone, the better. I guided her away from the window. "Aye."

My hospitality toward Sam Milham was quickly vanishing, and his planned departure the next morning couldn't come soon enough.

I awoke during the night, as I often did. But this time something seemed amiss. Turning onto my side, I propped myself on one elbow and looked around. The room appeared brighter than usual, but why? The sky beyond the window was dark, and the fire in the fireplace between the children's and my bedchambers remained banked.

The door. Light glowed from beneath and alongside it. Surely Isaac had banked the fire in the common room hearth before retiring to the forge quarters for the night. Had it restarted?

I got out of bed and grabbed the lap quilt from the rocker. After wrapping it about my shoulders, I opened the door. A low fire burned in the fireplace, flickering its light throughout the common room and onto a form lying by the hearth.

Isaac! I rushed toward him.

My concern eased as I neared. He slept on his back with his hands clasped behind his head and a woolen blanket pulled halfway up his unclothed chest. His shirt and waistcoat lay folded beside him, along with his stockings and boots.

Stooping, I reached out to shake his shoulder but stopped at seeing an odd black drawing on his skin over his heart. About the size of my fist, it appeared to be the outline of a turtle with two lines within it that intersected below the turtle's head.

He sat up so quickly that I cried out and toppled over, landing on my hip and elbow.

"Elisabeth." The next thing I knew, he was on his knees helping me sit up. "Is thee all right?"

I covered my fluttering heart with my hand. "Other than the fright thee gave me at finding thee on the floor and then now, I'm fine." I glanced at the bedchamber doors, but no sound came from either room. At least we hadn't woken the children. I returned my attention to him. "Why is thee sleeping here?"

He covered his face with his hand for a moment. Going by how quickly his chest rose and fell, I'd startled him as much as he had me.

Then I realized why he'd stayed in the common room,

saying he would retire after he finished his Bible reading, when I'd bid him good-night. What I didn't understand was why he had not told me he intended to sleep in the house. We'd agreed to our Meeting elders' decree that he could live on the property only if he slept in the forge quarters, but I wouldn't have begrudged him one night. "Thee could have told me thee gave Sam thy quarters and needed a place to sleep. Thy old bed in the loft would be more comfortable."

He exhaled. "Sam isn't in my quarters. He's sleeping in the barn."

"Then why . . ." My stomach turned cold. He could have only one reason to stay in the house. I swallowed. "Thee thought he might try to harm us?"

He didn't respond, but the solemnness of his expression answered my question.

Standing, I adjusted the quilt around me. "Thee didn't tell me?" I walked to the front window nearest the door. That did little to calm my nerves, however, since I could see only darkness beyond the glass.

The floor creaked, and he stepped around to face me. "I didn't want to worry thee, especially if my concern was unnecessary, which I hoped it was. But I wouldn't take any chances either."

My face warmed. Never had I been in the presence of a man so undressed, save for when Papa burned with fever and we cut off his shirt. Yet 'twasn't the immodesty that unsettled me. 'Twas my lack of discomfort with it. Isaac stood unabashed with his arms folded across his chest, and while I should have averted my eyes, instead I found beauty in the broadness of his shoulders and the distinct contours of muscle beneath his bronze skin.

An odd sensation stirred in my belly, and I pressed my

hand into it. "At meeting, thee wasn't comfortable with his visit from the start."

"I had suspicions," he finally said.

I walked away from him, my lips pressed together to keep myself from saying something antagonistic. When I could speak calmly, I turned around. "Thee should have told me. I'm not a child, and I'd appreciate if thee would stop treating me like one."

In a few strides he reached me. "I'm sorry."

"I don't want thee to be sorry. I want thee to be honest so thee need not apologize. Thee claims to want the friendship we once had, but how am I to trust thee when thee is not honest with me?"

"'Twill not happen again."

In the glimmer of the firelight, the sincerity that knit his eyebrows eased my irritation but not my curiosity. If we were in any danger, I needed to know as much as I could. "Why did thee think Sam might harm us?"

He glanced at the front windows. "Come sit with me."

Moments later, Isaac sat beside me on the settle, having donned his shirt and partially tucked it into his breeches. He stared at the fire, his brow creased. Whatever his thoughts, they greatly troubled him.

I closed my eyes. *Father, give him peace, and give me patience.* Thoughts of Mary, Susannah, and Hannah's visit last week filled my mind. Mary's parting words of wisdom resounded: *"Thee and Isaac prayed together often before he left. Have you done so since he returned? 'Tis nigh impossible for the heart to harbor animosity for someone 'tis praying with."*

How was it that now, as we sat so close together, I missed him just as much as I had when he was away?

"The Lenape sometimes use animal and bird calls to communicate, such as when they are hunting or traveling and don't want to be detected," he said.

"And that is why thee ordered me inside?"

"I didn't know what would happen." He kept his tone temperate despite the brusque edge to mine. "I feared for thy and Jon-Isaac's safety, and I wanted you inside until I knew there was no danger. It seemed unlikely that the Lenape would follow me here, but I couldn't ignore the possibility. When I recognized Sam's call outside the meeting house, I didn't know if he was trying to locate me or communicating with others with him."

He paused. "At least at first, Sam felt betrayed by my returning home, and some of the warriors turned against me." He slowly released a breath. "One of them wants me dead."

I tried to swallow but couldn't. "Dead? Why?"

"I shamed a young warrior." He now spoke much more softly as he again stared at the flames. "Two weeks before I left Chinkanning, Sam and I traveled down into Northampton to trade our peltries for provisions. On our return trip, we came upon a band of young warriors burning a homestead. They had . . . murdered all but a small boy."

He closed his eyes and shook his head. "He wasn't much older than Ethan. The warrior was going to scalp him as well, and I shoved him off the boy and called him a coward. I traded our provisions for the boy's life, but the warrior vowed revenge."

The thought of such a horror threatened to turn my stomach, but at the same time his courage and honor begot great respect.

"When we returned to Chinkanning, word of what happened had already reached there. Many in our village thought me a traitor." Leaning forward, he rested his elbows on his knees and rubbed his hand over his face. Tears shone in his eyes when he turned his head to look into mine. "I'm as much white as I am Lenape. Yet how am I to claim either as my people when both have done such horrific things to the other?"

My heart went out to him. "Isaac." I placed my hand on his shoulder, brushing his loose hair onto his back. "Thee is both but neither. We are Friends, bound not by the color of our skin or by our culture but by our love for Christ and others. Thee may not belong with the Lenape or with the white settlers, but thee does belong here . . . with we who love thee. Above all, thee belongs to God."

He eventually nodded. "'Twas then I knew any hope for reconciliation was lost. Weeks earlier, while we were still in Wyomink, a party from our village had set out on the warrior path. Teedyuscung, who once shared my dream of peace, led them. The rest of us left for Chinkanning, a day's travel to the north, and days later, they rejoined us, bearing scalps and captives."

Captives—in his village? Never had I expected that.

"No matter how I tried to persuade him, Teedyuscung wouldn't release them. Then when Sam and I returned from Northampton, he instructed me to leave, for the sake of the tribe as well as my own welfare. There was talk of moving again to Diahoga, another few days' journey to the north, and I couldn't bear traveling farther from here. So I left."

Silence, save for the crackling of the fire, filled the common room. I searched for words of comfort, but what could I possibly say to ease the anguish wrought by what he had endured?

Father, speak through me what thee wants him to hear.

"Isaac, thee endeavored for peace, just as Christ did when he was on earth." When my mouth opened, I allowed the Light Within to direct my words, just as I did when giving testimony at meeting. "If thee was thought a traitor to the Lenape or to the white settlers, so be it. Christ was mocked as well. Thee was faithful to thy beliefs, and to the heart of God himself, no matter the cost. At the end of thy life, when thee stands before him, that will be all that matters."

A grin eased some of the sorrow from his face. "Why can I try to convince myself of something but believe it only when I hear it from thee?"

I smiled. "I have always felt the same about thee. Could we . . . pray together, as we used to?"

He straightened. "Indeed."

"I want thee to get a bit more sleep," Isaac said when we finished praying.

Though his face now reflected peace in his heart, the reality of our situation rushed back to me. "Nay. I can help thee keep watch."

He glanced at the wall clock, then to the window. "The sky will be lightening in the next hour. If anything were planned, 'twould have happened by now."

We stood and walked toward my bedchamber. At the

door, he faced me. "I'm still not used to thy height. When I left, I'd stopped growing but thee had not."

"Susannah says I was a late bloomer."

He stared into my eyes. "Sometimes the late bloomers are the most lovely of all. They bring beauty when 'tis needed most—when the splendor of all else and hope for rebirth has faded away."

"Isaac." I looked down only to be taken aback by my attire. Having left my bedchamber without taking time to dress, I stood before him wearing merely a shift and the quilt. His immodesty seemed almost acceptable, much like the traditional dress of the Lenape we'd seen in Philadelphia several summers before, but my own disconcerted me.

He lifted my chin. "No more secrets between us, agreed?"

I nodded, though unable to look into his eyes—and this time not because of propriety. I had no right making such a promise, hypocrite that I was.

CHAPTER 11

Isaac

Second Day, Fourth Month 5th

By the sun's station in the sky, the time neared ten in the forenoon when Sam and I returned from hunting. We emerged from the wood into the clearing surrounding the house, and right away my stomach sank.

A horse and carriage sat by the garden fence, and Hester White and Dorothy Evans, weighty Friends from our Women's Meeting, stood with Elisabeth by the half-full laundry line. Ethan and Jon-Isaac sat on a blanket nearby.

"Isaac!" Ethan ran toward us and stopped before me, taking in my buckskin and trade-cloth. "Is thee an Indian again?"

Sam laughed. "Isaac will always be an Indian."

Ethan looked from Sam to me, confusion crumpling his face. "Thee is not a Friend anymore?"

"Of course I am. I will always be a Friend as well." I lifted him into my arms, then glanced at Sam, who held the arms of the travois bearing the deer I'd shot. "Thee can take that to the tree beside the forge. I'll be right there to help dress it."

He dragged the travois away, nodding at Elisabeth and the women as he passed.

Hester and Dorothy watched me approach, their faces— one elderly and the other middle-aged—devoid of the smiles they'd worn at meeting for worship the day before. I didn't know what unsettled me more, that or Elisabeth's soberness.

I set Ethan on the ground. "Hester. Dorothy."

"Isaac." Hester looked me over from behind her spectacles. "On our way here, we came upon a Friend who informed us he'd seen thee earlier this morn and thy appearance did not befit a Friend. Apparently, he spoke the truth."

Of all the days for them to come calling—rigid Hester especially—it had to be today? "I wore this only to hunt. Elisabeth has enough washing to do already"—I jutted my chin at the hung laundry—"and I didn't want to increase her burden by soiling my good clothing." They were female, so surely they could appreciate my reasoning even though both employed young women from our Meeting to assist with household tasks.

"I see. This manner of dress, then, is not a regular occurrence?"

"Indeed not." Hopefully my explanation would appease them and Elisabeth as well. "I intend to change my clothing as soon as our deer is dressed."

Dorothy, a lifelong good friend of Susannah's who knew

me well, canted her head. "Is thy friend staying longer than expected?"

"Just a day. Lord willing, he'll continue his journey to Wilmington tomorrow." I looked from her to Hester, glad for the opportunity to change the subject. "Would you care to come in and visit?"

Hester sniffed. "Another time. We came to speak with Elisabeth since yesterday she made it known to Dorothy that she wished to discuss a serious matter with elders from the Women's Meeting." She glanced at Elisabeth. "But it seems she now feels 'twould be best to remain silent. So we shall be on our way."

Dorothy gave Elisabeth a sympathetic smile. "Should thee change thy mind, we would be happy to discuss what is on thy heart."

Elisabeth nodded stiffly. "I thank thee."

After they'd climbed into the carriage and started toward the road, I sighed.

"Thee did nothing wrong," she said, then pressed her lips together. "I do not understand why Friends cannot accept thee. Yesterday they were commending thy moving testimony in meeting, and yet today they are quibbling over matters of no significance."

What a relief that her annoyance wasn't directed at me but in my defense. "It matters not. I suspect they were simply addressing me because they felt they must mollify whoever approached them."

Her discomposure didn't abate as easily. "I just don't want thee disowned again."

Such a consequence seemed doubtful. "Fear not. But I'll wear my plain clothes from now on if thee prefers."

"For thy own sake, I do"—she crossed her arms—"but not

because I believe it would be wrong for thee to dress otherwise."

I longed to embrace her but resisted. "Let's keep that between us though, aye? No need for thee to be taken to task too."

Her eyes suddenly teared, and I stepped closer. Something had her distressed, and she couldn't truly believe I would be disowned again for something so trifling. Perhaps 'twas her original reason for the women's visit that upset her? "Thee asked to speak with them about something?" Odd that she would go to others when Mother was a Women's Meeting elder—unless she wished to speak about me. She had just defended me, though, so that seemed unlikely.

She shook her head and turned back to the laundry. "'Twas a decision made in haste."

Unsure how to respond, I glanced at the forge. Sam stood with his hands on his hips, smirking at me from next to the tree where he'd hung the deer by its hind legs. Elisabeth's demeanor asserted she would say no more, so I headed for him.

"I'm not sure how you do it, my friend," he said when I neared.

"Do what?" I sounded annoyed, but so be it.

He chuckled. "Stand so close to her without wanting more than just that."

I looked back at Elisabeth, who bent forward to brush something from Ethan's cheek as he looked up at her. She smiled and kissed his forehead, and I couldn't help feeling a bit envious, even despite my misgivings about the women's visit. "'Tis becoming more and more difficult," I muttered.

Facing the deer, I pulled my knife from its sheath at my waist. "Let's make quick work of this."

Sixth Day, Fourth Month 9th

"Isaac? Hello." A man's voice interrupted my thoughts as I stoked the fire in the forge on Sixth Day forenoon.

When I looked over at the doorway, an involuntary growl rumbled in my throat. "Hiram." I stopped pumping the bellows. "Elisabeth and the boys are out visiting with my mother and Susannah. Did she know thee would be calling?" Elisabeth had received his letter, which included regrets that another business trip kept him away, but as far as I knew, he hadn't mentioned visiting today.

He pushed his spectacles farther up on his nose. "She did not. This was a bit of a speedily planned trip, although I shall tarry if she shan't be long. Does thee know when she will return?"

"In time to prepare dinner, so anytime now."

He pulled a gold watch from the pocket of his wide-cuffed, bright-blue coat. "Excellent. Actually, I came to see thee as well. Does thee remember the hinges that Jonathan made for me—the ones I picked up on my last visit here?" He pulled one from his coat pocket. "I was hoping thee would be able to forge more of them."

I wiped my hand on my shirt, then took the piece and examined every surface and angle. 'Twas a bit more intricate than a simple hinge, but surely he could have found a closer blacksmith who could replicate it—had he wanted to. I carried it to the iron bin and searched for the material Jonathan used.

He joined me there, though keeping his distance from anything that would mar his fine clothing. "I'm curious about thy relationship with Elisabeth. You seem quite close."

As much as I wished to confirm that—vehemently—I refrained. Besides, I expected he'd already asked David about the nature of my relationship with Elisabeth. "We have been friends for as long as I can remember. My mother's house is only a short walk from here, and we played together nearly every day as children and even started school together."

"But thee is older, is thee not?"

"By two years." I continued to peruse the contents of the bin, finally pulling out the iron bar I was looking for. "I knew no English when the Lukenses adopted me, and they tell me I didn't speak at all for close to a year after my first parents died. For that reason, they waited until I was almost eight to send me to school. Elisabeth, on the other hand, was reading by the time she was six, so the school committee allowed her early entrance."

"And thee lived here for several years?"

I moved around him to the hearth, then pumped the bellows before sliding the iron into the coals. "My Quaker father died when I was twelve, and my mother apprenticed me to Jonathan. I came to live here, sleeping in their loft."

He followed me again. "Elisabeth tells me she has no next of kin aside from her half-brother. This is true?"

I hesitated, displeased with the direction of this question. "She has family in England, I reckon, but none with whom she is acquainted."

"How is that?" He turned sideways to face me and clasped his hands behind his back.

"Jonathan was orphaned as a boy. Friends in London took him in, and my uncle's family paid his ship fare here to

Philadelphia, where he lived with them and learned black-smithing. As far as I know, Jonathan had no contact with family in England after arriving here."

"And Elisabeth's mother?"

"A similar story. The family paid her ship fare from London, and she assisted my aunt in running the household. She and Jonathan married and moved here after she fulfilled her contract of service." Needing more heat to soften the iron, I pumped the bellows. The fire blazed, radiating into the already warm room.

Hiram stepped back and took a handkerchief from his waistcoat pocket. "My, it gets oppressive in here." He mopped his forehead.

Even in my light linen work shirt with sleeves rolled above my elbows, sweat dampened my back and beaded on my face. He had to be nearly suffocating in his suit and frock coat.

He cleared his throat. "So Elisabeth truly has no kin, then. How unfortunate."

I searched his face, hoping to find the sympathy his tone lacked. Not even a hint tinged his expression. Pity for his physical discomfort evaporated like water dropped onto glowing coals.

He smiled. "From whom, then, if Elisabeth and I were to decide to marry, would we obtain parental consent before writing our letters of intention?"

Marriage? I grabbed the iron bar with the tongs and removed it from the intense heat. A discussion of such signif-icance required my full attention. "I suppose thee would speak with our elders. Under the circumstances, Meeting would most likely appoint my mother and Susannah to give consent."

Elisabeth had asked to speak with elders from the Women's Meeting earlier this week. Maybe this was her reason for going to Dorothy? If so, Elisabeth's declaration that it was a decision made in haste was a grave understatement.

"I see."

I inhaled slowly and spoke with as much nonchalance as I could muster. "Have thee and Elisabeth spoken about this?"

"Some."

Her prior innocence about Hiram's intentions now seemed even more unlikely. But she'd also seemed confused —and perhaps she still was.

"Has thee any idea what thy Meeting intends with regard to the children?" Hiram went on. "I expected they would've appointed a committee to determine their custody by now."

Fire spread through me, and it had nothing to do with the hearth. "Elisabeth is the only mother Jon-Isaac knows, and Abigail and Ethan adore her as well." I paused to moderate my tone. "Placing them with another family would be like the death of yet another parent for them, and it would devastate Elisabeth. The children are her family. They're stability for her."

He dabbed his forehead again. "But also a great responsibility. And as her husband, would I not become her stability?" He shrugged with a shake of his head. "No matter. We shall have time to discuss such details."

I seized the iron bar with my tongs and shoved it back into the coals.

Whatever honorable qualities Elisabeth found in Hiram escaped me. I just hoped she'd soon see that the children's best interests, as well as her own, seemed of little importance to him.

~

"Isaac, is thee sad?" Abigail's green eyes watched me as I sat on a ladder-back chair beside the bed she shared with Ethan.

Her sweet concern brought a smile to my lips but did little to alleviate my gloom. "A bit."

"Does thee miss Papa too?"

I smoothed a few strands of blond hair behind her ear. "I do." My heart ached more as I looked from her to Ethan. The children's sorrow kindled my own grief—not only for Jonathan but also for the parents I'd once loved dearly but now couldn't remember. "I miss him a lot."

"Does thee cry too?" Ethan asked.

I swallowed. "Sometimes."

"Thee did not cry when Papa died," Abigail said.

This wasn't the conversation I'd expected—or hoped for—but I would never be dishonest with them. "I did, just not while I was with you."

"Was Elisabeth with thee when thee cried?" she asked. "She says God wants us to bear each other's burdens, so we shouldn't cry alone."

Remarkable words from Elisabeth, since I hadn't seen her cry since Jonathan's funeral. Not that it would be the first time she didn't heed her own astute advice. "Not this time. But she is quite right." I adjusted the quilt over them. "'Tis time we said your prayers."

After both had prayed, I stood.

"Sleep well," Elisabeth said and leaned down to kiss them. I hadn't even realized her presence.

We returned to the common room, my candle in hand, and she closed their door, then faced me.

I looked away, lest her stare bore through to my soul. "How much of that did thee hear?"

"I'm sorry. I just love listening to thee talk with them at bedtime."

That encouraged me, but . . . "Thee didn't answer my question."

"Enough to know thee is struggling with melancholy today, although I already sensed that. Thee has eaten little since breakfast. Would thee like something now?"

"A cup of tea would be appreciated."

"Is thee unwell?" Concern lined her brow, which came as a comfort. So much of her time went into the care of the house and the children—as well as the sobering ruminations that plagued her mind, whether about the loss of her father, her possible marriage to Hiram, or whatever—that she was often preoccupied.

"Nay. Just not hungry."

We walked to the hearth, and Mwekane wagged her tail from where she lay nearby. I scooped her up and sat on the settle, petting her while Elisabeth made tea. When she brought our cups, I set the puppy on the floor and took one from her.

She sat beside me. "When we left to go visiting this morning, thee seemed fine. Yet when we returned, that had changed. Thee barely ate any dinner or supper. 'Tis not like thee."

I watched the fire. "Some days are more difficult than others. I greatly miss thy papa, Sam, and my Lenape and Mahican friends—and, strange as it may seem, I find myself missing my first parents." I sipped my tea. "Ethan and I were talking about thy papa this afternoon, and seeing the sadness in his eyes and hearing it in his voice, I saw myself when I wasn't much younger than he—a little boy loved and yet overcome by loss."

"I'm sorry thee is hurting so. But I am also glad he has thee. All of the children admire thee, but he does especially. He said you were playing a game while Hiram and I were walking."

The thought of them strolling across the yard, her holding on to his arm, disquieted me as much now as it did then. "We made a wicket to play a game the Lenape and Mahicans played in Wyomink. Thee had an enjoyable time with Hiram today?"

"Aye." The tightness that usually accompanied our conversations about him edged into her voice.

Starting another quarrel wasn't my intention, but I needed to know their intentions. "Hiram and I spoke for a time before thee returned. He asked who would provide parental consent should you decide to marry. Is that . . . something you are considering?"

She placed her teacup on the table beside her and folded her hands in her lap. "Although I didn't think it a possibility, he did mention marriage a few times over the months. We also spoke about it today. Now that I know him better, and considering the circumstances—"

"Does thee know him better? And considering what circumstances?" She couldn't be seriously debating this.

She stood and moved toward the hearth. "The children need a father, and I cannot care for the homestead and them alone."

Alone? "Thee is not alone. I'm here, and—"

"But for how long?" she asked, turning around.

Had I not already made that clear? I got up. "In Horsham? Indefinitely. Here in particular? For as long as thee wishes me to be here."

"Isaac, I didn't mean . . ."

Then what did she mean? "Hiram and I also spoke about the children today," I said, determined to open her eyes to his thoughts about them. "If anything, he is hesitant to become a father at the same time he becomes a husband."

"That isn't true."

But it was, and her weak retort proved she knew it. "Marriage is one of the weightiest choices we make in life. 'Tis not a decision thee should make unless thee is fully certain."

"And what if I am fully certain?"

"Is thee? Less than three weeks ago, thee told me you weren't courting. So thee considered him simply a friend. Yet now you are contemplating marriage. Does thee love him? I mean truly love him like thee always said would be necessary before thee married. Like thy papa and mama loved each other."

She crossed her arms and pursed her lips. "I was young and naive when I said that. Philadelphia Yearly Meeting has affirmed that friendship, respect, and companionship is a solid foundation on which to build a marriage. I may not have believed that before, but now I see the practicality in it."

"Is it practicality, or is it settling for less than God intended for a marriage?" I moved toward her. "I just don't want thee to make a harried decision and then regret it."

"I have no intention of doing that. Thee just doesn't like Hiram. That was obvious from the moment thee met him. He is a respected man in good standing with his Meeting. So he is older than I. That doesn't mean he wouldn't be a good husband." She sat on the rocker, then snatched a stocking from the darning basket on the floor and retrieved her sewing hussif. "I'm not discussing this any further."

I released the breath I'd been holding. My intuition told me we wouldn't be discussing anything else tonight either.

~

Smoke pricked my eyes and stung my throat. The cabin and barn in the clearing before me burned, fully in flames. Gunshots boomed, followed by shrieks of terror and triumphant whoops. Within the haze, a settler family fled, hunted by black-painted warriors.

Yet my legs wouldn't propel me forward and my mouth wouldn't open. I couldn't halt the warriors, nor could I lead the family into the prospective safety of the forest.

"Isaac!" A woman's scream came from near the cabin. Strangely, it now looked like the Alden home.

A tall warrior, his face fully blackened, shoved a woman to her knees. He grabbed the white cap from her head, loosing long blond hair, then drove her to the ground with a foot atop her back. Clutching her hair and twisting it around his wrist, he raised his other hand, brandishing a knife above her forehead.

"Isaac!" Her terrified cry, this time dreadfully familiar, echoed again.

The warrior yanked her head upward, revealing the lovely face and bright-blue eyes I knew so well.

Elisabeth!

Suddenly I was sitting up. Darkness surrounded me, and the only sounds were my gasps for air. The night's coolness chilled the clammy skin of my chest and back, making me shiver.

Between my feet, Mwekane stirred on top of the quilt and crawled closer. She nestled beside me, and I lay down and stroked her back. "Good girl." Inhaling deeply, I wiped my brow with the back of my hand and measured my breathing to slow my hammering heart.

"Isaac!"

I sat up again, certain I'd heard my name this time.

The door to the forge entrance clunked open, and a flickering light glowed beyond the quarters' doorway.

"Isaac!" Abigail.

I jumped out of bed and rushed into the forge. She neared, dressed only in her shift. The light of the lantern she carried illuminated her pinched face.

"Abby, what is it?"

"Please, come quickly," she said, near tears. "Ethan can't breathe."

CHAPTER 12

Elisabeth

Seventh Day, Fourth Month 10th

I could barely breathe myself as I paced before the hearth with Ethan in my arms, wrapped in a blanket. His harsh, stridulous breaths continued as his head lay on my shoulder, interrupted only by fits of tight coughing that restarted his crying and gripped me with fright.

How I wished for clarity. None of the children had ever suffered such a cough before, and weariness and apprehension expunged my mind of what Dr. Crossley recommended when children took ill with it.

The back door opened, and Isaac, his shirt untucked, followed Abigail and Mwekane inside. His long strides quickly brought him to where I stood, and he set the lantern on the table by the settle. With a hand on Ethan's back, he stepped around beside me to look at his face.

"How long has he been like this?"

I searched his countenance for any indication of his level of concern. It reflected equanimity, which annoyed and comforted me alike. "He awoke coughing about ten minutes ago. Abigail said he was 'snoring' for a while beforehand, keeping her awake. He can't say more than a word or two at a time."

He moved his hand to Ethan's forehead and brushed the hair from his face. "Has he had croup before?"

Croup. My heart pounded harder at the reality brought by hearing the word aloud. Just last week, a family from Gwynedd Meeting had lost their daughter, just a year younger than Ethan, to the horrid illness. I shook my head, too overwhelmed to speak.

Another coughing fit racked Ethan's body, leaving him crying when it ended. "Hurts," he whimpered.

Isaac rubbed his back. "I know it does. Try not to cry. 'Twill only make it worse. We'll get thee feeling better." He looked at me. "Wrap him and thyself warmly and take him outside."

Was he daft? Despite how spring approached, the temperature had dropped significantly overnight. I'd even seen his breath when he and Abigail came into the house. "But 'tis so cold."

"Thanks be to God for that. Often the cold helps ease the breathing."

I stared at him. He couldn't be—

"Elisabeth, I need thee to trust me. Some of the children in Wyomink took ill with croup this winter, and I helped their medicine woman treat them. Please. Wrap him and thyself and take him outside." He turned to Abigail, who stood beside him clutching a buckskin satchel to her middle. "Will thee help me here inside?"

She nodded eagerly.

I held Ethan tighter, my mind and my heart rivaling for control. While hesitant to take an already sick child into the bitter cold, never had I not trusted Isaac's advice. And if he'd treated croup before, he had more experience with it than I.

We headed for the bedchambers to gather the warmest blankets we could find.

I had no idea how long I'd sat outside with Ethan on my lap. At least fifteen minutes had passed. Following Isaac's instructions, I'd wrapped Ethan in the quilt from the bed he shared with Abigail, then allowed Isaac to swathe both of us in the woolen blanket and quilt from my own bed once we sat on the bench beside the front door on the porch. We were plenty warm but breathing the chilly air as the three-quarter moon and stars glowed in the clear night sky.

Ethan's raspy breathing persisted, heightening my anxiety but also providing some comfort by confirming that he still breathed. His coughing had waned, and his stillness and even breaths told me he was drowsing. "Father, have mercy," I whispered, closing my eyes.

The door opened and Isaac stepped out. "How is he?"

"He coughs less, and his breathing seems easier."

"Good. Bring him inside." He helped me to my feet, then guided us into the house.

There, he slipped the blanket and quilt from around us and started toward the settle. He had placed the rocker and a ladder-back chair behind it with their backs facing it, and on the floor between them sat our biggest pitcher and a large copper bowl filled with fist-sized stones from the back garden. Abigail, with Mwekane by her side, crouched by the hearth, peering into a small kettle that sat on a trivet.

Isaac placed the blanket and quilt over the settle and chairs, forming a hut of sorts by ensuring coverage of the frame to the floor except in one area. "Bring him here."

I slowly moved closer. "What is thee going to do?"

"The Lenape use what they call a sweat oven for rituals and to treat illnesses and ailments. It's a roundhouse they heat and fill with steam. The medicine woman used a similar construction, much smaller and without the heat of a fire, for the children with croup. The steam lessened the cough and eased the breathing. It'll not harm him."

I held Ethan tighter. "Thee is certain?"

"I've seen it with my own eyes."

Although hesitant, I nodded.

He unwrapped Ethan and then took him and gave me the blanket.

Ethan stirred. "Lisabeth?" he croaked.

"I'm right here, sweet boy," I soothed, stroking his hair. "Isaac has thee. He will help thee feel better."

He gave a noisy exhalation and laid his head on Isaac's shoulder.

"I'll take him inside and sit in there with him," Isaac told me. "Once we're in there, pour the water from the pitcher onto the stones in the bowl. Be careful not to touch the stones or the bowl. The stones have been in the fire. Once thee has poured the water onto the stones, cover the opening with that blanket to hold the steam in, then refill the pitcher and do it again, until I tell thee to stop. Does thee understand?"

I nodded again. At least it seemed like a fairly innocuous treatment.

He carried Ethan to the makeshift hut and set him on the floor, then crawled in and pulled him in onto his lap, ensuring he didn't touch the bowl or stones.

I knelt by the pitcher at the opening and looked inside. I could barely see them in the darkness. "How long will you be in there?"

"As long as it takes for his breathing to quiet. More stones are in the fire, and I will have thee switch them when these cool." He craned his neck to look down at Ethan. "'Twill be even darker in here when Elisabeth places the blanket over the opening, but I will be right here with thee."

"Will thee . . . tell me . . . a story?" he rasped.

"As many stories as thee wants." Isaac looked back to me. "Pour on the water now, then quickly cover the opening and get more water."

I drew a breath and did as he said.

When Isaac finally said I could stop, Abigail watched me from by the hearth as she petted Mwekane. Isaac's satchel sat on the table.

"I'm making a tea for Ethan," she said. "Isaac said not to let it boil."

I joined her. What looked like pieces of wood floated in a slightly red-tinged liquid in the kettle. "What is it?"

"The inner bark of a red oak tree. Isaac said 'tis good for treating coughs and hoarseness. He said the Lenape know about all sorts of teas and salves and other cures that white folks have never used." She smiled a little. "He said he'll teach me all about them."

My legs suddenly felt heavy, and I backed up and sat on the bench at the table. "Is Jon-Isaac still asleep?"

"I don't know. He hasn't cried."

I leaned forward and rested my forehead in my hands. "Would thee peek in to check on him for me?"

She crossed the floor, and my bedchamber door creaked open. A few moments later, the door creaked again, and her footfall returned. "He is sleeping."

"Good."

She sat next to me. "Is thee praying for Ethan?"

Nay. I'd been listening to the muted sound of Isaac's voice as he told Ethan a story within the blankets. "I wasn't, but that is a fine idea. Let's pray for him. Jesus is the Great Physician, and he loves Ethan very much."

"May I pray for him?"

I stroked her hair. "Thee is such a good sister."

She grinned. "Isaac said that too."

Isaac. Guilt stabbed me as I remembered my insolent words to him earlier in the night.

I owed him a sincere apology—again.

The hearth fire lit the common room with an undulating glow when I awoke. All was quiet except for the sporadic snapping of the flames behind me, and alarm gripped my middle. Ethan lay on his back between Isaac and me, now silent.

I pushed myself onto one elbow and yanked down the blanket that covered all three of us.

Beneath his shirt, his little chest rose and fell.

"His breathing quieted about an hour ago." Isaac's soft assurance startled me since he lay on his side with his eyes closed. "He has been sleeping soundly."

Ethan sighed with only a hint of hoarseness.

Isaac opened his eyes and drew the blanket over us.

I lay down again, lulled by relief and the warmth surrounding me. While I'd balked at the greasy scent of the bearskin Isaac had brought in from his quarters for us to sleep on, the fur proved far more comfortable than I'd expected. "Has thee been awake all this time?"

He propped up his head. "I've been half sleeping."

"Half sleeping?"

"Sleeping with one eye open. Another of the many skills I acquired on the frontier."

I swallowed. "I cannot thank thee enough. Knowing what could have happened—" My voice wavered, and I rid my mind of such a thought. "I also must apologize . . . for not trusting thee as I should have. I know thee cares for the children and would never do anything that could harm them."

"At times, 'tis difficult to agree to the unfamiliar."

True. But that was no justification for my distrust. He deserved the apology—more than one, really. I inhaled and slowly let out my breath, determined to hold his gaze despite how I wished to look away. "I know thee cares for me as well and that thee would never intend to hurt me either. I shouldn't have said what I did last night. Thee was only speaking out of concern, and I responded in anger."

"I just . . . I want thee to be sure, Beth," he said. "Thee is not a child and I know that, but I care too much for thee to remain silent. Thy grief is still so deep, and I sense thee feels pressured in thy decision. Not necessarily by Hiram, but because of thy situation. I want thee to make certain in thy heart that marriage to this man is what thee truly wants. Will thee take the time to do that?"

'Twas hardly an unfair request. "Aye."

Mwekane whined from where she lay curled by Ethan's feet, then jumped up and trotted to the back door. She faced us and whimpered again.

Isaac slid from beneath the blanket and followed her. After opening the door to let her outside, he closed it so it was ajar only about a foot, then stood at the gap watching her.

The light in the room dimmed, and a look over my shoulder confirmed that the backlog in the hearth would soon crumble into embers. I pushed the blanket down and rose to get another log. After placing it atop the backlog, I stooped to coax the fire with the bellows.

The back door closed, and moments later Isaac knelt beside me. He prodded the logs with the poker until the new log burned. A soft laugh escaped his throat, and I turned to find him watching Ethan. He had rolled over to where Isaac had been sleeping, and Mwekane now lay at his side with her head on his belly.

"Abigail said he squirms like a worm in his sleep."

"He does." When I returned my attention to Isaac, my gaze settled on his chest. With its front laces loosened, his shirt hung to the side, revealing the black line drawing over his heart.

He glanced down, then helped me stand.

We returned to the bearskin, and I slipped under the blanket next to Ethan. Isaac hesitated when I held the blanket aside for him, but then he lay down on his side facing me and rested his head on his hand. His shirt drooped, partially baring the figure on his chest.

I upheld myself on one elbow and, with mettle that surprised me, used one finger of my other hand to move the fabric aside so I could see it more closely.

He swallowed audibly. "Does thee recognize what that is?"

The cross within an upright oval was surrounded by an outline that formed a head at the top, a short leg at four corners, and a pointed tail at the bottom. "A turtle with a cross?" I traced the head with my finger, but pulled back when his muscle tightened beneath it. "Does it hurt?"

"Only when it was first painted. I can't feel it now."

"'Tis paint?"

"A type of paint that's etched into the skin using a porcupine quill. The turtle is for my mother who gave me life, because I believe she was from the Turtle Clan. The cross is for my father who gave me life and my Quaker parents, as well as for my own salvation in Christ our Lord."

I smiled. What a perfect representation of who he was. "'Tis beautiful."

"It doesn't bother thee?"

His eyes captivated me. Never had I met another person with eyes the color of his, though they now seemed more gray than blue with his back to the firelight. "Of course not. 'Tis who thee is."

He took my face in his hand and brushed his thumb across my cheek. "No one understands me as thee does."

The intensity of his countenance and the tingle of his touch took my breath away. How I longed to know what distressed him. "Isaac—"

"We should sleep while Ethan is comfortable." He dropped his hand to my shoulder, then pulled it back.

I nodded. While I may have understood him better than any other, he still held back from even me. Not that I could fault him that, for I likely withheld as much from him, if not more.

If only I had the courage to speak the truth.

CHAPTER 13

Isaac

Second Day, Fourth Month 12th

What sounded like raised voices from within the house stopped me as I exited the woodshed early on Second Day morning. I returned to the chopping stump and grabbed the axe from atop it, then continued the few paces to the front corner of the house to listen.

"'Tis unfair!" Abigail's accusation emanated from the partly open casement window. "Thee never expects Ethan to do everything thee expects of me!"

"Abigail, thee is older and more capable than he," Elisabeth responded. "At his age, thee also had fewer responsibilities."

While I'd witnessed some pithy interactions between Elisabeth and Abigail over the last month, never had they argued in anger and only once had Abigail spoken with disrespect. More brazen words came from Abigail, and I tossed the axe onto the ground and headed for the open front door.

"Ethan has his chores as well," Elisabeth said as I stepped into the house. She gathered the porridge bowls from the table and started toward Jon-Isaac, who sat in the high chair smearing bread topped with peach preserves on his face. "Ethan, thee mustn't give Jon-Isaac thy bread. He is too little to eat that."

Ethan set down the cup of milk he'd been drinking from. "My bread. He took my bread."

She set the bowls on the table and removed the bread from Jon-Isaac's hands, then gave it to Ethan.

Jon-Isaac let out a screech and started to cry.

"I shall give thee more pap in a moment, sweet boy." As Elisabeth walked behind Ethan, he knocked his cup over. She quickly righted it, but not before the last of its contents spilled onto the table.

"Sarah and Anna will soon be here." Abigail stalked into her and Ethan's bedchamber and returned carrying her horn-book and slate. "We were late for school one day last week because thee insisted I wash the bowls before leaving."

Elisabeth grabbed a towel and dropped it onto the spill. "Abigail, I asked thee to do something, and thee needs to—"

"Thee is *not* my mother."

I'd heard enough. "Abigail Edwards."

She spun around and then stilled, her eyes wide.

I looked to Elisabeth, who'd jumped at my voice and now looked close to tears as she held the wet towel and tried to quiet wailing, red-faced Jon-Isaac. "Does thee need help?" I asked.

She shook her head, then gathered the bowls and cup and carried them to the wash basin.

I held out my hand to Abigail. "Get thy cloak. I would speak with thee while we wait."

Staring at the floor, she handed over her hornbook and slate, then lifted her cloak from its hook on the wall by the doorway. Once she had donned it, I followed her outside and shut the door behind us. Inside, Jon-Isaac's crying quieted.

"Sit down."

She did, and I lowered myself onto the bench next to her. "Thee is struggling with indignation and disobedience in thy heart this morning?" Anger added to anger accomplished nothing of benefit, so I spoke gently. The last thing I wanted was to undermine the trust she now had in me.

"Aye."

"Why does thee think that is?"

She gulped, and her chin quivered. "Elisabeth always wants my help . . . with the cooking, with the cleaning, with washing, with Jon-Isaac, with everything." Tears streamed down her flushed cheeks when she looked at me. "But Ethan never has to do any of that. He just gets to play with Jon-Isaac."

Elisabeth did expect a lot from her, but Abigail had never seemed bothered by that. In fact, she seemed to enjoy responsibility. "So thee is feeling overburdened by thy duties? Or is thee feeling some resentment that Ethan has fewer duties? Or a bit of both?"

She wiped her face with the edge of her cloak. "A bit of both."

"And thee understands Ethan is younger and his abilities are fewer, as well as that when Ethan plays with Jon-Isaac, he is helping by allowing Elisabeth to accomplish her duties with less interruption."

She sighed.

"Does thee understand that?"

"Aye. But Sarah and Anna don't have nearly as many chores. Anna is two months younger than I, and she's already working on her third sampler. I haven't yet finished my first one because I rarely have time to work on it."

Ah, so that was it. My brother Daniel's young daughters had four older siblings, two of whom were girls only a few years shy of marriageable age. With the chores divided amongst seven children, Sarah and Anna feasibly had a lesser workload. "So thee also feels resentment because thy friends have more free time."

She bit her lip. "I'm being selfish."

I took her hand in mine. "Thee is human, Abby, and as humans, we're naturally inclined to selfishness. 'Tis only through extending the love of Jesus Christ to others that we overcome that. We must learn to love them as much—or more—than we love ourselves."

Movement caught my eye, and I glanced up to see Daniel and Hannah's school-age children walking up the lane. "Thee must go so you are not late for school. But I want thee to consider what we have spoken about and especially what thee said to Elisabeth. She may not be the mother who gave thee life, but has she not loved and cared for thee and thy brothers as though she is?"

She nodded. "I didn't mean that. I don't know why I said it."

I did—mainly because I'd spoken hastily so many times myself. "That is what happens when we are quicker to speak than we are to listen. God gave us two ears but only one mouth. Remember that." I patted her back. "Go now. We will discuss this more later."

She stood and hugged me, then took her school materials from my lap and hurried to meet Sarah and Anna, who now walked ahead of their brothers and sisters. They all waved to me, then turned around to head to the schoolhouse.

Now, to check on Elisabeth.

Elisabeth was nowhere to be seen when I entered the house. In the sitting area, Ethan knelt on the floor playing with his blocks while Jon-Isaac watched from his baby-tender and Mwekane lay nearby.

"Not in thy mouth, Jon-Isaac," Ethan said, then took the block the baby gnawed.

Jon-Isaac protested loudly, and Ethan jumped up and ran to the table by the settle. He retrieved Jon-Isaac's coral teething ring, then took it to him and went back to playing while Jon-Isaac gummed it.

I walked to the bedchamber doors, but both were open and Elisabeth wasn't in either room. My next thought was that she had gone outside by way of the back door, but I found her sitting on the footstool in the corner where she placed the children when they needed to contemplate unsuitable behavior.

With one elbow on her knees, she had her forehead against her wrist as she clutched a handkerchief in her fist. Soft sobs shook her shoulders.

Empathy welled within me. "Thee is not the one who needs to contemplate thy actions," I said as I sat cross-legged at her feet.

She lifted her head, sniffed, and wiped her eyes. "But I do. I have been too demanding of Abigail, and I know that full well. While only seven, she is so mature and independent that I forget her tender age. She is right. I have been unfair."

There was so much more to it than that. "Thee has also been struggling with sadness over thy papa, weariness from the sleep thee missed the last few nights, and concern about Ethan's health. Aye, thee spoke shortly to Abigail, but she was disobedient."

She shook her head and dabbed her nose. "I have been so distracted by my own condition that I have failed to consider hers." She closed her eyes. "Perhaps Hiram is right."

The hairs on the back of my neck prickled, and I held my tongue for a few moments to ensure civility of my tone. "About what?"

Tears slid down her face when she looked at me. "The children. He believes raising three young children is more responsibility than should be expected of a woman of my age and position. I've always refuted it, but . . ." She took a shaky breath.

'Twas no wonder she doubted her abilities. Still, I did not. "I don't believe that at all, Beth. Not for a moment. Aye, thee is young, but 'tis not uncommon for women to be married and have a child at thy age."

"But I'm not married, and I have three children. Does thee know of other women who have just turned twenty yet have three children—and no husband?"

"Nay. But I do know thee was like a mother to Abigail and Ethan even when Barbara still lived and that thee has been their—and Jon-Isaac's—only mother since her death. I also know thy loving care and gentle guidance have played a large part in why they are such kind and loving children. I have no doubt that if anyone can do this, 'tis thee."

She wiped her eyes again. "Thee truly believes that?"

"Have I ever spoken with frivolity about something of such consequence?"

"Never." She nodded a few times and managed a smile. "Thee is right. God has placed the children in my care, and he doesn't give more responsibility than that which we can handle with his grace. Lately, though, I've just felt so unfit to be the mother they need."

"Perhaps because Hiram has"—I almost said *undermined thy self-confidence* but quickly rephrased—"suggested that 'tis a more difficult plight than someone in thy position can handle."

She sighed. "He is only concerned for my and the children's welfare."

The children's welfare? How such an intelligent woman could be so trusting of him escaped me. "He wanted to know if Meeting would be forming a committee to determine their custody. How is removing children from the care of the person who loves them most showing concern for their welfare?"

"But he does care for the children. When he visited last, we spoke at length about them."

I knew nothing of that. "So he has no qualms about becoming their father?"

"Actually, he proposed that if we marry, Abigail and Ethan could be taken in by his brother and sister-in-law, who live next door to him. They are respected Friends and would love to have children but were never blessed with any. Abigail and Ethan would still be in the family, and we would see each other daily."

And she concurred with such an arrangement? Had Abigail and Ethan not suffered enough losses and changes in their short lives? "This is acceptable to thee?" Somehow I concealed the exasperation that surged within me. "This is what thee truly wants?"

"Nay. But I agreed to consider it. He is older and wiser than I, and—"

"Nonsense!"

She started.

"I'm sorry." I took her hand in mine. "'Tis just . . ." Unable to determine how to finish, I started again. "Beth, I have no doubt that Hiram is a learned man. I'm sure he is quite knowledgeable about many things." I forced a smile, hoping to lighten our conversation. "However, having seen his mannerisms during visits, I'm also quite certain that children are not amongst those things."

She looked down but grinned. "Indeed."

"Then does it not seem apt that thee would trust thy own judgment—and thy heart's decree—concerning the children? They adore thee, and thee loves them dearly." I squeezed her hand and tilted my head to see her face. "Aye, raising children is a great responsibility. But God has seen fit to place them in thy care, and thee has done a fine job shouldering that duty."

She nodded.

"What Abigail said to thee, she did not mean at all. She knows she must speak to us when she gets home."

"I need to apologize to her as well."

We stood, and she took my arm when I started for the back door. "I thank thee, Isaac."

Resisting the urge to pull her close, I placed my hand

over hers. "Continue to seek the Almighty's will in this, and I'll do the same."

"I shall."

Now I just needed to curtail my ire adequately enough that I wouldn't throttle Hiram Biddle when he visited later that week.

~

Sixth Day, Fourth Month 16th

The forenoon sun shone brightly in the clear blue sky and a warm breeze shifted through the budding tree limbs as I loaded the crates of Hiram Biddle's hardware into his carriage. Having had three and a half days to pray, read Scripture, and seek the Inward Light, I'd managed to greet him with kindness.

Now, although I had work to keep me busy in the shop, I exchanged my soiled work shirt for a clean one and accompanied him to the house. Dinner would soon be ready, and knowing Hiram's proposal for the children's custody, I intended to hear every word he spoke to Elisabeth.

She stood in the doorway, smiling, as we approached.

"Greetings, dear heart." Once we were inside, Hiram rested his hand on her arm and kissed her cheek. "Thee looks lovely. Is thee faring well?"

She stepped back, clearly flustered by his boldness, and it took all my self-control to keep from moving between them.

"We are. Ethan was ill for a few days, but he is quite well now." She hesitated when he held out his arm, but then took it and walked with him toward the sitting area. "How are Friends faring in Philadelphia?"

He settled on the couch while she remained standing. "The winter scourges are diminishing now that spring weather is here, fortunately. Of course, Robert Morris's latest declaration in response to the Indian attacks on the frontier has many Friends now fervently protesting."

If Friends were objecting, that could only mean the governor's edict brought more antagonistic treatment of the province's Indian tribes. Not surprising. "What declaration would that be?" I retrieved my waistcoat from the peg on the wall and donned it as I walked to the wingback chair.

Hiram arched his eyebrows behind his spectacles and unbuttoned his yellow silk coat. He smoothed the fabric of his waistcoat and folded his hands. "Essentially, he has placed a bounty on the heads of Delaware men, women, and young boys."

Elisabeth pressed a hand to her chest. "A bounty? Meaning what?"

"Payment for scalps or prisoners." By his nonchalant tone, one would think he spoke of animals, not people.

"Whatever for?" she asked.

"'Tis been some time coming." As I spoke, Ethan got up from where he played on the floor next to the chair. I sat and lifted him onto my lap. "After the raids in Lancaster and Berks Counties in Eleventh Month, many settlers demanded such a bounty, but Conrad Weiser opposed it because he suspected it would have the most effect on friendly Indians."

"He is the Indian interpreter?"

"Aye. He acts as mediator between the Indians and the province."

Hiram looked at her, the combination of a smile and a

scowl on his face. "I bring the latest *Pennsylvania Gazette* each time I visit. Does thee not read it?"

She crossed her arms over her middle. "I do, betimes. Papa always read it and informed me of that which he thought I should know. Isaac does the same."

But I had refrained from keeping her abreast of frontier affairs. 'Twasn't a subject I wished to discuss, and I knew the weekly lists of settlers murdered, captives taken, and habitations burned—at times in gruesome detail—would weigh heavily on her already saddened heart.

Now I had no recourse but to explain. "Morris originally agreed with Weiser, but back in First Month he approved rewards for the heads of Shingas and Captain Jacobs, Lenape chiefs who led many of the raids on the frontier to the west."

Hiram pulled a folded *Gazette* from within his coat and held it out to her. "Now Morris has declared war on the Delaware and any other unfriendly tribes, proclaiming a bounty for prisoners and scalps."

Elisabeth paused, then took it. "But the Lenape aren't unfriendly." She looked at me.

"Many are not," I said. "But more and more are allying with the French and participating in the raids."

Her gaze shifted between Hiram and me. "What's the bounty?"

Hiram nodded at the newspaper. "'Tis there on the second page, near the bottom. One hundred fifty pieces of Eight for male prisoners age twelve years or older, one hundred thirty pieces of Eight for a male scalp or prisoner under the age of twelve years, one hundred thirty pieces of Eight for a female prisoner, and fifty pieces of Eight for a female scalp."

Elisabeth flinched. "This bounty is for any Lenape?"

"Nay, dear heart. Just those deemed hostile." Hiram adjusted his spectacles.

"But how would that be proven? What would stop men from capturing and bringing in friendly Indians, stating they are hostile, for payment?"

Which was what Conrad Weiser had initially feared.

Hiram shrugged. "Naught, I suppose. 'Twould be their word against that of an Indian."

"And 'twould be easier yet to turn in a scalp." The pitch of her voice continued to rise. "How—"

"'Tis all right, Beth," I said.

Ethan, sitting sideways on my lap, appraised her with confusion.

She faced me. "Thee is half Lenape. Now having knowledge of this proclamation, how can thee not fear for thy life—or thy scalp?"

"What's thy scalp?" Ethan asked.

Elisabeth inhaled quickly, then walked over and took his hand. "Come now. Let's get thee seated at the table." She led him toward the kitchen area. "Dinner should be ready."

I stood and swept Jon-Isaac from his baby-tender into my arms. "Is thee hungry?" Hopefully my cheerful banter with him would ease her angst.

He answered with a gummy smile that revealed his two tiny teeth on the bottom and one on the top.

Hiram followed me to the table. "He speaks?"

I laughed. "He is only nine months old, Hiram. But he hears perfectly well." At seeing how Elisabeth struggled with the hearth spit that roasted our chicken, I handed Jon-Isaac to him. "Here. Would thee put him in the high chair?"

Hiram stilled, holding Jon-Isaac nearly a foot from himself. "I . . . How do I do that?"

"Never mind. Just be seated." After taking Jon-Isaac, I walked around the table to place him in his high chair, aware of Elisabeth's eyes following me.

Concern still lined her brow when I joined her at the hearth. Whether she fretted about the bounties or Hiram's discomfort with children, I didn't know. But I truly hoped it was the latter.

CHAPTER 14

Elisabeth

As delicious as the roasted chicken and sweet potatoes had smelled while they were cooking, by the time I sat down at the table, my appetite had vanished.

Hiram and Isaac ate heartily as they discussed goings-on in the city, their conversation fortunately so intent that they made no mention of the neglected food on my plate. I occupied myself by mashing sweet potato with goat's milk and spoon-feeding Jon-Isaac.

"So tell me, Isaac." From next to me, Hiram's voice broke the silence that had fallen for close to a minute. "Having lived with the Delaware people, what are thy thoughts about the strife on the frontier?"

Isaac raised his gaze from his plate and swallowed. After several moments, he drew a breath and let it out. "'Tis an already complicated struggle that will only be aggravated by Morris and the Provincial Council's decision. Morris calls the raids savage, yet his response is nothing less than savagery itself."

"Indeed," I murmured.

He glanced at me before his eyes snapped back to Hiram. "The Lenape have been stripped of their homes, their land, and their way of life, and settlers and the government continue to take advantage of them. They have always been a generous, peaceable people, but they are no longer treated with the love and respect they received from William Penn. Some now feel their only resort is retaliation."

Hiram had lifted a forkful of chicken to his mouth but now lowered it. "Does thee think the raids will continue for some time, then? Or even increase?"

Isaac kept his gaze on his plate. "Only the Almighty knows that."

Hiram nodded slowly as he chewed and then swallowed. "But surely thee has a better understanding of the Delaware mindset than most. Does thee—"

"I do." Isaac set his fork beside his plate and looked Hiram in the eye. "But in no way do I comprehend malice. Nor is such cruelty the way of most Lenape."

"Of course not. I only meant that thee certainly has a different insight into the situation." Hiram sipped his tea, seemingly unbothered. "Knowing that, I am simply interested in thy opinions. For example, on the spread of the raids. Just this month the *Gazette* reported raids in Hereford —only about forty miles from here. Even Friends and the Anabaptists, people who once lived in peace alongside the Indians, are no longer spared. This has Philadelphians concerned the attacks will move farther south. Would thee deem that a possibility?"

Surely Isaac would refute his words. But when he did not answer, the skin on my arms tingled with trepidation. "This is true?"

Isaac's expression sobered.

Hiram clucked his tongue. "Thee truly has not been reading the *Gazette*, has thee, dear heart? Just about every issue includes several letters from the frontier settlements detailing the atrocities befalling them. Some in Philadelphia now fear the war that rages may draw disturbingly near."

Isaac stood so quickly that the bench almost toppled backward, taking Ethan with it. He steadied Ethan and righted the bench in one motion, then rushed to the high chair beside me. In it, Jon-Isaac flailed his arms and grimaced, his face bright red.

I jumped up, but Isaac grabbed him before I could. He gave him three firm slaps to the back, and with the fourth Jon-Isaac gagged and spewed down the front of himself and Isaac's waistcoat.

"Oh dear," Hiram exclaimed.

I glanced at him as I turned to get a towel. "'Tis all right. He's fine."

Hiram tucked his chin against his chest, his ashen face contorted in revulsion, and pressed a fist to his mouth. "Pardon me. Suddenly, I need the necessary." He rose and hastened toward the back door.

I stared after him as he disappeared, my mind whirling. Then I remembered Jon-Isaac. Snatching a towel from beside the wash basin, I dipped it into the bucket of clean water on the floor and returned to Isaac.

He held Jon-Isaac, the hint of a grin on his lips. "We need to work on thy table manners, young man."

Jon-Isaac smiled. "Aah-gaah."

I wiped his face and dabbed the front of his shirt and petticoat, then folded the towel and used its unsoiled side to clean off Isaac's front. My request that he wear a waistcoat over his work shirt for meals now seemed petty. While he had looked more presentable, it added more work for me. "I shall need to wash this."

"Is Jon-Isaac sick?" Ethan now stood next to me.

"Nay, sweet boy."

"Babies sometimes choke when they're learning to eat," Isaac said. "He's as happy as can be now. See?"

Jon-Isaac leaned forward and reached for the bowl of mashed potato on the table in front of his high chair.

Ethan giggled. "I think he's hungry."

"I expect he is, now that his belly is empty again." I carried the towel to the basket of soiled linens beside the back door and dropped it in, then peeked out the window at the necessary. Hiram was nowhere in sight. Finally, I turned around.

Isaac had set Jon-Isaac back in his high chair and was unbuttoning his waistcoat. "I'll go change this, and check on Hiram as well."

"I thank thee." Upon returning to the table, I lowered myself onto the bench beside Jon-Isaac and sighed.

Could this day become any worse?

~

The day indeed became worse. My stomach threatened to turn as I stared at the first Fourth Month issue of the *Penn-*

sylvania Gazette that evening. Still unsettled by Hiram and Isaac's discussion at dinner, I'd collected the last four issues of the newspaper, wanting to see with my own eyes what they'd described. Now I almost wished I had not. The accounts proved much more disconcerting—and the disturbing events closer—than I'd expected.

At the bottom of the second page, a letter from Fort Shirley, a few days' journey to the west, detailed one man's capture and escape from an Indian town. It continued with a warning that Shingas and Captain Jacobs had set out with war parties to fall upon the Conegocheague settlements.

Following that, encompassing much of the first column of the third page, more letters detailed the horrors enacted on the frontier, including one relating the raids in Hereford. Tears blurred my vision as I read the conclusion of the letter:

That the Enemy killed George Zeislof and his Wife, a Lad of Twenty, a Boy of Twelve, and a Girl of Thirteen Years old, four of which they scalped: That another Girl was shot in the Neck, and through the Mouth, and scalped; notwithstanding all which she got off, and was alive when the Letter was wrote: That a Boy was stabbed by them in three Places, but the Wounds not thought to be mortal: That they killed two of the Horses, and five are missing, with which thought the Indians carried off the most valuable of the Goods that were in the Waggons.

In the same Letter Notice is taken of another Misfortune that happened on the Sixth of March, in Lynn Township, in Northampton County, viz. That three Indians attacked the House of David Bielman, murdered his Wife and two Children, and carried off some of his best Effects.

Men, even women and children, murdered so callously. While I'd known there were problems on the frontier— Friends reminded us during each meeting for worship that we must pray for and afford aid to those who suffered there— never had I considered the extent of the calamity.

Guilt riddled me. In my sorrow over the unfortunate happenings in my life, I'd overlooked the plight of others who fared far worse. The loss of Papa stung, but the children and I were still together. We had a home and a community in which we felt safe, and we had Isaac, who ensured we lacked naught. My heart ached for those who'd lost so much, both white and Indian.

The floor creaked on the other side of the room. Isaac closed the door to the children's bedchamber and started toward me.

"I had no idea," I said as he neared. "Why did thee not tell me?"

He sat with me on the settle. "Thee has had so much to bear. I didn't want to add to thy burden." Leaning his head back, he closed his eyes. "And just thinking about it sickens me, much less speaking of it."

I set the newspaper atop the other issues on the table next to me. "What can we do to help?"

"What we are already doing." He opened his eyes and stared at the ceiling. "Praying for peace. Collecting food, supplies, and alms for those affected."

"But that will not bring back husbands, wives, and children lost or taken captive. 'Twill not prevent more violence." I shifted toward him. "Isaac, there must be a better way. For years we lived in harmony with the Lenape. Surely we can find a way back to the amicable covenant we once had. Thee knows the Lenapes' hearts. Would they be open to such a dialogue?"

"They would. But not if Morris and the Provincial Council continue to walk this path of deception." He sat straighter. "I feel a burden to travel to Philadelphia."

Philadelphia? "Why?"

"Israel Pemberton and a group of Philadelphia Friends also feel there is a better way. From what Hiram told me after dinner, they have a plan of sorts to compensate the Lenape for the land they have lost. Earlier this week they petitioned Morris and the Provincial Assembly not to declare war on the Lenape, although at the Council's urging, Morris did not oblige.

"Now these Friends are meeting with Conrad Weiser to discuss how to approach the Lenape. I have taken part in such mediation, and as both a Friend and a Lenape, I can provide insight and understanding for both sides. In the last few hours, I've strongly felt God's leading to visit Israel Pemberton and offer assistance."

I swallowed. While I yearned to accompany him, that seemed implausible. Making the journey with the children would double the travel time and be much more of an imposition. "When would thee go?"

"Tomorrow. I'd do the morning chores, visit Daniel to ensure that he and the boys can help thee until I return, and finish the hardware order I'm working on. If I leave by nine and ride Midnight, Lord willing, I shall be there by noon."

"And where would thee stay?"

"With David. He lives only minutes from Israel Pemberton. I have wanted to call on him anyway, being he is the only sibling I have not visited since returning."

Clearly he had thought this through. Even so . . . "With

this scalp bounty, will thee be safe traveling alone? I cannot help fearing that someone will see thee as a way to acquire quick compensation."

He chuckled. "That doesn't concern me, nor should it thee. I cannot imagine that a man with any common sense would look upon me, with my plain clothes and speech, and surmise he could present me to Morris as an unfriendly Indian."

Plenty of people in the province were without common sense, though. The government's follish treatment of the Lenape and other tribes, among other things, proved that. "But they wouldn't need to present thee if they took thy scalp."

"I truly believe the scalp bounty poses no threat to me, as do I believe this area is safe from attacks. Convicted as I am that 'tis God's will that I make this trip, I also trust his hand will protect us."

I looked away but nodded. How could I deny that—and how could I expect him to forsake such an opportunity to help bring God's healing and hope to such a perilous situation?

"But I will go only if thee approves."

I raised my gaze to his, and the sincerity on his face brought tears to my eyes. "Thee must go. Thy wisdom and knowledge will be invaluable. My only regret is that I cannot accompany thee and provide any assistance I could offer."

The intensity of his expression eased. "'Twill be for only a few days."

I nodded. A few days I hoped would pass quickly.

❧

Seventh Day, Fourth Month 17th

I had just finished washing the front windows when Mary and Susannah's carriage drove into the yard. After lifting Jon-Isaac from where he sat on the rug amongst the children's blocks, I went out to meet them.

"Isaac has not departed, has he?" Mary said as I reached the carriage.

"Not yet." I took her hand and helped her climb down, then kept my arm around her. "Abigail and Ethan are helping him pack and ready Midnight." Just then, the three emerged from the barn with Isaac leading the shiny black horse as the children sat astride and Mwekane followed at his heels. My heart sank a bit, knowing he would soon leave. "Here they come."

Mary walked toward him, limping slightly and holding a letter in one hand.

Having finished tying their horse to the garden's corner post, Susannah approached me. "I assured her he wouldn't have left yet. How is thee faring?"

"We shall be fine. Isaac expects he will be away only a few days at most, and Daniel and the boys will be helping us."

Isaac lifted Abigail to the ground, then Ethan. Before he could set him down, Ethan wrapped his arms tightly around his neck. Isaac rested his forehead against Ethan's, speaking to him. The tenderness of their interaction brought a lump to my throat.

Susannah rested her hand on my back. "I love watching him with the children."

As did I. "If only Hiram were as good with them." The quiet words spilled out before I realized I'd said them aloud.

Susannah met my gaze, her eyebrows raised, then looked at Isaac and Ethan again. "Children—boys especially—need a man in their lives. Isaac knows too well the hurt of losing the man in his life, and I suspect his relationship with the children is as good for him as it is for them."

Indeed. Abigail had been so distraught about his leaving that I'd allowed her to forgo her Seventh Day half day of school. And my heart ached at the thought of Ethan losing yet another man who meant so much to him. But Isaac wouldn't do that. He cared too much for the children, and he'd already pointed out how another major change in their life would affect them. Surely he would return just as he said he would.

Isaac set Ethan on the ground, then led Midnight to the garden fence and tied the horse there. He walked around the carriage before embracing Mary with one arm and guiding her to us.

My throat tightened further, and I swallowed. "I readied food for thee to take along. 'Tis inside."

We all went into the house, and Isaac followed me to the kitchen table while Mary and Susannah, now holding Jon-Isaac, took seats in the sitting area.

I faced him. "Does thee have time to visit with us?"

"'Tis later than I'd hoped to leave already."

I knew that. But—

"And gray clouds are moving in from the west."

I nodded. Any bad weather he encountered would only lengthen his journey. "Thee should go, then." I picked up the biscuits I'd smeared with apple preserves and wrapped in linen. "Thee has water and anything else thee might need?"

"I do." Instead of taking the biscuits from me, he covered my hands with his.

I longed to set the biscuits back on the table and embrace him, but abstained. Mary and Susannah sat only five paces from us, and if I appeared upset by his leaving, the children would follow suit. Abigail and Ethan had both cried when he told them he would be away for a few days, and I doubted I could handle more tears from them without weeping as well.

After saying his good-byes to Mary, Susannah, and Jon-Isaac, he picked up Abigail with one arm and Ethan with the other. "You mind Elisabeth." He grinned as he held each of them on a hip. "And when I return, Lord willing, I will bring you something."

Abigail's eyes sparkled. "Like what?"

"I'm sure Philadelphia's mercantiles carry some lovely little toys and confections. 'Twill be a surprise."

Ethan stuffed a dried apple slice into his mouth. "I like surprises."

"I wish we could go with thee," Abigail said. The longing in her tone told me she wished to accompany him almost as much as I did. "I've never been to Philadelphia."

"Maybe next time. I have some business to attend to on this trip."

They each wrapped an arm around his neck, and he hugged them. "'Tis time." He set them on the floor.

I reluctantly carried the biscuits to him. "Safe travels. May God go with thee, and may his Light direct thy path as thee strives to discern his will for peace."

He took the biscuits in one hand and slipped his other arm around my middle to draw me close. "Lord willing, I will return by Third Day eventide."

Oh, how I wished he would stay—or we could go with him. I nodded, knowing it would be futile to try to answer verbally.

He released me and then headed for the front door.

When the door closed behind him, I steeled myself and joined Mary and Susannah.

Surely the Almighty would provide Isaac protection, and I prayed the Lord would use this opportunity to bring harmony—not only to end the war that shed so much blood but also to assuage Isaac, who longed for peace between the two peoples he loved.

CHAPTER 15

Isaac

A low blanket of gray clouds obscured the sun, making it difficult to determine the hour when I reached David and Deborah's home in Philadelphia. I'd made good time, so the time likely neared quarter of one at the latest.

Halting Midnight on the pebblestone street, I looked over the grounds beyond the wrought iron fence and then guided him through the brick columns on either side of the long lane.

The two-story brick mansion with its white-framed windows and black shutters looked just as it always had. Its large carriage house and front walking garden brought back memories of the weeks Elisabeth and I had spent at Lukens Hall with Mother and Susannah each summer. The property's only difference now was the fragrant pink blossoms that graced the cherry trees lining the horseshoe-shaped lane.

As I neared the carriage house, a middle-aged man in a brown suit and black boots emerged. His red hair, tied in a queue, brought instant recognition.

"Jamie Gibson," I called as I dismounted.

"Well, look who's come visitin'!" He slapped me on the back, his light blue eyes twinkling. "How long's it been now? Two years?"

I cringed at the thought of my last visit, when I'd come to question David and Deborah about my first parents. David had greatly discouraged my leaving Horsham, even pleading with me to stay with them for a while. Still, I'd refused. "A bit longer."

"Is David expectin' you?"

"He isn't."

"No matter." He took Midnight's reins. "Go on up to the front door and knock. Moira'll show you in."

Moira. Elisabeth and I had always loved their kind maid. A young woman when we were small children, she had kept us out of entirely deserved trouble more than a few times.

I headed for the front steps as Jamie led Midnight away. At the white double front doors, I rapped with the brass knocker and dropped my head so Moira would see only the top of my hat when she answered.

The door soon opened. "Welcome to Lukens Hall. May I help ye?"

Grinning, I looked up at her.

She squealed and then covered her mouth with one hand. "*Och*, come in, come in." She hugged me when I stepped into the foyer. "'Tis so good to see ye, dearie."

"Moira?" David's concerned voice echoed into the hallway. Moments later, his tall, slim frame emerged from the office. "Is everything—" A smile spread across his face, and he hastened toward us. After embracing me for several moments, he stepped back and laughed. "'Tis about time. How glad we were when Mother sent word that thee had returned. How is thee? Everything is well at home?"

"'Tis." I pulled Mother's letter from the inside pocket of my coat and handed it to him. "She and Susannah send their greetings."

"Come in. David Junior is working, and Jacob and the younger ones have not yet returned from school. But Deborah, Rachel, and Bernice are here." He stopped by the doorway to his office. "Has thee eaten?"

"I have. Elisabeth sent food with me."

His brow pinched. "How is she? So grieved we were to hear of Jonathan. Such a tragedy."

"The last several weeks have been difficult."

"For thee as well, I'm certain. Thee should have brought her along."

"I contemplated that, but she is caring for the children now, and I'm unsure how long I will stay. Hiram Biddle visited last week and informed us of Israel Pemberton and other Friends' intention to seek peace with the Lenape, and the Almighty has burdened me to visit him and offer assistance."

He nodded. "I had planned on sending word about that. I was unsure if thee would be interested, not knowing thy encounters on the frontier, but those at the Albany Congress spoke highly of thy compassion and efficacy with intercession. Thee will stay with us while thee is here?"

I smiled. "If 'tis no imposition."

"Never." He raised his hand, gesturing toward the back of the house. "Come. Deborah and the girls are out on the veranda. They shall be thrilled to see thee."

As we walked through the affluent splendor of the house, plain by Philadelphia high-society standards but more extravagant than any of the homes of Horsham Friends, more memories rushed back.

How I wished Elisabeth could be by my side, to share not only the musings but also her support in my endeavor.

~

First Day, Fourth Month 18th

"David! David Lukens!"

A man's voice interrupted our conversation as I strode outside the meeting house with my brother and his four sons. With meeting for worship concluded, we had set out through the masses of Friends in search of Israel Pemberton, whom I'd attempted to visit the previous afternoon.

When I turned, a man of about five and forty years, with dark hair and blue eyes, approached us. Shorter than I, he wore expertly tailored plain clothing and exuded a confident air.

"Israel." David clasped his hand.

"Hello." He smiled at David's sons and then held out his hand to me. "Thee must be Isaac. Mary gave me thy note when I arrived home late last night. It came as a pleasant surprise. I'm quite interested in hearing thy story and about thy time with the Lenape. Would thee be able to join us for dinner today?"

Just as I'd hoped. "I would be honored."

"Excellent. We look forward to it. Does thee know the location of our home?"

Surely all of Philadelphia did. "In Chestnut Street west of Third?"

"Aye. I look forward to it."

Matthew, David's twelve-year-old son, stepped closer after Israel walked away. "Wait till thee sees their house. 'Tis one of the grandest in all the city."

I had passed by the magnificent home several times over the years, but never had I seen the inside. Today that would change, but my keen interest wasn't in the exquisiteness of the Pembertons' house.

'Twas Israel's plans for reconciliation with the Lenape that garnered my anticipation.

After dinner, Israel and I retired to the Pembertons' parlor. We sat in comfortable wingback chairs on either side of a tall window and drank the tea that one of their servants had brought to the room for us.

Israel met my gaze as he held his teacup at chest level. "I did not want to question sensitive matters in front of the entire family, but I must say I'm intrigued by thy story. David has spoken of thee in the past, but we never discussed how thee came into the Lukens family. Would thee care to expound upon that?"

I swallowed my sip of tea. "My parents and I traveled to Philadelphia during the winter of 1735. We contracted influenza a few days after we arrived, and the Friends' Almshouse took us in. Despite the care we received, my parents died."

He nodded slowly. "I remember that winter. Many people took ill."

"At the time, Deborah and her sisters were regular volunteers at the almshouse. David's parents—now mine as well—were here in the city to visit, and Mother was helping there. She cared for me during my illness, and when my parents died, she felt burdened to take me in. Since my first parents spoke little English and soon became too stricken to provide much information, Friends had no way of searching for next of kin for me, so they consented. The Lukenses took me home to Horsham and reared me there."

"I see. And it was thy search for original family that led thee to Wyomink?"

"Aye."

He raised his eyebrows. "Was thee able to locate any of them?"

I shook my head.

"I'm sorry to hear that." He set his cup on the small circular table beside his chair, then folded his hands on his middle. After several moments of silence, he proceeded. "I'm certain I need not explain the very desperate circumstances in the northern and western portions of the province. While Friends in no way condone the barbarous acts perpetuated, we do recognize the Delawares' plight as a result of their mistreatment. Many of us wholly believe that by extending consideration and the love God commands of us, as well as financial aid to compensate them for some of which they have lost, we can rekindle the friendship we once shared."

I couldn't have agreed more. "I believe the same."

"As does Conrad Weiser. We met with him, knowing his great familiarity with Indian affairs, and he confirmed that the Delaware feel aggrieved by the loss of their lands without adequate, and in many cases a complete lack of, recompense. He also approves that endeavoring for peace with them, by pacific measures, is the only way to save the province from ruin."

He cleared his throat. "He has since sent to me William Locquies, the friendly Delaware, proposing him as a suitable messenger of peace. With that in mind, Anthony Benezet and I have waited upon Robert Morris to allow us to meet with the Six Nations chiefs now visiting the city, to take notice of them and endeavor by a friendly conversation to manifest our good disposition toward them."

Impressive. While I'd expected Israel would have made some progress in his effort, he had achieved more than I'd anticipated. "And has Morris agreed?"

"He has, with our assurance that we will promptly acquaint him if anything with a prospect of tending to public interest should occur."

That in itself was an accomplishment. "What welcome news."

"With his consent, I have invited the Six Nation chiefs, as well as Conrad Weiser and two other interpreters, to dine with me and other concerned Friends tomorrow so we may converse and strive toward peace between the Delaware and the province. If thee is able, I would be pleased if thee would join us."

Clearly, though he was no longer an assemblyman, Israel's political influence had not waned. "Of course. I would be honored."

"Excellent." He smiled and gave a satisfied sigh. "I'm encouraged, Isaac. Mary and I have prayed much about this, and I believe way will open."

Great optimism swelled within me. "As do I."

"May the Almighty continue to guide our thoughts and

interactions, and may the Prince of Peace be present amongst us as we endeavor toward reconciliation."

As I later departed the house, the only way I could have been more elated was if Elisabeth awaited me at David and Deborah's. How I longed to share this wonderful turn of events with her.

~

Second Day, Fourth Month 19th

The following day, after dinner at Israel Pemberton's, I returned to Lukens Hall even more confident that peace with the Lenape could be achieved. I closed the front door behind me, breathing in the delicious smell of chocolate, and turned to find Deborah stepping into the hallway from David's office.

She looked up from tucking her neck kerchief into the bodice of her gray gown. "The meeting went well?"

I smiled and stepped toward her. "Very well."

"Praise be to God. We just sat down to talk. Come in and tell us about it."

In the office, David sat on the large navy velvet couch with his legs crossed and a cup of chocolate in his hand. Deborah poured a cup for me, then picked up her own from the table by the couch and sat close beside him.

I lowered myself onto a chair across from them and savored my first sip. The thick sweetness warmed me—as did the thought of Elisabeth's delight when she received the canister of grated chocolate I'd bought that forenoon.

David grabbed his spectacles from the table and donned them. "So who was in attendance?"

"Seventeen of us. Israel and Mary, of course. Six Nations chiefs Scarroyady, Canachtogo, the one they call Old Belt, and Cayanquiloquoa. Cayanquiloquoa's wife and son. Interpreters Conrad Weiser, Andrew Montour, and Daniel Claus." I paused, trying to remember the Friends' names. "And James Pemberton, Anthony Benezet, Abraham Farrington, Joshua Dixon, and me."

He nodded. "And the dialogue was well received?"

"Very much so. After dinner, Israel addressed the chiefs, expressing Friends' hope to restore the peace our peoples once shared, and Scarroyady responded that the Six Nations, including the Delaware under them, wish for the same."

"How wonderful," Deborah said.

I took another sip. "He also agreed to take to the Lenape our extension of goodwill along with the assurance that Friends will do all we can to have them forgiven, should they forbear further mischief and repent of their conduct. Truly, I don't believe the meeting could have been more fruitful."

David smiled. "And what particular action has been suggested or decided?"

"Nothing as yet. The chiefs asked for another meeting, and we plan to confer again on Fourth Day morning, with several more Friends as well as Indians who are in the city also invited to attend."

Fourth Day. My stomach sank at the realization, and I leaned my head against the chair's back.

Deborah cocked her head. "Is aught amiss?"

"I told Elisabeth I should be back in Horsham by Third Day eventide." While I wanted to be present at the Fourth Day meeting, that would mean delaying my return. And if more meetings were necessary, my stay would be prolonged even further. "I have no way to get word to her quickly enough, and surely she'll worry." Especially considering how my last trip had stretched to more than two years' absence.

After some thought, Deborah brightened. "Why don't you bring her and the children here? Jamie could follow thee home with our coach in the morning and then bring you all back here. Have them pack whatever they would need to stay a few days with us."

"That is a fine idea, my love." David took her hand, then turned his attention to me. "Bearing in mind the events of the past several weeks, some time here should give Elisabeth a much-needed respite."

Indeed. With all the servants at Lukens Hall, Elisabeth would have few responsibilities to bear. Having time for herself would be a welcome change.

Deborah looked to him. "Perchance Mother and Susannah would visit as well?"

David grinned at me. "There is thy resolution. We would thoroughly enjoy having everyone here, and if you leave at first light on the morrow, Lord willing, you could return by eventide and be able to attend the Fourth Day morning meeting. Does thee think Mother and Susannah would accompany you?"

"'Tis likely. Mother has talked of visiting."

"Perfect. I shall inform Jamie to have the horses and coach readied by first light."

'Twas settled, then. My only concern was that between the anticipation of the talks with the Six Nations chiefs and the prospect of bringing Elisabeth and the children back to Philadelphia with me, I'd get little sleep tonight.

CHAPTER 16

Elisabeth

Third Day, Fourth Month 20th

Shh. Thy brother is still napping," I reminded Ethan as I opened the back door of the house. Jon-Isaac usually slept in my bedchamber, but that morning I'd placed him in the cradle by the rocking chair so I could clean the bedchambers. "Thee must play quietly for a while longer."

"I will," he said.

I tousled his hair, then watched as he headed for the sitting area, where he had been building with his blocks before he needed the necessary. The aroma of chicken stew beckoned me to the hearth to check our dinner.

"Lisabeth, look!"

I spun around at his excited squeal. "Shh."

Jon-Isaac stirred but fortunately did not awaken.

"But look." Ethan's loud whisper held awe as he stood by the bench at the table, pointing. On the table sat a canister that, by its familiar shape, held my favorite grated chocolate. Beside it was an unmarked paper box of what I expected was candy, as well as two toys—wooden cups on a long stick with a ball attached by a tether.

My initial confusion turned to joy. The appearance of such gifts could mean only one thing.

Movement caught my eye, and I looked across the room to see Isaac step from behind the wall in the children's bedchamber into the doorway. A grin spread across his face.

"Isaac!" The gifts forgotten, Ethan hastened across the floor into his arms. He hugged his neck when Isaac picked him up. "We missed thee."

"Don't wake thy brother." Isaac carried him toward me. "And I missed you as well. Did thee and Abigail listen well while I was gone?"

Ethan nodded eagerly.

"One of the toys on the table is for thee. And if Elisabeth agrees, thee may have a comfit from the box." He set Ethan on the floor and turned his smile to me.

I stepped forward to embrace him but stopped at recollecting Mary's gentle admonishment to me after Isaac left for Philadelphia. *"Thee and Isaac are no longer children, and thee is courting Hiram,"* she'd said. *"Take care that the affections between thee and Isaac are blameless."*

"Welcome back," I greeted him.

He pulled me close, enfolding me in his arms. "I missed thee as well."

What a comfort to hold him. No matter how I'd tried to tell myself I was fine with his temporary absence, having him back brought tremendous relief. Finally, I stepped back and looked at him. "And I thee."

He slid his hands down my arms. "Close thy eyes."

Laughing softly, I did as he said. A moment later, something rounded touched my lips. I took a bite, and the sweet thickness of a chocolate almond conceit filled my mouth. Savoring both the taste and the solace of memory brought by my favorite childhood treat, I let it melt. Then I remembered his trip and opened my eyes. "How was thy visit? Was thee able to meet with Israel Pemberton?"

He lifted the remainder of the conceit to his lips, grinning mischievously, but then fed it to me. "'Twas better than I'd even expected. I dined and visited with Israel after meeting for worship on First Day, and then yesterday we met with chiefs from the Six Nations, interpreters, and a few other Friends. The chiefs believe the Lenape want peace as do we, and think they will be open to a dialogue on such."

Just what we had hoped and prayed for. "How will you proceed?"

"The chiefs have asked for another conference, which we have planned for tomorrow morning with more Indians and Friends invited."

Tomorrow. "Thee will be returning to Philadelphia forthwith, then?" My tone reflected my disappointment despite my attempt otherwise, and I lowered my gaze to his chest, focusing on the buttons of his waistcoat.

"I will." He lifted my chin. "And I want thee and the children to come with me. David and Deborah have invited all of us, including Mother and Susannah, to visit for the week. Jamie returned with me in their carriage and is seeing to the horses."

I couldn't think of anything I'd enjoy more. The weeks

I'd spent at Lukens Hall each summer starting at the age of nine had been a welcome reprieve from chores and an interesting change of scenery, and I adored David, Deborah, and their children. "Of course. If thy conference is on the morrow, we would need to leave right away."

"As soon as possible, anyway. A rest for the horses would be prudent."

I pressed a hand to my chest, thinking of everything to be done. "I'll need to gather our necessary belongings . . . and Abigail is at school, and—"

"Gather whatever we'll need. I'll get Abigail from school, ask Daniel and the boys to care for the animals, and visit Mother and Susannah. We'll still arrive before nightfall."

I smiled, surely brighter than I had in weeks.

"We're all going to Philadelphia?" Ethan looked up at us as he held his ball and cup. Beside him, Mwekane waited for Isaac's attention with her tail wagging.

Isaac leaned down and rubbed the puppy's head. "Would thee like that?" he asked Ethan.

"Oh, I would. We can take Mwekane, can't we?"

I hadn't pondered that. Lukens Hall was immaculate, and while Mwekane was well behaved, she could be high-spirited at times. Abigail and Ethan would be devastated to leave her behind, even at Daniel and Hannah's.

"Of course we can." Isaac scooped up the dog and let her lick his chin. "David's boys have two dogs, and I'm sure she would like to play with them. I have a few things to attend now, so I want thee to help Elisabeth in any way she asks, understood?"

He nodded. "Abby will be excited."

So was I.

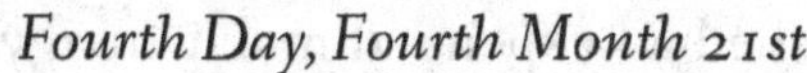

Fourth Day, Fourth Month 21st

"'Tis good to see thee looking so serene, Elisabeth." Deborah Lukens's kind words seemed to read my thoughts as I sat on the veranda at Lukens Hall with the other women.

I set my sampler in my lap and met her gaze. Despite her smile, I suddenly feared I'd come off as too gratified by the respite from my usual responsibilities. "I hope I have not appeared displeased with my life as it is. The Almighty has truly blessed me, and I thank him each day for his favor."

"Not at all, dear. Thee has always been quite content, and 'tis obvious how much thee loves thy sister and brothers." Deborah looked out over the back lawn to where Abigail, Ethan, and her youngest, Rebekah, played with Mwekane. Nearby, Rebekah's nurse, Adele, held Jon-Isaac as she supervised the children. Deborah returned her attention to me and nodded once. "Thy faith and strength amidst the circumstances of the past year are venerable."

Warmth tingled on my cheeks, though I couldn't determine whether it resulted from her compliment or how much I relished the family's servants taking care of my every need. "Being here—having the chance to spend time with all of you again—is certainly a blessing for us."

"And the service of the staff as well, I'm sure," Bernice added with a wry grin.

Deborah gave her a stern look. "Bernice."

She lowered her teacup from her lips. "Oh, Mother, I'm not being facetious. I'm just stating fact. We're all quite grateful for their assistance, thee included. Why shouldn't Elisabeth be as well?"

Seated between Bernice and me, Rachel opened her mouth but then closed it. For as long as I could remember, she had expended much energy attempting to curb her bold younger sister's outbursts, and their differences now extended to more than just demeanor.

While Rachel adhered to her parents' strict beliefs about plainness, Bernice had clearly strayed. Her emerald-green silk gown more resembled the current popular style, with double flounces adorning her sleeve hems, and her smaller cap revealed more of her dark hair, which she'd set in curls around her face.

Bernice raised an eyebrow when our eyes met. "And should thee marry Hiram Biddle, thee would appreciate a similar life. He has as many servants as we have—if not more—and I should think thee would not be expected to lift a finger except to host get-togethers, accompany him to parties, and bear him children—"

"Bernice, thee has said enough." Deborah's tone, carrying a firmness I had never heard before, silenced her daughter. "Do take care that thy words reflect the benevolence, propriety, and content appropriate for a Friend."

"Aye, Mother." She sighed quietly.

Our conversation continued with Deborah, Mary, and Susannah discussing current Philadelphia happenings, but my thoughts wandered to Hiram.

In the last weeks, I'd often pondered how my life would change were I to become his wife. With servants to perform all the menial tasks, I would have much more time to spend with Abigail, Ethan, and Jon-Isaac—and any other children Hiram and I might have.

Except that he had little interest in the children.

Out on the lawn, Abigail and Rebekah, only slightly

different in height, swung their clasped hands between them as they skipped. Ethan threw a ball for Mwekane, while Adele followed the girls, holding Jon-Isaac's hands as he slowly put one foot in front of the other.

The door opened behind us, and Moira appeared. "Pardon the interruption. Hiram Biddle is here."

Hiram—here? I stood and placed my sampler on the seat of my chair.

"Send him out, Moira." Deborah rose and rested a hand on my back when I walked to where she stood closer to the door. "Hello, Hiram."

He stepped out onto the veranda, looking me up and down. He then nodded at the women seated before returning his tight smile to me. "I crossed paths with Isaac on his way to the Pembertons' this morning. How surprised I was when he informed me that thee was also here in the city."

Though his tone wasn't unkind, I sensed he was bothered that I had not informed him. "I planned to send word to thee today."

"Of course. Well, no matter." He held out his hand, and when I took it, he drew me nearer, staring into my eyes with a countenance of sweet adoration. "Thee is here, and that is what is important. I have come to invite thee to supper today." He glanced out over the lawn. "And the children as well, of course. Would thee do the honor of joining me?"

The children too? That I hadn't expected, especially after his last visit. But I might have simply misread his unfamiliarity with them as uneasiness. Or perhaps, considering my wishes, he'd decided to get to know them better. "We would be delighted."

"Excellent. Four of the clock, then, so we'll have ample time to visit before the meal?"

The boys napped until about half past three, so that time would do nicely. "Four of the clock it is."

"Would thee care to join us for a cup of tea?" Deborah asked him.

"Another time." He lifted my hand to kiss the back of it, then stared into my eyes. "I look forward to our time together this afternoon."

I smiled, surprisingly not self-conscious of his affection this time. "As do I."

~

Abigail, Ethan, and I arrived at Hiram's home right at four of the clock, having left Jon-Isaac at Lukens Hall with Adele due to his irritability upon waking from his nap. Jamie jumped down from the box seat and opened the carriage door, then lifted the children out and helped me alight. Once on the ground, I faced the house.

Three stories and brick with white trim and black shutters, it resembled Lukens Hall, although it sat only fifteen paces from the street. A brick walkway led to the front door, flanked on each side by a tall tree, and black iron fencing separated the yard from the street.

The front door opened, and Hiram stepped out onto the brick steps. After descending to the walkway, he smiled. "Welcome, my dear." He took my hand and kissed its back, but this time held it to his lips for several moments.

"What time will you be needin' me to return, Elisabeth?" Jamie asked.

"No need," Hiram said. "Thee may let David know that I shall escort them home."

I nodded when Jamie looked to me. "I thank thee."

He tipped his hat. After climbing back onto his seat, he slapped the horses with the reins and drove away.

"Does thee always thank the help?" Hiram wore an amused grin when I returned my attention to him.

"I suppose." Not that I frequently interacted with servants. "The Lukenses always have, and I follow suit. Surely nothing is wrong with expressing gratitude to those who provide assistance."

He scowled, contemplating that. "I reckon I always deemed the wages I provide them as my thanks. No matter. Shall we go in?" He held out his elbow to me.

I took his arm, although a bit disappointed. I'd anticipated Hiram showing more consideration for the children—after all, he had invited them—yet he had not so much as glanced at them or mentioned Jon-Isaac's absence.

My disparagement then brought remorse. Perhaps he just needed time to learn how to relate to them. From what I knew of his family, he was the youngest child, so he might not have grown up interacting with young children.

Abigail and Ethan walked hand in hand beside me, practicing the quiet obedience we had discussed on the ride there. I gave them a smile and an approving nod, and they grinned. Truly, even with their occasional rambunctiousness, they were two of the sweetest children I knew.

Upon entering the house, we were greeted by a grand foyer. Hiram's residence may have resembled Lukens Hall on the exterior, but the interior certainly did not. While David and Deborah's home was quite large and lovely in its decoration, and provided many comforts, it also abounded with modesty, simplicity, and practicality—not at all like the house in which we stood.

The children's eyes widened at the gleaming marble floors, wallpapered walls, elaborate moulding, and exquisite artwork that surrounded us. Even I had to curtail my disbelief. Never had I been in a home so extravagantly bedecked, and especially not one owned by a Friend.

Uneasiness edged at my stomach. But from what? The lack of the plainness I'd always embraced—or the thought of raising energetic little boys in such a pristine environment?

Hiram glanced around the two-story foyer, then eyed the curved staircase that led to the second floor. "Quite different from the cabin thee is accustomed to, but I assure thee 'tis quite homey." He winked at me. "And thee would certainly need not concern thyself with the upkeep. That is the staff's responsibility. Come. I have guests I'd like you to meet."

Guests? He had not mentioned inviting others to join us. Not that it mattered. 'Twas his home, and he might wish to acquaint us with his friends. While he had observed my life in Horsham, what I knew about his life here came only from our conversations.

Taking Ethan's hand to keep him close, I followed.

Hiram led us to a wide doorway near the staircase and then into a large parlor. Sunlight from the many tall windows lit the room, which boasted the same elegant décor as well as an immense fireplace and the finest furnishings I'd ever beheld. A stout middle-aged couple, the man wearing a brown velvet suit similar to Hiram's and the woman dressed in a dark-blue silk brocade gown and a lacy cap, stood from the couch.

Hiram placed his hand on my back, guiding me toward them. "Lemuel. Eleanore. I'd like you to meet Elisabeth Alden and her siblings." He shifted his gaze to the children. "This is Ethan and Abigail. How old are you, children?"

Both looked at me, and I nodded.

"I am almost eight, and Ethan is four and a half," Abigail said.

The woman stepped forward, smiling warmly at her. "How polite you both are. Does thee attend school?"

Abigail nodded. "I like school."

"Wonderful." She addressed Ethan. "And look at thee, young man. Four years old and already breeched?"

"Our papa is . . ." I swallowed at realizing my words. "He was a blacksmith, and Ethan loved to sit in the forge and watch him work. For safety, Papa insisted I breech him when he turned three."

"Ah. A most reasonable choice. Hiram has mentioned an infant sibling as well?"

At least someone realized his absence. "Aye, Jon-Isaac. He's cutting teeth and has been a bit ill-tempered today, so I left him in the care of Lukens Hall's nurse."

Hiram nodded. "A most sensible decision." Then with a smile, he said, "Elisabeth, this is my brother, Lemuel, and his wife, Eleanore, about whom I have told thee. They have been eager to meet thee—and the children, of course."

Suddenly, the air seemed sucked from my lungs. Heat washed over me, setting me off-balance, and I stepped closer to him for stability despite myself.

Before me stood the couple he hoped would become Abigail and Ethan's new parents.

❧

No matter how I tried, I couldn't sleep that night. After striving to keep up a happy, sociable appearance at Hiram's, I'd returned to Lukens Hall to learn that Isaac was out, meeting with a woman who cared for his parents before they died. Now, as I lay on my trundle bed in the bedchamber I shared with Mary and Susannah, my aching stomach and more-aching heart besieged me.

I sat up and listened to ensure Mary and Susannah both slept in the bed, then checked on Jon-Isaac, who slumbered deeply in the cradle beside me. As quietly as possible, I rose and donned my gown and petticoat. Moments later I slipped into the hallway, then tiptoed to the stairs and crept down to the parlor. With the time nearing quarter past ten, Isaac should soon return.

Only moments after the grandfather clock tolled its single bong at half past ten, the front door clicked as it unlatched. I stood from my chair and walked to the doorway to the foyer.

Isaac quietly closed the door, then turned around. He started at seeing me, placing his hand over his heart as he exhaled. "Beth. 'Tis late. Why is thee still awake?"

A few truths would have applied—that I worried because he still had not returned, that I'd had a horrible evening and just wanted the comfort of his company, or that my stomach hurt from forcing myself to eat supper despite my lost appetite. Then he came closer, and the moonlight through the transom above and alongside the door showed the weariness on his face.

"I wanted to see thee. We have not had more than a few minutes together at a time since we arrived." I stepped nearer, looking him in the eye. "Deborah told me thee went to visit a woman who knew thy parents."

He looked away but nodded. "Lydia Stanton. I came here when I left Horsham, in search of anyone who might have cared for my parents at the almshouse, and I learned of her. I was told since she spoke French, she was able to converse with them before they became too ill to speak. But she was in Virginia then." He glanced back at me. "One of the Friends at the Pembertons' this morning mentioned her, and I questioned where I might find her."

I suspected whatever information she'd provided had not been much, or it had upset him for some reason. "What did she tell thee?"

With a sigh, he combed his fingers into my hair, which hung loose to my waist. His hand caressed where it fell over my shoulder, which sent an odd shiver down my spine when he met my gaze.

I swallowed. "Thee is upset. Why?"

His eyebrows knit together. "'Tis late, Beth. I need to be up early to meet with Israel and other Friends tomorrow, and thee must be tired as well."

Which meant he had no intention of telling me—just as he had distanced himself from me after Margaret Roberts deceived him. Refusing to allow that to harden my heart toward him again, I stepped closer and slipped my arms around his waist.

He held me, burying his face in the top of my head, then turned us toward the staircase.

"Thee go ahead." I released him and stepped back, my vision suddenly blurring with tears. "I need to get something from the kitchen." Barely able to see where I was going, I hastened down the dim center hallway but continued through the house to the double doors that led outside onto the veranda.

Outside, I dropped into one of the chairs and cried until my tears were none and I barely had the strength to return to my bedchamber.

CHAPTER 17

Isaac

In my bedchamber, I stripped off all but my breeches and lay on the bed, staring at the ceiling. My eyes ached with exhaustion, but that hardly compared to the weariness that plagued my soul. This evening's visit, though it provided more information than expected, left me overwhelmed by conflicting feelings—joy in the gained knowledge that I'd so long yearned for, yet heartache in the loss of those I'd once loved most.

Then there was Elisabeth.

Would I ever understand my actions when it came to her? I'd been so pleased to find her waiting for me, to know she sensed my frame of mind and cared that I was troubled. Yet I had pushed her away. As soon as she had shown concern, hoping I would confide in her, I used the simplest excuse not to.

'Twas no wonder she couldn't trust me. Why would she share the difficulties she faced when I so often failed to share mine with her? I longed for the closeness we once had, when we shared our every feeling without a second thought, so why was it so difficult to confess my struggles?

I sighed heavily. Distancing myself from Elisabeth wasn't my intention. She had always known me best, and no doubt she still did. Only with her had I shared the horrors of what I'd experienced while away, and 'twas her reassurances —and her arms around me—that had comforted me since I'd returned. Even tonight, embracing her had eased the emptiness that gnawed within.

But that posed a problem as well. Elisabeth's beauty enchanted me, and her sweet affection stirred my heart in ways I dared not act upon. Her courtship with Hiram was now quite evident, whether or not I approved, so we could share nothing more than friendship.

In light of that, my earlier aloofness was a necessity. Her best interest required that we take care in our actions, and I'd never forgive myself if her reputation were to be called into question because of me. While that had not been the reason I'd held back from her downstairs, part of me was now glad that I had.

Still, I cared so much for her. There was no denying that her relationship with Hiram could have grave consequences, but I struggled to discern the extent of my responsibility. Should I respect Elisabeth's maturity and capability to make her own decisions? Or should I honor my word to Jonathan and do everything I could to protect her and the children? Both choices could result in more sorrow.

"Father, give me wisdom," I whispered. "Show me what to do."

Be still and know that I am God. The familiar words of the psalmist came to me in the darkness.

In my apprehension, I'd somehow lost sight of the Almighty. He loved Elisabeth, the children, and me, and I knew he had great plans for all of our lives. Throughout my years he had proven that his goodness could be trusted even in the bleakest of circumstances.

I needed to allow and esteem his sovereignty in this situation as well.

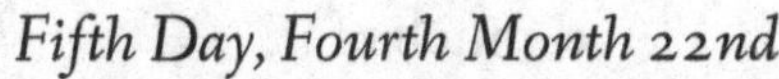

Fifth Day, Fourth Month 22nd

The women were visiting on the veranda when I returned to Lukens Hall after dinner at the Pembertons' the following afternoon. Susannah and Deborah each worked on samplers while Mother, whose weakening eyesight no longer permitted detailed handwork, knitted as they conversed.

"Isaac." Mother smiled and patted the empty half of the two-seated rocker she occupied. "Does thee have a few minutes to spare?"

"I have the rest of the day to spare." Guilt prodded me as I sat with her. 'Twas our second full day in Philadelphia all together, but I'd spent considerably more waking hours away from Lukens Hall than I'd spent on its grounds with the family. "I know I've been gone a lot."

"Thee is needed elsewhere right now," Susannah said. "We know that, and we're thankful for thy willingness to further Friends' strivings to bring peace to the province—as are many others. Thy favored testimony regarding Indian relations was well received in meeting for worship."

She paused as she held my gaze. "Thee does look tired, though, and I'm not surprised. Thee did not return until late last night and then left before breakfast this morning." As always, Susannah spoke her mind with no hesitation.

I shook my head. "I had some things I wanted to discuss with Israel before meeting. We're conferring with the Six Nations and Friends again tomorrow morning, but I believe we're nearing a final resolution on how best to address the Lenape."

Deborah set down her sampler. "How was thy visit with Lydia Stanton? Was she able to provide the information thee hoped for?"

"Aye, much of it."

The door opened, and Rebekah traipsed outside bearing a basket containing three dolls and a porcelain tea set. Behind her, Abigail carried another doll.

"Isaac!" She hastened toward me, then climbed onto my lap and wrapped her free arm around my neck. "We missed thee."

I hugged her. "I've missed thee too. Thee is enjoying thy time here?"

"Oh, I am!" She pulled back enough to look at me, grinning. "Deborah said Lord willing, we're all going on a picnic to the river tomorrow afternoon. Will thee go along too?"

A picnic sounded like the perfect retreat after this week's busyness. "I wouldn't miss it."

She embraced my neck again, then climbed down.

"Mother, may we play tea with the dolls in the garden?" Rebekah asked.

"You may," Deborah said. "Are Ethan and Jon-Isaac still napping?"

"Aye." Rebekah headed for their walking garden. "Come, Abby. 'Tis almost teatime."

Abigail skipped to catch up with her, glancing over her shoulder to wave at me, and I smiled.

"A child's love is a balm for the soul," Susannah said.

Indeed it was, for just a few moments with Abigail had greatly uplifted me. Before any more could be mentioned about my soul, I asked, "Where are Rachel, Bernice, and Elisabeth this afternoon?"

Deborah continued to scrutinize her needlework. "Rachel and Bernice left for the mantua-maker's right after dinner. Elisabeth has not felt well today, so she is resting with the boys."

Perhaps that was why I couldn't find her this forenoon. I'd scanned those assembled in the meeting house for midweek meeting for worship but never caught even a glimpse of her. I looked at Susannah. "Is she ill?"

"Just a bit of indigestion, she suspected. Something she ate at Hiram's seemed not to agree with her."

Or possibly it was the company?

I rebuked myself for such a thought. Either way, I now wanted to see her even more. "Well . . . I believe I'm going to rest a bit as well." I stood.

Susannah caught my arm as I passed her chair. "She is in our bedchamber. Just knock quietly so thee does not awaken the boys."

Meeting her gaze for only a moment, I nodded once.

Either she presumed my intentions or her words were meant as an encouragement to act. Whichever was true, she knew me well.

The door to the bedchamber Elisabeth, Mother, and Susannah shared was open several inches, so I rapped on it softly and then stuck my head into the room. Ethan and Jon-Isaac slept on the trundle bed on the floor, but Elisabeth wasn't on the bed as I expected.

"Isaac." Her whisper drew my attention to the far side of the large room. There she sat sideways on the large window's deep sill, her knees drawn to her chest.

I slipped into the room and quietly crossed the floor. Seeing her out of bed heartened me, as did her smile as I neared. "Thee is feeling better?" I sat by her feet.

"Aye." She searched my face.

I leaned forward, resting my forearms across my legs, and stared at the wooden plank floor. "I'm sorry about last night."

"Thee was right. 'Twas late."

"'Twas, but thee was right too. I was upset."

She touched my arm. "Because of the situation with the Lenape, or because of thy visit with Lydia Stanton?"

"The talks with the Six Nations have been demanding at times, especially considering their great importance, but they have gone well."

"And last evening?"

"Lydia answered every question I asked." I shook my head and snorted. "If anything, I should be grateful, but . . ."

"I have never known thee to be ungrateful, and I do not think thee is now." She swung her feet off the sill and onto the floor, turning so she was beside me. "Betimes the truth is like a finely sharpened knife. It can release the bindings that hold one captive, but it can also pierce the most tender of places."

I rested my forehead on my hand, rubbing one eyebrow. Common sense cautioned me to halt the conversation at that, but I suddenly longed to share with her what had me so troubled. "I just . . . Beth, I don't understand."

"Don't understand what?"

"Just . . ." How did I explain it when even I couldn't describe the process of my sadness? "At Lydia's last night, she took my hands in hers. 'Twas so hard for me to let go, because I knew her hands had also held the hands of my mother and father—that the skin touching mine had touched theirs." I cleared my throat. "Then when I left, I walked down to Friends' Almshouse and sat on a bench across the street, just staring at its arched entrance and trying to remember being there with—" My voice cracked, and she slipped her hand under my arm to clasp the crook of my elbow. "I can't remember them at all. How is it we can miss people so terribly even when we have no memory of them?"

She leaned her head against my shoulder. "Our minds may forget but our hearts do not?"

I had not expected an answer, certainly not one so strangely consoling.

Lifting her head, she looked at me. "Thee always said that if nothing else, thee wished to know thy parents' names. Was Lydia able to tell thee?"

More names than I'd ever expected. "My father was Jean-Luc Billiou, and my mother's name—or rather, the French name he called her—was Angelie."

"Ahn-zha-lee," she repeated, emphasizing the last syllable as I had. "What a beautiful name."

"And mine was Christian."

"Jacob and Mary changed thy name?" Her tone confirmed she was as surprised to learn that as I'd been.

I nodded. "I asked Mother about it this morning. She said she never spoke with Lydia while helping at the almshouse. Friends had separated me from my parents because they were much sicker than I, and Mother was never told my name."

She smiled, albeit sadly. "Thee has lived up to the name thy parents gave thee, just as I suspect they hoped thee would. They would be so proud of the man thee has become."

Her sincere encouragement uplifted me. "I hope so."

"I *know* so."

I pulled my arm from her grasp and slid it around her. "Thee always has known just what to say."

She looked into my eyes. "I'm only speaking what I know is truth. I'm glad thee told me."

How lovely she was, and the beauty within even eclipsed that of her countenance. All my life I'd loved her, but never as much as I did now.

Sixth Day, Fourth Month 23rd

I had no sooner entered Lukens Hall on my return from our Sixth Day meeting with the Six Nations and Friends than David stepped into the hallway from his office.

"Thee is smiling," he said. "That is a good sign."

"'Tis indeed." I shut the front door and walked toward him. "We have come to a decision we hope the Lenape will receive as our extension of the peace and respect they once shared with William Penn. Scarroyady is most hopeful 'twill put an end to the theater of bloodshed on the frontier."

"Praise be to God for that. Can thee join me? I'd love to hear the details." He followed me into the office and shut the door behind us. There, he motioned to one of the navy velvet wingback chairs in the sitting area in front of his massive desk, then took a seat on the couch across from it. "'Tis good to see true happiness on thy face. When thee arrived, thee seemed hopeful yet quite reticent. That has changed."

I lowered myself into the chair and kicked my feet out. "I'm heartened. The Almighty has made straight the way, and I believe 'tis his will that peace will come of this effort."

"What has been decided? Will messengers be sent to the Lenape, as thee suspected?"

"Aye, three men."

"And will thee be one of them?"

"Nay. Scarroyady has suggested Indians who were present at the meetings: Newcastle and Jiggera of the Six Nations and William Locquies the Lenape from the Jerseys. Israel and William Logan will be waiting upon Robert Morris for approval, and pending that, the three will travel to the Lenape and Shawanese with a message that we wish to treat with them to restore peace."

He canted his head. "Thee knows Scarroyady well from thy time with the Lenape. He did not consider thee as a messenger, with thy apposite experience as a mediator and thy ability to represent both sides?"

I dropped my gaze to my boots and sighed. "Some Lenape—those who turned to violence and retaliation—no longer welcome me as one of their own. Scarroyady felt for the sake of the peace process, as well as for my own safety, 'twould be best not to send me."

"I see. Is that a disappointment?"

I looked up at him. "'Tis, but I also see God's providence in it."

"Because of Elisabeth and the children?"

Primarily. "I gave Jonathan my word that I would care for them. I will not go back on that, and I couldn't do that to her—leave again—especially now. Her responsibilities, when combined with the grief of losing Jonathan, are overwhelming. Right now, she and the children take precedence over anything I want."

He smiled lightly. "Thee cares deeply for her."

I scanned his face for some hint of his intent. "Of course I do. She has been my dearest friend. I have cared deeply for her all my life."

"I think thee knows what I mean."

Aye, and I suspected he had assistance in coming to that conclusion. "What I think is thee has been talking to Susannah."

"That I have. But I also have eyes that see quite well—with spectacles, at least—and 'tis obvious that thee is fond of her and she of thee."

True, but that mattered little. "She's courting Hiram. 'Twould be improper for me to attempt to undermine their relationship."

"Not necessarily. Has thee pondered sharing with her how thee feels?"

Many times, but 'twasn't nearly as simple as he made it sound. "I have, but I fear dire consequences if I make my feelings known. I'm unsure how Elisabeth would react, and I also don't want to risk tainting her character in any way. We live on the same property, and although Meeting has agreed to that, they did so with the expectation that our relationship was and would be nothing more than a friendship."

I shook my head and stood to pace. "Then there is the likely chance that Hiram would complain so loudly to Meeting elders that I would be taken to task for unbecoming behavior, which I would have difficulty defending since he is an esteemed Friend and I have only recently been reinstated in Meeting. And I don't want to even think about the quandary that could put Elisabeth—and the children—in."

My brother pulled at his chin and gave a few slow nods. "All valid points."

Indeed, and I had not broached the complication of my heritage. While whites and Indians marrying wasn't uncommon on the frontier, Horsham was not the frontier, and my courtship with Margaret Roberts had resulted in some Friends—even a few from Horsham—questioning the wisdom of supporting such a union.

Facing him, I finished, "I have thought this over many times. Maybe in time, but if I said anything now, I fear 'twould end in detriment for all involved."

He considered that. "But time is not in thy favor. Is thee, then, holding this in the Light and seeking the Almighty's guidance?"

Was I ever. "Each and every day."

CHAPTER 18

Elisabeth

First Day, Fourth Month 25th

There thee is." Hiram's voice in my ear surprised me, as did how close he stood when I turned.

Stepping back, I bumped into a Friend walking by.

"Take care, dear heart." He drew nearer again. "Meeting for worship was well attended today."

Most definitely. The benches had been filled when I'd taken Jon-Isaac outside toward the end of meeting, and a swarm of Friends now moved about within the high brick wall surrounding the meeting house.

Beside me, Abigail tugged at my sleeve. "May we go find Isaac now?"

"Not yet." I lifted Jon-Isaac higher onto my hip. "Stay close, lest thee lose sight of us." Even with Mary, Susannah, and Rachel with us, 'twould take only a moment for her or Ethan to disappear in the crowd.

Deborah joined us then, accompanied by an older woman. "Elisabeth, this is Betsy Tyson."

Betsy Tyson. I recognized the name, but I'd been introduced to so many people and heard so many names while in Philadelphia.

The woman smiled, her flushed round face reflecting both delight and sympathy. "I was so saddened to hear about thy father. He made a delivery to my husband and me about six weeks ago."

Of course. Charles and Betsy Tyson. The couple to whom Papa and Abner had taken Samson, Ruthie, and their baby. "But Abner said you would be moving to North Carolina."

"We had to postpone our departure. My Charles suffered a terrible attack of the gout and couldn't walk for three weeks. Lord willing, we shall commence our trip at the end of next week."

My breath caught. "Then . . . are they still here?"

Her grin brightened. "They are. Would thee be free to join us for dinner?"

But the children. She had not mentioned them, and they'd been cared for by others on several occasions since we had been in Philadelphia, so I hesitated to leave them again.

Susannah took Jon-Isaac from me. "Go. They have a special place in thy heart. Way has opened for thee to see them one last time."

I smiled at Betsy. "I would be honored."

"And thee is most welcome as well," Betsy said to Hiram. "Thee remembers where we live?"

"In Sassafras Street." The flatness of his tone implied he

was not happy about something, though I couldn't imagine what. "We shall leave shortly and will meet thee there."

"I thank thee, Betsy."

Hiram stood in silence as I explained to Abigail and Ethan that I would return to Lukens Hall sometime that afternoon.

"But thee and Isaac said you would take us for a walk down to where you used to play when you were children," Abigail said.

I placed my hand on her shoulder. "And we will. Lord willing, I will return by the time Ethan and Jon-Isaac have finished their naps." Glancing around, I found Isaac nowhere in sight. His involvement in the conferences with the Six Nations as well as his poignant testimony in meeting this forenoon would surely have many Friends searching him out. "Would thee let Isaac know that?"

Hiram took my arm, then led me through the crowd to the nearest gate and out onto the sidewalk along Second Street. "Would thee care to enlighten me as to whom we shall be visiting besides Charles and Betsy?" he asked as we headed north.

People were everywhere, and as we neared the corner, he pulled me to his side. A group of older boys ran past, one turning to yell to someone behind him. Another boy called back, laughing.

Hiram exhaled in exasperation. "Friends would have done well to consider relocating to a less raucous location instead of rebuilding the meeting house here."

I glanced down High Street at the courthouse and butcher's shambles that occupied the center of the road between Second and Third Streets. 'Twas a rather bustling area—and loud at times despite the First Day noise ordinance—but that was of little importance to me. I merely wished to get to the Tysons'.

"Thee did not answer my question."

I looked at him, tempted to respond that his outburst had precluded me. "Several weeks ago . . ." Nay, not here. Too many people could hear. "I shall explain when we get there."

"Mmm." His eyes remained fixed ahead of us. "For some reason, I sense 'tis something thee should have shared with me before now."

My stomach twinged, but I refused to allow any discomfort with him to steal my joy. Soon I'd see Samson, Ruthie, and the sweet little girl who'd been the first baby I'd delivered on my own.

~

My heart quickened as we reached Sassafras Street, and I tempered my pace so not to get ahead of Hiram. Barely a word had come from him since we had crossed High Street, although my thoughts were so occupied by Samson, Ruthie, and the baby that I didn't mind.

Never had I thought I'd see them again. Abner told me he and Papa left them in the care of Charles and Betsy, who had plans to leave soon for North Carolina to join Friends at the New Garden settlement. From there, Samson, Ruthie, and the baby would be assisted south to Spanish Florida.

"Here we are." Hiram led me to a three-story brick house with black-painted window frames and dark-green shutters.

The front door opened, and a tall, dark-haired man of perhaps thirty years greeted us warmly. "Do come in. Father and Mother told me you would soon be arriving." He stepped back so we could enter, then closed the door. "I'm

Enoch, their oldest son. Thee must be Elisabeth. I've heard some wonderful things about thee."

I smiled. "I cannot thank thy mother enough for seeking me out today. I had no idea thy parents were still in Philadelphia."

"Only for another week, Lord willing. Mother has two sisters already in New Garden, and she and Father have been talking about joining them for some time now." He grinned. "Father's gout, if nothing else, has allowed Ruthie a proper period of lying in, and she and her infant are quite hardy now."

How glad I was to hear that. I'd worried for both of them when Papa and Abner whisked them away to Philadelphia barely three days after the baby's birth.

Hiram cleared his throat. "Since we are now here, perchance thee could share thy secret with me?"

I pressed my hand to my chest. "Oh, forgive me. Several weeks back, one of the Friends from our Meeting brought us two young people who had escaped from the man who enslaved them. The girl had reached her time of confinement, and I delivered the baby. We kept them in our root cellar for a few days, then Papa and Abner brought them here."

His eyes narrowed. "I see."

"Our deepest condolences on thy loss," Enoch said.

I nodded my gratitude.

"Come. They are in the parlor. I'm sure thee is eager to see them." He led us down the center hallway to the doorway of the large room.

"Elisabeth!" Ruthie stood from the parlor couch, where she'd been sitting next to Samson. With the baby cradled in one arm, she hurried over and flung her free arm around me.

We hugged for a long time, both laughing and crying. Finally, I stepped back to look over her. Clad in a calico gown and petticoat, and with her hair tucked into a linen cap, she hardly resembled the scrawny child who'd shown up at our home in labor. Much-needed weight filled out her figure, and her face glowed with healthy color. "Thee looks wonderful." I peered down at the infant in her arms. "And look at this sweet child."

She placed the swaddled baby in my arms, and the little girl peered up at me with the most beautiful dark-blue eyes. Her skin coloring, rather light when she was born, now matched Ruthie's medium brown, and she certainly favored her mother. "Thee is just precious," I crooned, stroking her cheek.

"Reckon her eyes'll turn brown eventually," Ruthie said. "My mama once told me mine were blue when I was born too."

I smiled. "She looks like thee."

"Just like we prayed for."

Tears of joy filled my eyes again. I'd pled with God to not let the baby resemble her father—so Ruthie wouldn't be reminded of the terrible acts he had committed, and so there would be little indication that the baby wasn't Samson's. God in his mercy had granted that.

Samson approached us. With his hair closely shorn and having gained weight too, he also looked much different. "We named her Elisabeth."

Ruthie touched the baby's cheek. "Couldn't think of a finer name for her."

I covered my mouth, trying not to choke up, as I stared down at the sweet little one who bore my name. "I've never been so honored." Then remembering Hiram, I turned toward where he stood in the doorway with Enoch. "Come meet them."

He joined us, his hands clasped behind his back, and nodded at Samson and Ruthie.

"Elisabeth mentioned you," Ruthie said.

"Hmph." Hiram raised his eyebrows but would not look at me. "I do wish I could say the same about you."

"So was thee planning on eventually telling me of thy proscribed anti-slavery activity?" Hiram whispered soon after we had left the Tysons'. He had remained quiet throughout our visit, mainly speaking when spoken to, and I'd suspected our walk to Lukens Hall might be accompanied by tense words.

"I wasn't intentionally keeping it from thee." Though no one else was anywhere near us, I kept my voice equally as low. "And just because the government declares slavery legal doesn't mean 'tis right in the eyes of God. No one has the right to subjugate another."

"Nay. But surely thee knows of the consequences should thee be caught."

"I also know the consequences should I ignore my conscience. Samson and Ruthie showed up at our door bone thin and filthy. His back bore scars from beatings, and she had been violated by their master. How could I not help them?"

He sighed. "This isn't thy first time participating in such activity, is it?"

I shook my head, tempted to release his arm and move away from him.

Stopping, he faced me. "Please tell me thee was not party to the escape of Thomas Graeme's Negro-Indian slave a few years back."

I searched his face, trying to gauge his thoughts. Aye, Hiram was good friends with the Philadelphia physician who spent summers at his family's plantation in Horsham, but surely he did not condone the man's keeping of slaves. "Nay, I was not." That had been Isaac's doing, as well as that of a laboring man of Dr. Graeme who went with Will, planning to pose as his master, though I dared not say so.

He slid the backs of his fingers down my cheek and rested his hand on my shoulder. "I do not wish to contend with thee, Elisabeth. Truly I do not. But if thee is to be my wife—which I dearly hope thee will, and soon—thy transparency with me is imperative. Thee knows the position I hold in society, and thee must understand what thine will be as my wife."

I swallowed. "Thee is saying I must deny my conscience for the sake of appearances?"

"Nay." He spoke almost loudly this time. Glancing around, he exhaled and then took my arm and started walking again. "I'm saying that care must be taken in our activities."

I pursed my lips. "'He hath showed thee, O man, what is good, and what the Lord requireth of thee: surely to do justly, and to love mercy, and to humble thyself, to walk with thy God.'"

He frowned but continued to look straight ahead. "Thee need not quote Scripture to me, Elisabeth. There is little, if any, of the Bible that I have not read several times over."

I paused. Initiating an all-out argument would be fruitless, but I would not flout the truth. "My intention was not to remind thee of Scripture." I kept my tone light. "I'm simply defending my actions."

He blew out his breath again and squeezed the bridge of his nose beneath his spectacles. Finally, his expression softened, and he released my arm to take my hand. "Thee is here only for one more day, and the weather is lovely." The gentleness of his tone eased my apprehension a bit. "Shall we put aside our differences and enjoy our time together while we can?"

I forced a smile. "Of course."

'Twas only half past two, so we strolled through the streets of the comelier sections of the city, appreciating the fine brick homes and blooming trees and flowers. The sun warmed us from a cloudless sky, and a lovely floral aroma accompanied the light breeze.

Several people stopped to converse with us, and I began to truly understand Hiram's station in society. He was highly regarded not only by Friends but also by other prominent Philadelphians, and he introduced me to each one we met. His honoring words and others' attention made me self-conscious at first, but soon I found myself almost appreciating it.

As we strolled along Third Street, he pulled a chained gold watch from his waistcoat pocket. "'Tis just about quarter past three now. As much as I despise to return thee to Lukens Hall, I know thee assured them of thy presence this afternoon, so I fear I must." He met my gaze. "Will thee join me for dinner on the morrow, just the two of us this time?"

I stopped, facing him. "I would love to have dinner with thee, Hiram, but for the sake of propriety, I could not agree to an unchaperoned visit."

"Mmm. In that case, perchance a visit to the London Coffee House?"

"William Bradford's establishment? I've heard David speak of it. But he's said slaves are sold on a platform in the street before it, and how would we enjoy our time there should we encounter such atrocity?"

"Of course." He lifted my hand and kissed it. "Thy moral philosophies are noble yet wearying, dear heart. Shall we just take another walk after dinner, then?"

Where were my manners? He wished to spend time with me, and I was complicating it. "Would thee join us for dinner at Lukens Hall, and then we could walk?"

He nodded. "Agreed. I only wish to make thee happy, Elisabeth."

We started in the direction of Lukens Hall, and I tried to ignore my uneasiness. Aye, we had our dissimilarities, but Hiram cared for me. He had made that quite clear in his conversation with those we met today. Certainly he would also show that in his respect of my principles.

Second Day, Fourth Month 26th

Another beautiful spring day greeted Hiram and me when we set out for our walk at Lukens Hall after dinner the next afternoon. Taking his arm, I breathed in the sweet scent of cherry blossoms. The lovely flowers graced the trees that lined the brick lane, and when the breeze heightened, their petals fluttered down around us like pink snow.

Hiram smiled as he plucked a petal from my neck

kerchief. "Thy time here has passed far too quickly. I shall greatly miss having thee so nearby."

My heart warmed. Despite our disagreement the day before, he couldn't have been sweeter to me afterward or today. "And I thee. My time here has been a joy, and part of me yearns to stay."

He chuckled. "I hope 'tis a sizeable part, and I should think so. Who, if given the chance, would forgo the amenities of Lukens Hall—or my home—to return to a place so removed from civilization and that requires such exertion to maintain?"

'Twas a fair question, I had to admit. "Even so, I do love Horsham."

"Of course thee does." He met my gaze. "I have been contemplating that of late. Considering thy fondness for Horsham and its charming appeal, I was thinking we might build a country home there. A place to which we could retreat seeking quietude as well as relief from the city's summer heat and humidity."

Build? "That is a fine idea, but a house already sits on my land."

He laughed again. "The cabin is quaint, dear heart, but it would never suit our needs. Especially when children make us a family."

But Papa had built our house. 'Twasn't Lukens Hall or Hiram's home by any means, but it had served us well enough. Then I realized his remark about children. 'Twas as if Abigail, Ethan, and even Jon-Isaac did not exist in our future.

"Think about it. Having a home there would be advantageous, and surely the ability to remain close to Friends there would make thee happy?"

That I couldn't deny. "Aye."

We walked in silence for a few moments, and as we neared the street, I stopped. Suddenly, I no longer wished to leave these grounds with him. "Might we just sit in the front garden instead? 'Tis so beautiful here."

He glanced around. "If thee prefers."

We strolled back to the nearest path into the walking garden and followed it to a white-painted cast-iron bench beneath a flowering dogwood tree. Sitting beside me, Hiram took my hand.

I closed my eyes, breathing in the fragrant scent that surrounded us, and listened. While I'd waited on God's still, soft voice regarding my relationship with Hiram several times, discernment had never come. I longed for the stability and leisure that life with him would offer, but also feared that our differences would conflict and plague us with disagreement. God had spoken so evidently in the past, and my heart ached for his wisdom in this.

"I have also been contemplating our visit with Lemuel and Eleanore." Hiram's words broke me from my thoughts. "Thee seemed to appreciate meeting them, but thee has said naught about what we discussed beforehand. They and the children certainly enjoyed each other, and there is no doubt in my mind they would make a splendid family."

I swallowed, my throat suddenly dry. "They are delightful people, Hiram—so kind and generous—but . . . ." The right words simply wouldn't come.

"Thee has considered it, at least?"

"I have." Although scarcely, as to do so was like a knife to my heart. "And I have sought discernment, but it has not yet come. This is a weighty decision, for the children's sake especially, and I must make it with absolute certainty."

"Mmm. Thee needs more time, then?"

I nodded, though I couldn't imagine that any amount of time would be enough.

"I assure thee, dear heart, Lemuel and Eleanore will make fine parents. The children would receive loving care, the best of schooling, and every opportunity. And thee would be right next door. They and our children would grow up as cousins and close friends."

Aye. But—

He patted our entwined hands. "Having thee here has shown me just how much I want thee for my wife, and I'd like us to meet with Mary and Susannah to discuss parental consent for thee and write our letters of intention to marry. I plan to visit Horsham on Fifth Day to pick up more hardware from Isaac. We can obtain consent and write our letters at that time, so they can be submitted to be read at our next meetings for worship with a concern for business. Can thee make a decision by Fifth Day?"

Only three days away? My heart wrenched, torn between the rousing prospect of marriage and the dread of relinquishing Abigail and Ethan to the care of others. Part of the reason I'd entertained thoughts of marriage to Hiram was that our matrimony would provide the husband and father for the children I so desperately needed. Now that seemed unlikely, and shame pricked me for my self-regard. Unable to speak, I nodded.

He kissed my cheek. "Fear not, my dear. This will benefit all involved."

And yet his kiss brought to mind one of the most fateful kisses ever given—that of Judas on the cheek of Jesus Christ.

CHAPTER 19

Isaac

Third Day, Fourth Month 27th

Elisabeth Alden!" a shrill voice called from behind us as we walked along High Street's sidewalk on our way back to Lukens Hall.

We all turned around. A middle-aged woman bustled toward us, waving frantically. Behind her a Negro girl of about fifteen years carried a stack of several packages wrapped in paper.

Elisabeth smiled, but something about the way she lifted Jon-Isaac higher on her hip and pulled Abigail closer belied the cheerfulness she attempted to express. "Hello, Eleanore. How nice to see thee again."

The woman wiped perspiration from her brow with a handkerchief. "Hello! And hello again to you too, children.

What an opportune encounter. Hiram said you were returning home today." She looked to me. "Thee must be Isaac. Hiram told me 'twas thee who spoke so eloquently in meeting for worship." She smiled at Ethan, whom I held, then addressed Susannah. "Thee spoke in meeting for worship as well. Thee was also favored in thy testimony."

Susannah nodded her thanks.

"Eleanore is married to Lemuel, Hiram's brother," Elisabeth told us.

That explained her sudden reticence. While she'd divulged little about her and the children's time at Hiram's house the previous week, she had admitted that Hiram's brother and his brother's wife—the ones he wanted to take custody of the children—had also been guests.

A young boy ran by us, grazing the Negro girl and sending her packages wobbling. Despite how she attempted to balance them, the one on top slipped off and fell to the ground.

"I will get that for thee." Abigail released Elisabeth's hand and stepped forward.

Eleanore grabbed her arm as she tried to bend down. "Thee will not. 'Tis Jane's duty to tend the packages, not thine, and she will see to it that this one finds its proper place."

"But that boy ran into her. 'Twas his fault the package fell, not hers." Abigail leaned down, only to be yanked up straight again.

"Hold thy tongue, child. I said 'tis her duty."

Abigail quickly returned to Elisabeth's side and hugged her waist. Elisabeth opened her mouth as she put her arm around Abigail, but then closed it again. When our gazes met, she gave a barely perceptible shake of her head.

Eleanore, who had turned to Jane, nodded at the ground. "See to the package."

"Aye, mistress." Jane quickly knelt, set the stack on the ground, placed the wayward package on top, and then carefully stood holding the full stack.

Eleanore's glower had disappeared when she turned her attention back to us. "Well, you will be leaving for home soon, I'm sure, so I shall let you finish your business. I'm so glad we had the chance to see each other again." She patted Abigail's head, seeming not to notice how the little girl clutched Elisabeth even tighter, then grinned at Ethan. "I so look forward to our time together in the future. Safe journey."

Once she'd left, Abigail faced Elisabeth, her chin quivering. "Did I do something wrong?"

"Nay, sweet girl, not at all." Elisabeth handed Jon-Isaac to Susannah and took Abigail's face in her hands. "'Tis never wrong to treat another with kindness. Remember that, no matter how people react or what they say."

"But why did she—"

"Some people, even some Friends, believe they need not treat Negroes—or Indians or others who are different—as they treat those like themselves." Elisabeth spoke quietly. "But we know God loves everyone equally and that his Light shines within all of us. Thy attempt to help Jane shows the tenderness in thy heart for her plight, and thy actions were compassionate." She smiled lightly. "Thee treated her just as Christ would have treated her."

Abigail grinned.

My heart warmed. I longed to take both of them in my arms, commend Abigail for her love, and remind Elisabeth that she was indeed the mother the children needed. But knowing I couldn't show such affection here, I held out my free hand to Abigail instead. "Come now. 'Twill be time for us to take leave soon. Would thee allow me the honor of escorting thee?"

Giggling, she grabbed my hand with both of hers, and we started walking.

"'Teach a child in the trade of his way, and when he is old he shall not depart from it,'" Susannah softly quoted to Elisabeth as they followed us. "Thee is training them as well as any mother I have ever met."

Elisabeth said something in response, but I couldn't quite hear it. Still, I understood what she said next. "Suddenly, my heart longs all the more for Horsham."

My heart also longed for Horsham—and for her.

Fourth Day, Fourth Month 28th

With our dinner finished at home the following afternoon, Elisabeth stood from the table. She lifted Jon-Isaac from his high chair, then carried him to the sitting area, there placing him on the braided rug with Ethan and their toys. By the time she returned, I'd collected our plates and utensils and taken them to the wash basin.

"I thank thee." She stopped beside me.

I lifted her chin so she would look me in the eye. The sadness that marred her lovely face wounded me, both in that something weighed on her and that she felt she couldn't share it with me. "Thee has barely spoken a word today." She hadn't seemed herself since we returned from Philadelphia, even more so today.

She sighed. "I know. I'm sorry."

"Would it help if thee talked about what has thy heart so heavy?"

She opened her mouth but then closed it and shook her head. "So much vexes me. I need to sort it all in my own mind, and seek God's wisdom and his will, before I can even attempt to explain it to another."

So much meaning what? Our telling encounter with Eleanore Biddle, her courtship with Hiram, the stark difference between her responsibilities in Philadelphia and at home? All three had to be on her mind. Or had she made a decision she knew would have deleterious consequences? I hoped not, but people in grim situations sometimes made impetuous choices.

"What can I do?" I asked.

She drew a breath and met my gaze. "Would thee be willing to stay with the boys, even if just for an hour, so I can go to the meeting house?"

I had smith work waiting for me, but that mattered little. The meeting house had always been a place of solace and clarity for her, and she needed it dearly. "Of course. Go now. We'll be fine."

Her smile returned, this time more genuine.

She left, and after I tidied the kitchen area and put Ethan and Jon-Isaac to bed for their naps, I settled into the wingback chair in the sitting area. Sighing, I rested my head back and rubbed my face. Sleep had escaped me much of last night, replaced by thoughts of Elisabeth and the children, and I closed my eyes.

I awoke to the sound of footsteps on the porch. Moments later, Susannah followed Mother through the doorway.

"Isaac." Susannah appraised me curiously. "Did we wake thee?"

I stood and started toward them. "I was just resting my eyes."

"Is Elisabeth in with the boys?"

"Nay. She asked me to stay with them while she went to the meeting house."

"'Tis a good place for her." Her gaze held mine. "I suspect thee slept as little last night as she did."

Probably. "Was she aware you would be visiting?"

"Aye. Although with everything on her mind, I'm not surprised she forgot."

My gut told me they hadn't come simply to enjoy tea and conversation, and the fact that Mother had forgone her afternoon rest to be there further suggested the gravity of their visit. "What is this about?"

Susannah paused, a gesture that told me she hesitated to answer since I didn't already know. "Hiram has proposed that they write their letters of intention to marry when he visits on the morrow. On our journey home yesterday, while thee rode with Jamie and the children napped, Elisabeth asked if we would give our approval as parental consent."

Marry? So soon? "Surely you did not agree."

Neither responded.

I shook my head. 'Twas much too hasty, and Elisabeth had to realize the risk she was taking. Hiram wasn't a man who would allow his wife to voice opinions he disagreed with—of which Elisabeth had many—and she wasn't a woman who'd be persuaded to remain diffident.

Moreover, how could she not tell me? We'd spent two hours sitting before the hearth fire last night, talking about our time in Philadelphia, yet she had made little mention of Hiram at all.

"We queried and advised her as we would anyone in a similar situation, and we plan to meet with them both," Mother said. "When Abigail awoke, we agreed to finish our discussion today."

I eyed Susannah. "She showed no interest in a courtship with him until after Jonathan's death. Thee knows that. 'Tis been less than two months."

"They have known each other for several months now, Isaac."

"But you can't think marrying him is in her best interest—or the children's. Has she told you what he's suggested for Abigail and Ethan?"

"She has. And 'tisn't an unreasonable resolution. The Women's Meeting has already determined that a committee should be appointed to ensure the proper care of the children. That will not be necessary should they declare their intention to marry."

"So if she marries Hiram, she must give Abigail and Ethan to Lemuel and Eleanore, and if she doesn't marry him, the Women's Meeting will take them from her." 'Twas no wonder she was so distraught. "How could they do that in good conscience? You know what that would do to the children—and her."

Mother placed her hand on my arm. "The Women's Meeting is tasked with addressing concerns regarding the children of the Meeting. Thee knows that, Isaac. As a young, unmarried woman, 'twould be a hardship for Elisabeth to rear three children alone, even with the care of Friends. And while we would work in conjunction with Philadelphia Meeting to ensure Lemuel and Eleanore's clearness before placing Abigail and Ethan in their home, we did not enjoin the arrangement. 'Twas Hiram's suggestion, not ours."

"Elisabeth is an intelligent woman who continually seeks God's will," Susannah added. "We know she will act on his leading, and we must respect that. We love her too, and the children. Certainly we would prefer that they remain in Horsham, but God's place for them may be in Philadelphia. We must bear that in mind."

"But she is being forced to make one of two decisions, neither of which she would otherwise choose. Has she not suffered enough?"

"What other options does she have?" Despite my growing anger, Susannah kept her tone gentle. "How would a young, unmarried woman rear three children and care for this house, the livestock, and the property? Even if she sold much of the land, she has no income, and the money received would last only so long."

"I'm here. We have my income from taking over the forge, and together we have managed fine since Jonathan's death."

"But she is in a courtship with Hiram," Mother said. "She has assured us that she cares for him and that she intends to speak with him further about their rearing Abigail and Ethan as well as Jon-Isaac. Unless the clearness committee from his Meeting or ours reports back that they do not approve of the marriage, 'tis her decision to make."

More anger welled within me, and agitated, I paced away from them. Amidst my ire toward Hiram for his selfishness and Mother and Susannah for their leniency with him, indignation toward myself burned deep in my gut. I should have strived harder to help Elisabeth see how—

"My apologies." Elisabeth hurried inside, short of breath

and close to tears. "I forgot you were coming. I left as soon as I remembered."

"Thee is here now," Mother said kindly. "That is all that matters."

Unable to stay in their presence another moment without uttering words I'd later regret, I brushed past all three women and walked out the door, ignoring Susannah's calling of my name.

~

"Surely we have enough firewood to last us weeks." Elisabeth's soft voice came from behind as I dropped the axe to the ground.

I glanced back at her, both annoyed and relieved that she had sought me out. With a long sigh, I started to gather the cut firewood from around the chopping stump. Depositing it in the woodshed proved she was right. Two hours of chopping wood before supper and an hour afterward had not only expended much of my ill temper but also produced plenty of firewood.

Her solemn eyes watched me as I stepped out of the shed. "The children are ready for bed. They asked if thee would come pray with them."

I wiped my forehead with the back of my hand and grabbed my waistcoat from where it lay on the ground. "I shall be in momentarily."

By the time I'd returned the remaining uncut logs to their pile, put the axe in the woodshed, and stepped inside, Elisabeth had already rocked Jon-Isaac to sleep. Guilt prodded me, but at least Abigail and Ethan were still awake.

Ten minutes later, I emerged from their bedchamber

with my heart even heavier. Their recounts of the day and simple but earnest prayers had lifted my spirits but also reminded me that our time together was limited. While I'd always adored children, my love for these two was different. A life devoid of their innocent curiosity, silly humor, and sweet affection seemed unthinkable. And yet it might soon be a reality.

With Elisabeth still in her bedchamber, I sat on the settle. My head ached with fatigue, so I rested it back and closed my eyes.

Within a few minutes, her door opened and then closed. Her footsteps drew near, and the settle creaked beneath her weight beside me.

"I'd planned on telling thee last night," she said. "But then we started talking about thy meetings with the Six Nations and my visit at the Tysons', and I just . . ."

I opened my eyes and leaned forward, resting my elbows on my knees. Despite my hurt and frustration, I felt for her. 'Twas difficult enough knowing what awaited Abigail and Ethan, and I couldn't imagine the bitterness of the decision she faced. "Did thy time at the meeting house help thee?"

She sighed. "Never before has God been silent when I've sought discernment. Even in the meeting house, where his Light has always shone brightest, his words did not come." She shook her head. "Isaac, this is the weightiest decision I shall ever make. Never have I needed wisdom more, yet . . ."

I straightened. "Keep listening. When the time is right, his words will come."

She swallowed hard. "But we are to write our letters of intention on the morrow."

"I know." I inhaled deeply, then let out the air, praying

for apt words. "Has thee considered that thy reservations may be God's leading? When we faithfully seek his will and know his heart, which thee always has, our intuition reflects his wisdom. Thy misgivings may indicate that Hiram is not whom he intends for thee . . . or that he is but the time simply isn't right yet."

She wouldn't look at me. "My reservations aren't with Hiram. I know he loves me."

"But he doesn't love the children thee loves."

She stiffened. "That isn't true. Even if his love for them is only the Christian love we're called to extend to all, I'm certain once he has more time to spend with the children and get to know them, he will be a fine father."

"How? He has proposed that Lemuel and Eleanore rear them instead."

She met my gaze with weary eyes. "I'm going to ask him to reconsider."

"And if he refuses?"

She looked down, staring at her folded hands in her lap. "I do not think he will. He knows how much the children mean to me."

"But he has always known that, and 'tis been of little concern to him."

Setting her mouth, she shook her head. "This is why I hesitated to tell thee. No matter what Hiram does, he will never be acceptable to thee."

Now we were back to the subject of my opinion about him—as if this were my fault. "Beth, I want thee to be certain. Thee said thyself that this may be the weightiest decision thee ever makes."

"And thee said thyself, 'tis *my* decision." Tears filled her eyes. "While my mind can make more than one decision, my heart has only one choice—to do whatever I must to ensure that which is best for the children."

Even if it meant marrying a man not fit for her? And even if what was best for them was what they already had—a home and community that provided the care and steadfastness that every child needed.

"If he insists that Lemuel and Eleanore take the children, they shall still be close by, and we shall see each other daily." She brushed a tear from her face. "But if the Women's Meeting places them in another home, we may end up miles apart."

Then marry me, I longed to plead with her. *Marry me, and we'll raise the children together, here in the home they know and love.*

Yet when my mouth opened to speak, I felt such a stop in my heart. The caution to keep silent stilled my tongue with such intensity that I immediately knew its source. Many times throughout my years the Inward Light had illuminated my next steps, but only a few times had I felt it this strongly.

The gravity of Elisabeth's decision urged me to dismiss it, but I knew better. When I'd done so in the past, even when my actions seemed in no way harmful, I'd later regretted it. And this was a situation where regrets would be heartrending.

I leaned forward and covered my face with my hands. Again the temptation to propose marriage rose up within me, but I clenched my teeth in submission.

Father, give us wisdom.

Chapter 20

Elisabeth

My throat ached at the realization of my selfish ignorance.

In all my ruminating about how marriage to Hiram would affect the children and me, I'd never considered Isaac. The children loved him, and my marriage would take them not only from their home and friends but also from the man who'd stepped into their father's place when Papa died. Isaac showed them the same patient, unconditional love Jacob Lukens had given him, and he in turn thrived on their adoration and dependence.

Yet he had no safe recourse. His only option would be to propose marriage so we could rear the children together, but he had to know how fervently Hiram would contest his actions. Such a situation could have exacting results for him.

And that was if he even wanted to marry me. Never had he implied that he did.

Sitting beside him, I longed to apologize but could not. That would only confirm the consequences of my decision.

Isaac uncovered his face, wiping his eyes as he did.

My composure, already wavering, dissolved. He had never been comfortable weeping in front of people, and even when Papa died, he had shed only a few tears in the presence of others. Knowing 'twas my doing that now pierced him hurt almost as much as the decision I loathed. "I'm so sorry," I choked out.

He shook his head as he drew me close. "Do what thee must for the sake of the children," he whispered in my ear as I clung to him. "They have lost so much. They need thee."

But they needed him too—and there wasn't a thing I could do about that.

～

Fifth Day, Fourth Month 29th

'Twas nearly eleven of the clock when I heard the sounds of a horse and carriage coming down our lane. I checked our dinner stew, then peeked into my bedchamber at sleeping Jon-Isaac as I headed for the open front door. A fresh breeze cooled me when I stepped outside, a welcome relief from the heat of the hearth and oven.

Hiram's coachman halted the horse by the garden's corner post, then climbed down and opened the carriage door. Hiram alighted, looking around. He smiled when his gaze reached the forge, and Isaac soon appeared from beyond the side of the house. Ethan hop-skipped alongside him, holding his hand as he wore the child-sized leather apron Isaac had fashioned for him.

"Isaac. Hello." Hiram clasped his hand when Isaac reached him, then gestured all around them. "Is it me, or is today not one of the most beautiful spring days we have ever seen?"

"Lisabeth says all days are beautiful 'cause they're gifts from the Almighty," Ethan said.

Hiram sniffed, his eyebrows disappearing above the brim of his hat. "Is that right? Well, thy sister is as smart as she is beautiful." He turned and then smiled when he caught my eye. Starting toward me, he left Isaac and Ethan standing by the carriage with his coachman.

The flush that had warmed my face at Hiram's compliment intensified as he stepped into the house and slowly looked me over. Placing his hands on my waist, he moved us away from the doorway, then drew me against himself and pressed his lips against mine.

My stomach twisted. I stumbled back, grasping at his hands to get him to release me, but he moved one hand to the back of my head to hold me there. Barely able to breathe, I dug my fingers into his arms and fought to turn my face away. "Hiram, stop."

He released me, grinning again. "My apologies, dear heart. Do forgive the impropriety." He chuckled in amusement, a sentiment that alarmingly couldn't have been more different from my own.

I backed away, my chest still heaving and heart pounding. Aye, and if we were to marry, I'd need to get used to such familiarities with him. I'd considered that before, but never had I thought being touched like that would be so staggering.

Fighting a wave of instability, I drew a shaky breath and

fled toward the kitchen area so I could regain my composure. "Would thee like a cup of tea"—my voice wavered—"or chocolate?"

"Tea is fine." By the way he nonchalantly walked to the sitting area, removed his hat, and sat on the couch, he seemed to have no idea he'd unnerved me. Perhaps I had simply over-reacted?

I made the tea, uncomfortably aware of how he watched me, then carried the tray to the side table. After handing him his teacup and saucer, I sat beside him, although not as close as usual. My fingers still shook as I reached for my tea, so I left it where it sat.

He took a sip. "Thy hands are trembling, my dear. Certainly thee is not nervous about our meeting with Mary and Susannah?"

If only 'twere as easily resolved as that. "Nay."

"Then what is vexing thee?" He placed his cup and saucer on the table, then took my hand and smiled. "I'm soon to be thy husband. Speak freely."

I resisted the urge to pull away and, having been given an unsolicited invitation to share my concerns, determined to speak plainly. "Over the past few days, I have been seeking God's will and wisdom with regard to Abigail and Ethan, and I believe 'tis in their best interests that they stay with me."

He sobered but said nothing. Hopefully, he was taking my words to heart.

"I have cared for them the past two years, and for the last ten months I have been their mother. They have lost so many beloved ones in their short lives already. Moving to Phil-adelphia would be a significant adjustment itself, and I cannot bear the thought of them enduring more change than necessary."

He remained silent for a few more moments. "Does this have aught to do with thy meeting with Eleanore on Third Day morning?" Despite the seriousness of his expression, his tone remained light, which heartened me.

"Eleanore?"

He smoothed his hair. "Aye. When she and I spoke later that day, she feared she had been a bit too hasty in reprimanding Abigail for how she offered assistance to her slave."

A foreboding coldness clutched my stomach. "Jane is enslaved?"

"Thee did not know that?"

Indeed I had not. "I thought she was simply a servant, a hired girl. Is she their only one, or do they have others as well?"

"There are three others."

A more alarming thought came to mind. Hiram's servants were also Negroes, even the one outside my home right now. "What about thy servants? Are they enslaved as well?"

"Nay. None of them." He uncrossed his legs and shifted to face me. "Elisabeth, dear heart, I know thee harbors a tenderness in thy heart for slaves, but thee must understand that not all people treat them harshly. Lemuel and Eleanore's slaves have never been ill treated by them. Moreover, Yearly Meeting has not prohibited the keeping of them."

"Just last year they ordered that Friends who imported or purchased slaves should be admonished," I said. "And the year before, they published 'An Epistle of Caution and Advice Concerning the Buying and Keeping of Slaves.'

Although they have not declared that participating Friends should be disowned, 'tis only a matter of time."

He removed his spectacles and pinched the bridge of his nose between his thumb and fingers. "Elisabeth—"

"And even though Lemuel and Eleanore's enslaved may not be beaten or brutalized by them, that doesn't make their bondage any less wrong. In God's eyes, all are created equal, are we not?"

"Elisabeth—"

"Are we not?" I stood and faced him. "All of us are made in God's own image, Hiram. 'Tis a disgrace that so many people, Christians especially, treat his children as mere property to be bought and sold and treated as livestock. How does that follow the Lord's instruction to love others as we love ourselves? In his eyes, enslaved people have as much value as you and I. 'Tis not our place to decide otherwise."

He rose too, but I gave him no chance to speak.

"I know Lemuel and Eleanore are thy family, but I cannot in good conscience allow Abigail and Ethan to be reared to believe that slavery is acceptable. Papa and Barbara would have never approved, nor do I."

"I'm merely trying to provide the best solution to our dilemma," he said. "Does thee have a better idea? Perchance having thy Women's Meeting place them?"

A *dilemma*? That was what he considered the children? I stared at him, all fondness for him now gone. "Nay. I will remain their mother."

"Dear heart, we have discussed this. I travel often for business, and I want thee to accompany me. Traveling with one child will be troublesome enough. Doing so with three children, even with a nurse to care for them, would only complicate—"

Pursing my lips, I crossed my arms. "Then I cannot marry thee."

~

Hiram's eyes widened as if I'd renounced my faith before all Friends in attendance at Yearly Meeting. "Elisabeth, come now. Listen to thyself. Thy principles have gotten thee all fired up, and thee is not thinking clearly. Sit down, and we shall discuss this calmly. I am certain we can come to a suitable agreement."

But I didn't want an agreement. I wanted a marriage—to a husband I not only loved but with whom I also shared the same philosophies. And while I did care for Hiram, with Christian love if nothing else, it wasn't just his beliefs I didn't like. As much as the revelation convicted me, 'twas also *him* I didn't like.

"Hiram, thee has made thy decision regarding the children, and so have I. But our decisions are not the same or even similar," I said softly. "All along I have hoped we could come to a resolution, but now I realize we cannot. Our principles differ greatly, and I see that in our case it would result in a marriage weakened by disunity."

He grasped my arm. "Let's be reasonable. Surely with more conversation we can come to an agreement."

Be reasonable . . .

As the words resounded in my mind, an odd feeling washed through me, quickening my pulse. I shook my head, attempting to rid myself of it, then withdrew my arm. "Even if we could, how long would it be before we disagreed again —about slavery, or plainness, or whatever else?"

"Plainness?" He sniffed, looking around. "Aye, thy home

may be plain, but thee harbored no qualms about the indulgences of Lukens Hall. In fact, thee appeared to quite enjoy them, did thee not? Wouldn't that make thee a hypocrite?"

I fought the urge to snap back at him. Responding to mean-spiritedness with the same would serve no purpose. "Nay. Lukens Hall, while large and lovely, is hardly extravagant, and there is no vice in employing properly compensated help."

His face reddened. "Mmm, I see. But thee finds my home extravagant, I expect?"

"I do not want to argue with thee, Hiram." I took a step back, fighting the light-headedness that set me off-balance. Uncomfortable warmth overwhelmed me, and I yearned to end our conversation so I could step outside. "I'm sorry, but I have made my decision."

He took my arm again. "Elisabeth, be reasonable."

My vision darkened, followed by flashes unlike I'd ever seen. Within me my heart thudded, and no matter how hard I tried I couldn't get enough air.

His grip tightened. "Elisabeth?"

I needed to get away—outside, anywhere. Isaac. He worked in the forge. If only I could get to him . . .

Wrenching free, I tried to move around the couch toward the door, but that set the room in motion around me. The floor heaved upward, and suddenly I lay sprawled on it.

"Elisabeth!"

"Nay! Stop!" My attempt to get up and flee sent me lurching forward, and I hit my forehead on the wall before landing back on the floor. Covering my head, I curled up on my side.

"Hiram! Get away from her." 'Twas Isaac's voice, but it sounded far away. "What did thee do?"

"Nothing at all. She started acting peculiarly and lost her balance. I only tried to steady her, and she pulled away and fell."

A hand rested on my arm.

My body recoiled seemingly of its own volition.

"Beth." Isaac's voice and the pungent scent of hot iron and leather assured me 'twas him. "What's amiss?"

I gasped, fighting the unbearable weight upon my chest. "My heart . . . can't breathe . . . such giddiness."

"Go, Hiram. The path through the wood by the garden goes to my mother's house. Tell Susannah that Elisabeth's taken ill."

An arm slid beneath me, and the world tilted again as Isaac cradled me against him. "'Tis all right, Ethan. Get a clean cloth, dip it in the water bucket, and bring it to me." Fingers loosened the ties of my cap. "Let me wipe thy face, Beth."

My entire body felt as heavy as lead, but I managed to lower my hands and hold my arms against me. A wonderfully cool rag dabbed my face and neck, then was placed on my forehead.

I opened my eyes slightly and then fully. My vision had returned. While the giddiness remained, it had lessened, and even my breathing and fluttering heart seemed to slow.

Isaac gazed down at me, his brow furrowed, and touched my cheek with the backs of his fingers. "Thee is burning up. Just rest. Hiram went for Susannah."

Fever? But that didn't explain my terror at . . . what? I didn't know.

Now shaking uncontrollably, I turned my face into his chest. For some reason, I started to cry, and once started, I couldn't stop.

CHAPTER 21

Isaac

Unable to remain still, I paced the common room floor again. Susannah tended to Elisabeth in her bedchamber, and while I could hear their muffled voices whenever I neared the room, what they said was unintelligible. At least Susannah hadn't felt the need to send me for Dr. Crossley. Still, my concern swelled with each passing minute.

Father, be with her. She needs you.

And we needed her.

Ethan. In all the commotion, I'd forgotten about him. He still sat silently on Elisabeth's rocking chair, where I sent him when Susannah arrived and I carried Elisabeth into her bedchamber.

"I want Lisabeth," he whimpered, his chin trembling.

I swept him up into my arms. "I know. We just need to be patient a little while longer."

Ethan laid his head on my shoulder.

On the couch, Hiram sat stiffly upright with his hat in his hands. He'd said nothing since returning with Susannah, with the exception of insisting again that he had acted in no way unbecomingly. His face showed scant emotion, but his fingers nervously worked the brim of his hat.

I glanced at the clock on the wall. Half past twelve. Jon-Isaac would soon be awake if he wasn't already—and wanting his pap. The aroma of stew and freshly baked bread filled the house, but the heaviness within me rendered it untantalizing.

Elisabeth's bedchamber door opened, and Susannah exited carrying Jon-Isaac in one arm and her medical bag in the other hand. With her foot, she gently closed the door behind her.

"How is she?" I asked.

"I think she will be fine. I've given her laudanum, and she's feeling considerably better, albeit a bit tired." She set her bag on the floor by the couch and addressed Hiram, who'd stood up. "She asked to speak with thee."

"Of course."

Watching him move around us toward her bedchamber, I rebuked the jealousy that rose within me, returning my attention to Susannah instead. "Laudanum? For what?" I kept my voice low.

She stepped around to my side and placed her hand on the back of Ethan's head as she looked into his face. "Fear not. Thy sister should be just fine."

He squirmed. "May I have some dried apples?"

I set him on the floor. "Aye. Just be careful getting them down. Take the ones farthest from the fire."

He started for where the slices were strung across the hearth, and I turned back to Susannah. "Is she ill?"

Jon-Isaac fussed and reached for me, and she handed him over. "I expect not. Her temperature had come down by the time I got her undressed and into bed. Her breathing difficulty and chest pain also diminished as we talked and I examined her. We'll need to monitor her for further signs of illness, but I'd be surprised if any manifest." She canted her head. "The last year has been difficult for her, Isaac. Grief and distress can manifest themselves in physical ailments."

Surely she couldn't mean . . . "Hysteria?"

"I'm not saying that at all. I'm simply explaining that emotional distress can cause physical symptoms. She and Hiram were engaged in a heated discussion when she started feeling ill, and—"

"Does thee think he acted inappropriately?"

She shook her head. "He stated he did not, and she confirmed the same."

I released my breath and rubbed a hand over my face. That came as a relief, yet my concern remained. Impatience drove my gaze toward Elisabeth's open bedchamber door.

Susannah grasped my arm, her expression drawn with sympathy. "Give them time."

I nodded. But time together was the last thing I wanted them to have.

Fifteen minutes later, Hiram emerged and donned his hat. "Has thee loaded my order?" His expression and quiet voice conveyed solemnness that seemed odd from a man whose future wife wasn't as ill as feared.

"I have." I stood from the bench at the table and handed Jon-Isaac's bowl of panada to Susannah so she could continue feeding him. "'Tis all there. Will thee need any—"

"I should have sufficient for some time now." He nodded at Susannah. "I thank thee for thy assistance. I trust she is in competent hands. However, with this turn of events, I will take my leave." He looked at me. "Elisabeth asked for thee."

I didn't know what gladdened me more—that she had asked for me or that he was leaving. Remorse quickly convicted me of such an un-Christian thought. "Safe journey home."

I couldn't get to Elisabeth's side quickly enough. She lay in bed propped against two pillows and with the quilt over her for modesty. Her muslin cap sat on the bedside table while her gown and petticoats were draped over the rocking chair. As I sat on the edge of the bed, she opened her heavy-lidded eyes.

"How does thee feel?" I asked and pressed the backs of my fingers to her cheek. Her skin felt no warmer than that of my hand, and the red flush of her face had faded almost completely.

She averted her eyes to the quilt. "Embarrassed at making such a spectacle of myself."

I took her hand in mine. "Don't concern thyself with that. We're just thankful thee isn't as ill as we feared." When she sighed, I squeezed her hand. "Does thee have any idea what happened?"

She closed her eyes for several moments, then her forehead creased when she opened them. "I don't know. Hiram and I were talking, and I started feeling unwell. I became hot and light-headed, and I wanted air. But when I tried to walk, I couldn't keep my balance. He tried to help me, I think . . .

and suddenly, I was terrified. But of what I don't know. 'Twasn't him, but . . ." She shook her head. "Isaac, I'm so confused."

It took my every resolve not to gather her in my arms and comfort her. Instead, I smoothed loose wisps of hair back from her face. "Thee needs to rest now, not worry. There is nothing to fear. Susannah is going to stay until Abigail gets home from school, and I will be no farther away than the forge."

"The boys. Are they all right?"

"Susannah's feeding Jon-Isaac, and Ethan knows thee is fine." I grinned. "He's now at the table, stuffing his mouth full of dried apples."

She laughed softly. "Don't let him eat so many that he spoils his dinner."

I smiled at the sweetness of her concern for him and its reassurance that her condition had to be improving.

She closed her eyes again, and I patted our entwined hands. As much as I didn't want to leave, sleep would be best for her. "Thee should rest now. We'll be here if thee needs us."

She opened her eyes again but only briefly. "Aye."

As I stood, I leaned over and kissed her forehead. 'Twasn't my place, but I couldn't refrain. Who knew how many days I had before the person who knew me best—and whom I adored more than I'd ever imagined possible— became the wife of another.

The floor creaked behind me as I sat by the children's bed, listening to Abigail tell me about her day at school. Elisabeth stopped beside me and, once Abigail had finished, leaned down to hug and kiss her and Ethan.

I stood from my chair and tucked them in. "Sleep well now."

Elisabeth and I left the room, closing the door partway behind us, and she glanced at the open front casements. "'Tis a beautiful night. Shall we sit outside?"

This day had been the warmest in months, and I welcomed the chance to enjoy the fair weather—and her presence while I could.

Outside, we sat on the bench in the refreshing cool air. The sun had fallen below the horizon, but it still gave an orange glow to the edges of the few clouds that had darkened to gray. A fragrant breeze shifted through the trees as song sparrows serenaded with their calls.

Elisabeth watched two yellow finches that perched together on the garden fence, smiling slightly as they appeared to play. One fluttered into the air before landing again, and the other followed suit.

"How is thee feeling?" I asked.

"A bit tired, but well otherwise." She met my gaze. "Thee has asked that at least three times now, and each time my answer has been the same. May I simply tell thee if that changes?" While her tone held a hint of wit, I knew she wished I would stop asking.

"Agreed."

"I also would not mind if thee slept inside the house tonight."

Susannah had suggested the same. Still, I'd hesitated to mention that. While Susannah's recommendation would absolve us of impropriety in the eyes of Friends, I couldn't predict my nightmares. It had been nearly three weeks since my last one—a longer reprieve, fortunately—but I never knew when another would violently wake me. "I can sleep in the loft—or in the common room if thee wants me closer."

She turned her gaze to the front yard and the lane to the road, then swallowed. "I . . ."

The time I'd dreaded had come. She'd said nothing about her and Hiram meeting with Mother and Susannah another day, but I suspected they'd made those plans. "Go on."

She looked down at her lap and scratched at a stain on her apron. "Hiram and I have decided not to marry."

Not marry? Joy surged through me, but I dared not share that. With effort, I kept my appearance and tone as neutral as possible. "Was it thy decision or his?"

"Mine. Well, and his. Before I took ill, I told him I couldn't marry him. He tried to change my mind, but when he came in to see me before he left, he told me he had thought everything over and agreed that 'twas in both of our best interests to part ways." She looked up. "I'm afraid thee may lose his smith work."

As if that mattered a bit to me. "'Twill be fine. The Almighty has provided plenty of other customers. I'm not worried"—if anything, I was thrilled—"and thee shouldn't be either."

She nodded. Strangely, the decision had originally been hers, yet she seemed disappointed—or remorseful. Unless . . .

"Does thee love him?"

"I do, but merely with Christian love." She whispered the words as she wrung her hands. "I had started to believe those feelings went deeper, but they do not. Today I realized the great extent of our differences . . . and how selfish I've been."

Selfish? "In what way?"

"I allowed the thought of the comfortable life I would have as his wife—and the idea that marrying him would resolve all the challenges I face—to tempt me to wed him even though I don't love him as I knew I should." She shook her head. "He, too, wishes for a marriage built on love exceeding that of friendship and respect, and that is not what I feel for him."

Oh, what happiness that brought me.

She sighed. "'Twould have been deceitful of me to feign such for my own benefit."

"Aye, if thee had proclaimed that kind of love and married him, but thee did not. 'Tis humans' nature to be tempted. Giving in to temptation is what leads to sin, and thee saw the error of thy ways. Thy motives have never been malicious. If anything, they've been gallant in thy pursuit of the children's needs."

She shifted to face me. "But now they will likely be taken from me."

I took her hand in mine, again prompted to propose marriage. But her ended courtship with Hiram wouldn't absolve us of all consequences should she agree. If she were to suddenly inform our Meeting elders that she wished to marry not Hiram but me, a man who'd been living on the same property as she, some would surely question our propriety—and possibly even deny to marry us under the care of Meeting.

And that would be if Elisabeth agreed to it. While our relationship had certainly improved in the time since I'd returned, that did not mean she was ready to be my wife.

"The Women's Meeting cares for thee and the children, and that will help guide their decision."

She stared out across the yard again. "I'm sorry for how

contentious I've been. Thee suspected Hiram and I wouldn't be compatible, and I should have considered thy opinions instead of arguing."

Our conversation was so very different from what I'd expected, and the unity we were building—so much more like the companionship and deference we'd once shared—encouraged me to move past our quarrels. "'Tis easy to rationalize when we desire something strongly, and sometimes rationalizations blind us to truth. Thee feels disappointment, but 'tis a blessing that thy realization came before marriage and not afterward."

"Does thee think I should go to the elders before a committee can be appointed?"

I'd pondered that option as well. "Maybe. I'd like to speak with Mother and Susannah first." I squeezed her hand gently. "If thee does, I will stand with thee . . . if thee is in agreement."

She stared at me, seemingly surprised, but then smiled. "I would appreciate that."

"But I'd like thee to repose for another day or two, until we are certain of thy health," I added.

"With three young children?" She gave a quiet laugh. "If only that were possible."

~

First Day, Fifth Month 2nd

"Isaac Lukens!"

An unfamiliar voice called soon after Elisabeth, the children, and I started home following First Day meeting for worship. When I turned, a white-haired Friend approached us. He had joined meeting halfway through and given an uncharacteristically hurried testimony right before the rise of meeting.

"I'm Elkanah Willing, Lydia Stanton's neighbor." He spoke just as quickly now. Even his nod and smile at Elisabeth seemed almost fitful. "When she learned I would be heading north today to visit my brother in the Great Swamp, she asked if I would carry this letter to thee." He pulled a folded and wax-sealed sheet of paper from the pocket of his waistcoat and handed it to me.

I stared at it. Considering the hours Lydia and I had spent talking about my parents, I couldn't imagine what we might not have discussed.

"We thank thee," Elisabeth said. "Would thee care to join us for dinner?"

I looked up. "Aye, my apologies."

"Thy hospitality is greatly appreciated, but I must continue on my journey." He grinned again, nodding one last time. "I shall be on my way now. Good day."

Abigail giggled as he headed for the horse sheds. "He's funny."

Elisabeth squeezed her shoulder. "Abigail. 'Tis just his way. He was very kind in taking the time to carry the message here." She turned to me. "Does thee know what 'tis regarding?"

I broke the wax seal. "Nay." Unfolding the letter, I found only a few lines of Lydia's shakily written script:

Dearest Isaac,

> *Last evening I remembered something thy mother told me about her brother, who was some type of Lenape leader. His English name was Black Snake. I still cannot*

*remember the name of their village or his Indian name, but
I pray this information will be of assistance.*

   God's blessing on thee,
   Lydia

Black Snake. Sukachgook, to the Lenape. I stared at the name in disbelief and then reread the sentences.

"Is it about thy family?" Elisabeth asked.

"She remembered my Lenape uncle's name." I folded the letter and placed it in my pocket, then glanced at the sky. "Let's get home before the rain."

Elisabeth took my arm when we started walking again but said nothing more, for which I was most grateful.

CHAPTER 22

Elisabeth

Isaac had lapsed into pensive silence after reading Lydia Stanton's letter. Although eager to question him about it, I'd abstained. The information Lydia provided either stunned or troubled him, and the way he responded to my question about the letter's content conveyed that he wouldn't say more in front of the children. Fortunately, Abigail was tired and agreed to nap with Ethan when I put the boys to bed after dinner.

Isaac sat on the settle when I returned to the common room. The dismalness of the now-rainy day provided meager light, and the glow of the fire flickered on his face as he again read the letter. He placed it in his pocket and rose, then stepped to the hearth. After grabbing the bellows, he knelt and coaxed the fire brighter.

I stopped beside him, appreciating the emanating heat.

The unseasonably warm weather we had been enjoying made today's cool dampness seem like a stark return to early spring. "Would thee like some chocolate?"

He smiled, albeit slightly, for the first time since we'd left the meeting house grounds. "'Tis a fine day for chocolate."

I grinned. "Every day is a fine day for chocolate."

He stood and then returned to the settle as I went to the kitchen area. He again held the letter when I brought the tray, and handed it to me when I sat down with him.

I opened it and read the lines. "Does thee know who Black Snake is?"

"A Lenape warrior, Sukachgook. His father—my grandfather, Achwangundowi—was a great sachem who strived to keep peace in the Lenapes' hearts, both with other tribes and white settlers." He took the letter and tucked it in his waistcoat pocket. "Sukachgook forsook his father's pacifism and allied with Captain Jacobs."

I'd heard that name before—but where? The *Pennsylvania Gazette*, I believed. "He was one of the Lenape chiefs the governor put a bounty on?"

"Aye. I've never met Sukachgook, but we all knew him by reputation. He left Shamokin, the village of his family, and journeyed to Kithanink, beyond the western mountains, to join the warriors bent on revenge." He released his breath slowly. "I knew 'twas possible my family participated in the bloodshed on the frontier, but I never expected this."

With a sigh, he shook his head. "Shamokin's about seventy-five miles downriver from Wyomink. Twice I visited it, but never did I imagine my mother's family was so close. What I don't understand is why no one there claimed to know my mother. Unless . . ." He paused, staring at the floor by the hearth. "She and my father told Lydia they lived above the Forks of the Delaware, so perhaps she never went west with her family? I don't know."

I lifted my cup from the tray and took a sip as my mind whirled. While his uncle's deeds would likely prevent Isaac from searching for him, the rest of his family embraced peace.

Isaac had already posted a letter to Tom and Jerusha McCue before we had left Philadelphia, asking if they knew of anyone in the Bethlehem area by the name Billiou. The thought of him leaving us again—whether for Shamokin or Bethlehem—disconcerted me, and yet how could I expect him not to seek out those he so longed to meet? "How far is Shamokin from here?"

"Several days' journey." He looked at me, his slate-blue eyes stoic. "I wouldn't make the trip without first trying to ensure they're still there."

My unease quelled. His going to Bethlehem would at least be less dangerous. "Would thee even be safe returning there?"

"In Christ, we are safe wherever we trod."

Indeed, but . . . "That doesn't mean harm cannot befall thee. Many people have lost their lives despite the strongest of faiths."

"'And fear ye not them which kill the body, but are not able to kill the soul,'" he quoted, a grin tugging at his mouth.

I didn't share his amusement. "Isaac. I would prefer both thy soul and body intact."

He chuckled. "As would I." With another sigh, he sobered. "If only I'd known this before the messengers to the Lenape departed the city. I could've sent a message to inquire about Sukachgook's family in Shamokin. Though Achwangundowi has died, his wife may still be alive." He picked up his cup. "I mustn't dwell on such. Lydia has provided more information, and I should be grateful. If I'm meant to find them, way will open."

"Aye," I whispered.

Just as long as the Almighty, if he did lead Isaac to them, would also make straight the way for his return.

~

Fourth Day, Fifth Month 5th

Jon-Isaac stirred in the cradle as I returned to the common room after putting Abigail and Ethan to bed. He whimpered, kicking his legs beneath the quilt, but then smiled as I neared.

"There's my sweet boy." I stooped beside him and loosed his covering to lift him out. After feeling under his petticoat and pilch to find his clout still dry, I carried him to the kitchen area. He fussed as I dipped a cup into this evening's pail of goat's milk and then poured the milk into his baby feeder, only quieting when we settled into the rocking chair. Sucking contently, he snuggled against me, staring into my eyes.

I kissed his hand, praying the Almighty's blessing on his health as I did each night. Upon Barbara's death, Susannah had warned me that hand-fed infants were less likely to live than those who nursed, but Jon-Isaac now thrived on pap, panada, and milk.

His eyes gradually closed, making me sleepy as well, and I glanced at the clock on the wall. Ten minutes past eight. Isaac expected he wouldn't return from visiting until nine. Weary, I closed my eyes to rest them for a few moments.

I awakened suddenly.

Isaac stood above me, his hand on my shoulder and a gentle smile on his lips. "I was hoping thee hadn't retired yet. I stopped at the Crooked Billet on my return from Moreland, and this had arrived for thee." He pulled a letter from his inner coat pocket.

I took it, my interest stirred. He was the one anticipating correspondence, not I—his reason for stopping at the tavern in Hatborough—and I didn't recognize the handwriting.

"Shall I put him to bed?" he asked.

I nodded and then stood when he carefully lifted Jon-Isaac from my arms. As Isaac carried him to my bedchamber, I walked to the kitchen area, where the combined light from the hearth and the chandelier above the table was brightest.

The wax seal loosened easily, and I unfolded the letter. My eyes immediately went to the signature at the bottom, but I couldn't make it out, so I started with the salutation.

> *My Dear Sister in Christ Elisabeth,*
>
> *I hope this letter finds thee and thy family well. I have sent word to John Cadwallader, so he could inform thy Meeting, but I also wished to inform thee, so this sad news would not come to thee secondhand. On Fourth Month 15th, my companion in ministry, Linus . . .*

My stomach turned, and I dropped the letter. I knew only one Linus, and I'd hoped to never hear from or of him again.

The letter landed on the table, and the candlelight glimmered over the script. Gritting my teeth, I reached for it, compelled by the words *sad news*. As much as I didn't want to even touch the paper that bore his name, I needed to know what it said. My hand trembled as I lifted the letter.

> *. . . succumbed to quinsy here in Virginia. He had the highest respect for thee, and I always suspected his care for thee went deeper than he voiced aloud. I hope thee finds comfort, as I do, in knowing that he is now with the Father in heaven.*

His care for me went deeper than he voiced aloud? Nothing could have been further from the truth. Anger heated me like a fire from within, but my whole body shook as if I stood outside on the coldest night of winter with no cloak. I rounded the table on wobbly legs, tearing the letter into pieces before casting them into the hearth fire.

Satisfaction replaced the fury as the flames consumed the pieces from their edges inward, but that soon yielded to chest-crushing remorse and despair. With the Almighty's help, I'd forgiven Linus—or so I had thought.

Papa's words resounded in my mind: *"Forgive him, daughter. They that forgive wrongs will be forgiven, but revenge is prepared for those who revenge."* What if I hadn't—

"Beth?"

Isaac's voice spun me around. Seeing the concern on his face as he neared broke my resolve, and tears slipped down my face.

"What is it?"

No matter how difficult, 'twas time I told him. Isaac had shared with me the unspeakable things he experienced, and I owed it to him to be as forthcoming with mine. "Does thee remember Josiah Smith, the public Friend?"

"Of course. He has visited Meeting many times in his traveling ministry. Has something happened to him?"

I shook my head. "The last few years, a young man accompanied him. Josiah had introduced him to Christ, and he became a convinced Friend and began traveling with him because Josiah's eyesight was failing." I tried to swallow the lump in my throat. "Josiah wrote to inform me that his companion . . . died of quinsy last month."

Unable to look at Isaac, I pulled my handkerchief from the pocket of my apron and wiped my eyes. "He and I . . . We became . . ." Whatever I said, the words seemed wrong.

"You were fond of each other?"

I shook my head. "Well, we were, but . . ." I could say no more.

"Would it help if I read the letter?"

A glance at the hearth proved that not a shred of it remained. This would only increase Isaac's confusion, and rightly so. "I threw it in the fire," I whispered.

He glanced at the hearth. "Perhaps thee could tell me what happened?"

Lord help me, I was trying.

"Elisabeth?" Abigail's voice came from across the room, and she appeared near tears herself as she approached in her shift.

"Is aught amiss?" Hopefully she wasn't poorly. 'Twasn't even summer yet, and some children from Meeting already suffered from the flux.

"I had a frightening dream."

Poor girl. I drew her close. "About what?"

"Indians," came her muffled reply as she buried her face in my side. "Tench Davis said Indians have been burning homes and taking people's scalps, even those of Friends."

Not surprising, considering the boy's father tended to be a disorderly walker. "Never thee mind Tench Davis. His is idle talk. We have always been friends with the Lenape."

"But if they come here?"

Isaac turned her toward him and squatted. "Thee remembers why I met with Friends and Six Nations chiefs last week? We discussed how to bring peace between white settlers and the Lenape, and we believe our message to them will stop their violence."

Her countenance softened and she nodded.

"Thee has nothing to fear. Shall I return thee to thy bed now?"

She grinned, wrapping her arms around his neck.

He stood and carried her toward the children's bedchamber.

As I watched them step into the dimness of the room, the silhouette of him holding her and the tenor of their hushed conversation stirred such admiration for him that tears filled my eyes. I paced to the hearth, my hand over my heart.

Isaac was so special to me—so needed in my life—and I feared what I was about to tell him would rescind any esteem he had for me.

I sat on the settle when he emerged from the children's bedchamber a few minutes later. He lowered himself beside me and leaned forward to look into my downcast face.

Shame, though the Almighty had taken it from me over the last year, threatened again, seeming to lash down my tongue. Even so, I couldn't just sit in silence. "In Fifth Month of last year, Josiah and his companion visited

Meeting for a week. His companion and I had become friends during their prior visit, exchanging letters on occasion, and last year he visited me each day. We grew closer."

My throat threatened to close, and I cleared it. "The evening before they left, Papa and Barbara went visiting, but I remained here with the children since they would be returning late. The Friend came to call, and I knew I should have declined his visit since I was alone . . . but I didn't."

Isaac said nothing, but his breaths now came heavier.

"We sat down for chocolate, and then I looked in on the children because he thought one of them called for me. They were both asleep, though. When we finished our chocolate, he invited me outside to look at the stars with him. I agreed, and as we walked near the forge, I grew terribly weak. So weak I could no longer stand. He helped me into the forge quarters, and—"

A growl sounded deep in his throat.

"The next thing I remember is awakening in bed with Abigail and Ethan . . . feeling very unwell." A sick feeling rose in my throat, and I cleared it, determined to finish. "My clarity returned by morning, and I realized then what he'd done. I confronted him when he and Josiah stopped here so Papa could file one of their horses' hooves before they traveled on, and he insisted that . . . that I'd pursued him and that he'd spent the night seeking forgiveness for capitulating to my wiles. He said I needed to be reasonable. I remembered none of it, so I told no one lest I wrongly accuse him. But Susannah knew something was wrong, and a few days later I told her . . . and she informed Papa."

"I'd put him in the ground if he wasn't already there," he said through clenched teeth.

Humiliation trained my gaze on the floor, and I hurried

to conclude. "Susannah and I wished to notify the elders, but Papa refused."

Isaac shook his head. "As Friends, we stand for truth."

"I told him that, but he wouldn't listen. He feared people wouldn't believe me, that I might even be disowned for deception, and that no man would ever consider marrying me."

He dropped his chin to his chest, inhaling through his teeth.

My throat seized. Even if Isaac believed I had not consented to commit sin, I had withheld vital information from our Meeting. "Isaac, I'm sorry. I—"

He looked at me, the anger contorting his face giving way to anguish. "Beth, thee did nothing wrong."

But I had. "I withheld truth."

"At thy papa's command, and against thy will."

I stood, crossing my arms, and moved away from him. Tears again filled my eyes when I turned. "And I've despised myself for it. After Papa died, I resolved to go to the elders and make everything known so they could address the Friend's conduct appropriately. A few weeks later, while talking with Dorothy Evans after meeting for worship, I gathered the courage to ask to speak with Women's Meeting elders. But when she and Hester White visited the next day to discuss what I wished to share, I couldn't do it. I was a coward, even though I feared he would one day return, and even though I knew my silence might allow him to do the same to others."

He rose and gently took me by the arms. "Thee is not a coward, and he can neither return nor harm another now."

What a joyous relief that was, though I didn't know what brought more relief—being freed from the guilt I carried or knowing that I no longer hid anything from Isaac and that he didn't fault me.

Drawing me closer, he lowered his head so his forehead rested against mine. "No more secrets between us. Promise me?"

I nodded. "I promise."

~

Fifth Day, Fifth Month 6th

Abigail turned from where she stood at the open front door with her hornbook and slate the next morning. "They are here."

I placed Jon-Isaac in his baby-tender and went to join her. Outside, Daniel and Hannah's children walked up our lane carrying their own school materials.

Abigail stepped out onto the porch and looked around. "I want to say good-bye to Isaac. Does thee know where he is?"

We couldn't see the forge or the doors to the barn from the porch, so I followed her into the front yard. Still no sign of Isaac. "He probably went hunting at sunrise. Thee may see him on thy way to school."

She sighed, scanning the area as if that would make him appear. "But he's always back by now."

I hugged her to my side. "Thee mustn't be late for school. Go on now."

She did, although reluctantly, and I waved to the waiting children.

When I stepped back onto the porch, Ethan stood in the doorway. "Where is Isaac?"

"I'm not certain." And Abigail was right. Isaac was

always back by now. 'Twas possible he had not gone hunting after all. "Stay with Jon-Isaac while I check the forge and barn."

He did as instructed, and I rounded the side of the house. Since the barn doors were still closed, the forge seemed a more likely place to find him. I opened its door and stepped inside. "Isaac?"

Only silence answered. To be certain he wasn't still in his quarters asleep or ill, I walked through the shop to the room I despised. Pressing my hand into my middle to ease my apprehension, I knocked on the door. Again, no answer. I knocked a second time and then forced myself to slowly unlatch the door.

Light slid into the room, and I clapped a hand over my mouth as my stomach threatened to rid itself of the porridge I'd just eaten. Save for the bed, washstand, clothing press, and mirror on the wall, the room was empty. All Isaac's belongings, what few he had, were gone.

I backed away, crying out. The next thing I knew, my knees slammed onto the floor.

He was gone.

CHAPTER 23

Isaac

The scents of hay and livestock hung thick in the dank air. Exhausted and with my head aching, I buried my face deeper into the crook of my arm. Surely it couldn't be nearing dawn. Hadn't I fallen asleep only minutes ago?

But 'twas always the oily, metallic smells of the forge that greeted me each morning, not the odors of a barn. I sat up and got to my feet. Not only was I in the barn, but the light that streamed into the stall through the small window above told me sunup had come some time ago.

Elisabeth.

Thoughts of last night revisited at once, reminding me why I'd chosen to sleep there. Fury welled within me again, and oversleeping only fueled it.

I dressed quickly and headed for the door. As I left the dimness of the barn, my head throbbed harder. At least dense gray clouds obscured the sun's brightness. I hesitated, tempted to return to the stall to retrieve my satchel of healing herbs, but then continued on to the house, scattering the flock of chickens on the way.

As I neared the back door, Elisabeth called my name from behind. I expected to find her nearing me when I turned, but she was nowhere to be seen. The door to the forge stood open, so I started in its direction.

A plaintive wail echoed within as I reached the doorway, and I hurried inside. She knelt on the dirty brick floor, her petticoat awry as she sobbed into her hands. "Elisabeth!"

She looked up and cried harder as she struggled to get to her feet. Although she choked out words, I couldn't understand them.

I righted her, keeping an arm about her waist when she stumbled again. "What? What is it?" Fear that injury or illness had befallen one of the children—or that she was truly having a hysterical episode—speared my gut. "Tell me."

She clung to me as if she would never let go. "I came looking for thee." I could barely understand her breathless explanation. "All thy possessions were gone. I thought . . ."

That I'd left again.

Oh, what had I done? I tightened my arms around her, holding her head to my shoulder. "I'm here. I simply slept in the barn." When I tried to put her away from me, she clutched me with surprising strength. Finally, she released me enough that I could grip her shoulders and step back.

She wiped her eyes, staring at the floor. "Thee must think I've lost all my mental faculties."

God forbid it. I guided her to the bench against the wall and sat her down, then pulled over the chair from my desk and sank onto it, facing her.

Twisting her hands in her lap, she stared at them. Her mouth opened but then closed again.

I rubbed my hand over my face, trying to gather my thoughts. Never had any woman vexed me so much or in so many ways. I blew out my breath. "Thee truly thought I had left? With everything thee has gone through, thee still believed I would do that?"

"Nay, I . . ." She inhaled and then swallowed. "Thy belongings were gone. After thee just learned more information about thy family—and after what I told thee last night— what was I to believe?"

As much as I hated to admit it, her conclusion hadn't been implausible. Besides, she wasn't the one who deserved my anger. I pressed my pounding temples. "I know I left before, but I'll never do it again, not without thy approval. As long as thee wants me here, I will stay. Understood?"

She lifted her face, attempting a smile, but wouldn't look at me. "Aye."

"Is thee all right now?"

She nodded.

"Good. 'Tis later than I planned to get started today."

She stood. "I shall get thee some porridge."

"A slice of bread with jam will do. I told Mother I'd be there early to till the garden." When she headed for the door, I rose. "Elisabeth—"

"Thee best be going"—she didn't look back at me— "before she worries."

Aye. I had soil to till, and Susannah had explaining to do.

Susannah opened the back door as I emerged from the wood into the backyard. She smiled, waving, but her expression sobered as we met by the garden fence. "Thy countenance says thee is troubled this morning." Her eyes peered into mine, concern lining her brow. "Is aught amiss?"

"*Amiss* doesn't even begin to describe—" I gritted my teeth. Already my tone edged with irritation, though she didn't deserve it either. "Elisabeth told me about what happened."

She closed her eyes and nodded. "I've been praying she would." When she opened them, she placed her hand on my arm. "Come inside and we can talk."

Sitting at the table for tea and conversation, Susannah's usual remedy for struggles of the heart, seemed a doubtful cure today. Still, she might provide information Elisabeth hadn't.

I followed her into the house and then paced the kitchen floor.

"Thee has broken thy fast?" she asked.

"Aye." She didn't need to know that amounted to only two bites of bread with jam. I glanced through the doorway into the center hall. "Is Mother awake?"

"She's napping in the parlor. Her hip has been sore, and she slept fitfully last night." She sat at the table, so perhaps our subject of conversation had rendered her unable to stomach anything—even tea— either.

"Does she know?"

"Aye."

"Who else?"

"With Barbara and Jonathan now with the Lord, no one. How much did Elisabeth share?"

I crossed the floor to the table and folded my arms. "The man who did this. Who was he?"

She looked up at me only after a few moments of thought. "She didn't tell thee?"

"Not his name. Only that he was a convinced Friend traveling with Josiah Smith, and that he met a deserved fate while in Virginia." Except Susannah was still unaware of his demise. "Yesterday Elisabeth received a letter from Josiah informing her of his death as a result of quinsy."

"I see." She kept her tone even, but her expression seemed to brighten as she blinked. In relief maybe? Then her expression took on an air of skepticism. "But I do not for a moment believe 'a deserved fate' was her particular wording."

Unbelievable. The tension swelling within me threatened to explode. "How is it that both thee and she are so indifferent? The thought of a man doing to her . . ." I turned away, shaking my head. Suddenly, I longed to spend the morning in the forge, putting the hammer to iron with as much force as I could muster. "It sets my blood boiling."

"As it should. And we are not indifferent, not at all." Impatience now tinged her usual calmness. "What he did was reprehensible, taking advantage of her innocence and trust. For months I have walked with her as she has borne burdens no woman should ever have to endure—confusion, despair, guilt."

"There is nothing for her to feel guilty about."

"Nay, but she remembers little of what happened—"

"And he insisted she pursued him," I finished. "I don't

believe that. She would never . . ." I couldn't even say the words.

"I agree. But she was lonely and quite taken with him, as were many of our Meeting's young women. He had a beguiling air about him, and his astute testimonies belied the depravity within. She basked in the attention he paid her, and because of that, part of her feared he spoke the truth."

Nauseated, I walked to the hearth. The warmth of the flames heated my face but didn't come close to the burning inside me. Never had I despised a man more. 'Twas fortunate for both of us that he had already left this life, for I feared what I would do if we were ever to cross paths.

"Isaac, thy anger is not unfounded." Her gentleness had returned. "But keep in mind that Elisabeth has had time to come to terms with what happened. With the Almighty's help, she has even forgiven this man."

"That makes it no less horrific."

"Nay. The episode she suffered last week serves as confirmation of that."

I turned around. "What does thee mean?"

She stared at her hands folded on the table. After several moments, she looked up at me. "Some believe our minds remember more than we realize. Elisabeth's spell during Hiram's visit was accompanied by fear she couldn't explain."

Aye, that was exactly as she described it.

"I have no doubt this convinced Friend gave her something so she wouldn't resist—laudanum, we suspect, since she thought her chocolate tasted slightly bitter and she knew he used it for his cough—but I wouldn't be surprised if some remnants of memories return in time. Hiram's doting on her may have brought them closer to the surface." She lifted a hand to indicate the chair across from her. "Isaac, please sit."

Struggling against the frustration that coursed through me, I obliged. My body stilled, but I couldn't halt the unceasing thoughts that plagued my mind. It seemed unlikely that Susannah would identify the man either, which made little sense. I could ask anyone from our Meeting about Josiah's traveling companion and get an answer.

Then there was her willingness to not report his heinous wrongdoing. He should have been sitting in a jail, not traveling with a highly respected minister, gaining the esteem of Friends himself and possibly preying on other young women.

I shook my head. "How could you keep silent? What happened to our Quaker tenet of truth?"

"The truth?" Mother rasped from behind me. "The *truth* broke our hearts."

Mother hobbled to the table and took the chair beside me. "Elisabeth wished to acknowledge to the elders what happened, but Jonathan forbade it. She honored her father's command, and after much time seeking wisdom, Susannah and I agreed to do the same."

"She was suffering enough." Susannah's eyes now glistened. "Consider what would have happened had we gone to the constable and had this man arrested. He would have told the court the same thing he told Elisabeth—that she pursued him and consented. She remembers nothing, so she couldn't have denied that, and the case would have been dismissed. Would thee have aggrieved her further by making her calamity public knowledge and putting her at risk of being charged with fornication?"

How foolish my quick judgment had been. "Nay."

"Even if she weren't charged, her reputation would have been tarnished," Mother added. "Our decision was made with much care and contemplation."

Susannah reached across the table and took my hand. "Isaac, nothing will change what's been done. Hating her wrongdoer will benefit neither thee nor her."

I swallowed, unable to deny that either. "I know."

Mother placed her gnarled hand on mine and Susannah's. "The Almighty promises us that he works things together for the best if we love him. That assurance has carried Elisabeth, and though she still struggles, the love of Christ holds her fast. Even this cannot separate her from him." She searched my face, her eyes crinkling with sadness. "Do not let it separate her from thee either, because that is what thy indignation may well do if thee does not take care."

Guilt sickened me further as I remembered this morning's events. Elisabeth had been distressed, and instead of comforting her, I had taken offense and questioned her trust in me. "I fear my indignation has already separated us."

Mother looked out the window behind Susannah. "My bones tell me rain approaches. I think 'twould be best if we waited till tomorrow to till the garden, when the soil will be more workable."

Oh, how I loved her. I leaned over and kissed the side of her head. "Was that my hint to go apologize?"

She grabbed my hand and squeezed it. "Such a smart son I've reared."

Just not smart enough to realize that my inability to temper my response was further hurting Elisabeth, who'd already endured far more pain than deserved and was the last person I'd ever want to harm.

When I opened the front door and stepped into the house, Elisabeth stood from where she sat on the braided rug with Ethan and Jon-Isaac.

"Thee is finished with the garden?" she asked.

"Mother suggested we wait till after the rain." I joined her in the sitting area, again riddled with remorse. "'Twasn't thee I was angry with, even if it may have seemed that way."

She nodded but wouldn't look at me.

Jon-Isaac squealed before I could say more, and I turned to find him standing by the couch using its arm to stabilize himself. His little hand reached toward us, opening and closing.

"Watch this." Ethan jumped up from where he sat playing with the whittled farm animals I'd made for him. He knelt by Jon-Isaac and folded up the hem of his petticoat, then took his hand. "Come on, Jon-Isaac. Show Isaac what thee can do."

Jon-Isaac bounced in excitement, grinning and showing his three little teeth. His one bare foot stepped forward, and he took two steps away from the couch. After three more steps while holding only Ethan's hand, his balance faltered, and he fell into Ethan. They both laughed themselves silly.

"Well done, young man." I lifted him into my arms, my mood suddenly lighter.

He clapped his hands and squealed, garnering laughs from all of us.

I turned to Elisabeth. "Thee is in trouble now. These little boys will have thee even busier yet."

"So I fear," she murmured.

"Thee managed me when I was a boy. Thee will be just fine."

Her expression became a combination of a smile and a scowl. "Thee was older than I."

Grinning, I took her face in my hand. "Yet thee still kept me out of trouble more times than I could count."

She laughed softly and turned her face into my palm as her cheeks flushed the most lovely pink.

I would have savored the gesture if not for its evidence that she could not look me in the eye for more than a moment or two.

CHAPTER 24

Elisabeth

With the kitchen tidied, Isaac in the forge, and the boys abed for their nap, I settled into the rocker to work through my mending pile. The hearth fire provided only paltry light, and soon the scent of spring rain wafted in the windows and beckoned me outside. I gathered my hussif and the basket of clothing, then carried them to the front door, prepared to make use of the bench on the porch.

At crossing the threshold of the open door, I halted. Isaac sat on the bench, his elbows on his knees as he stared at the floorboards between his boots. He turned his head to look at me, then straightened.

The solemnness of his gaze fixed my feet to the floor, but I couldn't just stand there. "I wondered why I wasn't hearing the usual clanging from the forge." Even my words felt awkward as I sat down with him.

"I wanted to talk to thee after the boys were abed."

Not surprising since our conversation had been interrupted by Jon-Isaac's attempt at walking. I set the basket on the floor and my hussif on my lap. "And thee knew I'd be coming out here?" Isaac's intuition was surprisingly keen at times, but even I hadn't known I'd be coming outside until moments ago.

"Nay. I was just giving thee time to settle the boys. And trying to get my thoughts in order." After releasing his breath slowly, he swallowed. "I need to apologize . . . for my actions and how thee thought I'd left."

I traced the embroidered flowers on my hussif with my finger. "Thee slept in the barn last night. Why?" Once voiced, it seemed a needless question.

"I couldn't stay in there. Not knowing what . . ." His voice wavered, and he cleared his throat and shook his head. "So I gathered my things and went to the barn. Even there, sleep wouldn't come, and then I slept much later than usual. I hadn't expected thee would need to come looking for me." Despite how he clenched his jaw, his lip quivered the slightest bit.

Touched by how deeply this troubled him, I laced my fingers with his.

He pressed my hand between both of his. "I should have been more sensitive to thy feelings instead of questioning thee. I allowed my ire toward another to influence my treatment of thee, and I never meant to do that."

His brusqueness had indeed stung, but the candor of his apology eased that. While I'd told myself 'twas not his intention to dismiss me, now I had proof of it.

He rubbed my hand with his work-roughened palm. "I don't want this to come between us."

Nor did I. Yet I had to wonder how it wouldn't affect our relationship. How much time would need to pass before he could look at me without thinking about what happened? And for how long would discomfort stir within me when I looked into his eyes?

Even so, I lifted my chin. "Then we shan't allow it, whatever it takes."

"Had thee told Hiram?"

I glanced out across the yard. "Papa forbade me from telling anyone. But when I started to entertain thoughts of marriage to Hiram, Susannah advised that I should marry him only if I could confide in him. But each time I planned to do so, I felt such a stop in my heart." Considering how our courtship had ended, I now understood why the Lord had halted my words.

"I'm glad thee confided in me."

For the first time since I'd sat down, I looked at him. His eyes, more gray than blue beneath the cover of the porch, had misted, and that brought tears to mine. "As am I."

The rain fell harder, pattering on the slate roof above us, and the sound of it combined with the fresh dampness of the air invoked breath-catching memories of the countless times we had sat there talking as rain fell. Now here we were again, yet everything was so very different. While part of me longed for the past, when our lives had been simpler, my heart also swelled with thankfulness for the present—and the presence of one I held so dear.

Sighing, I rested my head against his shoulder.

Amidst all the changes, one thing remained—us.

"Elisabeth, these cookies are delicious." Susannah's tone conveyed her delight as she inspected what remained of the brown-speckled white cookie in her hand. "Are they thy creation?"

"Actually, Abby deserves the credit." I smiled at Abigail, who along with Ethan sat on the other side of the table between Isaac and Susannah. Both children had their mouths stuffed full of cookie, so she couldn't have answered if she wished. "She and Rebekah baked them with Deborah at Lukens Hall, and we came up with a similar receipt."

Abigail swallowed. "I call them chocolate moons. They are quite simple to make, although Elisabeth had to help me with beating the egg white properly."

Beside me, Mary swayed on the bench, her shoulder bumping into mine. She jolted awake, and I slid a steadying arm about her.

She patted my leg. "Forgive me. Between meeting for worship and this wonderful meal, I'm wearier than usual."

Meeting for worship had lasted close to three hours, with many addressing the escalating discord between the British and the French. Friend after Friend had testified, reminding us that we must uphold our doctrines of nonresistance and care for all those in need. By the quiet snores throughout the room at the rise of meeting, a number of elderly Friends had tired.

"We shall get thee home, then." Susannah stood and gathered her plate and utensils, then carried them to the wash basin. As she passed Isaac on her return to the table, she stopped, peering down at Jon-Isaac, who drowsily sucked his thumb as he lounged on Isaac's lap with a full belly. "Looks like someone else will soon be sleeping as well."

"Aye." Isaac then grinned, looking down. "Oh. Thee means this young man."

She patted his shoulder, chuckling, then moved around the table to collect the children's plates.

I rose and helped Mary to her feet.

"We thank thee for another lovely dinner." She hugged me and kissed my cheek, then glanced at Isaac. "Sitting around this table as a family brings such joy to my heart. We are truly blessed."

Papa's presence was still terribly missed, as was many others', but I had to agree. "Aye, we are."

Abigail approached Susannah. "If Elisabeth approves, may I go home with you? Thee said some First Day afternoon we could work on our samplers together."

Susannah hugged her close. "I did say that. But what if I brought my sampler here? Then we could work on them while Isaac and Elisabeth take a walk. When they were younger, that was their favorite thing to do on a First Day afternoon."

Aye. So why did uncertainty hedge at my happiness to enjoy a walk with him again?

I looked at Isaac, who nodded his agreement, and I repeated the gesture.

Abigail bounced on her heels, then set about gathering the utensils from the table.

Isaac tousled Ethan's hair. "'Tis nigh time for thy nap. Go out and use the necessary, then I'll come in thy bedchamber with thee after I put Jon-Isaac to bed." He stood, cradling Jon-Isaac in one arm, and rounded the table to Mary and me. After offering her his free arm, he led her toward the front door.

I followed, stepping into pace beside Susannah. "I thank thee for offering to stay with the children."

She smiled. "Thee and Isaac work so hard. I see your sweet friendship returning, and no doubt you both would welcome a chance to enjoy the Lord's creation as you once did. I shall return as soon as Mother's settled for her rest."

We bid our good-byes at the door, and Isaac shut it behind them.

I stepped closer and kissed Jon-Isaac's chubby cheek. "Sleep well, sweet boy."

He smiled, snuggling against Isaac's chest while still sucking his thumb, and my heart warmed. A lump inexplicably formed in my throat, and I swallowed. "No falling asleep together this time." How I'd giggled at finding the two of them sound asleep on my bed after dinner one day this week.

"Not today. Ethan would search me out, I'm sure." Isaac's eyes twinkled. "Besides, it seems I have plans with an old friend. I wouldn't miss that for anything."

As I stared at him, the most unusual feeling, almost a fluttering, stirred in my middle. No discomfort accompanied it, yet my breath caught.

I inhaled, searching for a response. "Nor would I."

With the boys napping and Susannah and Abigail happily working on their samplers, Isaac and I stepped off the porch, then rounded the newly planted garden to the pathway through the wood. The brightness and warmth of the sunny day diminished as we entered the canopy of tall trees, and the potent scent of tilled soil gave way to the cool, heady combination of damp earth and foliage.

Isaac slowed when we neared the plank bridge over the stream, offering his arm.

After my reaction in the house, looking into his eyes seemed precarious, but I obliged. "Where are we headed?" Fortunately, the forest offered much nature to peruse.

He placed his hand over mine. "I came upon the fishing pool while I was hunting last week. I thought we'd go there first, unless thee has another preference."

"Nay. I have not been there in—" My voice suddenly gone, I stopped. The last time I'd been there was with him, before he'd left. I cleared my throat. "Years."

My chest ached, and I steeled my wits, vowing not to become maudlin. This time was meant for enjoying ourselves and the beautiful day, not exhuming the difficult sentiments we had been striving to overcome.

Neither of us spoke as we followed the stream, although that didn't bother me. From early childhood, the importance of silence had been etched on my heart, with Papa regularly reminding me that the Almighty's whisper could be heard more clearly when our mouths are closed and our ears and hearts are open to his still, soft voice. As well, Isaac and I had spent countless times simply enjoying each other's presence with few words between us.

After about ten minutes, we came to the area where the stream was deepest, nearly a fathom in the center. Branches of the trees that grew along the bank's edge hung over the water on both sides, shading it and the large slab of rock where we had always sat. The breeze rustled through the leaves, and the water gurgled over the rocks in the much shallower area downstream.

Isaac held my arm as I lowered myself onto the slab, then he sat next to me. "We caught some large catfish here. And remember that eel you caught?"

I nearly shuddered at the thought. Seeing the slimy creature knotting itself all around my line, I'd been sure it was a foot-and-a-half-long snake. Isaac, about thirteen at the time, insisted on removing the hook instead of cutting the line. Then he carefully worked to ensure not only that the eel didn't bite him but that no harm came to it. "I was terrified it would take off thy finger."

He chuckled. "I'm not sure if that was integrity or follishness."

"The former." I lifted my knees and smoothed my petticoat over my legs. "Or a bit of both."

With another exhaled laugh, he patted my knee. "'Twouldn't have been the first time."

I leaned back on my hands, closing my eyes and savoring the freshness of the air and the sounds of the babbling water and chirping birds. After some time, Isaac's presence seemed gone, and I opened my eyes. His hat, waistcoat, stockings, and shoes lay beside me while he waded in calf-deep water near the bank. His ability to move inaudibly never ceased to amaze me.

"The water must be quite cold," I said.

He glanced back as he rolled up his sleeves. "Not when compared to the waters in Wyomink. And the Lenape women dunk their infants in the river every morning, no matter the season."

Surely he jested. I couldn't bear the thought of doing something so cruel to Jon-Isaac. "They do not."

"They do. It makes them strong and healthy, they say." He leaned down and began turning over the rocks on the creek bottom. I had no idea what he was looking for but found pleasure in watching him as I'd done so many times before.

The leather cord that tied the end of his braid to its beginning at the nape of his neck loosened, and the braid slid over his shoulder, hanging toward the water. When he moved, the blackness of his hair shone in one of the rays of light that slid through a break in the canopy.

That brought to mind the question of how he had looked this time last year. I'd seen the way he dressed while with the Lenape in wintertime but had never considered how they dressed in spring and summer.

Years before, we had seen traditionally clad Lenape men during a visit to Lukens Hall. While the Philadelphians perspired in layer upon layer of clothing—and covered the resultant odor with strong perfume—most of the Lenape wore only breach clouts, leggings, and moccasins. Some even had their legs uncovered, and I'd marveled at their darker skin and the definition of each muscle beneath it. Isaac had likely dressed similarly in Wyomink, and that thought brought back the odd feeling in my belly.

Warmth rose to my face at the possibility I entertained improper thoughts, and I again forced my attention to my surroundings.

Isaac approached with his right hand behind his back. After stepping up onto the bank, he dropped down beside me. "Thy cheeks are flushed. Is thee too warm?"

"Nay, I'm comfortable." Just too brazen, apparently.

"I brought thee something." He swung his concealed hand around, revealing a four-inch-long speckled, reddish-brown crayfish. As he held it by the carapace, it moved its spidery legs, tucked its tail, and snapped its claws at the air.

I grimaced, having never liked them since one clamped my toe while I was wading.

"I caught one almost twice this size last summer. Biggest any of us had ever seen. Boiled with the proper herbs, they're palatable."

I looked at him. "The Lenape eat them?" I couldn't imagine touching one, let alone putting it in my mouth.

He watched it thrash about, his expression almost respectful. "They call them *shahëmwisàk*." Even his tone held reverence. "*Wanishi*," he whispered, then leaned forward and released it into the water.

As it slowly sank, it propelled itself backward in spurts.

"Last summer, *shahëmwisàk* helped keep us from starving."

"*Starving?*" I echoed before I could stop myself.

Aside from the stories he told the children at bedtime, he spoke of Wyomink only occasionally, and he had certainly never mentioned near starvation.

He watched the crayfish disappear into the shaded water. "A great drought plagued Wyomink last spring and into the summer. At the end of Fifth Month, a late frost—the second since our corn had come up—destroyed most of our crops. Deer were scarce, and the streams ran so low that the fish migrated or died. Sometimes we went days without food."

Horsham had also experienced a drought but fared far better. Friends shared food with those in need, and none under the care of Meeting had come close to starving. "Did thee not consider returning?"

He nodded, his eyes still fixed on the water. "I longed to sit at thy table and fill my gnawing belly. But I couldn't. My leaving would have meant one less hunter to find food, and I couldn't in good conscience abandon our women, children, and elderly—my people—to starve so I could enjoy sustenance." He met my gaze, his expression drawn. "Our hunger, and Governor Morris's refusal of aid, were two of the reasons many Lenape allied with the French."

The words *my people* stabbed my heart. He loved the Lenape, perhaps as much as he did those who'd reared him, and at times he seemed to relate to them more. As well, his time with Sam Milham, a man as Lenape as any white man could be, had generated a vigor in Isaac that I had rarely seen in all my years. That troubled me. "Does thee ever . . . consider returning to them?"

He took my hand in his, resting both on his thigh, and his eyes appeared to darken as he scowled toward the creek. "I am Lenape, and I am white. I love things about both cultures. And yet at times I must choose, one or the other. 'Tis a difficult choice, and I loathe how I feel so torn by it."

Air hissed through his teeth as he inhaled slowly. "The Lenape who have allied with the French call me Walks In Two Worlds. At first I despised the name, but now I realize its truth. I am Lenape, and I am also a Friend who will follow Christ even unto death because he gave his life for mine."

I waited, my breath held in anticipation of his next words as I stared at our entwined hands.

The differences between Isaac's and Hiram's struck me. Weeks before, while beholding Hiram's and my hands in a like position, I'd marveled at his delicate fair skin, even softer than my own.

In contrast, Isaac's were darker and considerably roughened. Forging iron had so blackened around his fingernails and in the deep grooves of his skin that even treatment with lanolin didn't remove it. Yet these same hands—*perpetually soiled*, in Hiram's words—were the hands that provided for and comforted me. In them I found beauty beyond compare.

His thumb stroked mine. "While I loved my time with the Lenape, I never fully enmeshed with them. I look more Lenape than white, but some couldn't comprehend my devotion to what they consider the white man's God. Of course, I don't fully enmesh with Friends either. Even though I hold to their beliefs, I don't look like them, and some of the Lenape ways I've embraced are difficult for them to grasp." He squeezed my hand gently and smiled. "But then there is thee. With thee, I need not be one or the other. I'm simply myself, and thee loves me as I am."

I smiled, yet his words didn't assuage my concern.

"So I stay. Not because I'm no longer welcome amongst many of the Lenape, but because women, children, and elderly whom I love need me here. And because thee is here, and when I'm with thee, I belong."

I swallowed, unsure how to respond amidst all the sentiments stirring within me. In light of the despair I'd felt when I'd thought he'd left again, his desire to stay brought such joy. But as I looked into his eyes, I didn't know what to make of the intensity that sobered his countenance, nor did I understand the way it captivated and yet unsettled me.

Even so, I needed to answer. "I'm glad," I whispered.

CHAPTER 25

Isaac

My eyelids grew heavy as I lay on the couch in the sitting area that evening. Although the wall clock hadn't yet chimed half past seven, my difficulty sleeping the last few nights had finally taken its toll. Jon-Isaac slept soundly on my chest, and the pleasant combination of the lavender scent of his just-washed hair and the sounds of giggling and splashing from the kitchen area, where Elisabeth bathed Ethan, lulled me.

"Isaac?" A small hand patted my shoulder.

When I opened my eyes, Abigail stood by the couch wearing a clean shift, her hair still damp.

"May I practice braiding with thy hair?" She smiled sweetly, revealing the gap where her top front tooth was missing.

I grinned, unable to deny her. "Aye." Moving carefully so

not to wake Jon-Isaac, I lifted my head from the arm of the couch and untied the cord that held my hair, then let the braid fall down over the arm before lowering my head.

She knelt alongside the couch and released the braid, then combed her fingers through my hair. I closed my eyes.

A hand on my shoulder again woke me. This time Elisabeth stood by the couch, her hand over her mouth. If only 'twere that lovely countenance I saw every time I awakened.

"I will take him," she said, then slowly lifted Jon-Isaac. Her lips twitched as she strove to keep a straight face, so something tickled her fancy, and I suspected it wasn't simply that both Jon-Isaac and I had been sleeping. She started toward her bedchamber. "The children are abed waiting for thee."

I rose, and my hair slapped against me. A glance over my shoulder explained her amusement, and I felt around for the extent of my fate. Abigail's braiding practice had resulted in a multitude of long, thin braids protruding from the sides and back of my head.

In their bedchamber, Abigail and Ethan lay side by side with Mwekane curled up at their feet. Both grinned, and Abigail pulled the quilt up to her nose.

I eyed them mock-solemnly as I sat on the edge of the bed. "And what, may I ask, is so humorous?" I petted Mwekane, who wagged her tail and licked at my hand.

Ethan pointed. "Abby made thy hair pretty." He burst out with the pure laughter of a small child, and Abigail, unable to contain herself any longer, joined in.

What joy these two and their silliness brought me. Even on the days when Jonathan's absence and my longing for blood family weighed on me, they brought lightness to my spirit. I grinned. "Indeed she did. Has Elisabeth prayed with thee?"

Both nodded.

"All right. Sleep well, then." After standing, I collected the candle from their bedside table, then returned to the common room. Mwekane followed, and I shut the door behind us.

Elisabeth stepped out of her bedchamber at the same time. She pursed her lips, trying not to laugh. While I didn't want to think about how long it would take to pull out each braid, the cheer that crinkled her eyes made any amount of time worthwhile.

I held out the braid that hung in front of my ear. "She is quite good now, doesn't thee think?"

She took it in her hand and then stepped to the side of me to look at the braids down my back. "Quite. Would thee like my help in taking them out?"

I shrugged. "I may leave them. Jabez Holt is to come by tomorrow with a horse in need of reshoeing. The expression on his face would be worth any reprimand received, I'm sure."

"Thee will do no such thing." Though her words held vehemence, she could no longer suppress her smile. She pushed me toward the sitting area. "Let me get my hussif. She tied off each braid with embroidery thread, so I may need my scissors."

She soon joined me on the couch, and I turned my back toward her. "How many are there?"

"Hmm." She fingered the braids, sending tingles from my scalp down my spine. "Looks like thirteen."

By the time she finished, I could barely take in a breath. Neither of us had spoken a word as she worked, but the sensation of her releasing the braids and then smoothing my hair stirred such pining for her touch that it took me aback.

I longed to take her face in my hands and kiss her lips but dared not. She'd never shown sign of desiring that type of affection from me, and if she were upset by it, that could have a ruinous effect on our relationship.

I stood. "'Tis getting late. I'd best get to bed."

She looked from the wall clock to me. "'Tisn't even half past eight." Confusion marred her face and her tone.

"I know. But I'm weary, and thee must be as well." I started for the back door, and Mwekane trotted after me.

Elisabeth trailed a few steps behind. Upon reaching where I waited at the door, she tried to smile. "Today was a lovely day," she said softly. "I truly enjoyed walking with thee this afternoon." She raised her hand as if to place it on my arm, but then dropped it to her side and looked away.

Remorse riddled me. The last thing I wanted was to rebuff her, and seeing her bewilderment, I ached to take her in my arms and reassure her. But that would be unwise. Drawing a breath, I squeezed her shoulder. "'Twas. Sleep well now."

I headed for the forge before I could do anything that might impair our friendship.

～

Third Day, Fifth Month 11th

When I stepped out of the forge on Third Day afternoon, Abigail, along with Daniel and Hannah's children, approached the house in a group. I waved, watching them as

I continued toward the springhouse. Odd that they would walk her all the way up our lane.

Abigail stopped at seeing me, dropping her slate and hornbook to the ground. She then turned and clung to much-taller Esther, who had been leading her with an arm around her shoulders. By the time I reached them, she sobbed.

"Abby, what is it?" I tried to turn her toward me, but she only cried harder. The other children appeared solemn but not upset, so I couldn't imagine what would have her so distraught. "Esther, what happened?"

She frowned. "Schoolmaster rapped her knuckles three times . . . for dishonesty."

Lying? 'Twasn't like Abigail at all.

"Abby, let me see thy hand."

She allowed me to turn her around but refused to look at me as I took her left hand in mine. Her knuckles were slightly bruised and swollen, and tears streamed down her cheeks faster than she could wipe them away with her other hand. Surely she hadn't deserved such punishment.

"'Tis all right now." Dropping to one knee, I lifted her downcast face. "I'm not cross with thee. Just tell me what happened."

She continued to sob, and I returned my attention to the children.

"Tench Davis and Conrad Warner called her an orphan. She told them she isn't because Elisabeth is her mother and thee is her father. Schoolmaster overheard." Esther frowned as she placed her hand on Abigail's head. "The boys received only a verbal reprimand, but he disciplined her with the ferule."

How dare he? 'Twas not the first time this schoolmaster had enacted an overly harsh punishment on a student, and our Meeting's school committee would be hearing about it. Forthwith. "Thee didn't deserve that, Abby," I assured her.

"I'm sorry," she choked out. "I shouldn't have said that, but I didn't like what they called me."

Nor did I, especially since I'd also been called an orphan as a child and understood how much it hurt. "'Twas cruel of them to say such a thing. Come now. Let's go inside."

Anna picked up Abigail's hornbook and slate and handed them to me, and the children all bid Abigail a quiet good-bye.

I thanked them, then walked Abigail to the house.

Inside, Elisabeth sat at the table spoon-feeding Jon-Isaac while Ethan sat across from her, munching on moon cookies.

Ethan turned. "There thee is, Abby. We have thy milk and cookies waiting for thee."

Elisabeth stood from the bench and came toward us. "Is aught amiss?"

Abigail looked up at me, her eyes wide.

I smiled to ease her apprehension. "I'll talk to her. Go sit and eat awhile."

Elisabeth neared, watching Abby pass by on her way to the table. "What happened?"

I jutted my chin toward the door, then followed her out to the porch. "Some boys were teasing her, calling her an orphan. She told them she isn't, that thee is her mother and I her father, and Schoolmaster overheard and rapped her knuckles for dishonesty."

Her eyes widened. "How badly?"

"Enough that her hand is bruised and swollen. And enough that I'm going to Benjamin's right now to speak with him." My sister Alice's husband was not only a member of our Meeting's school committee but also known for his fairness and wisdom, so if anyone could help, 'twould be him.

She sighed as she glanced through the window at the children. "Isaac, she *was* dishonest."

"Aye, but this shouldn't have happened." I stopped at hearing my terse response, then shook my head and softened my tone. "She's a child, and she wasn't being dishonest with wrongful intent. She just wanted the boys to stop mocking her. A verbal warning would have sufficed. There was no need for him to injure and humiliate her."

Elisabeth pondered that. "Thee is right. But thee is also upset. 'Twill not help if thee goes to Benjamin so full of fire."

I couldn't deny that. Anger, as righteous as it felt, would only complicate the situation and undermine the path to an agreeable resolution. Even so, I had no intention of tarrying. "The two-mile ride to their place will be time enough to determine the most constructive way to present my perspective." I stepped around her and headed for the barn. "Lord willing, I'll be back by suppertime."

I returned from Benjamin and Alice's less than two hours later but said nothing about the visit until the children were in bed. Elisabeth also held her tongue until we sat at the table with slices of the pecan pie she'd made that afternoon.

"How was thy discussion with Benjamin?" she asked after swallowing her first bite.

I grinned. "I kept my spoken words and demeanor a reflection of Christian concern and goodwill."

She laughed softly. "I would never think otherwise. Thee was obviously cross when thee left, though."

I was, but seeking the Inward Light as I rode had allowed me the calm disposition to convey what had happened with concern instead of frustration. Benjamin's rapt attention and thoughtful questions and dialogue had further consoled me, allowing us to converse with everyone's best interests in mind.

"I shared what happened and my thoughts about the harshness of Abigail's reprimand, and Benjamin agreed that my concern is not unwarranted. He concurred that her behavior has rarely required even a mild reproach at school or in Meeting, and that her punishment shouldn't have been so exacting."

"And what will happen now?"

"Benjamin will pose my concerns—and his—to the school committee. This isn't the first time a family has disagreed with Schoolmaster's discipline. The committee will deliberate and appoint representing Friends to converse with him, hear his point of view, and labor toward defining apt correction of scholar misconduct."

Elisabeth nodded but said nothing as she prodded her pie with the fork. Something troubled her, though I couldn't determine what.

"Something vexes thee?"

She sighed and set her fork on the table beside her plate. "What if this brings more attention to us? Concern about the children's custody already exists. I fear that if 'tis made known to all that Abigail is now identifying us as her mother and father, Meeting will be emboldened to proceed with forming a committee."

I hadn't considered that. "It may. Though chances are good that many will find out anyway. The other children are likely to mention it at home, and word will eventually make its way to those who do not have children in the school."

She stared at her plate.

"What is thee saying, then?" I asked. "That thee would prefer Benjamin not go to the committee?"

She eventually looked at me, her eyes serious. "Nay. Thee is right. And 'tis still a matter to be addressed. A school cannot be a proper environment for learning when children are fearful or ridiculed, either by their schoolmates or the schoolmaster."

My pie finished, I stood from the bench, rounded the table, and sat next to her. "The last year has been difficult enough for her. 'Twas merciless of the boys to call her what they did, and Schoolmaster's dealings with them and her weren't exemplary."

"I know. And so we must do what is right and let the Almighty take care of the circumstances."

"All things work together for the best for those who love God and are called according to his purpose."

She continued to push at the remainder of her pie. "During our visit yesterday, thy mother reminded me of that as well, and Susannah asserted its truth in her own life with regard to Philemon."

Although I had been only six years old at the time of his death, I still remembered fishing with Philemon Palmer, Susannah's beloved who died of scarlet fever only a week before they were to marry. His loss, albeit devastating enough that she never married another, led her to study medicine and then midwifery, which had greatly benefited our community.

Elisabeth raised her gaze to mine. "I pray my trust in the Lord is as honorable as hers."

It most certainly was, so much so that her sweet humility touched me. "Fear not. Thy conviction is venerable. And our Father in heaven is ever faithful." I grinned. "Now finish thy pie before I do it."

She smiled. "I thank thee, Isaac."

I shifted to face her and brushed a loose tendril of hair behind her ear. Given the chance, I could stare at her for hours and enjoy every moment of it. "For what?"

"Taking such noble care of us these last two months. I've acted less than appreciative at times—too many times—but I don't know how I would have managed without thee."

"Truly, 'tis been my pleasure." After moving my hand to the nape of her neck, I drew her closer and pressed my lips to her temple.

She inhaled and clutched my arm.

"I'm sorry. I didn't mean to . . ." I dropped my hand to my lap.

Swallowing, she shook her head. "Of course." Within moments, she had gathered the pie dish from the center of the table and my plate and fork from across it. I quickly had another piece of pie in front of me, though her hands trembled slightly as she worked.

Oh, what had I done? My intention of encouraging her with a brief kiss on the forehead—something I'd done on occasion in the past—apparently came off as more than that. Maybe it *had* been more than that.

Either way, it surprised or upset her, just as I'd feared such a show of affection would on the night she'd removed Abigail's braids from my hair. How I wished I could retract my impulsivity.

Afraid I'd only worsen the situation by trying to explain, I dug into my pie and hoped I would be able to down it.

Fifth Day, Fifth Month 13th

I'd just finished forging another hatchet blade when movement drew my gaze from the hammer and anvil. John Cadwallader stood inside the wide doorway to the shop with an axe in his hand.

With a nod in his direction, I set down the hammer and thrust the tongs holding the blade into the water bucket, then started toward him. "John. Is thy axe in need of repair?"

He handed it to me. "I think 'tis time for a new one, unless thee can restore this."

Age had pitted the blade and roughened its edge, and the handle was starting to crack. I handed it back to him. "'Tis time for a new one."

"Then I would like to order a similar axe." He looked from the tool to me. "I was also hoping thee would have a few minutes to speak with me."

I'd wondered if we would receive a visit from weighty Friends in light of the incident at school earlier in the week, but they visited in groups of two or more. John was alone, so hopefully this would be more informal. "Certainly. Would thee care for some tea?"

"I thank thee, but nay. And I'd like to speak with thee alone."

Without Elisabeth? Perhaps this wasn't regarding Abigail, then. I couldn't decide if that brought relief or greater unease. "Let's step outside where 'tis cooler." I led him to the open rear door of the forge, then followed him out. There, we sat on the hewn-log bench along the back wall of the building. "What is on thy mind?"

"After meeting for worship this forenoon, Benjamin shared with me what happened with Abigail this week and that the school committee will be meeting to ascertain the next steps."

I wiped my forehead with my arm. Suddenly, the outside air seemed just as warm as that inside the forge. "Elisabeth and I have spoken to Abigail about the importance of being fully truthful."

He smiled kindly. "Knowing thee and Elisabeth as I do, I suspected as much. However, I also wanted to converse with thee because I believe there is truth in what she said."

I hesitated, unsure if I'd heard him correctly. "What does thee mean?"

He crossed one leg over the other and folded his hands on his knee. "Abigail told the boys that Elisabeth is her mother and thee is her father. Did Elisabeth not assume the role of mother to the children when Barbara died?"

"Aye."

"I have also watched thy interactions with the children since thee returned. Today thee had Ethan and Jon-Isaac sitting with thee in meeting for worship, and Jon-Isaac seemed quite content to fall asleep in thy arms. Clearly they love thee, and thee loves them. Has thee not assumed the role of father for them?"

"Indeed, but . . ." Not knowing the direction of this conversation, I couldn't finish.

"Let me ask this. Would thee consider becoming their father in a legal sense?"

Legal sense? "I . . . Of course." While child-rearing was a great responsibility, I both adored and felt a special kinship with Abigail, Ethan, and Jon-Isaac. As well, I'd given Jonathan my word that I'd care for them, and I intended to do everything I could to keep that promise. "Having lost my first parents at a young age, I understand the blessing of being taken in and loved as a child born into a family. I can think of no better way to honor my Quaker mother and father than by doing what they did."

His grin widened. "I cannot agree more." Then after staring at the wood behind the forge for a few moments, he looked back to me. "Isaac, let me speak plainly. The children need a mother and a father. Thee and Elisabeth have provided a fine, godly home for them since Jonathan's death. Thee and she also care for each other. You have been friends all your lives, and the Christian love and respect you share for each other is a firm foundation on which to build a marriage—and a home for children."

How I knew that, especially since my care for Elisabeth went so much deeper than Christian love and respect. Still, I—

"Has thee considered that?"

Countless times. But how Elisabeth had reacted to my affection two nights ago made it clear how she would feel about marrying me. Susannah had cautioned that Elisabeth's assault had damaged her trust in any man, and—with great sorrow—I'd realized that misgiving might extend to me as well. But I couldn't tell him that.

"Aye, but she ended a courtship only two weeks ago. Would Meeting even agree to appointing a clearness committee should we declare intention to marry?"

"Thy mother is a Women's Meeting elder, and thy family has been esteemed in Meeting since its beginning," he said. "We all know thee and Elisabeth well, and—"

"My heritage?" My throat tightened as I leaned forward and stared at my folded hands suspended between my knees.

He shifted toward me. "That is of no concern. I cannot speak for all Friends, but I know the sense of our Meeting. Most were appalled by Hugh Roberts's treatment of thee. Of more importance is thy faith, and since returning, thee has shown true devotion to our Meeting, Elisabeth and the children, and Friends' desire for fairness toward and peace with the Lenape."

That came as a relief. But I'd still need to persuade Elisabeth to marry me. Straightening, I nodded.

"Give it thought, Isaac, and seek wisdom from the Father. Then, if thee feels conviction that marriage is his will, share that with Elisabeth." He stood.

I rose to see him out. "I truly appreciate thy insight and honesty, John."

If only 'twere as simple as he made it seem.

CHAPTER 26

Elisabeth

Second Day, Fifth Month 17th

'Twas quite common for Susannah to visit in the afternoon, but I'd learned that when Mary forewent her midday rest to accompany her, something weighty required discussion. So when both women walked in the open front door, my thoughts immediately went to the children.

We chatted about community news as we sipped tea and ate sweet biscuits, but eventually I could beat about the bush no more. Looking from one to the other, I prepared my heart for what might come. "I sense something else is on your minds."

Mary smiled from her place beside Susannah on the

319

couch. "Thee has always had an intuitive spirit. We do bring news, though I dare say most would not consider it unwelcome."

Praise be to God for that. "Go on."

"Ellis Fitzwater asked to speak with me after meeting for worship yesterday." Susannah spoke more slowly than usual, and while her calmness usually brought comfort, this time I detected hesitancy in it. "Since hearing of thy ended courtship with Hiram, he has been considering thy plight with regard to the children. In light of his own situation, he wished to ask my opinion on whether thee would be receptive to marriage—with him."

The bite of biscuit I tried to swallow got caught in my throat, and I coughed and fought to clear it. When that didn't help, I gulped a mouthful of tea, which burned all the way to my stomach. "Marriage—with Ellis?" Hearing the squeak of my voice, I cleared my throat again.

"He is in need of a wife and a mother for his children," Mary said, "and he is aware that thee wishes to rear Abigail, Ethan, and Jon-Isaac, and that thee will need a husband and father for them should thee do that. He is an upright man, stable in his finances and in good standing with our Meeting, and he was certainly a devoted husband and continues to be a loving father."

Indeed. But marriage to a widower with seven children, all of whom were boys except for the oldest, who was nearly of marriageable age? Although I knew Ellis well, as I did all Friends from our Meeting, never had I considered him a prospective husband.

I set my teacup on the table beside my chair. "While I appreciate his proposal, I . . . 'Tis nothing against him. I'm sure he would be a fine husband, but I've always told myself I would never marry simply for convenience."

Mary arched her wispy eyebrows. "I have seen many such marriages grow into deep devotion and love."

I glanced at Susannah, but she remained silent, and her expression gave little evidence of her thoughts. "Only a few weeks ago, Hiram and I were preparing to declare our intention to marry. How could I so quickly declare intention to marry another?"

"Mother and I shared with the Meeting elders thy reasons for ending thy courtship with Hiram, and all agreed that thy decision was made with wisdom," Susannah said. "'Tis also understood that thy situation requires more hasty decision making."

Mary looked upon me with sympathy. "Elisabeth, thee must realize that little time remains should thee wish to retain custody of the children."

Of course I did. But marrying Ellis? No matter how good a husband and father he would be, I recoiled at the thought of the physical affections he would expect.

Or that any man would require of his wife.

Remembering how I'd reacted the one time Hiram kissed me with passion, the gravity of what I faced stole my breath. If I couldn't tolerate that, how would I ever manage anything more? "I can't."

"But—"

Shaking my head, I stood. My feet carried me toward the door, seemingly without my consent, but I stopped and faced them. "I cannot marry anyone." There was simply no way, and I'd lose the children because of it.

Susannah stood. "Elisabeth—"

"Thee doesn't understand. I cannot bear the thought of a man—any man—touching me. How would I be a proper wife? And 'twould be unfair if I didn't admit beforehand what Linus did, yet what man would marry me knowing it?" My lungs ached to fill, and I turned toward the door only to collide with Isaac.

He caught me by the waist, keeping me from toppling. "'Tis all right."

But it wasn't. Everything was *not* all right, nor would it be. And he had heard everything I'd just said. If he had not already questioned my rationality, he likely did now. Heat emanated from deep within me, and I covered my face with my hands and leaned it against his chest.

He held me close. "'Tis all right," he whispered again, this time into my ear. "Just be still."

I squeezed my eyes closed, trying to breathe and praying for peace. The desire to flee soon eased, as did the feeling that my chest was being crushed. Isaac still spoke softly, and though I couldn't make out what he said, my apprehension settled. Finally, I lifted my head.

Susannah now stood with us, her countenance sad. "Sweetheart, we didn't know thy discomfort was so—"

I shook my head again and drew a breath. "Even I didn't realize it until Hiram—" Realizing how my words sounded, I stopped. "He did nothing wrong." Except it hadn't felt that way at the time. "I just . . . I didn't want him to . . ." Oh, trying to explain was only making everything worse. Again I turned my face into Isaac's chest.

Susannah placed her hand on my back. "I shall speak with Ellis. He said he would not be hurt should thee decline. He just wanted to present the option to thee."

I swallowed, suddenly contrite. The man was thoughtful, if nothing else.

"Elisabeth." When I looked over to where Mary still sat on the couch, her head was tilted with compassion. She held out a hand. "Come."

Isaac released me, and though I immediately missed the solace he provided, I did as she asked.

With her teacup now on the table beside her, Mary took my hand in hers when I sat down with her. "God loves thee, and he is merciful. He knows what thee needs, and he goes before thee. Trust him."

I nodded, staring down at our hands as they lay on my leg. The dark spots on her skin and the arthritis that misshaped her knuckles spoke of how many years she had placed her faith in the Almighty. Even through many heartaches, he had never forsaken her. "I know."

"Way will open, for thy healing and for thee and the children. He has a plan."

How right she was.

I just hoped with all my heart that God's plan would keep the children and me together.

I'd just blown out the candle on the nightstand when the front door unlatched and creaked open. Isaac had told me he would be out late visiting with Daniel, so I need not wait up for him, but I had not expected him to come inside when he returned. Unless it wasn't him?

My heart quickened as I slid out of bed. The moonlight through the window allowed me to see the rocking chair, and I grabbed the quilt from the back of it and wrapped it around myself. While instinct bid me to stay put, Abigail and Ethan slept unprotected in the next room. I inched the door open just in time to see a familiar silhouette cross the threshold onto the porch.

"Isaac."

He stepped back inside, followed by Mwekane. "I didn't mean to wake thee. I thought thee might still be up, and wanted to get her even if thee was not." True to his word, he took care of the dog's every need.

"I wasn't asleep. I shall be right out." We had seen little of each other after Mary and Susannah left that afternoon—mostly due to our busyness, although I'd also avoided any situation where he could question me in confidence. But I'd missed his company tonight.

By the time I'd dressed and joined him, the common room glowed with the light of the chandelier candles. "Is thee hungry?"

He smiled and held up a hand holding three of the sugar wafers I'd made that morning. "Not anymore," he said through a mouthful.

I stopped as he rounded the table, suddenly feeling self-conscious. While I wanted time with him, looking him in the eye was difficult. "I'm glad thee came in."

"I didn't want to turn in without trying to ensure all was well."

My well-being was questionable at best, and surely he knew that as well as I did.

He sat on the bench and leaned back against the table's edge. "Is thee all right? Truly?" Concern etched his forehead above gentle eyes.

The Scripture I had read this evening came to mind. "God's grace is sufficient, for his power is made perfect through our weakness." I grinned. "So all is not lost."

Chuckling, he patted the bench next to him. "For either of us."

I lowered myself beside him. "Thee is one of the strongest people I know."

"I feel the same about thee."

"Even after what I said?" My cynical words came out before I could stop them. Unable to take them back, I stared at my clasped hands on my lap and steeled myself for his answer.

"Especially after that." He turned toward me and tucked my unbound hair behind my ear so it no longer hid my face. "Because now I better understand, and that is all I want. Well, and for thee to rest assured that nothing could change my feelings for thee."

Admiration and appreciation of him brought tears to my eyes and urged me to embrace him, but I refrained. We already treaded close to disobedience by his being in the house at such a late hour without justification. "Thee has never given me reason to think otherwise, but thy conviction is heartening. I hope thee realizes how grateful I am for thee."

He smiled and placed another cookie into his mouth. After resting his arm on the table behind me, he swallowed. "There *is* something I would like to discuss, unless thee is too tired."

My curiosity piqued. Our topics of conversation rarely required introduction. "Speak freely."

"When John Cadwallader came by about a new axe last week, we spoke for a bit. He brought up what Abigail said at school, and he believes there is some truth to it because we *have* taken on the roles of mother and father for her."

At least some from Meeting realized that.

His gaze held mine, and he smiled faintly. "He also proposed that in light of our friendship and desire to rear the children, we might consider marrying."

My heart skipped, and I tried to swallow past the sudden dryness of my throat. In my early adolescence, I'd often imagined wedding Isaac one day—until the incident with Margaret Roberts and his leaving Horsham, anyway. I'd thought about it after ending my courtship with Hiram as well, but now he knew what happened last year and how that still affected me. Whyever would he want to marry me when . . .

I cleared my throat. "Isaac, thee knows how much I care for thee. And that is why I hesitate, because I wouldn't be a suitable wife for any man. 'Twould be—"

"I know thee is uncomfortable with some aspects of marriage. I understand that and would fully take it into account. In many ways, little would change. We would live here, I'd continue to run the forge, and we'd rear the children together."

Except that I would be his wife in every sense but one. "'Twould hardly be fair to thee." Even so, was I a fool? The children needed parents who were approved by our Meeting —quickly—and our marriage would provide that.

Nay. I'd permitted a wrongful reason to drive my willingness to consider marriage with Hiram, and I couldn't do that with Isaac.

He shook his head, his solemn expression easing. "That isn't my concern. Thee and the children are. We both know time is of the essence." He slid his arm from behind me and leaned forward, resting his elbows on his legs, then looked at me again. "I know thee will need time to ponder this and seek wisdom, as I have. But I believe I would be a good husband and father."

The sincerity in his voice brought more tears to my eyes. Truly, I doubted another man would care for the children and me as Isaac did. Which made the decision all the more troubling, because he deserved better. "'Tisn't thee I'm concerned about."

He straightened. "This is difficult for thee. I know that. And tonight may not be the best time to address this after Mother and Susannah's visit today, but time slips away. Will thee at least consider it?"

If nothing else, I owed him that. "Aye."

Long after I returned to my bedchamber for the night, sleep eluded me. The day had been filled with such contrasting feelings that my mind swirled. In addition to the usual concern about the children's future, others followed in succession—the anxiety brought on by the proposition of marrying Ellis Fitzwater, the realization that I would not be a seemly wife, and the combination of both embarrassment and gratitude I'd felt when Isaac consoled me.

The tumult within had only intensified when he offered marriage also. While his suggestion seemed quite sensible— our marriage would not only allow the children to remain with the family they knew but would bind dear friends—qualms about myself plagued me. Since returning, Isaac had re-proved himself one of the most compassionate and honorable people I knew, and he deserved a proper wife. 'Twould be selfish of me to marry him knowing I couldn't fulfill that role.

Sobs shook me, and I turned my face into the pillow so not to wake Jon-Isaac. How unfair that something I'd played no part in now begot such turmoil and anguish in my life. A year had passed, yet I suddenly felt just as angry as when I'd confronted Linus.

Bitter animosity clutched my throat, choking me. Oh, I despised Linus. Even though he no longer walked upon the earth. Even though he would never harm another. Even though I knew he could never conceal from the Almighty the iniquities he had hidden so well from Friends.

And if I loathed him so, did that mean I had not forgiven him as I'd thought? Christ taught that we would be forgiven of our sins as we forgave others of theirs. Enmity would harden my heart, and unforgiveness would endanger my soul. Linus had already entered into eternity, so the only one to suffer under the weight of my animosity was me.

God forbid that I let him wound me further. I wouldn't allow it.

"When darkness closes in all around thee, seek the Light, daughter." Papa's repeated advice to me when I'd struggled came to mind. *"Light is always greater. His Word is a lantern unto thy feet and a light unto thy paths."*

His Word.

I slid out of bed and entered the common room. After my eyes adjusted, I made my way to the sitting area to get the candle from the table beside the couch. I lit it in the hearth's banked embers, then retrieved my Bible from the table and settled into the rocker.

Allowing the Bible to fall open on my lap, I shifted it so the candlelight flickered across the small typescript. *Come unto me, all ye that are weary and laden, and I will ease you.*

How remarkable that the Almighty spoke so aptly through his Word.

Take my yoke on you, and learn of me that I am meek and lowly in heart: and ye shall find rest unto your souls. For my yoke is easy, and my burden light.

How I needed that, for Christ to take my burden. "Father, take this," I whispered. "I can bear it no more."

Third Day, Fifth Month 18th

With Abigail at school and Isaac and Ethan delivering some smith work to a widow from our Meeting, I couldn't bring myself to get on with the day's chores. Laundry needed washing and hanging, the house could use tidying, and numerous other small tasks awaited.

Even so, I found myself on the sitting area rug with Jon-Isaac, who had made a game of filling a play bucket with his toys, carrying it around as he held on to furniture, and then dumping the toys and starting all over again. Even his smiles and giggles couldn't rid me of the weariness that made any task unfinishable.

A horse's snort sounded outside, and then footfall crossed the porch. "'Tis another lovely day," Susannah said as she strode through the open doorway.

Jon-Isaac babbled to her, reaching out a hand and opening and closing it in his sweet baby wave. I couldn't blame him. Her unexpected visit delighted me as well.

I rose. "Is thee headed out for a visit?"

"Returning from one." She smiled as she neared. "One of

the Walton families in Mannor of Moreland welcomed a hardy son early this morning."

"Thee must be weary, then." And she still looked more lively than I felt.

"I am, though tending an uncomplicated birth always gives renewed energy." Her eyes searched my face. "How is thee today?"

I longed to pour out how Isaac had proposed that we marry and my paralyzing doubts about becoming a wife, but held my tongue. Susannah knew me well and would pose poignant queries, including ones for which I had no solid answers. If I were to be conversing about it with anyone, it should be Isaac, though I hesitated to do that as well.

"Better."

She accepted my response with no further questions. Instead, we discussed the latest news from Friends at Byberry Meeting, as conveyed to her by the Waltons, whose kin attended there.

As I saw her out to her horse a half hour later, Midnight trotted into the yard with Isaac and Ethan astride. Isaac halted him, then swung down and lifted Ethan to the ground.

"Isaac has an uncle!" Ethan said as he ran toward us.

Of course he did. He had several uncles.

Isaac approached quickly, holding out a folded paper. "'Tis a return letter from Tom McCue. He spoke with a Moravian in Bethlehem who was visiting from their community in Nazareth, about fifteen miles to the north. The man confirmed there is a Philippe Billiou, in his fifties, who lives near Nazareth." He turned to Susannah. "According to Lydia Stanton, my mother who gave me life told her my father had a brother, though Lydia could remember only his last name."

Finally, Isaac had credible word of a prospective family member. His joy lightened my heart. "How wonderful."

"'Tis indeed," Susannah agreed. "Did thee send word back? Or I suppose thee would just write directly to this Philippe Billiou, would thee not?"

He shook his head. "Nazareth is two days' journey by horse if the weather holds. I can be there myself sooner than a letter would arrive. I'll leave first thing on the morrow"—he looked at me—"if thee is agreeable, that is."

Tomorrow morning. For Nazareth.

Everything in my being wished to plead with him to stay. The children and I needed him here, and he'd nearly lost his life the last time he was in that area. Yet he'd hoped and prayed for such an opportunity for so long, and at least he wasn't talking of Shamokin. "Of course I am."

Besides, how could I tell him otherwise? I wasn't his wife, and with how I'd balked last night, he likely expected I never would be. Who was I to deny him the chance to find his family?

Fourth Day, Fifth Month 19th

Though I again slept fitfully during the night, the next morning came too swiftly. Isaac had retired to the forge quarters soon after the children were abed, planning to get as much sleep as possible, and I knew we would have little time together this morning as well.

He readied Midnight while I prepared food and drink

for his journey, then the children and I accompanied him to the front yard, where he'd tied the horse to the garden fence post.

The children said their good-byes with as little ado as they could manage, just as I'd instructed, but I found it difficult to heed my words to them. As thankful as I was that Isaac finally had a chance to meet family, his leaving brought considerably more apprehension than his trip to Philadelphia a month ago.

He would be traveling much farther this time—and venturing into an area not far from the turbulence on the frontier. Though his Lenape heritage was less evident with him dressed as a Friend, who knew what peril might await him there.

After stowing his food and drink in the bags behind his saddle, Isaac faced me. He rested his hands on my shoulders and then ran them down my arms before taking my hands in his. "Daniel's boys will be here at sunrise and eventide to care for the livestock, even Sally." He grinned but sobered quickly. "And don't hesitate to send word if thee needs help, either from them or the older girls, with anything else. Assuming two days' travel time there and back, I shouldn't be gone more than a week, Lord willing."

Lord willing. *Oh, Father, please will his return.*

I nodded, striving to keep an optimistic demeanor. The last thing I wanted was to make him feel guilty—or to give the children reason to fuss. "God go with thee, and may he bless thy time there greatly."

He drew me close and held me for a long time, then moved his hands to the sides of my face and kissed my forehead. "I will miss thee."

His lips and whisper against my skin sent tingles all

through me, much like when he'd kissed me two nights before. Except this time I wasn't startled by it. "And I thee." I tightened my arms around him, savoring each moment until he gently put me away from him.

After mounting the horse, he nodded to us.

I forced a smile as I placed my hands on Abigail's and Ethan's shoulders. Abigail, holding Jon-Isaac on her hip, encouraged him to wave.

With one last good-bye, Isaac trotted Midnight down our lane toward the road.

Even before he was out of sight, I missed him.

CHAPTER 27

Isaac

Fifth Day, Fifth Month 20th

'Twas near sunset when *Der Gasthof zur Rose*—the Rose Tavern—came into view ahead. Having passed Nazareth a bit more than a mile back, I would soon arrive, but even that knowledge had not prepared me for such respite. The stockaded inn, barn, springhouse, and garden alongside the Minisink Road confirmed that I would soon be in the company of blood family.

The hostler raised a hand as he headed from the inn, a two-story mansion of muted red weatherboard, toward the stone-banked barn. *"Hallo!"*

"I'm hoping thee can help me." I dismounted Midnight and led him. "I'm looking for Philippe Billiou. I'm told he lives north of Nazareth."

He nodded. "Billiou. Da voodsman, *ja*." His thick German accent reminded me of Dieter Kolb's. "Go in. Herr Klotz tell you da way. I tend da horse."

I intended to stay only long enough to obtain directions, but handed him the reins. Midnight was a strong, spirited horse, and I'd paced our journey—thirty miles to *Der Siebenstern* in Saucon yesterday and thirty miles from there to Nazareth today—but he deserved a rub down, feed, and watering.

Inside, the tavern bustled with patrons eating, drinking, and conversing in both English and German. Provincial troops occupied three tables, and several men—locals, I presumed—gathered around two large tables along one wall. The air was thick and warm, but the delicious aroma of roasted chicken and potatoes made my stomach rumble.

A middle-aged woman approached carrying two tankards, but she stopped as soon as I removed my hat. All eyes now watched me, and the conversing stopped.

Two of the soldiers stood and walked toward me. "Where are you headed, traveler?" one asked.

Their wariness came as no surprise to me. In light of the raids, unfamiliar Indians were seldom welcome and never trusted—even if clad in the garb of a Friend, apparently.

I cleared my throat, fighting off the reminder of what happened on the Nescopeck Path. "My name is Isaac Lukens. Long ago, before I was adopted, I was called Christian Billiou. My parents were Jean-Luc and Angelie Billiou, and I've been told that Philippe Billiou, who I believe to be my uncle, still lives in this area."

"Well," a strained voice said. An older man struggled up from a chair at one of the large tables and made his way closer, leaning on a cane. "Christian Billiou, you say." His eyes narrowed as he scrutinized me in the fading light from the windows mixed with the glow of candles and the hearth fire. "Philippe has a painting of you and your parents on his mantel. You look like your mother but have the Billiou height."

My heart swelled. Hearing that I resembled my parents—and realizing I'd soon know what they looked like—brought an unexpected surge of emotion that almost evoked tears. Those around us seemed to relax, and my nerves followed suit. "If someone could direct me to his place, I'd be much obliged."

"Direct you, we can." The woman set the tankards before two men sitting at a round table, then faced me. "But you'll never make it there tonight. His cabin is about six miles from here, deep in the forest. You'll need daylight to find your way."

Several men nodded amidst widespread mutterings of confirmation.

But I needed to get there as soon as possible, and darkness had never hindered me before. "I'm certain I could—"

"You can't be going out there now," the man with the cane said. "Philippe likes being alone. Folks rarely call on him, and certainly not late at night. You'd likely end up shot before you could identify yourself."

Which meant I'd have to tarry till morning.

The woman neared me, wiping her hands on her soiled white apron. "Are you wanting a bed for the night, then?"

Nay, but what choice did I have?

I blew out my breath. "Aye."

Sixth Day, Fifth Month 21st

Soon after sunrise, I set out for Philippe Billiou's homestead, following Albrecht Klotz's directions. They indeed took me deep into the forest, and 'twas true that I never would have found my way in the dark of night.

Even with the sun shining, some areas within the wood were as dim as dusk. The anticipation and joy that pulsed like my own blood urged me to quicken Midnight's pace, but I resisted. Arriving a few minutes sooner wouldn't matter if it resulted in a lame horse.

After over an hour's ride, a clearing appeared at the end of the path up ahead. "Come on, boy." I clucked my tongue, pressing my heels into the horse's flank, and he tossed his head and trotted. As soon as we reached the clearing, I slowed him and dismounted.

The square-beam log cabin, much smaller than the Alden home and not as well kept, sat at the center of the glade. Oddly, no smoke curled from the chimney. Only a small, decrepit barn and an untilled garden shared the clearing, but the barn door stood open.

"Hello!" I called, leading Midnight in its direction. "Philippe Billiou?"

A slim older woman emerged holding a hunting gun by its barrel. Dressed in a buckskin skirt and a trade-cloth tunic belted about her waist, she had her gray-and-white hair in a long braid and appeared quite robust for her age. "Can I help you?"

Could Philippe have a wife? Nay, the barmaid at the

tavern had said he lived alone. As well, this woman was probably fifteen years older than he.

"I'm looking for Philippe Billiou."

She stopped five paces away, rested the butt of the gun on the ground, and looked me over from my hat to my boots. "He died. 'Bout two weeks ago. Heart just gave out on 'im, I reckon."

Died? Surely she was mistaken. I'd just received Tom McCue's letter a few days ago, and he'd written it less than two weeks before. "But—"

"He's with the Lord now. Certain as I'm standin' here, and I oughta know. I found 'im." She looked around me to the edge of the clearing, about twenty paces from where we stood. "Gave 'im as proper a Christian burial as I could."

An oblong mound of loose dirt piled a few inches above the surrounding ground confirmed a recent interment. Its length told me the man beneath it had been quite tall. And the old man at the tavern had mentioned my having the Billiou height, implying my father and uncle had also been taller than average.

A hand on my arm took my attention from the grave. The woman's eyes, previously narrowed with caution, now held sympathy. "You knew him?"

"Nay. Well, I suppose I did—once. I don't remember him, but . . ." My words sounded as bewildered as I felt, and I paused, trying to make sense of everything. Not that I wanted to accept the reality of it. "Long ago, I was Christian Billiou. I believe Philippe was my uncle."

Her mouth opened as her hand fell to her side. "Jean-Luc and Angelie's boy?"

Hope sparked amidst the empty numbness within. "Did thee know them?"

"I didn't, but Philippe has a portrait and some sketches of you and your parents in the house. Didn't speak much about you. Too difficult for him, I reckon." She proffered her hand. "Name's Damaris Harlow. I live through the wood there." With a nod, she indicated a narrow path that cut through the forest. "If you *were* Christian, who are ya now?"

I took her hand. Though toughened by work, it was gentle in touch. "Isaac Lukens. My Quaker parents named me since they didn't know my original name."

"Your parents died, then."

"Aye, in Philadelphia. Influenza."

She released my hand. "When you never returned, Philippe was certain you'd all perished on your journey. He'd been livin' here alone for 'bout four years when my husband and I bought land from him and built our cabin."

"Thee knew him well?"

"He and my husband spent plenty of time together when both were still livin'. Couldn't ask for a more loyal friend."

And if I'd known about him only a few weeks ago, I would've been able to meet him. That brought such bitterness that I could almost taste it.

She grasped my arm again. "Why don't we go inside? This was where you lived too. Philippe and your parents didn't have many material goods, but whatever ya might want of theirs is yours."

I turned to face the cabin. A portrait and sketches of my parents and me awaited us inside, and possibly some other possessions. I should have been thankful for that—and for Damaris, who, while not kin, offered me a connection to those who were. But that offered little comfort.

What I'd truly hoped for was now gone from this earth forever.

~

Philippe Billiou indeed had few possessions. The common room of his cabin, only half the size of the Aldens' common room and lit by four small windows, was sparsely furnished and already smelled musty.

Much of it was set up as a kitchen, with a table and two sitting benches, a worktable with a wash basin, and a few cooking pots and tools on the hearth floor. Otherwise, the room contained only a tall chest, two rocking chairs by the hearth, a chest of drawers, some candlesticks and lanterns, and a worn French Bible that lay open on the table. On the mantel sat something rectangular—the portrait I anticipated?

The floor squeaked with every footstep as I crossed it to the hearth. My eyes adjusted to the darkness of the room, and at reaching the mantel, I could make out a painting in a gilt frame. The portrait wasn't large, measuring about eleven inches wide and fourteen inches high, but even in the low light its quality clearly rivaled those I'd seen in extravagant Philadelphia homes. Yet here it was in a cabin in the wilderness.

"Philippe was a fine artist—self-taught," Damaris said with reverence as she came beside me. "He painted this as a gift to your parents on your second birthday." She looked from it to me. "Take it to the window so ya can see it in the light."

My hands trembled, but I lifted it down and carried it to the window. She dragged over a rocking chair, then stood beside it when I sat down.

In the portrait, my father—about five and thirty years old, tall and broad-shouldered, clean-shaven with blond hair and blue eyes—sat with his arm around my mother. She was much younger, certainly no older than Elisabeth, and quite beautiful with captivating dark eyes, pronounced cheekbones, and waist-length black hair that contrasted against her dark-red dress. In his smile I saw mischief, and in hers, gentleness.

The slim child my mother held on her lap was no doubt me, and I certainly resembled her. We bore the same eye and face shape, and my chin-length hair was as straight and dark as hers. Only my blue eyes, lighter skin, and how the man and I both wore dark-red trade-cloth shirts and buckskin breeches gave indication that he was my father.

A mix of joy and despair welled in me, threatening to explode within my chest, and I tried to blink away the tears that filled my eyes. Crying in front of others had always brought embarrassment, and I didn't even know the woman beside me.

She placed her hand on my shoulder. "I'll leave ya alone. Those two doors on the wall there"—she nodded toward the other side of the room—"are to the bedchambers. One on the left was Philippe's, the other your parents'. Both have dower chests. Not sure what's in your parents', but I know Philippe kept a lot of sketches in his—and in his Bible as well."

She walked to the open front door, then turned around, her body illuminated in the sunlight that streamed onto the bare floor. "Take whatever time ya need. If ya get hungry or need anything else, my place is a short walk through the wood on that path I showed ya. I'll take your horse in the barn and tend 'im."

Midnight. In my haste to come inside, I'd left him tied to a post by the barn. "I thank thee, Damaris."

She smiled sadly. "The Bible talks about us havin' a great cloud of witnesses, Isaac. Philippe may not be here in body, but no doubt he's watchin' over you, encouragin' you to endure. Your parents too, and all you've loved who have died in the Lord. Take comfort in that." Before I could answer, she was gone.

At once I missed the presence of one so kind yet thanked God for the solitude to grieve without an audience. I returned my attention to the portrait on my lap and ran my fingers over the faces of my parents. If nothing else, I now knew what they looked like, though that cut more deeply than expected. Hopefully the bedchambers held more information about them.

I stood and placed the portrait back on the mantel. *Father, give me strength for this.*

Darkness greeted me when I opened the door to my parents' bedchamber. The tiny room had no window, and the light from the common room brightened it only enough that I could make out silhouettes of furniture. The bed, small table beside it, dower chest, and washstand left just enough room to walk along the side and foot of the bed.

Stale air and dust made me sneeze and step back.

I'd seen a brass tinderbox at one end of the mantel when I replaced the portrait. A hearth fire would allow me to light the lanterns and candles, which I'd certainly need come evening, so I set to work. At least the time needed to kindle a fire would also give the room a chance to air out.

Once I'd lit one of the lanterns, I returned to the bedchamber. Flickering light glowed on the walls and cast my shadow as I set the lantern on the table. Except for the patchwork quilt on the bed, the room had no decoration. Not even a hat or an article of clothing hung on the pegs that crossed the wall beside the door.

And where had I slept? I'd seen no cradle, not that one would have contained a curious two-year-old. The rambunctious smile I wore in the portrait indicated that. So I might have slept with my parents. My throat tightened as I looked at the bed. Imagining myself snuggled comfortably between them, the lumpy straw tick beneath us and the quilt over top, brought the burn of tears behind my eyes. No matter how I tried to remember them, nothing ever came to mind. Neither the glimpse of a face nor the trace of a voice.

Unwilling to cry, I averted my attention to the chest at the foot of the bed. Its resistant hinge groaned as I lifted the lid, which then blocked most of the light from falling upon the contents of the chest. All the items inside appeared to be wrapped in linen, and I lifted each one out and placed it on the bed.

A plume of dust erupted around me when I sat beside the items, and I fanned it away and picked up the nearest one. Within the linen wrapping was a book with a mottled brown leather cover and *La Sainte Bible* engraved in gold on a burgundy strip on the spine. My parents' Bible. I opened the cover to find a few lines inscribed in French, along with names and what appeared to be birth and marriage dates:

> *Jean-Luc Billiou, né le 12 mai 1703*
> *Angelie, née en 1716*
> *mariage le 14 juillet 1731*
> *Christian Billiou, né le 2 octobre 1733*

I finally had a birthdate—Tenth Month 2nd, 1733—and my Quaker parents had been accurate in assessing my age.

Flipping through the book, I found two sketches between the pages—one of my father sitting in a chair holding me on his lap and the other of a side view of my mother's lovely face —as well as pieces of paper folded in half between the last page and back cover.

Unfolding them revealed two letters with the salutation *Mon cher Christian*, one dated 2 *octobre 1734* and the other 2 *octobre 1735*. Letters written to me on my first and second birthdays. They were in French, but my father's full name was signed near the bottom, as was my mother's first name in much plainer handwriting. If only I had paid attention when Elisabeth and I sat in on my cousins' French lessons while visiting Lukens Hall years ago.

The next wrapped item felt like cloth, which it was. A dark-red dress with a tiny floral print, folded perfectly. The dress my mother wore in the portrait on the mantel. Her wedding dress or just a favorite dress, since she treated it with such reverence?

I lifted it to my face, hoping for a hint of her scent, but it smelled only of the chest's wood. Still, it was hers, and she had worn it. Her skin had touched it, and now so did mine. Another priceless treasure.

Next I unwrapped a dark-stained, strap-hinged wooden box that measured about ten inches square. Its tiny key still sat in the lock on the front, and a slight turn of it unlocked the lid. Inside were several pieces of Lenape jewelry, mostly necklaces but also bracelets and earrings, made from various mediums: porcupine quills, glass beads, feathers, carved stones, shells. Beneath them were a belt of blue and white wampum that tied with buckskin fringe and a black trade-cloth medicine pouch embroidered with silver thread and decorated with quills, ribbon, deer hair, and beads.

The pouch held another necklace, this one strung with red beads and white cylindrical shells and bearing a flat black stone in the shape of a turtle. The animal's silhouette resembled the one inked on my chest, but whoever had carved the two-inch-round turtle had painstakingly etched the face, the claws on the feet, and the lines of the shell.

The delicateness and discoloration of the strung shells suggested the necklace was much older than my mother, and I wondered to whom else it had belonged. My grandfather? My grandmother? Or even a great-grandparent? No matter to whom, chances were good that its original owner had lived a content, peaceful life in a village north of the Forks of the Delaware.

Now where were they? Their time on earth had likely ended, and their descendants no longer walked the lands that had been their home for so many years. As well, where were my father and Philippe's family? Even if their parents had died, they could have siblings somewhere.

The answer to that might lay within Philippe's belongings, and as much as I wished to remain in my parents' bedchamber amongst their possessions, I needed to know more. After grabbing the lantern, I headed to the other bedchamber.

This room looked identical to my parents', except several pieces of clothing hung on the wall. Otherwise, it was just as sparsely furnished and undecorated. I opened the dower chest and lifted the contents out, then placed them on the bed.

A wooden box filled with painting and sketching supplies. Some unused paper. A few books in French, one containing the title to his land. And a tall stack of sketches—a few of my parents and me but many more of landscapes and animals. While they all held value because they belonged to my uncle, none revealed sought-after information.

That left me one last resource.

~

Damaris's cabin was about the same size as Philippe's, though a bit more inviting with rocking chairs and pots of herbs on the porch. A tilled garden and a barn that looked newer than the cabin also shared the clearing.

She appeared in the doorway as I climbed the steps, then smiled. "Was hopin' ya'd join me. C'mon in. My grandson's usually here for dinner, but he's out huntin' and won't be home till 'round suppertime."

So she didn't live alone. That eased my concern for her, as did the welcoming interior of the cabin. The common room was comfortably furnished, and the delicious aroma of what I suspected was rabbit stew filled the air. She and her grandson appeared to fare well even in the middle of the forest.

"Sit." She indicated the table and benches, then continued to the hearth. After stirring what simmered in the kettle hanging over the fire, she lifted a teakettle from a trivet on the hearth floor and carried it to the table. "Mint tea?"

"Please."

She filled two tin cups, then sat across from me. "Philippe was a man of few words and few worldly possessions. I suspect your parents were as well."

I inhaled the refreshing steam that rose from my cup. The tea too hot, I set the cup on the table and looked into her eyes.

Their color reminded me of Elisabeth's and intensified

the ache within. While the day's excitement had pushed thoughts of her from my mind, now in my disappointment, I longed for the one who'd been my comfort in difficult times. "Do you know anything about Philippe and Jean-Luc's or my mother's family?"

She scowled as if contemplating. "Some. Philippe and Jean-Luc were Huguenot trappers from Staten Island. If I remember right, they weren't too much older than you are now when they first came down here to trade with the Lenape. They liked the area and eventually made this their home."

I held my breath. "Do you know if they had more family in Staten Island?"

"None that I know of. Their parents had died."

So finding my father's family would be improbable. Another possibility lost. "What—" My voice faltered, and I cleared my throat. "What about Angelie? Do you know anything about her?"

"Well, that wasn't her birth name. She had an Indian name, but I don't know what it was. Her father was some sort of leader in their tribe. Philippe and Jean-Luc befriended him through trading, and that's how Jean-Luc and Angelie met. But then the tribe lost their land here and was sent west. Angelie went with them, but after a couple of days' journey, she left the tribe during the night and made her way back."

She stood and walked to the hearth, where she stirred the kettle again. "She'd already become a Christian"—she glanced over her shoulder at me—"and upon her return, she was baptized with the name Angelie, and she and Jean-Luc married."

Perhaps that explained why I'd never found any family

in Shamokin. I'd asked either the wrong people or the wrong questions. If only I'd known more then—or been more persistent.

Damaris moved about, filling two trenchers with stew and slicing bread.

I exhaled. Not that I wasn't grateful for the information she provided. I was, despite its lack. Yet if I intended to find those with whom I shared blood—and after I'd come this far, I did—my journey was far from over. My last chance for finding family was now in one place.

Shamokin.

CHAPTER 28

Elisabeth

Seventh Day, Fifth Month 22nd

With Jon-Isaac finally asleep in his cradle, I slipped out of my bedchamber and closed the door. Rambunctious giggling—much too loud for bedtime—emanated from Abigail and Ethan's bedchamber, and I hurried in to put a stop to it.

"Hush now. Jon-Isaac's finally sleeping." Finding them bouncing as they knelt on the bed with Mwekane, I set my candle on the bedside table and placed my hands on my hips. "Into bed with you—now."

Both hastily got under the covers. By the time I'd brought over the ladder-back chair and placed it by the bed, they lay on their pillows watching me with wide eyes and clutching the quilt up to their chins.

I sighed as I sat down. "Today was difficult." What an understatement that was. Rain had fallen hour after hour, keeping them inside, and they'd bickered multiple times since Abigail had come home from her half day of school. Their carrying-on had cut short Jon-Isaac's afternoon nap—again—and put him in a disagreeable mood. I'd even considered punishing them with no supper and an early bedtime.

"We're sorry," Abigail whispered.

Ethan nodded.

I couldn't help feeling a bit guilty. They truly did look contrite, and our challenging day had not been solely their fault. More than once, my response to their conduct, though meant to provide discipline, had only exacerbated the problem.

Exhaustion urged me to just accept their apology and pray with them so I could retire to the silence of the common room, but this was an opportunity to model the behavior I wanted them to embrace. "I must apologize as well. At times I responded in anger or frustration instead of working to bring about peace. Starting on the morrow, we all must strive for apposite actions. Understood?"

Both nodded this time.

"Aye, Elisabeth," Abigail said.

We should have discussed their behavior in more depth, but I simply couldn't. My mind was too tired to come up with supporting Scripture verses, and all I wanted was some time to myself before going to bed. Once we finished praying together, I kissed their foreheads and then stood. "Sleep well."

"Will Isaac come home tomorrow?" Ethan asked.

Oh, how I wished I could say he would. This was the fourth night he'd been gone, and the children missed him terribly. I suspected their off behavior in the last few days stemmed from his absence—no doubt a reasonable cause—and I knew better than to think my own disposition wasn't affected by it.

I sat again and stroked Ethan's soft hair back from his cherubic face. "Probably not, sweet boy. He expected he would be gone about a week. Lord willing, he'll return by Third Day."

His chin quivered. "I want him to come home."

"I know thee does. I do as well. We all miss him."

He swallowed. "If he comes home tonight, will thee wake us?"

Poor boy. He simply didn't understand. Not that I could blame him. "Of course I will. Sleep well now." After patting Mwekane's head, I left the room and closed the door partway.

The common room at eventide had become a source of comfort for me in the last few weeks, a place where Isaac and I talked and laughed together as we had years ago. But suddenly the solitude I'd yearned for no longer offered repose. I could go to bed early, but my body felt much less weary than my mind, which could lead to my lying in bed for hours with naught to do but ruminate.

Seeing the Bible at one end of the kitchen table, I carried my candle over and sat down. The last time I'd been in this particular spot had been when Isaac and I sat eating pie and discussing his conversation with his brother-in-law Benjamin. I'd thanked him for his care for the children and me, and he'd responded by kissing my forehead. His affection had startled me, and even now the memory of it brought a nervous flutter in my middle. Yet I longed for his presence beside me again. We needed him home.

Home. For seven years, he'd shared this house with my family. He now slept outside its walls, but it was still his home and the forge his workplace. Neither he, the children, nor I wanted any other arrangement.

But what did that mean now? He'd proposed marriage. If I refused, what would happen—not only to the children but also to our relationship? The children's fate seemed quite clear, and I knew all too well what had happened when a woman rebuffed him in the past. He had left, purportedly in search of his family but more likely in hope of finding something to ease the hurt inside him.

Not unlike his leaving earlier this week.

While he had no part in what day he received word of family, aside from the fact that he'd written to Tom McCue, that news came just one day after I'd hesitated at his proposal. How ironic, considering that his first quest for family had begun soon after Margaret Roberts's rejection. And how concerning, considering the result. That journey had changed his life irreversibly, as it had mine and others'. What if that happened again?

God forbid it.

Besides, 'twasn't him I had denied but the prospect of being a wife. He knew that and understood. But would it matter? Rejection was still rejection. Even though he had to know I would never treat him as Margaret did, my diffidence probably still smarted, especially since our relationships were so different. She'd been a mere acquaintance who suddenly showed interest in him. I'd been dear to him all his life. My indecision likely hurt even more—and gave him reason to again believe Horsham wasn't his true home.

My throat ached at the likelihood that my balking was one of the most follish things I'd ever done. Had I agreed to marry Isaac, we would have already written our letter of intention to the Women's Meeting. Pending approval of the clearness committee appointed to us—which I expected would consent to our marriage and custody of the children without reservation—we would marry and begin our life as a family. A family that, quite honestly, I already adored.

Tears filled my eyes.

Oh, Father, what have I done?

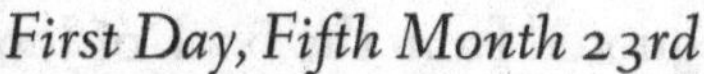

First Day, Fifth Month 23rd

Our meeting house had always been one of my very favorite places. Even as a child, I found joy and peace in the beautiful silence and the apt testimonies given. While many of my schoolmates merely tolerated First Day and midweek meeting for worship because they had no choice, I thrived on it, eager to hear what the Almighty might impress upon me. And he had spoken, my tender age notwithstanding.

If only he would speak now as I sat on the same meeting house bench the following morning.

For weeks I'd beseeched his wisdom, soliciting his word regarding the children. He had placed these three precious little ones in my life, and truly they had become my life—my highest priority aside from my relationship with Christ. But what did the Lord intend now? Was I to continue as their mother and even become a wife as well? Or did he have another plan?

When Mary and I last visited for tea, she had cautioned me that with our finite knowledge and foresight, we cannot always see the Lord's plan. She reminded me that things we will never comprehend this side of the heavens can happen. At the time, I nodded, for I'd already experienced such in merely twenty years of life.

"*Whether or not what we suffer is wrought of our own doing,*" Mary had said, "*our Father in heaven can give unto us beauty from ashes. 'Tis his hands that knit together our restoration, just as he knit together our being before birth, but 'tis our hearts that must trust wholly in his goodness. Trust him. Has he not shown thee, time and again, that he is faithful?*"

Indeed he had, so many times. What had Papa often quoted from the book of Job when he faced turmoil? *Though he slay me, yet will I trust in him.* Job had lost so much more than I—everything he had, truly—but he still trusted. *And I will reprove my ways in his sight.* Just as I must. God loved me, and he loved the children even more than I did. As well, his perfect plans for our lives far surpassed the strategies devised even by my best intentions. My place wasn't to tell the omniscient One what would be best but to obey him.

Except that to obey, I needed to know what was commanded of me. I had yet to find discernment, at least with regard to the children, about whether God truly intended me to rear them, or someone else. The Lord had showed me that marrying Hiram wasn't in his plan, but no further instruction had come.

The bench I sat on creaked and shifted as weight lifted from it, and I glanced to my right. On the other side of Ethan and Abigail, Hannah stood with her hands folded at her waist.

"'Trust thou in the Lord and do good: dwell in the land, and thou shalt be fed assuredly.'" Her clear voice echoed throughout the room, reciting from one of the psalms. "'And delight thyself in the Lord, and he shall give thee thine heart's desire. Commit thy way unto the Lord, and trust in him, and he shall bring it to pass. And he shall bring forth thy righteousness as the light, and thy judgment as the noon day. Wait patiently upon the Lord, and hope in him.'"

Wait patiently upon the Lord.

Four weeks ago, my question had been whether Hiram and I should marry. For several days and nights I prayed for an answer, but only with time did it come. Even so, God had made my path straight, not because of my faithfulness—admittedly, my patience had been lacking—but because of his.

"Most of us appreciate how worry can bind us so tightly, even to the point of physical discomfort," Hannah continued, her eyes closed. "We pray for an answer to what concerns us, and often it doesn't manifest as swiftly as we hope. But the sun rises and sets on the Almighty's time, not on ours. 'Tis he who sees our tomorrows and knows what each one holds. Likewise, 'tis in his time—and not when we wish but when he knows best—that he makes known the way. 'Wait patiently upon the Lord, and hope in him.'"

As she sat down, the peace I'd been yearning for washed through me. For at times God spoke directly into the heart in the silence, and other times his wisdom was imparted through the voiced words of one amenable to being used for another's benefit.

~

Following meeting for worship, Mary, Susannah, the children, and I all joined Daniel and Hannah's family for dinner. Abigail then stayed to spend the afternoon with

Sarah and Anna, and the rest of us headed home. There, I put the boys to bed for their nap, then settled on the couch to tackle my ever-present mending pile.

Soon after, Susannah came through the open front door. Not surprising. At Daniel and Hannah's, she had discreetly mentioned my change in disposition, and I'd confirmed it but didn't have the privacy to elaborate. I suspected she would visit after Mary lay down for her afternoon rest.

Smiling my greeting, I wove the needle into the fabric of the shirt I was mending and set it back in the basket by my feet.

She sat on the wingback chair Isaac often used. "Thy mind is clearly more at ease. I'm glad."

As was I. Today's dinner was the first true meal I'd eaten since Isaac left, and the knot in my stomach had finally loosened. Though she didn't say it, I knew she hoped for an explanation. "Hannah's testimony spoke straight to my condition, and I was reminded that I must wait upon the Lord with patience, trusting in his providence."

The hint of a smile appeared as she slowly nodded. "He is ever faithful. Even so, faith often takes effort."

"Aye. But Lord willing, Isaac will return in the next day or so, and I trust we'll be able to work through what we must."

"With regard to the children?" Her brow furrowed. "Or does thee mean with each other?"

After a moment, her perplexity made sense. I had not mentioned Isaac's proposal to anyone, but now I felt the desire to share it. Her advice had always been wise and trustworthy, and she knew both Isaac and me well enough to provide a gainful perspective.

I folded my hands on my lap. "The night before Isaac

received the letter from Tom McCue, he told me John Cadwallader had spoken with him the week before. John suggested that in light of our situation, Isaac and I consider marrying and rearing the children together." I swallowed, now feeling guilty, though I didn't know why. "Having sought God's wisdom, Isaac proposed marriage that night."

Susannah's mouth opened slightly and then closed. "I see. And how did thee respond?"

I glanced down at my hands, then released them at seeing how they wrung. "I gave no definitive answer." And then he left for Nazareth. Who could blame him?

"I see." She closed her eyes, listening.

My first instinct was to again convey my reasons why I shouldn't marry any man, but I waited. Susannah knew my fears, so interrupting her with what was already implicit seemed needless. Instead, I gave her time and prayed for clarity to come from our dialogue.

About three minutes later, she stirred. "Does thee love Isaac?"

I looked up. "Of course I do."

"And why does thee love him?"

Another question I didn't expect. "Well, because he pursues God and his wisdom, and because he cares deeply for the children and me. And because he is kind and gentle, and he makes me laugh." Truly, the list could go on indefinitely. "Because he knows me so well—the bad and the good—yet he still esteems me." And because nothing else of this world made me feel more safe and at ease as his presence—or as enlivened as his smile. I dared not be that honest, though. Just the thought of it brought warmth to my face.

She nodded a few times. "Does thee think those qualities would make him a capable husband?"

"Of course. 'Tis not his abilities as a husband I doubt. 'Tis my own that I fear would fall unacceptably short. Knowing that, 'twould be wrong of me to marry him." In a whisper, I finished, "That is what I told him."

"And how did he respond?"

Suddenly, discussing Isaac's proposal with Susannah seemed improper. The conversation with him had been disconcerting, but conferring about it with his sister—especially without his consent—unsettled me more. "He said he understood my discomfort with some aspects of marriage and . . . would fully take it into account." I forced my gaze from my lap to her. "But that would be unfair to him. As my husband, he would deserve . . ." Unable to finish, I pressed my lips together, trying to keep my poise.

Susannah rose and came to sit beside me. "Thee is not incorrect," she said. "The Bible tells us husbands and wives should not withhold themselves from each other in this way."

I nodded, but amidst my discomfiture with the subject, I couldn't produce an answer. A tear slid down my cheek, and I brushed it away.

"Oh, sweetheart." She took my hand in hers and squeezed it. "Isaac has assured thee that he would fully take thy apprehensions into account. Does thee not truly believe that?"

"I do. But 'twouldn't be proper of me to expect that."

"I agree."

Now I was confused. "Then what is thee saying?"

"I'm saying thee loves Isaac and trusts him. He loves thee and would never endeavor to harm thee. Does it not seem likely that in time and with the Almighty's guidance, your relationship would strengthen even further and allow thee to be his wife in every way?"

How could I answer that? I didn't know what would happen on the morrow, let alone over time should we marry. And how could I—

There is no fear in love, but perfect love casteth out fear.

The verse I'd memorized as a child interrupted, begging my contemplation. 'Twas true. And while Isaac's and my love for each other was not perfect—we were human, after all—it was sincere and devoted.

Even so, my fear was just as genuine.

I am able to do all things through the help of Christ, which strengtheneth me.

Another verse came to mind, this time one I'd proclaimed more times than I could count over my lifetime. Never had the Lord dismissed me when I begged his strength in the past, so how could I believe he would turn from me now if I—or we, Isaac and I together—asked for his favor?

A cord of three strands is not easily broken.

Throughout our childhood, Isaac and I had claimed that promise many times when we faced adversity—whether it was his academic difficulties in school, the loss of my sister and brothers, or the loss of his father and my mother. I'd even made a braided cord from long lengths of his and my hair and red-dyed lamb's wool yarn that symbolized Christ. Our paraphrase of the verse seemed just as applicable now.

Taking a deep breath and then releasing it, I raised my gaze from my lap to Susannah. "Thee always gives me plenty to think about."

A smile crossed her kind face. "Here is something else for thee to think about. When Mother and I were here last week, thee told us thee could not stand the thought of any man touching thee. Yet only moments later thee willingly went to Isaac, seeking the comfort of his arms. So it would seem that thee cannot tolerate the thought of any man touching thee, save one—and he is the man who wants thee to be his wife. Am I correct?"

Indeed she was. "Aye."

She squeezed my hand again. "I will give thee one last thing to ponder, and thee need not answer me. I just want thee to contemplate this. Were thee to refuse his proposal, and were he to then marry another, would that upset thee?"

'Twas fortunate I didn't have to reply, for I couldn't have responded if I'd wanted to.

Would I be upset? Nay.

I would be devastated.

Although weary, I lay awake long after retiring that night. What Susannah had said repeated in my mind, and all my thinking about Isaac had me wishing him home even more. I couldn't help wondering if he missed us as much. Certainly, spending time with his uncle took priority, but he'd said he would miss us. Moreover, I'd felt it in the way he held my face in his hands and kissed my forehead before he left.

How right Susannah had been. Though I hadn't thought about it before, I was quite comfortable with Isaac. Never had I retreated from his touch or felt anything close to trepidation with him. His kissing my forehead after I thanked him for his care for the children and me had startled me and evoked a peculiar feeling in my belly, but neither came from fear. In fact, when I'd had my episode while quarreling with Hiram, 'twas to Isaac I'd tried to flee seeking safety.

And then there was our parting when he left for

Nazareth. He had ended our embrace, not I, and my reaction to his tender good-bye had been . . . well, exhilaration, even if it was accompanied by the despair of his departure.

Turning onto my side, I pulled the quilt up higher on my shoulders and sighed. I'd told Susannah I loved Isaac, and I did—in a way I had never expected.

Truth be told, I couldn't imagine life without him.

CHAPTER 29

Isaac

On Seventh Day, Damaris and her grandson had accompanied me to the county court at Jacob Bachmann's Tavern in Easton, about ten miles from Nazareth, so I could petition the transfer of Philippe's land deed to me. That day passed quickly, but not the next.

On First Day, thunder, lightning, and teeming rain awakened me just before dawn. I'd planned to leave for Shamokin at first light, but the foul weather continued throughout the day with only occasional breaks, barring my travel and evoking a temperament that rivaled the fury of the storms.

While Philippe's cabin and land would become my property once the judge received confirmation of my claim to be Christian Billiou—from my brother David, a longtime friend of his—I couldn't leave Nazareth soon enough. The initial bittersweet feeling brought by my parents' and uncle's effects all around me now resulted only in bitterness, and I itched to start the next part of my journey. Instead, I was stuck in the cabin while the gusting wind pelted the windowpanes with heavy rain.

As the afternoon dragged on, I searched the house for what items I would take with me. Damaris had generously provided me a large oilcloth sack, but I still could take a limited amount. I packed only the necessities—my parents' and Philippe's Bibles, the portrait of my parents and me, my mother's dress and box of jewelry, and a stack of my favorite sketches by Philippe—then went through the drawers of the tall chest in the common room again.

In the top drawer, my hand came upon a drawstring calico bag with something rectangular inside. I pulled it out, and the faint scent of lavender followed. Inside was a bar of soap that overwhelmed me with fragrant familiarity. It smelled so much like the soap Elisabeth made that my mind returned to the night I'd fallen asleep on the couch with Jon-Isaac while she bathed Ethan and Abigail braided my hair.

Everything had felt perfect that night, and suddenly I missed them so much that my chest ached.

Guilt followed. I'd promised Jonathan I'd take care of them, and now here I was, gone for five days and planning to extend that journey—likely by weeks—to continue my search for family. All this only a day after I'd proposed marriage to Elisabeth. She hadn't given an answer, but she'd also had only a day to consider it. What kind of man offered marriage to a woman—and made a promise to a dying friend—and then reneged?

And taking into account my past actions, what would my

failure to return as promised do to Elisabeth and the children? She finally trusted me again, and the children learned from my behavior. Never would I want to hurt her or exhibit anything but upright conduct for them. As well, what would I do if I returned from Shamokin weeks from now to find the children removed from her custody or her unwillingly engaged to someone else to prevent that?

I held the soap to my nose again. In it I smelled Jon-Isaac's hair, heard Ethan's giggles, saw Abigail's gap-toothed smile, and felt Elisabeth's hands removing the tiny braids in my hair. I loved them so much, more than I could express with words. Yet I'd planned to forsake them in search of people who might not even still exist on the earth—like Philippe—or might try to take my life in revenge. While I certainly didn't regret coming to Nazareth, I'd be a fool to now go on to Shamokin.

I returned the soap to its place and closed the drawer. Raining or not, I needed to tend to Midnight, visit Damaris to thank her for all she'd done for me, and get some sleep. As soon as the weather cleared—hopefully by morning—I would begin the journey back to Horsham.

Third Day, Fifth Month 25th

Having left Nazareth at dawn, I neared Bethlehem at midafternoon. The weather, though dismal and misty, had held thus far, but in the distance clouds loomed dark and threatening. I'd hoped to make it another ten miles to *Der Siebenstern* in Saucon—far enough that I could reach Horsham by tomorrow evening—but the nearer Bethlehem became, the more I couldn't deny the conditions to come. Frustrated, I spurred Midnight galloping toward the McCue homestead.

Jerusha appeared in the doorway of the cabin as I dismounted Midnight. "Isaac!" she called, waving. "See to your horse in the barn and then come inside."

The wind had picked up by the time I left the barn, and I hurried across the front yard to the porch. She waited for me, smiling as she rubbed a hand over where her tunic shirt stretched taut on her rounded belly. From afar, I hadn't realized she anticipated a child.

"We were hoping we might be seeing you." She hugged me and then patted my arm. "You're cold and wet, probably hungry too. Let's get you some dry clothes and hot victuals. Tom's at the neighbors', but he'll be back by supper."

My ungratefulness convicted me as I followed her inside. Instead of being bothered that the coming storm was altering my plans, I should have been thankful for such good friends with whom I could shelter. "When is thy child due?"

A smile lit her face. "In about ten weeks. We've prayed for this little one for nine years now. Our Lord is faithful."

She brought me some of Tom's clothes and then had a large trencher of steaming stew and a thick wedge of bread on the table when I finished changing. As we sat at the table, I ate and described my time at Philippe's. Her sympathetic ear even encouraged me to share my proposal to Elisabeth, which I hadn't planned on doing.

Jerusha nodded when I finished. "I always knew you loved her."

Now if only she loved me as much.

Ready for another subject, I glanced toward the door, where I'd left my oilskin sack. "Would thee like to see my mother's belongings?" Being Lenape, Jerusha would surely appreciate them.

"I'd love to."

I retrieved the sack and set it on the table, then pulled out the dress and box of jewelry.

She cooed as she looked over the folded dress, but her eyes welled when she opened the box. Lifting out the pieces one by one, she examined each with reverence. Tears slid down her cheeks as she held the carved black turtle necklace in her hands. "My grandfather had a necklace similar to this."

Showing her might not have been the best idea after all. I placed the box and dress back into the sack, then lifted out the portrait, which I'd swathed in another piece of oilcloth to protect it from the elements. After unwrapping it, I sat beside her on the bench and held the frame upright on the table.

She gasped softly, covering her mouth with a hand. "How beautiful," she whispered as she touched my mother's face. "Her name was Mehokquiman. Red Bird, in English."

What? "Thee knew her?"

She continued to stare at the portrait. "Her village was several miles to the north of mine, but we played together as children several times, and we met a few times as adolescents. I can't remember her parents' names, but her brother's name is—"

"Sukachgook," we said together.

I added, "Her father was Achwangundowi."

"Yes." She shook her head and grimaced. "Her brother was most cruel. Even as a child, he did dreadful things. Many claimed he had a sickness in his mind."

Little about his behavior had changed, then. "'Tis said

that he has wreaked all manner of havoc on the western frontier."

She nodded, and seriousness drew her eyebrows together. "Isaac, you may believe your remaining family is in Shamokin, but you mustn't go there. No doubt you would be in grave danger. As a Friend, you wouldn't defend yourself, and . . ." She swallowed as she laid her hand on her belly. "Forgive me. I get overwhelmed at times these days. But no good would come from your being there."

Still, how could I forget my family? With her already upset, I dared not mention my plan to send a message to Shamokin when Newcastle, Jiggera, and William Locquies returned to Philadelphia. "My family is there. And the Lenape are my people—*our* people—and they're suffering. Many have told me I have a gift for mediation, and in the last few days I've come to believe God has given it to me for this reason. How do I go back to Horsham and just forget them?"

"You don't." She grasped my arm. "You will never forget them. I know that. Most of my family died before I joined the Moravians, but what has happened to the Lenape breaks my heart. Our lands lost. Our people scattered, impelled to take lives amidst the British and French war for land that truly belongs to neither. Our traditions and customs disappearing, our people as well." She took a napkin from the pile of them at the center of the table and wiped her eyes.

This wasn't going as I'd hoped. I laid the portrait on the table. "I'm sorry. Please, I don't want to upset thee."

She shook her head. "Listen to me, Isaac. The Lenape sent you away, refusing your wisdom and assistance. Do you remember what Jesus told his disciples to do when people wouldn't receive them or hear their words? He said, 'When ye depart out of that house, or that city, shake off the dust of your feet.'"

Shake off the dust of my feet? That was what God wished me to do? "But—"

"I know that sounds harsh, but going to Shamokin would have no benefit. Not now, anyway. There's too much strife, too much threat. God has given you the gift of conciliation, but it will be of no help to anyone if you go there and lose your life."

That I couldn't deny. "But is it any better to not use it at all?"

She stared at me. "You are already using it. Your letter to us told of your time in Philadelphia with Friends and Six Nations chiefs. Is that not where you can make the most difference, with those in power in the province?"

Oh, the truth she spoke. How had I overlooked that?

"You feel torn between the Lenape and the white settlers." Her tone had softened. "How could you not? Your veins carry the blood of both. But God has placed you in Horsham, with a woman and children you care for—and who care for you. And close to Philadelphia, where your gift is greatly needed.

"Whether Governor Morris and those in power will heed the wisdom you and the other Friends provide, none of us can say, but you will make a difference. If not with them, then with others who'll be encouraged to stand up for fair treatment of Indians—and with the children, because I know you will teach them to be voices for anyone mistreated." She smiled. "Three months ago you should have died, but God spared you for a reason. Trust him, as you have been doing, and follow where he leads."

"I cannot thank thee enough," I whispered as we hugged again.

How grateful I was that God had brought this kind, astute woman into my life when I needed her most. The first time we met, she saved my life with her healing hands. Today, she had likely saved it again—and helped me discern where I belonged—with her loving wisdom.

~

Fifth Day, Fifth Month 27th

Inclement weather continued to delay my trip home. I'd hoped to leave for Horsham at dawn the next day, but heavy rain continued until midmorning.

The sky finally started to clear then and I took my leave, but the last few days' storms had rendered the Minsi Trail even more rutted than usual and perilously muddy in some areas. Many times I dismounted and led Midnight. Despite moving as speedily as was safe, we were still more than ten miles from Horsham even after ten hours' journey.

I was tiring, but 'twas Midnight I worried about. We'd traveled at least thirty-five miles, and his slowing gait and occasional displeased snorts told me we should stop. He needed feed, water, and rest before we traveled any farther, so I stopped at Bartholomew's Tavern in Montgomery for the night. The next morning we left at first light, and his vigorous pace proved he had slept much better than I.

Like the night before, all I could think about was Elisabeth as we trotted down the road from Montgomery to Horsham. Though being so close to home brought anticipation and relief, I also wondered how she would react. She certainly hadn't wanted me to leave, but neither had she accepted my proposal. For the past few days I'd told myself this time away might help her come to a decision, but whether that was in my favor was yet to be known. Another aspect of my life that I'd have to entrust to the Almighty.

As the ascending sun cast a golden light across Horsham's rolling fields, up ahead the meeting house, burying ground, and school came into view. Never had I more appreciated the sight of them under the cloudless blue sky and amidst blooming trees.

Midnight quickened her gait as she always did when we neared home, and I turned her southwest at the crossroads and let her gallop up the hill past my cousin William's grist mill. I dismounted on the dirt lane that led to the Alden house, then sneaked Midnight around the back of the barn.

Inside, I tended her. A mere fifteen minutes later—but still not quickly enough—I left the saddle bags in the barn to empty later and carried the oilskin sack toward the house.

I'd seen the front door standing open, so I stole around to the front of the house and crossed the porch as silently as I could. Stopping in the doorway, I found Elisabeth and the children at the kitchen table.

Abigail and Ethan sat next to each other eating porridge while Elisabeth occupied the bench across from them, spoon-feeding Jon-Isaac, who sat in his high chair. 'Twas a scene I'd observed many times, but this time it tightened my chest with sentimentality.

I cleared my throat. "Did you save some porridge for me?"

They all looked over, and the children squealed and jumped up. "Isaac!"

Nails scraped across the floorboards as Mwekane bounced to her feet and scurried toward me.

Elisabeth stood and grabbed Jon-Isaac, then hastened after them all.

I set the sack out of harm's way and, as they neared, dropped to one knee.

Abigail and Ethan ran into my arms, almost knocking me over with their momentum. "Thee is home," they both exclaimed.

And I had no intention of going anywhere without them anytime soon. I hugged them, releasing them only when I realized Elisabeth stood beside us, waiting. She smiled, her lips trembling and eyes moist, as I straightened. On her hip, Jon-Isaac kicked his feet and reached for me, babbling gleefully. We all laughed, and I took him.

Elisabeth swallowed hard and pressed her fist to her mouth, though her smile couldn't be concealed.

I drew her close, wrapping my arm around her. When she clung to me as if she would never let go, emotion nearly choked me. "Has thee any idea how much I missed thee?"

She grinned despite her tears. "Not as much as I missed thee."

Oh, I loved this woman. And as I drank in the glow of happiness on her face, my fear that we had no future together seemed unfounded. I doubted she could have held me tighter.

She finally loosened her grip, but I kept her against my side. Abigail and Ethan began asking questions—too many to answer at once—and I looked down at myself. "We'll have plenty of time to talk. Right now I'm splattered with stinking mud, and you need to finish your breakfast and chores. Do that while I get washed and changed."

Abigail pulled at my arm. "May I stay home from school today?"

"Abby, despite thy excitement, thee needs to be in school," Elisabeth said.

"But—"

"I will be here when thee gets home," I told her.

She opened her mouth but then closed it when I raised an eyebrow at her. "Aye, Isaac."

"Did thee find thy uncle?" Ethan asked.

I'd hoped to not have to answer that question just yet, but getting it over with might be better. "I found his cabin, but he went to heaven a few weeks ago."

Abigail scowled. "He died?"

"He did. We can talk more later. I need to get cleaned up, and thee needs to ready thyself for school."

She hugged me again. "I don't care if thee is dirty. I'm just glad thee is home."

Elisabeth stared into my eyes when I handed Jon-Isaac back to her. "I'm so sorry."

I tried to smile and nodded. "Would thee heat some water for me?"

"Of course." She headed for the hearth.

Ethan raised his arms and then put them around my neck when I picked him up. "Did thee miss us too?"

I rested my forehead against his. "More than words can say."

A half hour later, I returned to the house clean and dressed in fresh clothing.

Ethan and Jon-Isaac played with their toys in the sitting

area while Elisabeth tidied up. She smiled at me as I hung the washtub on the wall by the hearth, but before I could go to her, Ethan jumped up and approached.

"Will thee build blocks with me?"

Jon-Isaac crawled to the couch, reared up on his knees, and used a seat cushion to push himself to his feet. "Zac!" He walked to the arm while holding on, then let go and slowly wobbled toward me. "Zac!"

I looked at Elisabeth. "Is he saying my name?"

"I believe so." She moved toward him, giving him space but staying close enough that she could catch him if he stumbled. "He started saying that yesterday. The walking without support started last night."

And if I'd gone on to Shamokin, I would have missed out on his first word—my own name, no less—and some of his first steps. I certainly needed no additional confirmation that coming home had been the right thing to do, but this only proved it more.

Ethan squatted beside me, clapping his hands. "Come on, Jon-Isaac. Just a few more steps."

Jon-Isaac grinned, showing his little teeth, then intentionally fell into my arms when I leaned over to pick him up. "Zac!"

Straightening, I held him close. Surely my love for him—and for the shaggy-haired little boy who looked up at me with pure adoration in his big brown eyes—couldn't have been any greater if they were children born to me. Jon-Isaac grabbed a handful of my hair, which hung loose since it was still damp from being washed, and babbled.

I bent down and lifted Ethan onto my opposite hip. "Were you boys good for Elisabeth while I was away?"

Ethan dropped his chin to his chest, glancing at her.

She neared us, looking even more tired than when I first got home. Still, even weary, she was the loveliest woman I'd ever seen.

"Did thee and Abigail misbehave?" I said.

He nodded. "But we apologized."

"Ah." I carried them to the braided rug and set them down. "Play awhile. I'll join thee in a few minutes."

Ethan went back to building with his blocks, while Jon-Isaac grabbed his teether from the floor and put it in his mouth.

Returning to Elisabeth, I raised my eyebrows. "A difficult week?"

She sighed. "Some days were better than others."

My heart went out to her, but I also couldn't help hoping that her taxing days had encouraged her to think of the good that could come from our marrying. "I'm sorry."

She dismissed that with a shake of her head. "No matter. I—"

"Isaac, will thee help me?" Ethan peered at me hopefully when I glanced over my shoulder. "Jon-Isaac keeps grabbing the blocks I need."

I took Elisabeth's hand in mine. Ethan's innocent coveting of my attention was endearing, but I wished for more time with her. I wanted us to discuss so much, both about our future and my time away.

"Go on," she said. "We'll have time this afternoon while they nap."

True. And if everything went as I hoped, we would need to get used to sharing each other with the children. 'Twasn't something most men my age envisioned when they considered their engagement and first year or two of marriage, but if we wed, it would be our reality—one I'd gladly welcome.

"Zac!" Jon-Isaac held out one hand toward me, opening and closing it. His teether now lay discarded on the rug next to him.

I laughed. "Coming. We can build with blocks until dinnertime if you like."

Elisabeth's blue eyes glimmered when I looked back to her. "Thee is such a good man. Thee is a blessing, to them and to me."

The sweetness of her countenance captivated me, but 'twas what she said, combined with everything that happened in the last week, that brought the sting of tears to my eyes. I'd longed to hear those words from her since returning to Horsham, and they were even more heartening than I'd imagined.

Aye, I loved these little boys, but naptime couldn't come quickly enough.

CHAPTER 30

Elisabeth

Never had I been so content as I went about my household tasks. In the last few days I'd fallen behind on them while struggling to keep the children and myself in good spirits and take care of the necessities, but now my initiative had returned. I felt less weary, and listening to Isaac and the boys play brought such quiet joy to my heart that no task seemed loathsome.

Once I'd finished in the kitchen area and bedchambers, I returned to the common room. Isaac sat on the floor against the couch while Ethan lay beside him amidst the children's blocks and carved wooden animals. Jon-Isaac, who'd been playing earlier, now lolled on Isaac's lap as he held a fistful of Isaac's hair in one hand and sucked his other thumb drowsily.

The sight of them roused happiness within me. "Looks

like somebody is all ready for his forenoon nap," I said, crouching next to Isaac. "Shall I take him?"

Isaac looked up from absently fingering Jon-Isaac's blond hair. Though he smiled, the sheen of his eyes belied it.

I lowered myself to my knees, tempted to ask if something was amiss, but that was an unnecessary question. His weeklong journey had to have been physically and emotionally exhausting. And though he had not expressed it, surely he despaired over the loss of his uncle.

As soon as I slid my hands under Jon-Isaac's arms, he squawked, arching his back and clutching Isaac's hair tighter.

"Leave him," Isaac said. "Once he's asleep, I'll put him to bed."

Jon-Isaac quieted the moment my hands released him, and I smiled. "There is no doubt as to what thee wants." Looking back at Isaac, I resisted the urge to question him. He wouldn't say much with Ethan there, so I stood to tidy the sitting area.

As I swept the floor, moving toward the front door to broom the dirt outside, I came upon a bag by the door. My first instinct was to set the broom aside and look inside, but I stopped myself. "Isaac, is this thine?"

"Aye. I forgot I brought that in," he said. "Thee can bring it here."

"What's in it?" Ethan stood, his eyes sparkling with interest.

Isaac watched as I neared. "Some of my parents' and uncle's belongings."

"Can I see them?" Ethan moved toward me.

"Aye. Some of what's inside is fragile, though."

I carefully set the bag on the floor and knelt beside Isaac. Ethan dropped down on the other side of me, reaching for the sack, but I stayed him. "Patience. Thee will get to see them, but we must be gentle."

Isaac one-handedly opened the sack and withdrew a rectangular object wrapped in more oilcloth, which he set aside. He removed the rest of the items one by one and set them on the floor. First two French Bibles, then a simple but beautiful trade-cloth gown and a box of Lenape jewelry. Finally, several sketches.

Ethan's eyes lit up. "Who made them?"

"My uncle Philippe was an artist." He shifted Jon-Isaac so he could use both hands to page through them. "He liked to draw the forest where he lived and the animals in it." After about ten drawings that depicted nature, the next one portrayed the finely detailed face of a young child with chin-length dark hair. "Can thee guess who that is?"

Ethan stared at it, then finally shook his head.

I recognized the child right away. "That is Isaac, when he was a very little boy."

He showed us the next picture, this one a side view of a lovely woman's face, neck, and shoulders. "And this is my mother."

I pursed my lips, trying to hold back a rush of tears. How amazing that he had such a gift—one that allowed him to see the mother he so wished he could remember—but knowing what he had lost had to strangle his heart each time he looked at it. Even more so than it did mine. "She is beautiful." A tear slipped down my cheek, and I quickly brushed it away.

Ethan scowled. "Why is thee crying?"

I stroked his hair. "I'm just happy for Isaac, that he has these things."

Isaac's jaw clenched as he showed us more drawings, one

of his father and two of a cabin, then he set the stack on the couch behind him. After glancing at Jon-Isaac, whose eyelids hung low, he touched my arm. "Would thee put these in the sack for me? I think he's ready for his nap." He stood with him still cradled in one arm, then headed for my bedchamber.

Ethan looked at me when Isaac closed the door behind him. "What's he doing?"

I forced a smile. "He probably wants to rock Jon-Isaac for a little while." That was a possibility, but I suspected otherwise. 'Twas more likely he wanted time to himself.

Ethan looked thoughtful, then returned to his blocks and animals. "I'm going to build a barn for when he comes back. He'll like that."

Such a sweet boy he was. "I'm sure he will."

While he got to work, I placed everything back in the sack and set it beside the couch where it would be safe. The broom I'd been using earlier caught my attention, and I resolved 'twould be best to resume my duties. Ethan was right there, and moreover, Isaac was in my bedchamber, a place where we certainly couldn't be alone together.

But, oh, how I longed to go to him.

Just when I feared Isaac had permanently joined Ethan for his nap that afternoon, the children's bedchamber door opened quietly and then closed. Moments later Isaac sat beside me on the couch.

I looked up from the framed portrait on my lap—the item we had not unwrapped earlier. His face gave little evidence of how he felt, unless he was feeling not much of anything. I doubted that. "I thought thee might have fallen asleep with him."

He chuckled. "That would mean giving up this time with thee. Never."

I didn't know what encouraged me more, the brightening of his disposition or the confirmation that he wanted time with me despite his weariness. And despite how I'd responded to—or, more aptly, skirted—his proposal. Lifting his hand from where it rested on his leg, I laced my fingers with his. "I'm so very sorry about Philippe." Already, my throat swelled.

He let out his breath slowly, his gaze fixed on the portrait. "He died about three weeks ago. Heart failure, the neighbor woman reckoned." He shook his head. "Three weeks, Beth. If I'd known sooner, I . . ." Standing, he paced away from me.

My heart ached for him. I set the portrait aside and got up to go to him.

He faced me. "Why? He was alive for twenty-two years of my life, and then only two weeks before I learned he existed, he died."

"I know. It seems terribly unfair."

He grit his teeth and shook his head again, focusing on something across the room. "Alas, but 'tis not. The Almighty has a plan, and far be it from me to question that. Nothing happens to us outside of his will and without his consent."

How many times I'd reminded myself of that in the last year. "But that doesn't allay the hurt."

"Nay." Tears pooled in his eyes, and he stepped closer, resting his hands on my sides and dropping his forehead to rest it against the top of my head.

The flutter in my middle tensed my muscles, but I stayed

myself from stepping back. Isaac needed me right now, and being close to him had never unsettled me before.

Of course, that had been when we were simply friends. Our relationship felt different now that he'd proposed marriage, and despite how Susannah had assured me, I didn't know what he would expect from me. That evoked pangs of the apprehension I'd felt with Hiram the last time he visited.

My chest tightened, and I inhaled and swallowed. Isaac wasn't Hiram, nor was he Linus, not in *any* way. Yet if I didn't take care, the aversion they triggered could imperil my relationship with him. Unsettled or not, I couldn't allow that.

Father, I need thy peace and wisdom.

Isaac lifted his head and released me. "It sounded like thy week wasn't easy either."

I missed his closeness right away, which confused me even more. I folded my hands at my waist but then dropped them to my sides when they ached at how tightly I twisted them. *Please. Still the unrest within me.*

"Tell me about it?"

The challenges I'd faced now seemed so much less significant, especially when compared to all he had endured. Complaining seemed absurd, even selfish. All the same, the genuine concern that lined his forehead told me he sincerely wanted to know.

"Abigail and Ethan quarreled several times, with each other and with me. They woke Jon-Isaac from his afternoon nap twice and then he was in a sour mood for the rest of the day." I shook my head, feeling like a telltale. "They weren't themselves with thee gone, and admittedly, I did not always respond in the most beneficial way."

When I dared to glance at him, he observed me sympathetically. "I'm sorry."

'Twasn't his fault. Moreover, unexpected good had come of it, and our discussing it now gave me the opportunity to bring up the decision I'd made, despite the apprehension I felt. "No matter. Thee is back now." I smiled, determined to hold his gaze as I spoke. "And if nothing else, thy absence helped me realize that as much as I wish to rear the children, I cannot imagine doing it without thee. The children love thee and need thee, and so do I."

His lips parted as he stared into my eyes. "Is thee saying that . . ."

I nodded. "I want to marry thee." That was, if he still wanted to marry me. "If thy proposal still stands."

The next thing I knew, he was swinging me around. I clung to him, unable to suppress a cry of surprise.

He laughed and set me back on my feet. "Of course it does." His joviality eased into earnestness as his hands moved to my waist. "And not just because thee needs a husband and the children a father. I want thee to be my wife." Just as Susannah said.

I grasped his arms more tightly, somehow thrilled, terrified, and guilt-pricked at once. "Even though . . ." Unable to finish, I stared at the buttons on his waistcoat.

"Beth, thee has been by my side for most of my life. 'Twould have been for all of it if thee had thy way. I want thee beside me for the rest of my days." He lifted my chin until I looked into his eyes again. "Nothing could change my feelings for thee. Even if thee were still uncertain today, my proposal would stand—for as long as necessary."

"Isaac," I whispered, then covered my mouth with my hand as happiness overwhelmed me. When he'd appeared in the doorway muddy and weary from arduous travel and so obviously elated to see us, I'd thought it impossible that I could love him more. Now the depth of his devotion proved that thought erroneous. Remembering his first words to me this morning, I rephrased, "Has thee any idea how much I love thee?"

He grinned and pressed his lips to my forehead. "Not as much as I love thee."

~

Isaac closed the door to the children's bedchamber after we tucked Abigail and Ethan into bed that night, then slipped his arm around my middle and turned me toward him. Clasping his hands behind me, he smiled.

A mix of angst and exhilaration twinged in my belly and stole my breath. While my mind exhorted me to put distance between us, my heart reminded me that 'twas Isaac who held me. Isaac who'd been my dearest friend for most of my life. Isaac who loved me and put my needs before his own. And Isaac whom I trusted implicitly. Fear of him had never played a part in our relationship, and I wasn't about to allow that to change. As the serenity of his expression eased the disquiet within me, I placed my hands on his upper arms.

"I cannot remember the last time I saw Mother so happy."

Nor could I. When we had visited her and Susannah that afternoon to request parental consent to marry, Mary had shed tears of joy that continued throughout our visit. Susannah's eyes had gleamed with delight as well, and she wasn't one to readily weep. "I agree."

He took my face in one hand, and the fluttering in my middle returned. No matter its reason, we were now close enough that he could kiss me. When I'd greeted him upon his return this morning, my sudden desire to feel his lips against mine had taken me aback, but now we were alone. Susannah had once warned that a tender kiss can easily gain in intensity, and I couldn't predict my response should that happen.

"Would thee like some apple pie?" I asked.

"Aye." He dropped his hand to my shoulder, then led me to the kitchen area.

I brought the pie, plates, and forks to the table. Once we each had a piece, I slid onto the bench beside him.

"Susannah wasn't as surprised as I thought she would be," he said after swallowing his first bite. "Is there any chance she already knew?"

I lowered the forkful I was about to put in my mouth. "Well, she didn't know, but she may have suspected. She visited on First Day afternoon, and I shared with her that thee had proposed. As we conversed, she helped me discern my feelings and afforded me much to think about."

His expression offered no intimation of his thoughts. "Thee was still unsure at that time?"

I had not meant for him to think— "Not because of thee. With only a few questions, she helped me see how much I care for and trust thee. My misgivings were with myself alone."

He set down his fork and placed his hand on mine. "There is no reason for thee to have misgivings. I know thy concerns, and I will give thee the time thee needs—however long it takes. If thee wants me to sleep on a trundle in thy bedchamber, I will. If thee wants me to sleep out here—"

"Isaac. Thee will be my husband." And for that reason, I needed to be able to discuss such things with him, even if it was uncomfortable at first—which it was. I drew a breath, determined to speak with confidence. "I don't want thee to sleep on a trundle . . . or out here. I want . . ." But what did I want? In this case, I wasn't sure—at least not yet. "I want us to be husband and wife . . . as God intended it."

He squeezed my hand gently. "And we will be. As it is, 'twill likely be two months before Meeting can declare us clear to be married and our marriage can be orderly accomplished. So we will bring this before the Almighty in prayer each day and allow his mercy and grace to lead us. Then if thee still needs time once we're married, thee will have it."

The compassion on his face as he watched me intently brought tears of gratefulness to my eyes. How I cherished him. "And I want thee to be happy."

"I will be. I love thee, and I love the children. That doesn't mean our life together will always be easy. Like all families, we will encounter difficult times. But with Christ at the center of our marriage, we will face nothing we cannot abide together."

How right he was.

Giving his hand a squeeze in return, I stood and retrieved my Bible from the table next to the couch. It opened to the page marker at Ecclesiastes 4, and I removed the cord we had braided from his hair, my hair, and dyed-red yarn. Even after twelve years, the embroidery thread tied around each end still bound it securely, just as the love of God bound Christ, Isaac, and me.

I set the Bible back in its place and returned to the bench. After sitting, I took his hand and placed the cord in it. "A cord of three strands is not easily broken."

Staring into my eyes, he pressed the cord between our palms. "Neither will we be."

Isaac

First Day, Fifth Month 1st, 1757
Philadelphia, Pennsylvania

The sun shone from a cloudless sky as I led Ethan through the crowd gathered outside Philadelphia Meeting. David and his sons had followed us out of the meeting house, but a glance over my shoulder confirmed they'd stopped somewhere to chat with Friends. After several minutes of searching, Ethan and I still hadn't found Elisabeth, Abigail, and Jon-Isaac. They had left through the door closest to where they sat on the women's side, while we'd exited through the door nearest our own seats.

Even my stature offered little assistance today. Far too many people gathered in groups or moved about within the brick wall surrounding the meeting house grounds. Finally, I lifted Ethan high against my side so he could see above people's heads. "Does thee see them anywhere?"

Holding his hat against the spring breeze, he scanned the crowd. "Nay." He pointed toward High Street. "Aunt Deborah, Rachel, and Bernice are over there."

Elisabeth had been sitting with them, so heading in their direction seemed reasonable.

"Isaac!" An elderly female voice carried over the din of Friends.

I turned to find Lydia Stanton leaning her thin frame on a cane as she slowly moved toward us in a dark-gray gown. Her hair was now pure white, but her twinkling brown eyes told me she was as sharp of mind as ever.

"Lydia. I was hoping we would see thee today. How is thee faring?"

"Well enough. I had a fall in the garden this week, but I'm on the mend, praise be to God." Stopping before us, she peered up at me. "I was ever so sorry to miss thy wedding. Each year I spend a few months in Virginia with my daughter, and last year I departed a month earlier than usual so I could be there for the birth of my first great-grandchild." Her gaze shifted from me to Ethan. "This must be one of the children thee and Elisabeth adopted?"

I lowered him to my hip. "This is Ethan. He's the best little helper a blacksmith could ask for."

"How delightful." She patted his arm. "How old is thee, young man?"

He smiled. "Five and a half."

"Ah. I'm sure thee is a fine helper. Thee has a sister and brother too?"

He nodded.

"And how old are they?" she asked me.

"Abigail will be nine next month, and Jon-Isaac is twenty-two months."

"How wonderful. My nephew tells me that thee continues to assist with the Friendly Association. Is that what has brought thee to the city?"

I set Ethan on the ground. "Aye, my intent is to attend as many meetings as possible. Most times I'm here for only a day or two, but with the peace conference in Lancaster next month, Israel Pemberton asked if I could afford more days for planning this time. With the weather now so fair, I brought Elisabeth and the children along, and we're spending a week with David and Deborah."

"Israel has said what an asset thee has been to the Association. Thy counsel has been indispensable."

I hoped so. Thus far, the Association had not been able to accomplish all it desired, mostly due to the underhandedness of Pennsylvania's government, but we continued to strive for peace and fairness. "I've decided not to attend any more conferences for a while, but I'm honored that God has seen fit to use me and that Israel has welcomed my assistance."

Ethan pointed. "There. I see them."

About ten paces away, Elisabeth approached with Abigail, who carried Jon-Isaac at her side. Elisabeth's cheeks were rosy, likely from the extraordinary warmth of the day and the close quarters inside, but her cheery smile assuaged any concern for her health. In fact, she couldn't have looked lovelier in the laced-bodice plum-colored gown and petticoat she'd picked up from the mantua-maker yesterday, a gift from David and Deborah.

Jon-Isaac squirmed in Abigail's arms. "Papa!"

Abigail lowered him, and he ran toward me as fast as the

little legs hidden beneath his skirted frock would carry him. She followed closely in case he stumbled.

I lifted him into my arms, then placed my hand on Abigail's shoulder. Elisabeth sidled up to me and took my arm as I made introductions, and Lydia's doting shifted from the children to her.

"Such a pleasure to meet thee, dear. Isaac told me about thee last spring when you all were here, and I knew thee was special to him. How thrilled I was to receive the invitation to thy wedding last summer. By the time my son sent it on to me and it arrived in Virginia, though, your marriage had taken place. But learning you had married brought such joy to my heart."

We continued to converse for a few more minutes, then parted ways. I led Elisabeth and the children toward the meeting house, placing Jon-Isaac on the ground when he wriggled to get down and walk. Abigail took his hand, and Elisabeth guided Ethan. As we neared where David and Deborah stood not far away with their younger children, Lydia called to me.

She again approached, and I quickened my pace to her so she wouldn't need to walk farther than necessary.

"I almost forgot to ask," she said. "After thy visit to me last spring, thee sent word that thee might have found thy father's brother. Was thee able to do so?"

I smiled, though sadness prodded me. "I found his homestead, but he'd already passed on. And from what I could determine, he and my father probably had no other relatives in the Colonies."

Her brows drew together in sympathy. "What about thy mother's family? Did the name of her brother help thee at all?"

It had, at least in determining who they were. I doubted I would ever go in search of them again, but I hadn't lost all optimism. "It did, but I believe her family is now far to the west, likely in Kithanink or the Ohio Valley. Even so, my work with the Friendly Association could someday bring us together." Considering Sukachgook's vile conduct, that was improbable, but I could hope. There was that of God in all of us.

She clucked her tongue. "I know how much thee hoped to find family."

The familiar sound of Jon-Isaac's giggle lightened my spirit, and I looked over to where Elisabeth and the children still congregated with David's family. Abigail again held Jon-Isaac, and David's son Matthew poked at Jon-Isaac's ribs, eliciting more baby laughs from him. Beside her, Elisabeth and Ethan joined in the joviality as she held his hand.

Elisabeth slid her other hand over her belly, from the side obviously rounded with the child we would welcome in three months. Then she smiled sweetly when our gazes met.

"I did find family," I said, returning my attention to Lydia.

A family I never could have imagined but loved more deeply than I'd ever thought possible.

A Cord of Three Strands
Discussion Questions

1. By the end of chapter one, Isaac Lukens has endured much heartache—physically and emotionally. He struggles with regret, particularly about the way he left Horsham, yet when the difficulties of his life overwhelm him, it's his family and close-knit community he longs for. Have you ever been in a situation like this, as either the one giving or receiving love and grace? How has this affected how you interact with others who've hurt you?

2. Elisabeth Alden resents her father's insistence that she keep a secret from their community. Speaking the truth is a stalwart tenet of the Society of Friends, and she fears that her keeping silent may put others in danger. Then her family takes in two runaway slaves and hides them from the men who are pursuing them. Elisabeth's father reminds her that there is a season for everything, including a time to speak truth and a time to conceal it. Do you believe this is true? Why? What would you have done in her situation? What would you have done in her father's position?

3. Before Jonathan Alden dies, Isaac gives him his word that he will care for Elisabeth and the children. Do you think he does this out of guilt, duty, or love (or perhaps a combination of these)? Did you expect that he would keep his word? Why or why not?

4. Elisabeth and Isaac's friendship is strained after Isaac first returns to Horsham. When do you think her resentment of him begins to wane, and what events lead to the strengthening of their relationship?

5. After Isaac goes to Lydia Stanton hoping for information on his parents, he asks Elisabeth, "How is it we can miss people so terribly even when we have no memory of them?" She responds, "Our minds may forget but our hearts do not?" Have you ever experienced what Isaac describes here—missing someone you've never met (or you've met but can't remember)? What do you think causes this type of feeling?

6. Elisabeth and Hiram Biddle have a complicated relationship. She cares for him and he for her, and it was common for marriages to be built on necessity and friendship during this time period. What do you think you would have done in her situation? Married for the sake of necessity and hoped for the best, or refused a marriage that would be "weakened by disunity"? Why?

7. Elisabeth talks about feeling "a stop in her heart." This is a Quaker term that describes felt but not easily understood scruples about an activity or action, although this feeling certainly isn't limited to those of the Quaker faith. Describe a

time when you felt a stop in your heart. Did you pay heed to it or ignore it? Looking back, would you do that again?

8. Isaac tells Elisabeth that the Lenape who had allied with the French call him Walks In Two Worlds, and that he originally despised the name but now realizes its truth. Have you ever felt like you walked in two different worlds, a part of each but not fully belonging in either? And if so, have you found a place where—or, as in Isaac's case, a person with whom—you belong despite it all?

9. At the end of the story, Isaac has found family, but not in the way he'd originally hoped for. In your life, with whom have you found family—either biological or otherwise—in a way you never expected?

10. Who is (are) your favorite character(s) in the story? Why? Which character do you relate to the most? Why?

11. What was your favorite scene in the book? Which was the least favorite?

12. What is your greatest takeaway from reading this story?

Author's Note

A Cord of Three Strands is a combination of fact and fiction. While Isaac and Elisabeth are fictional, some facets of the story, including several characters and Friends' role in relations with the Lenape and in refuting slavery, are not.

In the late-seventeenth century, proprietor William Penn opened Pennsylvania to Europeans enduring religious persecution. Among those who fled to Penn's "religious experiment" were Jan and Maria Thiessen Lucken, Dutch Mennonites who had found some religious tolerance in Crefeld, Germany. They reached Pennsylvania in October 1683 and settled the village of Germantown, which is now a part of Philadelphia. Peter Lukens, my eighth-great-grandfather and a son of Jan and Maria, came to Horsham Township, at that time a wilderness, around 1717.

The Lukenses, who at some point had joined the Society of Friends, were prominent Pennsylvanians, both in societal contributions and as devout Quakers. One interesting family member was Seneca Lukens, a well-known clockmaker and a grandson of Peter Lukens. His intriguing first name led me to consider the family's connection to Indian tribes (at the time, the Seneca lived in northern Pennsylvania and southern New York). From the possible Native American connection, Isaac Lukens—a half-Lenape, half-white young man who had been reared by Horsham Friends—made his way into a dream I had after an evening of genealogy research.

Further study on the family and the Society of Friends revealed men and women who followed Christ's instruction and example no matter the cost. Mennonites and Friends were the first colonists to denounce slavery and the gross mistreatment of Indian tribes, and Friends were instrumental in forging peace between Pennsylvania and the province's tribes, namely the Lenape, during the French and Indian War.

It is my hope that Isaac and Elisabeth's story embodies Friends' devotion to truth, equality, and love for others, as well as the plight of the Lenape people during a turbulent time in American history.

Much research went into this book. I have made every effort to write as accurately as possible, and at times had to make decisions about some facets of the story. Any errors within the text are my own. (History nerd alert: See www.christydistler.com/acts-research-resources for the full list of my research materials and resources. An abbreviated list is available at the end of this book.)

Spellings of Indian village names and the valley of Wyomink vary by source and even differ within the same source due to use of historical documents. I have employed spellings used in Harvey and Smith's *A History of Wilkes-Barre, Luzerne County, Pennsylvania*, choosing those that seem most common and closest to Lenape pronunciation.

Spellings of Lenape and other Indian names were

selected based on the commonness of their usage in historical documents and research materials. The Lenape language used is from Winton, Zeisberger, and Anthony's *A Lenâpé–English Dictionary* and Brown and Rementer's *Conversational Lenape*.

Scripture verses are from the 1599 Geneva Bible, which was used regularly by Friends and Mennonites during the seventeenth and eighteenth centuries.

In an interesting turn of events, I have recently learned, through Hatboro historian David Shannon, that Seneca Lukens was more likely named for the Roman philosopher Lucius Annaeus Seneca than for the Seneca tribe. A bit disappointing, but all is not lost. The imagination, whether piqued by truth or speculation, is a wonderful thing.

THE FRENCH AND INDIAN WAR

A Cord of Three Strands takes place during the French and Indian War (1754–1763). This war, although less renowned than the Revolutionary War (1775–1783), was a pivotal point in American history. The French controlled Canada and had their sights set on what is now the U.S. Midwest. They hoped to thwart English expansion to the west, especially in Pennsylvania, and tried to prevent the English from buying land that belonged to the Pennsylvania tribes—primarily the Lenape (called the Delaware by European settlers), the Susquehannock, and the Shawanese.

The Lenape were already distraught by the loss of their lands in eastern Pennsylvania, particularly the infamous Walking Purchase, and the gross mistreatment of the tribe by Pennsylvania's government and settlers impelled them to ally with the French and wreak havoc on the frontier to the north and west of Philadelphia.

While the non-Quaker population called for the raising of a militia for self-defense, the pacifistic Friends in the Pennsylvania Assembly refused. This political struggle finally ended in May 1756 when six prominent Friends resigned from the Assembly, allowing Pennsylvania to embrace military defenses.

THE FRIENDLY ASSOCIATION

To address the violence on the frontier, in 1756 Friends in Philadelphia formed the Friendly Association for Regaining and Preserving Peace with the Indians by Pacific Measures, under the leadership of Israel Pemberton, a former assemblyman. This group strove to forge peace with the Lenape through treating them with respect and love, working to compensate them for their losses, and acting as a liaison between them and the government. The Friendly Association continued to meet with the Lenape and the Six Nations (who controlled the Lenape) throughout the French and Indian War period, providing needed provisions and assisting with multiple peace treaties, some of which were more successful than others.

In 1758, Pennsylvania passed an act that created provincial stores to provide supplies to the Indians at reasonable prices. In addition, profit from the stores' sales would go toward the cost of schoolmasters for the Indians and other tribal expenses. The Friendly Association offered support, hoping the stores would benefit the tribes, but various problems developed over the next few years. After the outbreak of Pontiac's War (1763), the stores closed.

Quaker support of the Friendly Association dwindled in the early 1760s, and after Pontiac's War, so did Quaker influence in Indian affairs. The British Ministry now forbid those who had no official capacity to engage with the Indians, and while Israel Pemberton and Friendly Association leaders were still concerned for the Lenape people's welfare, many Friends became discouraged by the group's inadequate results and stopped contributing funds. Eventually the group could no longer carry out its mission and stopped meeting.

Over the years since, the Friendly Association has garnered both praise and criticism from historians, depending on their viewpoint. Many have concluded that whatever the outcome, the group certainly had the tribes' interests in mind and truly hoped to bring about peace during a turbulent time.

Still, the Friendly Association couldn't fix what the Pennsylvania government had destroyed and had no intention of mending. Despite the group's inability to accomplish all it hoped to, there is no doubt that the Friendly Association had its successes as well. The group did what it could to alleviate suffering, and one can only wonder how many other lives would have been claimed during the war—both Indian and white—had it not been for their dedication.

THE LENAPE TODAY

The Pennsylvania government's treatment of Indian tribes did not improve with time. By 1800, the Lenape had been forced out of Pennsylvania and into Ohio. They continued to be pushed westward, especially after the Indian Removal Act of 1830, which ordered that all Indians be moved west of the Mississippi River. In 2018 Native Americans made up only 0.2 percent of Pennsylvania's population (2018 United States Census).

The Delaware Tribe of Indians is now headquartered in Oklahoma, but Lenape culture is kept alive in the Delaware River Valley by museums, cultural centers, and individuals. For more information, visit:

The Museum of Indian Culture
Allentown, Pennsylvania
www.museumofindianculture.org

The Lenape Village/Churchville Nature Center
Churchville, Pennsylvania
www.churchvillenaturecenter.org

Woodruff Museum of Indian Artifacts
Bridgeton Free Public Library
Bridgeton, New Jersey
www.bridgetonlibrary.org/museum-2

The Nanticoke and Lenape Confederation Learning Center and Museum
Bridgeton, New Jersey
www.nanticokelenapemuseum.org

Delaware Tribe of Indians
www.delawaretribe.org

RESOURCES

Alderfer, E. Gordon. *The Montgomery County Story.* Norristown, PA: Commissioners of Montgomery County, 1951.

Arnold, Lisa Parry. *Thee & Me: A Beginner's Guide to Early Quaker Records.* Lisa Parry Arnold, 2014.

Bauman, Richard. *For the Reputation of Truth; Politics, Religion, and Conflict among the Pennsylvania Quakers, 1750–1800.* Baltimore: Johns Hopkins Press, 1971.

Brown, Janefer, and Jim Rementer. *Conversational Lenape.* The Delaware Tribe of Indians, 1999.

Bulletin of Friends' Historical Society of Philadelphia. Philadelphia: Leeds & Biddle, 1906.

Butterbaugh, Kelly Ann. *Upper Saucon Township and Coopersburg.* Chicago: Arcadia Publishing, 2010.

Crane, Elaine Forman. *The Diary of Elizabeth Drinker: The Life Cycle of an Eighteenth-Century Woman.* Boston: Northeastern University Press, 1994.

Harvey, Oscar Jewell, and Ernest Gray Smith. *A History of Wilkes-Barré, Luzerne County, Pennsylvania: From Its First Beginnings to the Present Time, including Chapters of Newly-discovered Early Wyoming Valley History, Together with Many Biographical Sketches and Much Genealogical Material.* Wilkes-Barre, PA: Raeder Press, 1909.

Hazard, Samuel. *Hazard's Register of Pennsylvania, Devoted to the Preservation of Facts and Documents, and Every Kind of Useful Information Respecting the State of Pennsylvania.* Philadelphia: W. F. Geddes, 1828.

Jenkins, Howard M. *Historical Collections Relating to Gwynedd.* Philadelphia: Published by the author, 1897.

Lippincott, Horace Mather. *Early Philadelphia, Its People, Life and Progress.* Philadelphia: J. B. Lippincott & Company, 1917.

MacMaster, Richard K., with Samuel L. Horst and Robert F. Ulle. *Conscience in Crisis: Mennonites and Other Peace Churches in America, 1739–1789.* Eugene, Oregon: Wipf and Stock Publishers, 2001.

Martindale, Joseph C., MD. *A History of the Townships of Byberry and*

Moreland, in Philadelphia, Pa., from Their Earliest Settlement by Whites to the Present Day. Philadelphia: T. Ellwood Zell, 1867.

Mathews, Alfred, and Austin N. Hungerford. *History of the Counties of Lehigh and Carbon, in the Commonwealth of Pennsylvania.* Philadelphia: Everts & Lemuels, 1884.

Michener, Ezra. *A Retrospect of Early Quakerism; Being Extracts from the Records of Philadelphia Yearly Meeting.* Philadelphia: T. Ellwood Zell, 1860.

Myers, Albert Cook. *Quaker Arrivals at Philadelphia, 1683–1750, Being a List of Certificates of Removal Received at Philadelphia Monthly Meeting of Friends.* Philadelphia: Ferris & Leach, 1902.

Osterhaut, Anne M. *The Most Learned Woman in America: A Life of Elizabeth Graeme Fergusson.* State College, PA: The Pennsylvania State University, 2004.

Parrish, Samuel. *Some Chapters in the History of the Friendly Association for Regaining and Preserving Peace with the Indians by Pacific Measures.* Philadelphia: Published by Friends Historical Association, 1877.

Smith, Charles Harper. *The Settlement of Horsham Township.* Ambler, PA: Trinity Press, 1975.

Tantaquidgeon, Gladys. *Folk Medicine of the Delaware and Related Algonkian Indians.* Harrisburg, PA: Pennsylvania Historical and Museum Commission, 1972.

Turner, Edmund Raymond. *The Negro in Pennsylvania: Slavery–Servitude–Freedom 1639–1861.* Washington, DC: The American Historical Association, 1910.

Turner, Edmund Raymond. *Slavery in Pennsylvania.* Baltimore: The Lord Baltimore Press, 1911.

Wallace, Anthony F. C. *King of the Delawares: Teedyuscung, 1700–1763.* Philadelphia: University of Pennsylvania Press, 1949.

Ward, Matthew C. *Breaking the Backcountry: The Seven Years' War in Virginia and Pennsylvania, 1754–1765.* Pittsburgh: University of Pittsburgh Press, 2003.

Watson, John F. *Annals of Philadelphia and Pennsylvania in the Olden Time.* Philadelphia: Elijah Thomas, 1857.

Weslager, C. A. *The Delaware Indians; a History.* New Brunswick, NJ: Rutgers University Press, 1972.

Winton, Daniel G., David Zeisberger, and Albert Seqaqkind Anthony. *A*

Lenâpé–English Dictionary. Philadelphia: Historical Society of Pennsylvania, 1881.

Woody, Thomas, PhD. *Early Quaker Education in Pennsylvania.* New York: Teacher's College, Columbia University, 1920.

ACKNOWLEDGMENTS

My first and foremost thanks, as always, go to Jesus Christ—my blessed Savior, sovereign Lord, and closest friend; the author and finisher of my faith; and the giver of any talent I may have. *Soli Deo gloria.*

Many thanks to my mom for being the greatest supporter of my writing (and, in true mom form, everything I do) and for introducing me to genealogy, which ultimately planted the seed of this book.

Much gratitude to my husband and children for giving me time to write, and for not complaining when dinner was late because I got lost in another century. And many thanks to my pups for being my writing partners (and leg warmers on cold days).

Anyone can write a book, but it takes a village to bring it to life. Unending thanks to all those who have helped take this story from idea to completed book:

Marlene Bagnull, for your friendship and invaluable knowledge of all things writing and publishing related.

Jean Bloom, for your exceptional editing skills, and Hannah Linder, for your graphic art prowess.

Kim M. Clark, for your friendship and hard-earned publishing knowledge.

J. M. Hochstetler, for your wonderful encouragement and endorsement.

My amazing critique partners (Verna, Vicki, Lori, Lisa, Carolyn, and the rest of the Thursday-night group; Lee Carver, Tanya Eavenson, Autumn MacArthur, and Ginger Solomon; and Joy Avery Melville), for your faithful friendship, wise input, much-needed laughs, and continuous encouragement.

Pegg Thomas, for providing the hand-dyed, hand-spun wool for the cord of three strands pictured on the back cover.

Hatboro historian David Shannon and Millbrook Society; Pete Choate and Horsham Preservation and Historical Association; and the staff at Friends Historical Library, Graeme Park, Churchville Nature Center, Historic Fallsington, Pennsbury Manor, Colonial Pennsylvania Plantation, and Moland House, for your dedication to keeping history alive and for answering all my questions.

The Friends of Horsham Monthly Meeting, many of whom have now left this life for eternity, for welcoming a curious teenager as family—and not just because I was distantly related. The love, knowledge, and wisdom you imparted over the years has followed me throughout my life and compelled me to give new life to Horsham's past.

Finally, a sincere thank-you to all my prayer warriors. You know who you are, and I'm forever grateful to do life with you.

About the Author

For as long as she can remember, Christy Distler has dreamed her most vivid dreams with her eyes wide open. Names became people—people who didn't exist in this time and place but couldn't have been more real in her heart and mind. So she did the only rational thing: gave them a voice by writing fiction.

Christy's novels, whether historical or contemporary, delve into betrayal and reconciliation, faith and grace, and involve the intertwining of cultures. When not writing, she works as an editor for publishing houses and independent authors.

Obsession with words (and history) aside, she lives with her family in Pennsylvania.

To connect, visit www.christydistler.com or scan this
QR code:

Single mom Janna Carpenter moves back to Lancaster County where she grew up, ready to start over with her young daughter. And her plans don't include another relationship.

But when her long-lost friendship with Luke Martin, now a widowed Old Order Mennonite father, rekindles into love, both will need to rely on their faith to guide them.

CHAPTER 1

A New Beginning

IF WHAT DIDN'T KILL you made you stronger, Janna could have singlehandedly upended the fifty-foot pine tree that had sliced through the second floor of her new home. As it was, she struggled to get a handle on her racing mind while steering her Honda CR-V to the curb and then shoving the gearshift into park.

"Mama!" Kayla's wail from the backseat suggested tears would follow. "What happened to our house?"

What happened was obvious. Horrifyingly so. But how? Everything had been fine twelve hours ago when they returned to their old apartment for the night before bringing the last carload of belongings to Akron this morning. The white clapboard house with its green trim, quaint front porch, and small flower garden had even felt like home already.

Oh no. Mrs. Bollinger. Their sweet seventy-something landlady who lived on the other side of the twin house had been sitting in a chair on the front porch when they left last night. Where was she now? Surely not inside. Yellow caution tape had been strung from the rightmost porch post to the street sign at the left corner of the property and along the side street. But had she been hurt? The tree barely touched her side of the house, but who knew what damage was inside.

Janna pulled the keys from the ignition, then glanced in the sideview mirror before getting out of the car. Hot, humid air enveloped her as she opened the back door.

Still in her booster seat, Kayla clung to her ratty stuffed rabbit and stared past her with wide eyes. "Our house, Mama."

Janna's chest tightened at the raw anguish in her daughter's voice. She released the seat's five-point harness and tried to portray a calm she didn't feel. "I know. But it'll be all right. Come on." She helped Kayla out, then held her hand as they crossed the street. A white pickup truck and a red-striped fire department SUV sat in front of the neighboring house, but no one was in sight.

Stopping where the sidewalk met the brick walkway, Janna stared up at the pine that had fallen sideways onto the roof above three of the four second-story windows. The middle two windows had cracked, but the one to the left of them fared much worse. Pine branches had broken through the frame from the inside, thrusting shards of glass and the old air conditioner onto the porch roof.

The tightness in her chest surged into her throat. That was the window of the bedroom Kayla had chosen.

"Don't go any closer!"

She turned at the deep voice's warning, clutching Kayla to her side. Two men, one maybe forty and the other old enough to be his father, approached from around the right side of the house. The younger one wore a navy-blue T-shirt with a fire department crest on the chest, so they had to be the drivers of the pickup and SUV.

The older one smoothed his thinning white hair. "You Joanna Carpenter?"

They knew her name—sort of. A good sign. "Janna, yes. We moved in yesterday. Is Mrs. Bollinger okay?"

The other, nearly a head taller, nodded once as the two stopped a few feet away. "She's fine. Gertie's outlived cancer twice. A tree in her roof barely fazed her"—he glanced down at Kayla—"though she was sure glad you weren't here. She wanted to call you but misplaced your number."

"Where is she?"

"At her son's place. A tree service is coming today, but no one can go in the house till it's inspected and deemed structurally stable."

Ugh. Not what she wanted to hear. "We can't even get our things from the first floor?" Only their bedframes, mattresses, and a dresser had been carried upstairs by the movers. "Almost everything's still downstairs."

The older one scrunched his face. "Sorry, hon. Justin's with the fire department. He can take your number and let you know what the inspector says. Probably won't be till Monday, though. Do you have somewhere to go?"

Hardly. Their old apartment was an hour and a half away, and she'd turned in the keys that morning. As well, everything she owned, save what filled their small car, was held hostage by the house.

"How'd that tree fall down?" Kayla scowled up at it, now looking more curious than upset. That wouldn't last long.

Justin leaned down and rested his hands on his knees. "We had a bad storm here last night. The ground was soft and wet from the rain, and the strong wind blew it over." Straightening again, he met Janna's gaze with concerned eyes. "Do you have somewhere to go?"

If only she could think straight. "Well . . . no." And she didn't want to go far in case they could get into the house sooner. Staying at a motel was an option, but finding a room in Lancaster County in late June would be nearly impossible. Except for one possibility. "Is the Flying Dutchman still the least-expensive place around?"

Both men eyed her. "It is," the older one said, "but for good reason. You don't want to stay there."

Not at all if its clientele were anything like they were years ago. But after paying the early termination penalty on their apartment, the movers' fee, and the first month's rent here, she needed to scrimp until she got paid again.

"It'll be fine . . . till we figure something out." Which she needed to do elsewhere. Swallowing down the lump in her throat, she returned her gaze to Justin. "If I give you my number, will you call me as soon as you know anything about the house?"

And for nothing else.

Goodness. She had no right thinking that way about him. Not every guy was bad news. Justin had to be fifteen years older than her, and he seemed nice enough. He also spoke with a hint of the accent common to *Deitsch* speakers, so he was probably Mennonite and married even though he wasn't wearing a wedding band.

"Sure." He pulled a pad of paper and pen from the back

pocket of his jeans and handed it to her. "Anything else we can do?"

Besides wave a magic wand and make this all go away? She clenched her jaw as she wrote out her name and cell phone number. "No. Thank you." She handed him the paper and pen, then grabbed Kayla's hand. "Come on, honey."

Kayla pulled away, her blue eyes alarmed below the curly wisps of damp strawberry-blond hair stuck to her forehead. "Where are we going? My toys are inside."

Janna picked her up and spoke quietly as she crossed the street. "I know. But we can't go inside the house right now. They'll let us know when we can." Thank goodness Kayla's favorites were in the car. "We have Rabbit and your blanket. We'll get the rest as soon as we can."

"But . . . Mama, noooo! I want . . . I want . . . Noooo!"

By the time they were both in the car, Janna was soaked with perspiration and wanted to cry just as hard as her wailing five-year-old in the backseat. She pulled away from the curb, only to slam on the brakes when a car horn blared alongside her. As soon as the street was clear, she headed toward Main Street.

Somehow, in less than twenty minutes, their fairy-tale new beginning had turned into a nightmare.

Ten minutes later, Janna turned off Wanner Road and onto Division Highway. Kayla had finally stopped crying and now clutched her rabbit and blanket as she leaned sideways against the headrest of her booster seat. Another ten minutes and they'd be at the Flying Dutchman. If nothing else, renting a room would give Kayla a place to take a nap—much needed after the move yesterday and their late night—while Janna decided what to do next. They had some clothing and food in the car, but not what they'd need for even a few days at a motel.

Suddenly, the car sputtered and slowed. Janna released the gas pedal and pressed it again, but nothing happened. Although K-LOVE still played through the speakers, the air conditioner blew warmer air and their speed gradually decreased.

"Mama?" Kayla already sounded sleepy.

"Hold on, Kay. Something's not right with the car." She glanced down at the dashboard. The only warning light lit was the low-fuel indicator, but that one hadn't gone out since the gas gauge stopped working six months ago. Since then, she'd been watching the trip meter to make sure she filled the tank every three hundred miles.

Except the full mileage was displayed instead of the trip mileage. "Please, no," she whispered as she tapped the trip meter button.

Three hundred and sixty-six miles.

No, no, no. Could this day get any worse?

"Mama? My tummy hurts."

What? *Oh, please not now.* A glimpse of Kayla's pale face in the rearview mirror confirmed her fear. Carsickness. Apparently, the day could get worse. Much worse. All because she'd taken hilly, curvy Farmersville Road so she wouldn't have to drive past the house where she and Mom had lived for six years of her childhood. "Okay, honey. We have to pull over anyway."

The car slowed even more as they climbed a hill, then Christian Aid Ministries' white wooden sign appeared on the opposite side of the road. Steering was much more difficult now, but if she could just get into the parking lot, they'd be safer than if she stopped on the shoulder.

"Please, God. Please, God," she whispered. "Just a little farther." At least no vehicles were oncoming.

The car was going too slow to make it fully into the parking lot. Cutting the turn into the driveway as soon as possible, she maneuvered the barely rolling car onto the grass between the sign and the bush alongside the exit lane.

Safe. Now to help Kayla.

She got out and opened the back door. Kayla peered at her through half-closed eyes, her usually pink cheeks almost colorless. What to do, what to do? Janna didn't want her to get sick in the car, but the late-morning sun beat down from a hazy sky and the temperature was already in the low nineties. Hardly comfortable for anyone, let alone a child who didn't feel well.

"Hello! Are you needing help?"

An all-black carriage—Old Order Mennonite—now sat on the other side of the car in the parking lot's exit lane, and its passenger was leaning her head out the side door. Before Janna could answer, the stout sixty-something woman wearing a muted pink dress climbed out. "Are you all right? Going by the look on your face, you're not."

Not by a long shot. "My daughter's carsick. And we ran out of gas." *Oh, and we're homeless.* She helped Kayla out of her seat. "Don't get out yet. Just sit on the floor with your legs out the door. If you need to get sick, tell me and we'll get to the grass."

Kayla nodded, still clinging to her rabbit, and sat down as instructed. Janna squatted and smoothed her hair back from her face.

The woman rounded the car door with a black thermos and a folded white handkerchief in one hand, then opened the thermos and poured water on the handkerchief. "My nephew used to get carsick whenever we hired a van, it seemed. Putting a cool cloth on his forehead or the back of his neck always helped. Here."

Janna took the offered handkerchief without looking away from Kayla. "Thank you." She wiped her daughter's face, then folded the handkerchief in half and placed it on the back of her neck, beneath her long ponytail.

"Can you call your husband to bring you some gas?" The woman dragged the back of her arm across her forehead, then adjusted the white head covering she wore over her graying dark hair. With dress sleeves that came below her elbows and black stockings and shoes on, she had to be sweltering.

"I . . . no. We just moved here and don't have family nearby."

"And a big tree fell on our house last night," Kayla added.

The woman gasped. "Oh my. Is that right?"

"Well, we weren't in it at the time." Janna stood, then looked into the woman's kind face for the first time—a face she knew well. "Malinda Martin?" No wonder the voice had sounded familiar.

"*Ya.* Have we . . ." She smiled brightly. "Janna. Oh my. We had no idea you were back in these parts." Malinda pulled her into a tight embrace.

Both were sweaty, but Janna didn't care. She needed a hug, and Malinda had always had a way of making things all right. "Just as of today," she said when they released each other.

Crazy. What were the odds that someone from the family that had once practically raised her would come to her rescue—just like they had when she was only a year older than Kayla. "I planned on stopping by once we'd moved in." Her lame excuse only made her feel worse. She should've done that long before now.

Malinda's grin didn't fade a bit. "Come home with us. *Mamm* and Luke will be so happy to see you, and he's got a little boy about your daughter's age."

Mamm and Luke. What about *Daadi* Eli? Her not mentioning him could only mean—

"What's your name, dear one?" Malinda bent forward.

"Kayla. But Mama sometimes calls me Kay." She held up the rabbit. "This is Rabbit."

"Janna, we always have gas on the farm. Luke can bring you back here with some and get your car driving again." She returned her attention to Kayla. "Have you ever ridden in a carriage?"

Kayla's face brightened. "No. But I love horses. Can we, Mama?"

Janna fought to rein in the conflicting emotions that threatened to overwhelm her. Malinda's offer of help was a huge blessing, but she hadn't seen or spoken to the Martins since she and her mother moved away almost fourteen years ago—not that she hadn't tried at first. "Are you sure? I wouldn't want to impose."

"Impose?" Malinda shook her head, her brown eyes crinkling with a combination of what looked like disbelief and sadness. "Never. And *Gott* calls us to show mercy to those in need. Please. Will you come?"

Only a fool would refuse such kindness, no matter how

awkward this might be. Nodding, she stroked Kayla's hair again. "Are you feeling well enough to go for a ride?"

Kayla stood. "Oh yes, Mama. My tummy doesn't hurt as much now."

Once the Honda was locked, they walked around to the carriage.

Beulah, Malinda's sister—and also sister-in-law since they'd married two Martin brothers—now stood by the passenger-side door of the carriage, glowering. Though the two dressed and even looked similar, their personalities had always been so different. "Plenty hot to be standing around," she grumbled.

At least Janna was wearing a calf-length summer dress and Kayla a knee-length skort and short-sleeved shirt. Her dress was sleeveless, but it covered more than the clothing she'd originally considered for such a hot day. Beulah certainly would have complained about their immodesty had they dressed in shorts and tank tops.

"*Ya*, 'tis. Especially when you're stranded." Malinda placed her hand on Janna's back. "Sister, you remember Janna, and this is Kayla." She winked at Janna. "Go ahead and get in. We'll be home in ten minutes."

Janna leaned into the carriage and pulled the back of the bench seat forward, then helped Kayla climb into the backseat. After following, she drew the front seat back into place. Her apprehension eased a bit at the ecstatic smile Kayla wore as she peered through the carriage's open back.

The sisters got in, then Malinda looked over her shoulder. She'd never been attractive by worldly standards, even when younger, but the warm, sincere smile that rounded her face gave it a genuine beauty. "*Ach*, Janna, *Mamm* will be so glad to see you," she said again.

Beulah grabbed the reins, huffing as she glared through the carriage's storm front. Her unpleasant demeanor was why Janna had spent six years of her childhood avoiding the woman as much as possible.

As the horse pulled the carriage out onto the shoulder of Division Highway, Janna slowly breathed in and out. If *Mammi* Salena would be so glad to see her, then why hadn't she or Luke ever responded to the letters she wrote to them fourteen years ago?

CHAPTER 2

The Reunion

LUKE REGRETTED PAIRING his cell phone to his truck's Bluetooth. Edie Stott, the most high-maintenance customer he'd ever built furniture for, had called four times this morning—the last two times during the fifteen-mile drive home from *Mamm*'s optician's office. Even more, he wished he hadn't given her his cell phone number. That had been his mistake of the century. At least one of them, anyway.

And now her phone number again appeared on the screen on his dashboard.

He glanced toward the passenger seat. His grandmother, though he now called her *Mamm*, had pursed her lips. She disapproved of cell phones, let alone a smartphone that could ring through the truck's speakers. While she no longer complained about the CD of a capella hymns he played whenever she rode with him, the phone ringing—multiple times, no less—was intolerable.

Sure he would regret this as well, Luke tapped the button on the steering wheel to answer the call. "Good morning, Mrs. Stott."

"Luke, I hate to bother you." Her high-pitched voice filled the cab.

He sighed. *Then don't do it.*

"My son and his family will be here to stay with us for two weeks starting next weekend. I just wanted to make sure our dining table and chairs will be delivered by then. The table we have right now won't seat all of us, and being Amish and all, you must know how important it is for families to sit down together for meals."

Mennonite, not Amish. Not that mentioning it would matter. He'd already done that at least twice. "Yes, I do, Mrs. Stott," he said as kindly as he could. "Lord willing, I plan to deliver the set on Friday at the latest."

"You swear to me it will be ready by then?"

Ach, he'd never sworn to anything and he never would. "The Bible says our yes should be yes and our no should be no—nothing more. But I can tell you I've never missed a delivery date." Hopefully, this wouldn't be the first.

After a few-second pause, she exhaled. "Well, I'll have to trust you on that, I guess."

"Thank you, Mrs. Stott. I'll talk to you soon, then, and you have a nice day." Before she could say more, he pushed the button on the steering wheel to end the call.

The acapella lyrics of "Though Troubles Assail" again filled the cab in four-part harmony. Fitting. Troubles were assailing, that was for certain.

Mamm folded her hands in her lap as she watched out

the side window. "She's making you earn every penny of this order, not?" The black bonnet over her head covering obscured her expression, but the empathy in her tone came as a relief. He didn't need chastisement right now, especially with Joah in the backseat.

"*Ya.* And I've explained why I'm a bit behind schedule and assured her I take my delivery dates seriously. I'll just have to go back out to the workshop after Joah's in bed each night."

"*Ach*, you work so much yet." Grimness now replaced the empathy.

"I know." But Mahlon was away till Wednesday at his grandfather's funeral in Ohio, which left Luke with all the work. On top of that, Joah had therapy appointments in Lancaster on Tuesdays and Fridays, and that cut close to two hours out of those afternoons.

He stopped at the red light at Martindale Road. "*Gott* always provides. He will in this too. After next week, things should slow down." Seemed like he'd been saying that for months.

"Daddy, can we go fishing today?" Joah asked.

Luke's stomach sank as he glanced in the rearview mirror. Joah peered out the back window at the tree-lined river on the other side of the intersection. They hadn't fished in close to a month, but he needed to be in the shop for the rest of the day. Cousin Miriam had been kind enough to tend any customers who came in this morning, but Saturday was their busiest day, and the customers who wanted custom furniture often expected to speak to him directly.

"I think it's a little too hot for fishing, son," he said. "But we'll go soon."

"Okay, Daddy."

Glancing in the mirror a couple more times, Luke saw Joah staring at the river as they crossed the intersection and then the bridge. His son said nothing more, but Luke knew how much he loved fishing—as much as Luke had when he was a child, if not more. The difference was *Daadi* had taken him often.

Luke blew out his breath, praying for wisdom. The furniture business was important to him. It was not only what he loved to do but also what supported his family. Yet sometimes he felt like it took precedence over what was best for Joah.

Something needed to change, and right quick.

Janna could see only so much through the carriage's storm front as they turned off Division Highway. The Martins' lane was now paved instead of gravel, but otherwise the property appeared mostly unchanged.

Beyond the two-and-a-half-story brick house stood the attached *daadi haus*, and the furniture and quilt shop and its parking lot sat across the lane. The *Conestoga Valley Quilts & Custom Furniture* sign still stood between the parking lot and the road, but it had been repainted. And the white picket fence that surrounded the house and *daadi haus* had been replaced.

The only other change stole her breath and brought a sting behind her eyes when she realized it. When they'd passed the row of five side-by-side black mailboxes—two for the house across the road—the one with the nameplate that read *Luke D. Martin* had once borne *Daadi* Eli's name. Her suspicion had been correct. He was gone.

"Mama, look!" Kayla whispered, her face animated as she pointed ahead.

Janna blinked her eyes dry. Behind the shop sat a large playset and a trampoline with a safety enclosure around it. Also new, they'd taken the place of the tall A-frame swing set where she and Luke had spent so many hours.

Malinda grinned back at her. "Perhaps you and Joah can play together."

"Oh yes, please." Kayla bounced on the seat, still holding Rabbit. At least her carsickness had resolved quickly this time.

After Beulah stopped the carriage, they all got out. A thin cloud veiled the sun now, and the breeze provided some relief, as did being out of the enclosed space of the carriage. Birdsong enveloped them, stirring reminiscence so strong that it brought goose bumps to Janna's arms.

Kayla pointed again. "Look at all the birds!"

Just as Janna remembered, the large martin house sat high on its pole, bright white against the dark-red carriage house beyond it across the lane. Birds perched on it and flitted all around, chirping. "They're purple martins."

A fairly new black pickup approached and slowly passed them. It continued toward the carriage house up the lane behind the *daadi haus*, then parked next to a black minivan. Strange. Customers always parked in the lot, and only one of the six parking spots was taken.

The truck's back passenger-side door opened, and a blond boy wearing black jeans, a light-colored plaid shirt, and white suspenders climbed down. Tugging his hat onto his head, he jogged toward them with an awkward gait.

Janna realized why as he neared. The poor boy wore a black cast and cast shoe on each foot.

"Here comes Joah now," Malinda said. When he stopped about twenty-five feet away, she motioned him to her. "*Kumm.* I have some friends for you to meet."

The truck's driver-side door opened, and a tall man got out. He was dressed much like Joah and wore the seagrass hat Old Order Mennonite men and boys wore in warm weather. But he drove a truck? "Is that . . ."

"Luke? *Ya.*" Malinda watched as he rounded the front of the vehicle.

"He left the *gmay* and married a Horning girl," Beulah said. Crossing her arms, she shook her head. "And now he's going to some *Funkeleit* church."

Well, that explained the two vehicles, but Luke and Joah still dressed Old Order. And how surprising. He'd once said he would never leave the *gmay*—although he'd been only a child at the time.

When Janna returned her attention to the truck, Luke was helping a slim elderly woman out of the passenger seat. She gained her footing, then smoothed her green cape dress as she started toward them.

Mammi Salena. Janna would've recognized her anywhere. Her gray hair was now whiter, and she wasn't as light on her feet, but she walked steadily. Luke followed and grabbed Joah on his way, swinging him up onto his hip.

Suddenly choked up, Janna covered her mouth and tried to blink away the tears that flooded her eyes. She'd thought about this for years, hoping to one day reunite with the Martins but also fearing that they would be standoffish with her. Now the time had come, and she almost felt sick.

Beulah climbed back into the carriage, muttering, and

the horse took off up the lane toward the large farmhouse she and Malinda shared with their husbands, two of Salena's sons. Janna hadn't used *Deitsch* in years, but the last two words of Beulah's jab—*dumme gedanke*—made her opinion clear: this is a foolish idea.

Perhaps she was right.

"Who're they?" Joah asked as Luke carried him toward the woman and little girl standing with Malinda near the carriage. "Malinda said they're friends for me to meet."

They didn't look familiar, but Malinda's kind heart earned her more friends—from inside their community and outside it—than could be counted. "I don't know, son."

Both wore a dress and had long hair, so they might belong to a somewhat-conservative church. The woman didn't wear a head covering, though, instead with her hair in a thick braid that hung over one shoulder.

As they got closer, the woman dropped the hand held over her mouth.

Janna?

He second-guessed himself, but it was definitely her. Many years had passed since her mother moved them to somewhere near Philadelphia, but the light-auburn hair, fair skin, and green eyes confirmed it. Tears streamed down her face, not unlike the last time he'd seen her. But then she'd been an almost-thirteen-year-old girl sobbing as she peered through the open passenger-side window of a beat-up Ford Fairmont. Now she was taller, and her pixie face and string-bean build had been replaced by natural beauty.

A few steps ahead, *Mamm* cried out and then hastened toward the three, her arms outstretched. She and Janna hugged each other, laughing and crying at the same time, while Malinda held the little girl to her side and wiped away her own tears.

Luke couldn't blame her. Though *Mamm* rarely spoke of her, she'd missed Janna. The *Ordnung* prohibited the use of cameras, but *Mamm* still had several public-school photographs of Janna in her hope chest.

He'd missed her as well, terribly at first. That had faded over the years, but he still thought of her on occasion, remembering all the time they'd spent together and wondering what had become of her. Now she stood before him, and by the way she responded to *Mamm*, she hadn't forgotten them as he'd assumed.

Malinda smiled as he neared. "Look who we found out front of Christian Aid Ministries. Their car ran out of gas right as we were leaving."

Mamm and Janna still showed no sign of releasing each other, so he set Joah on the asphalt and looked down at the curly-haired girl who hugged a scruffy brown stuffed rabbit. No doubt who she belonged to. "I'm Luke and this is Joah. What's your name?"

She didn't answer, watching him solemnly through long eyelashes.

Malinda patted her shoulder. "This is Kayla, Janna's daughter."

The little girl looked up at her, her face pinched. "How come Mama's crying?"

"*Ach*, not to worry, dear one." Malinda drew her closer. "She's happy, not sad. When your mama was not much older than you, *Mammi* Salena was like a grandmother to her, but they haven't seen each other in a long time."

Nee, Mamm had been like a *mother* to her, much more than Janna's own mother ever was. During the time the Carpenters lived in the rundown house across the road, Janna had spent many more nights sleeping in a bedroom next to his than she had at home. *Mamm* had cared for Janna when she wasn't in school and throughout each summer, all while her mother slept most of the day—not always at their house—and worked overnight at a nursing home.

"Joah is six," Malinda told Kayla. "How old are you?"

The little girl grinned, showing the gap of a missing tooth. "I'll be six in August. I was born on Mama's birthday." Her mouth then opened as she stared at Joah's feet. "How did you break your legs?"

Joah smiled. "They're not broken. They're getting fixed."

Hopefully, they were. "Lord willing, he'll have the casts for two more weeks, then he'll wear braces," Luke said.

"You can run with casts on your feet?"

Joah's grin broadened. "*Ya*. And I can climb the rock wall." He pointed to the colorful plastic climbing rocks attached to a slat wall on the playset. "And I can ride my scooter and my bike. I just can't jump on the trampoline 'cause I kept falling. Carin my therapist says after I get my AFO braces and can wear regular shoes, I can jump on the trampoline again."

"Luke." Janna's voice sounded much like it always had, kind and soft-spoken.

He faced her. For a moment he thought she might hug him as well, but she must've thought better of it. That was for the best anyway.

She smiled shyly. "It's good to see you again." Even with her eyes red and a little swollen, she was lovely.

Ach, he had no place entertaining such thoughts. He nodded, brushing them aside. "*Ya*, 'tis." It would've been better if she'd intended on visiting them, though. Their car had run out of gas less than two miles away. How many times had she driven by the farm but not stopped? "Are you living in the area?"

She swallowed as she swiped any last wetness from her cheeks. "We started moving into a twin over in Akron yesterday, but a tree fell on it in the storm here last night. Then we ran out of gas."

"All will be well." *Mamm* slipped her arm around Janna's waist. "*Gott* cares for the lilies of the field and the birds of the air, and so much more for us. 'Twas no coincidence that Beulah and Malinda came upon you."

Janna nodded, pressing her lips together.

"You're able to take her and a gas can to her car and get it driving again, not?" Malinda asked him. "If you don't have gasoline, we have plenty."

"I have some." Eating a quick dinner and getting over to the workshop would have to wait. Janna and her daughter's needs were more pressing, and taking care of car problems shouldn't be a woman's concern. "Do you want to go now?"

Her lips parted but then closed again. "If it's not too much trouble."

Why would she think that? "Of course it's not."

Kayla moved away from Malinda and peered up at Janna. "Can Joah and I play till you get back?"

"That's a fine idea," Malinda said, perhaps a bit too quickly. "If the clouds pass, it'll be too hot later." She shifted her attention from the children to Luke and Janna. "I can stay with them."

He'd intended to take Joah and Kayla along, but such eagerness brightened their expressions. "Is that all right with you?" he asked Janna.

She hesitated. "I . . . well—"

"Oh, please, Mama?" Kayla begged.

Janna stroked her hair. "Yes, that's fine. But you need to be careful and obey Malinda and *Mammi* Salena. And nothing to eat till I get back. Understood?"

"I promise." Kayla turned and grabbed Joah's hand. "Come on."

They skipped off toward the playset together.

Mamm released Janna and dabbed her eyes with her handkerchief again. "Go on now. When you get back, I'll have dinner ready. You'll eat with us, not?"

"We'd love to. Thank you." Janna looked and sounded more at ease, but then the seriousness returned to her expression. She pulled a long, thin insulated bag from her purse. "Kayla's allergic to peanuts. Her EpiPens are in this, but a lot of people aren't familiar with using them. If you'd rather she go with us—"

Malinda took it with a smile. "I know how to use them. But she'll be fine."

Janna hesitated, then nodded and looked at Luke.

"You can get in the truck a while," he said. "I'll get the gas can and be right there."

At least her car wasn't far away. Much had changed in his life, and no doubt Janna had plenty of questions, many of which had such complicated answers that he couldn't possibly address them on a short ride.

Especially since he still hadn't figured out some of the answers himself.